# ANANDA

Scott Zarcinas

# Also By
## Scott Zarcinas

### FICTION

*Roadman*

### THE PILGRIM CHRONICLES

*Samantha Honeycomb*
*The Golden Chalice*
*DeVille's Contract*

### NON-FICTION

*Your Natural State of Being*

# ANANDA

Scott Zarcinas

DoctorZed
Publishing
www.doctorzed.com

First published 2006 as Thanksgiving Day (ebook) by DoctorZed Publishing.

First edition print publication 2015

DoctorZed Publishing books may be ordered through booksellers or by contacting:

DoctorZed Publishing
IDAHO
10 Vista Ave
Skye, South Australia 5072
www.doctorzed.com
61-(0)8 8431-4965

ISBN: 978-0-9943054-0-4 (sc)
ISBN: 978-0-9943054-1-1 (e)

A CIP number for this book is available at the National Library of Australia.

Cover image Dreamstime.com stock imagery © Carodi | Burning fire cross

Printed in Australia
DoctorZed Publishing rev. date: 14/04/2015

For my girls

# ACKNOWLEDGMENTS

As with everything I have written to date, this book could not have been born without the emotional, financial and loving support of my wife, Martie Botha. I have given up everything to become a writer; she has given up more.

I would also like to thank the many individuals who were kind enough to examine the manuscript in its embryonic stages and offer valuable advice as to the eventual timing and mode of its delivery into the world.

Lastly, to God, who continues to show me that there is always more to life than meets the eye. I apologise if I am sometimes a little slow in seeing it.

*"You either believe miracles happen every day,
or not at all."*

Albert Einstein

# PART ONE

# ADELAIDE, 1995

# CHAPTER 1

THE LATE NOVEMBER sky had prematurely greyed by the time Michael Joseph trotted across the gravel of Wattle Gardens' parking lot. A gust of wind tugged the cuffs of his blue sweater like an annoying child trying to get his attention, then shook the branches of the eucalypt under which his VW Beetle was parked. The rustle of the leaves and the crunching of his footsteps drew his attention to the few remaining vehicles. On any other day the thought of an empty parking lot would have been disheartening, but not today. Empty was good. It meant he didn't have to pretend to be happy if he happened upon Norman Page on his way home after school, or any of the other teachers for that matter.

Halfway to his car another gust ruffled his long brown hair, bringing with it the smell of the nearby sea. He glanced at his watch, then up at the overcast sky. It was approaching five thirty; there would be another sixty minutes of useful daylight left, he guessed. If the rain didn't come first.

Irked with this recent bout of unpleasant weather, he hastened his lengthy strides. In fact, when he thought about it, everything irked him lately, and it didn't take a genius to work out why, either. He knew damn well why, and there was absolutely nothing he could do about it. That made things even worse. He hated feeling so helpless. If a problem needed fixing, he was always the first to roll up his sleeves and get to work on it. Yet, this was one problem he simply couldn't fix. There wasn't even anyone he could turn to for advice, except, maybe, his father, but he only wanted to do that as a last resort, when all else failed.

At the VW he noticed that he had forgotten to lock the door when he arrived this morning. "You idiot," he mumbled, and hopped in behind the steering wheel and started the engine. With a sense of relief, Wattle Gardens Primary School disappeared in the rear-view mirror as he steered the car out through the main gates onto the cul-de-sac and rounded the corner. Pulling up to the intersection with the main road, he was suddenly confronted with rush hour traffic and indecisiveness. Did he really want to be going home to a cold and empty house? Angie probably wouldn't be home till after ten. She would be working late at the office again, no doubt about it; she was all work and no play. Then again, what else was he going to do? All his friends had families to go home to; their wives only let them off the leash every once in a while, and certainly not in the middle of the week. Home it was then.

Michael pulled the car onto the busy road and the grey clouds seemed to darken with his thoughts. *Same shit, different day*, he mused, crossing to the outside lane. Someone honked and made him jump.

"Fuck you!" he muttered and gave them the finger.

It took almost half an hour longer to cross the city than usual. Rush hour, the rain, the traffic lights, everything was conspiring against him. To compound matters, it was almost dark. Finally, just as the rain began to ease, he turned onto Christopher Street and pulled into the driveway at number sixty-four. The headlights fell onto the low, redbrick parapet separating the house from the street and then onto the empty space where Angie's car should have been.

He parked the VW and got out to check the letterbox. It was empty. He should have known; not even the utility companies, it seemed, were bothered to bill him any more. Was it him, or had he become a Mr. Nobody overnight?

*Although it wasn't exactly overnight, was it?* he mused, running his hand through his hair. *Things have slowly been going downhill for over three years. Closer to four, even. Ever since Angie got her damn knickers in a twist over starting a family.*

He let the flap of the letterbox swing shut, then trudged across the small front lawn, shoulders slumped, feet dragging. In the dim light, he eyed the porch and the bluestone façade. Had it really been three years since he moved in here with Angie?

*Time flies when you're having fun, Mikey*, he mused, stepping up to the house.

The suburb of Tusmore wasn't the kind of environs he had ever expected to reside when he was a college student contemplating where and when he was going to live after he graduated. He felt out of place in this part of the city. For a start, he was too far away from the sea and the beach where he had spent most of his life. He needed to hear the seagulls squabbling, the crashing of the waves, the feel of the sand between his toes. Tusmore was about as far removed from that kind of life as he could imagine, an upper-class suburb with leafy streets and polite families where dogs didn't bark after the sun went down and young housewives dutifully looked after the children during the day whilst gossiping about the size of other husbands' pay packets. All wives, that was, except Angie. She was not your normal eastern suburbs woman.

Michael opened the front door and flicked on the hallway light. He was immediately confronted with a ghastly sight. Angie had inherited the house from her parents after the accident in 1990, and, for one reason or another, it was still furnished as it had been when they were alive—antique cabinets and sofas, wallpaper and carpets that were worn and faded, even a grandfather clock in the hallway and a rusty clawfoot in the bathroom. It reminded Michael of an old-aged home. It even had that old musty smell, which, he had to admit, was probably more attributable to the age of the building than anything to do with her parents. One day, though, he was going to stop procrastinating and do something about the yellow and white striped wallpaper and thinning blue carpet in the hallway. One day he was also going to refurbish the lounge room and the kitchen. One day he was going to do a lot of things.

He closed the door and headed to the kitchen at the end of the hallway to begin preparing dinner. The lights were off in all rooms, the lounge room and the study on the right, the main bedroom and Angie's old bedroom on the left, dark chambers that reminded him more of hidden caves in the bush than the living quarters of a house, places he just didn't seem to care about nor want to do anything with. Thankfully, there was still one place left he felt a modicum of peace and belonging, but before he entered the kitchen he stopped to wash his hands in the bathroom opposite the grandfather clock, a habit his hygienically minded father had drilled into him since childhood. Once done, he spent the next half an hour busy at the kitchen divider mashing the potatoes and spicing the mince for a cottage pie, keeping half of it heated in the oven for Angie when she arrived home.

"Whenever that's going to be," he said with a snort, sitting down at the dinner table. Some nights he didn't even see her at all.

Lifting the fork to his mouth, the telephone shrilled from down the hallway. He half stood, then sat back down and continued eating, letting the answering machine pick up the call. It wasn't until after he had cleaned the kitchen and washed the dishes that he went to the lounge room to check if the caller had left a message. Someone had. On the foot table next to the Steinway, the answering machine's red light was flashing on and off. He pushed PLAY.

"Michael, hunni. Are you there? Pick up the phone." It was Angie. Her voice sounded huskier than normal, the voice of someone working themselves far too hard. There was a pause, then she must have realised that he wasn't going to answer and continued with her message. "I'm still at the office. Something's come up. Stephen wants me to go through one of his divorce cases with him. It's kind of messy and I don't know how long we'll be, so don't cook for me, okay. I'll try to be home as soon as I can. Love you. Bye."

The news was disappointing, but half expected, really. He ran a hand through his hair and glanced over his shoulder at the couch. Yesterday's *Adelaide Sun* was lying folded on the cushions. Picking it up, he flicked on the TV and turned down the volume so that it was no louder than a hushed background murmur. Then he slouched lengthways along the couch, resting his head on one armrest, his feet on the other. Like the TV, the newspaper was merely a distraction to bar any thoughts of his problems with Angie getting through to his surface consciousness. He wasn't really reading the paper, not really taking in the story on the front page about the baby that had been abducted from the mall and was now feared dead, and it wasn't long before his eyelids began to droop.

At some point he dozed off, woken only when a beam of light swept over the lounge room ceiling some time later, headlights shining through the crack between the curtains. As he stirred, a car engine idled briefly before switching off. He glanced up at the Elvis Presley clock on the wall near the door. Strumming a guitar, Elvis sang into a microphone, his black legs swaying at the hips, his torso dressed in a blue jacket with black lapels. He was saying it was nearly ten, early for the likes of workaholics like Angie. Michael heard the car door shut, then silence as she crossed the lawn, then her hassled footsteps on the porch. After the keys wrestled with the lock, the front door opened and then slammed shut, shaking the Elvis clock on the wall. Almost immediately, her briefcase, heavy with cases and files she often brought home after a day in court, thudded onto the floor of the main bedroom, followed by the clomp, clomp of her shoes being removed.

Seconds later Angie appeared in the doorway, frowning. Michael could feel the stress surging from her like the pressure wave at the bow of a ship, and he braced himself for a rough ride; it had been another frustrating day at Sugarman Klein & Pickering. The blue suit jacket sagged on her slender frame, as if two sizes too big, and there was a large run riding up her black stockings, disappearing beneath the hem of her skirt. Her hair, normally held into a taut bun, was falling in loose strands around her face, and he caught her big brown eyes staring at him through the large rimless glasses perched on the tip of her nose, which she pushed to the bridge with a terse shove of her forefinger. The other hand was holding a woman's magazine. It was obvious something other than work was on her mind.

"What's the matter?" Michael asked, folding the newspaper onto the floor beside him.

Angie shrugged, a noncommittal twitch of the shoulders that Michael associated with apathy and disaffection. She glanced briefly at the magazine in her hand. "I, I saw an ad in the *Woman's World* that might help us with," and she paused, hesitant to continue, "with, you know, our problem." Her voice sounded even more tired than on the answering machine. Angie flicked through the pages to the ad, after which she stepped forward, the magazine splayed out.

Michael used his elbow to prop himself up and took the magazine. Her hands dropped to her side like a little girl awaiting approval from her father, and she continued to stand like this at the foot of the couch while he read the ad.

## FERTILITY PROBLEMS?

*Are you and your partner having difficulty conceiving? Are you worried you may never have the family you desire?*

*At St. Mary's Hospital Private Fertility Clinic we understand what you may be going through. We specialise in treating infertility in a discreet and understanding environment.*

*If you wish to inquire about our range of treatments, you can arrange a confidential appointment with one of our specialists by calling our toll free number below.*

Michael felt a cold finger of dread stroke his spine. Elbows on knees he stared at the words, unmoving at first, then ran a hand through his hair. "Do you think this is what we need to do?" he asked, glancing up at her over his shoulder. "It's going to cost a fortune."

Her hands shot to her hips and her scowl deepened. "Is that all you ever think about, money?"

"Of course not, but we're not exactly swimming in cash at the moment, are we?"

"It isn't going to cost us a thing," she said, sliding a strand of loose hair behind her ear. "I've read the health insurance package from work and in the fine print it says that if there's a legitimate cause of infertility, then the policy will cover the expenses of any treatment."

"You've obviously checked it all out," he said.

"Yes," she said. Her rimless glasses had slipped again. "I have. I just don't know why we didn't think of it before." Then thoughtfully, pushing her glasses back to the bridge of her nose, she said, "But it doesn't matter. What matters is that we're going to do something constructive about it. I've made an appointment for next Thursday. Five o'clock."

To Michael, this was all a bit of a surprise. He also felt left out. She had obviously been planning something like this for quite some while and he hadn't even had so much as a clue. They had never discussed the option of medical intervention at all before now, not even with his father, who was a doctor. Why now, suddenly? What was the rush? He needed time to think about it, long and hard, certainly longer than a week. This wasn't something they should just jump recklessly into. The situation wasn't nearly as desperate as she was making it out to be.

He suddenly remembered an appointment he had to attend, just the excuse he needed to delay matters. "I have a staff meeting after school that day," he said. "The headmistress won't give me leave. You know how she is."

"Why are you being so obstinate?" she said. Tears were starting to well in her eyes. "You don't care, do you? If we don't do anything about it now we may never have the chance. It's now or never."

"That's not true. I want a child as much as you do. I'm just not panicking about it."

Angie glared at him and crossed her arms. "Well, at least that shows I care. It's more than I can say for you. You just keep on saying not to worry. It'll be okay. We'll have a baby before Christmas. Well I've got news for you. I'm not pregnant and Christmas is almost here."

Michael stared at her. "Why are you working yourself into a frenzy? It's not good for either of us when you're like this."

"So it's my fault is it?"

"Angel, come on, now you're being irrational. No one is blaming anyone here."

"Really? Then why do I feel as if you blame me for everything?"

The next instant, Michael was addressing thin air. He heard her hurried scuffles down the hallway, then the slamming of the bathroom door. Slowly getting to his feet, Michael thought it odd how his legs could feel as heavy as his heart. He went to the bathroom and heard some muffled sobs through the closed door. He imagined her sitting on the toilet seat with her face buried in her hands, probably smudging her mascara. Then he tried talking to her, apologising for what he'd said, and when that failed he tried the doorknob. It was locked. Behind him, the grandfather clock said it was almost a quarter after ten. He figured there was no point in continuing like this. He'd just have to wait until she calmed down in her own time.

As he ambled up the hallway to the front bedroom, her crying faded until it fell silent. He felt a tug in his heart and a wrench in his gut, sad that she was so distraught, and angry that he couldn't do anything to help her over it. Angie deserved better than this. They both did. His greatest fear was that they were pushing each other so far away they'd soon fall out of sight, and he knew all too well it wouldn't take too much more before one of them plummeted over the edge.

Tomorrow, he promised himself, he would try and make amends.

THE NEXT MORNING began as normal. Angie was up at six, Michael at seven. When Michael sat down for breakfast at the kitchen table, she was dressed for work and drinking her obligatory cup of coffee, white, two sugars, from a mug with a yellow smiley face and a caption that said: DON'T WORRY, BE HAPPY. He smirked. Being happy wasn't high on his list of possibilities today, as with any other day in the foreseeable future. As usual, Angie had readied some cereal and a cup of coffee for him. There was an awkward silence while he tipped the cornflakes into his bowl and took a sip of coffee. They hadn't said a word since last night's argument and he tried smiling and making small talk, but Angie only brought the happy mug to her lips and smiled faintly in return. It was rather tepid, like his coffee.

Half giving up on the likelihood of any conversation this morning, Michael wiped a dribble off his chin with the back of his hand and gazed outside through the sliding glass doors that opened onto the backyard. The weather forecast was for cloudy skies and rain, hence his black sweater and jeans, and yet a plethora of dusty rays were shining onto the yellow kitchen walls. He should have felt enlivened, but his mood seemed unchanged. He was dulled this morning from lack of sleep, having tossed and turned all night, a fitful night filled with nightmares of being chased by unknown assailants.

Over a spoonful of cornflakes, he briefly glanced at his wife. Flicking through the magazine she had brought home last night, Angie stopped at an article in the "True Confessions" section, some of which he was able to peruse upside down, a tearjerker about the horror one woman went through when her baby was kidnapped two years ago.

Angie was captivated. She was frowning and taking quick sips of coffee, continually pushing her rimless glasses to the bridge of her nose. Her hair was tied into a professional bun, emphasising her large brown eyes and the fullness of her lips, and all of last night's creases had been ironed from her work suit. The gold crucifix she wore was dangling on the outside of her shirt between her breasts. She was wearing lilac lipstick, the same colour she had worn on their first date to watch the bonfire and fireworks show on Serena beach. Despite their recent troubles, he reckoned she still looked as gorgeous now as then.

He remembered that night with fondness. November 5, 1989, Guy Fawkes night. As they drove along the peninsula to Serena, they had discussed how many children they'd like to have. It was an odd thing to discuss on a first date, he had to admit, but discuss it they did, in detail, and the answer had been three. They were both single children, and they shared the common hope of starting a family in the future. He told her that he had always wanted to have a trio of little ones; it had been that way ever since he could remember. ("One for me, one for my wife, and one for the grandparents," he had joked at the time.) It was the same, he was happy to learn, for Angie, and the dream of having children was the seed that matured into the bond that eventually united them.

Back when he and Angie met, they were twenty-two and carefree and full of hope. Things were different in those days. Angie was different. They had a bright future, dreams to look forward to, a successful career, she as a lawyer and he as a teacher. After that, babies. There was a cheery purpose to their life. They seemed eager, if not ravenous, for each day, especially Angie.

Happiness, though, he came to realise, was only one side of a coin, misery the other. Your destiny was determined solely on the flip of that coin; heads you got lucky, tails you bummed out.

It was soon after they met that tragedy struck. They received news one night that her parents had died in a horrific bus accident on a local church outing. Angie, needless to say, was devastated. He tried imaging how he would have coped had it been his parents travelling in that bus and not Angie's. As the months passed, she somehow managed to pick up the pieces of her life. Her strength to carry on was admirable. She graduated with honours from Law School that same year and was one of only fifteen graduates to find employment. It was the middle of the recession, the one that followed the stock market crash of '87 and the one Paul Keating said was "the one we needed to have," (could you believe Australia still voted him in as Prime Minister after that?) and Michael was as proud of her achievements as he imagined her parents would have been. He knew then that Angie was the woman he would marry. She was going to be the mother of his three children.

*How things change,* he thought now, watching his wife. *Your dreams, your hopes, all of it decided on the flip of a coin that always lands bums up.*

Angie finished reading the article, sipped the last of her coffee, then stood up. "I have to go," she said, slipping the crucifix down the V of her shirt and out of sight. "I'm running late."

"But it's only quarter past seven," he said, glancing at his watch.

Angie took her mug to the sink. Michael saw her rub her temple as she went. If the mornings started like this, he knew she was sure to have a migraine by lunchtime.

"Don't start on me, Michael," she said. "I've got a lot of paperwork I have to get through at the moment. I don't need this."

It was a lie, pure and simple. He knew Angie took pride at being the most efficient worker in the firm, and he knew paperwork never mounted up on her desk. Unlike him, she needed the right conditions to be productive, namely a spotless desk where everything was in its correct place. If it weren't, then she simply wouldn't start until she had made it so, just as she always began the morning ironing her suit. He opened his mouth to say he didn't believe what she was saying, and then quickly shut it.

"I'll see you this evening," she said, flashing something tired that was supposed to be a smile, but was more like a forlorn grin. "I'll probably be late again. You know how it is."

Michael certainly did.

THAT EVENING AFTER school, Michael decided to call in on his father and fulfil the promise he had made last night. Though, if he were honest, Michael wasn't certain how he was going to approach the subject. How do you tell your father you think your wife is infertile and it's destroying your marriage? He could barely think it, let alone say it.

As he entered the house, a wave of nostalgia swept over him. Michael had been thirteen when the family upped and moved from Serena to Adelaide in 1980, a move he remembered with fondness. His dad had been following the lure of a partnership offer in a nearby doctor's practice and had bought the house soon after. Like the house in Serena, this one was situated just a few streets from the beach (so close, in fact, he could hear the waves crashing on a still night). Those years were filled with happy memories—high school, university, the early days of dating Angie—when things had been a lot simpler.

Robert Joseph was wearing a white apron with yellow flowers over his shirt and trousers when Michael walked into the kitchen. He greeted Michael with a smile and a playful slap on the back. "Good to see you, Mikey," he said, removing the apron and tossing it onto the edge of the sink. "What can I get you? A beer?"

Michael nodded. It was probably what he needed to help loosen his tongue. He stepped past the shorter, stockier man and sat down at the kitchen table. While his father rummaged inside the refrigerator, Michael looked around the room. On the near wall was a corkboard pinned with photos and lists of chores. One photo caught his attention in particular. It was a family snap taken last Christmas when nobody was looking at the camera, what he figured professional photographers would call a 'real life' shot. It was probably mid afternoon, after the presents had been exchanged, because there was wrapping paper strewn all over the carpet and everyone was sitting in the lounge room eating with plates on their laps. He saw himself sitting next to his mother, smiling lopsidedly. His nose was slightly hooked and prominent, salient almost, though by no means large, as were his chin and forehead, which others had told him suggested intelligence but which he just considered unappealing. How such a gorgeous woman like Angie could find him attractive, he was at a loss to explain. Perhaps it was his jade-green eyes; she was always complimenting him on their colour.

Robert now put two cans of West End Draught on the table. "I took that with the new camera you and Angie gave me," he said. "Not her favourite photo, is it?"

Michael didn't need to answer. Though almost everyone thought her pretty, it wasn't a flattering photograph. Angie was frowning and looking particularly grieved. Robert's present hadn't been well received, and Michael knew his father was feeling a tad guilty at the prank he had played that day. Michael opened his beer, took a sip and glanced back at the photo, also feeling a little bad at his role in the mix up. It had been his suggestion to buy her something to take her mind off her problems, but in the end it had backfired. It was best left unsaid.

Still gazing at the photo, Michael took another sip of beer. Angie was sitting next to his cousin, Julian Joseph, Jude to his family. Where Michael had the brains in the family, Jude had the looks, by far and away the most attractive of all the Joseph men. He had mesmerising crystal blue eyes that burned like polished sapphires and he was never without a different girl tagging eagerly onto his arm. His rise through the ranks of SAPOL, the South Australian Police Force, was as swift and dynamic as the number of women he seemingly bedded, so it was always a surprise to Michael that Jude soured his face with a perpetual frown, as if everything he'd achieved wasn't enough, as if everything and everyone, especially his family, was a source of constant disdain and contempt.

In the picture, Jude was slouching into the soft cushions of the couch, dressed all in black. His blonde hair, whiter than Angie's more golden colour, was neatly coiffed, befitting his newly promoted rank to Chief Inspector. Michael examined his expression more carefully. There was something on Jude's face he hadn't noticed on the day. Jude was staring at him with scorn, and even in the photo Michael could feel his blue eyes stabbing like daggers of ice. He wondered why Jude hated him so much.

"I know he's a cop," Robert said, following Michael's gaze, "and as his uncle I should be more understanding of his faults, but I don't trust him. I bet you a million bucks he's bullshitted his way into that promotion. Worse than that, he bullshits us, his own family." Shaking his head, he sat down at the table directly opposite Michael. Then he relaxed, like someone letting go of a troubling problem, and smiled.

"Is there something on your mind, Mikey, or have you just popped around to look at old photos?"

Michael didn't know where to begin. There were just too many things overwhelming him at the moment. He lowered his eyes to the can of beer, running his fingertip around its lip. Robert chuckled quietly. Michael flicked his eyes up to his father's face, then quickly down to the beer can again. A wry grin adorned his face. "Is it that obvious?" he asked.

"It's not that difficult when you've watched someone grow up over the last twenty-eight years of their life," Robert said. "You get to know them pretty well, but I wouldn't go so far as to say it was obvious."

Michael saw the kindly look of concern on his father's face and for the first time saw his true age, not the young man kicking the football with his son in the backyard, or playing beach cricket after work, but as a man only a few years from retirement and desperately keen to see his grandchildren grow up before he dies. That only accentuated the problem. As the months passed, it seemed more and more likely that it would never happen.

Michael's finger continued running around the lip of the can. Robert waited for him to begin. "You know we have been struggling to have a baby," Michael said, finally.

Robert cleared his throat and briefly glanced at the photo on the corkboard. "Everyone knows you and Angie have been trying for a while," he said. "I hope she wasn't too offended by the present I gave her for Christmas. It was only meant to lighten the situation."

"You mean the book of Kama Sutra?"

Robert nodded.

"She's over it now," Michael said. "We had a laugh about it later. It made trying for a baby more fun, at least."

Robert seemed happier. "So what's worrying you at the moment?"

Michael ran his hand through his long hair, contemplating the intricacies of how to put into words what had been only vague concepts till this moment. "It's been nearly three and a half years since we got married," he said, "and don't get me wrong, I love Angie and the fact that we're married, but I'm worried that not being able to have a baby is going to, you know," and then he stopped.

"You're worried it may split your marriage," Robert finished.

Directly hearing out loud what had been on his mind for some while made Michael feel somewhat dour. It was a reasonable reflection of his general state of being over the past six months, and he nodded, saying nothing for a while. "Angie seems to be taking it badly," he said, eventually. He reached for the beer can, then stopped halfway and withdrew his hand to his lap beneath the table again. "She doesn't say much, but I know it's affecting her, and not in a good way. Know what I mean?"

Robert shook his head in agreement, and said, "It's my experience, both professionally and socially, that in matters where a couple is unable to bear children, it's usually the woman who gets hit hardest. If a woman can't have kids she tends to blame herself, for lots of reasons. Sometimes she feels she's a failure, or worse, that she's no longer a woman. I suspect Angie is doing a lot of this blame at the moment."

Michael smirked; it was precisely what he had been thinking. Not that she'd ever said it outright, that was not her style, but he'd suspected that self-blame had been the problem for a while. "She won't talk about how she's feeling," he said, sighing. "She's using her work to avoid confronting the issue. Yesterday she left at seven in the morning and didn't come home until after ten at night. I wish I could do something, but I feel helpless. Whenever I try to talk to her I feel like she's deliberately avoiding me. I don't know what to do."

Pausing at first, Michael took hold of the beer can and brought it to his lips, not knowing how to proceed. The friendship he had with his dad was great, but he wasn't sure how much he should, or could, relate the depths to which he and Angie had fallen. The worst part was being invisible. He reckoned that was about as low as it could get, and when a man is no longer noticed he begins to think about other things, bad things, like which one of the partners at Sugarman Klein & Pickering was screwing his wife on the boardroom table after all the other staff had gone home.

He decided not to say anything; it was uncomfortable to say the least. Instead, he took another sip of beer. He could see his father was disappointed. Somehow he knew he wasn't receiving the whole truth.

"I can only begin to understand how you must be feeling, Mikey,"

Robert said, looking Michael firmly in the eye, "and I won't ever try to tell you what you should or shouldn't do with your own wife. But one thing this old dog has learnt in the past fifty-seven years is that honesty and patience always win through in the end, no matter how rough it may seem at present."

"It's getting rougher," Michael said. Robert cocked an eyebrow. "Angie wants us to go to a fertility clinic. She's even made an appointment for next week."

"And you don't think it's the right thing to do."

Michael sat back and ran a hand through his hair, glancing at the light above table. Why was he so averse to seeking treatment at a fertility clinic? Why, when he imagined himself walking into the waiting room, did he have this feeling of dread and despair, as if he was walking into a lion's den?

"I don't know what to think any more," he said, sighing. "There are good and bad things about it. Her health insurance is going to cover the costs and the clinic may actually be able to help us have a baby. That's something good, at least, but I'm worried for Angie. She seems to be pinning all her hopes on this. If they can't help, and we can't have any kids, she's going to be devastated. It'll be worse than when her parents died. At least then we could plan for a future and have something to believe in. I'm afraid that she'll have nothing left to hope for if the fertility clinic falls through."

"There's always hope, Mikey," Robert said, his voice and expression serious. "It's what's kept mankind getting out of bed ever since he emerged from the African jungle."

Michael was pensive. Hope, he thought, was about all he had left.

# CHAPTER 2

AS HE SLEEPS, Michael is aware of two things; firstly, he knows it is the night before the appointment at the fertility clinic; secondly, he knows he is in the middle of a frightening dream. In it, everything is in black and white. He is running down the street. His legs are heavy and his chest is burning. He thinks he is being chased, but he's not sure; he can't see anyone behind him, but he feels fear, terrifying fear. Suddenly, he trips and falls. A black shadow looms over him. He tries to get up, but he can't. He can't move. He can't run. He can't do anything. He screams, but no sound comes out. Then he feels horrendous pain, as if he's being stabbed in his stomach, as if his whole intestines are being wrenched out. He knows he is going to die. The black shadow is watching. He looks up at it and screams in horror. The shadow has no face.

Michael woke with a fright and sat immediately upright. The back of his throat was stinging sharply, like a bad case of tonsillitis, though he knew it was probably because he'd been breathing harshly through his mouth, like someone who'd been running, while he slept. He put his hand over his heart and felt it thumping against his ribs. He could feel sweat on his brow. Taking several deep breaths, he glanced at the clock on the bedside cabinet. It was 5:29 a.m.

Angie continued to sleep quietly, oblivious to his recent fright. Slipping out of bed, now wide-awake, he went to the bathroom. His hands, he noticed, were trembling. It had to be one of the worst nightmares he'd ever had, even worse than those he suffered as a child after he and Jude saw Billie die, when he'd wake up terrified and screaming for his dad to come and comfort him. He glanced at his fatigued reflection in the mirror and tried telling himself that it was only a dream, that it wasn't real. It took a minute or two, but it seemed to work. His mind began to calm and his hands lost their shivering tremble.

After relieving himself, he filled the bathroom sink with hot water. Steam misted the mirrored doors of the cabinet above, which was good because he didn't want to look too closely again at his bleary eyes and haggard face. He opened the cabinet and reached for his razor. The blades looked blunt, so he removed the disposable head and tossed it into the bin beneath the sink. He was surprised to see it land near a crumpled blue box and a white, plastic object that on first glance looked like a small toothbrush. He bent down and removed the box and object, only now recognising what it was, a home pregnancy kit. At one end of the plastic tester he spied a reading. It was negative.

He knew Angie used to test her urine every month like clockwork when they first began trying to conceive, but the sight of the pregnancy tester confused him. Angie hadn't bothered to do it for the last six months or so, when she came to realise that the likelihood of being infertile was more probable than possible. Why had she tested it last night? Was there something she wasn't telling him?

The thought that Angie was withholding something troubled him the whole time he showered and got dressed. The image of that pregnancy tester lying in the bin beneath the bathroom sink simply wouldn't leave his head, and by the time she arrived in the kitchen at quarter to seven, dressed and ready for work, he was in a rouseable state of scepticism. She had, after all, arranged the clinic appointment behind his back. What else had she been up to that he wasn't aware of?

The cuffs of his blue shirt were rolled half way up his forearms, as if ready for a fight, and his freshly washed long hair was hanging loose over his shoulder, occasionally falling in front of his face as he finished the last spoonfuls of his cereal. Angie seated herself at the table with her usual cup of coffee, paying no particular heed to him. She seemed neither surprised nor pleased that he had risen before her. She just stared outside through the windowpane sliding door, interested only in gauging the weather. He followed her gaze, glancing quickly outside. Several fluffy cumulus clouds were rising with the sun over the hills in the east. There was nothing of interest for him, just the same shit, different day, so he turned back to Angie with the intent of confronting her with the news of his earlier discovery in the bathroom.

Angie didn't give him the chance to speak. "Don't forget we have the clinic appointment today," she said, taking a sip of coffee. "Five o'clock."

"You know I don't like hospitals," he said, and then, almost as an afterthought, added, "Miss Schmetterling had a fit when I asked her if I could miss tonight's teachers' meeting. Are you sure I have to go?"

Angie rolled her eyes and sighed. "Yes. We've discussed this all before and we don't need to go through it again. You're my husband and we're in this together. If you don't meet me at the hospital, it'll be a total dereliction of your duty."

"Christ!" he said. "This is emotional blackmail."

"Don't you blaspheme!" she said, and slapped her palms down onto the tabletop. Tears formed in her eyes. She pushed herself up from her chair, knocking the underneath of the table with her upper thighs, and before Michael knew what was happening she was out of the kitchen and crying. He heard her footsteps hurry down the hall to the front bedroom.

He threw his hands in the air. "Christ!" he said, pushing the chair back and standing up. "Angie, I'm sorry," he yelled after her. "I didn't mean it, you know that." He waited for her reply. There was just the tic-toc of the grandfather clock. "Angel, come on!"

This was getting ridiculous, he thought. This whole thing was getting out of control. He couldn't say anything anymore without her running off crying. Staring at the ceiling, not knowing what to do, he absently ran a hand through his hair. He just wished the whole situation would go away and they could get back with their lives, the way they used to be when they just got married, happy and carefree, like when they used to find the time to go for dinner at their favourite restaurant, Piccolo Diavolo, and spend a romantic night together, or like when they used to go away on weekends to his father's holiday house in Serena and relax and enjoy each other's company. That was all he wanted, nothing more. He just wanted the marriage to get back to normal.

He followed her out of the kitchen, and as he walked around the dividing bench he glanced at the refrigerator's only two magnets, yet more reminders of Angie's deceased parents: JESUS LOVES YOU! and GOD GIVES WHAT'S RIGHT—NOT WHAT'S LEFT!

"Yeah, sure," he harrumphed, glaring at them. "God gives you nothing but shit and then complains that no one is grateful for it."

He wandered slowly up the hallway. Deciding to let Angie keep her distance, he stopped before entering the front bedroom and leant against the doorframe. The curtains to his immediate left had been pulled open and light was streaming through the window, forming a bright square on the quilt in the centre of the room. It was the only room in the house they had attempted to renovate. Angie, he recalled, had made all the decorating decisions. The result: purple. The whole room was one shade of it or another—lilac, mauve, lavender, violet— the walls, the linen, the curtains, the quilt, all were purple, even the bedside alarm clock and lamp. The only things not were the bare wooden floorboards (Angie had insisted they rip up the horrid blue carpet, at least in this room), the sliding mirrored doors of the built-in closet, and the oak dressing table at which Angie was now perched.

With her back to him, she was sitting on a stool directly ahead, peering into the dressing table mirror and rubbing foundation makeup into her cheeks and forehead. A cosmetic case sat open like a mini painter's satchel to her left. It was brimming with assorted lipsticks, eyeliners, brushes, creams, mascaras, and lots of things Michael didn't recognise. In the reflection he could see her face. She was trying her best not to cry and the whites of her eyes were streaked with red. He felt a tug of guilt and apologised for what he had said in the kitchen.

Angie sniffed and applied a touch of moon-dust colouring to her cheeks. Then she put the mascara brush down and began touching up her eyes with black eyeliner. She was deliberately silent while she worked, making him wait for her reply, and only after a minute or two did she turn around and face him. "If you're truly sorry," she said, holding his gaze, "you'll be in the lobby of the hospital before five o'clock this evening."

She turned back to the dressing table mirror and removed the lid to a tube of red lipstick. As she slid the lipstick across her lips, they were transformed into soft, alluring petals and Michael suddenly understood why bees were so attracted to flowers. After a few seconds, she puckered and smacked her lips gently together, then stood the lipstick on its end next to the cosmetic case and turned around.

"How do I look?" she asked.

Michael was about to reply when suddenly, as she stood up, Angie doubled over as if she had just been delivered a punch to the stomach. Her face was contorted—mouth gaping, eyes wide—and despite the recently applied makeup her skin had turned ghastly pale. He stared at her, momentarily immobilised with fright. Angie groped for the dressing table, the other hand clutching her lower belly. The tube of lipstick was knocked onto its side and it rolled off the table onto the floor next to her briefcase. Angie didn't seem to notice. She wobbled precariously, teetering like a toddler just learning to walk. Without a second to spare, Michael broke free from the paralysis of his initial shock and rushed over, catching her just before she fell.

Angie didn't speak. She didn't seem able. She just leant into his embrace and grabbed hold of his arm. He was horrified. He didn't know what to do or how to help, other than just hold on to her and hope the pain would quickly pass. His mind was racing. What was happening? Did he need to rush her to the hospital? Should he call an ambulance?

After a minute, her wrestle-like grip began to relax. To his relief, she was soon standing erect once again with the colour returned to her face. He stood by as she took several deep breaths and pursed her lips, blowing the air slowly out of her lungs. When she finally met his eyes he could tell the worst was over. "Are you okay?" he asked.

She nodded, regathering her composure. "I'll be all right," she said, after a moment. "Don't worry, I get it all the time." But her attempt to play down the seriousness of what had just happened only made Michael worry even more. She seemed to sense his unease. "It goes away by itself. It's just a little stomach cramp, that's all."

Her smile was weak and unconvincing, and he knew by her reticence that she was withholding the truth. She patted his arm in a poor attempt to allay his concerns and reached for her briefcase beneath the dressing table. Before leaving, she kissed him on the lips and reiterated their plans to meet after work. Michael knew he had no choice but to let her go. She left him standing alone in the bedroom, confused and worried.

LATER THAT DAY, Michael stood motionless at the blackboard with his back to the class. His hand was raised where it had stopped in mid-sentence, a broken piece of white chalk firmly fixed between thumb and forefinger. He had been in a daydream, lost in his own world. He had no idea how long he had been standing that way and was busily trying to figure out how he had managed to misplace his memories and what he had been saying to the class.

They were obedient and silent, damn good kids he reckoned. All he could hear was their shuffling bums on the seats and the anxious pacing of someone walking past the classroom in the corridor outside. It sounded like Norman's footsteps, heavy and discordant, like a clumsy elephant constantly tripping over itself. Running a chalk-covered hand through his hair, he tried to pick up from where he had left off. Only he couldn't remember.

Suddenly, the image of Angie floated in front of the blackboard like a vision of the Holy Mary. He remembered this morning's incident in the bedroom, her face contorting with agony, her body doubling over as if she had been stabbed in the stomach, and it made him sick with worry. Despite her words of consolation, he knew Angie was covering something up. She said that she was fine, but she wasn't; he had seen the alarm in her eyes flashing as brightly as lightning. For whatever reason, she was holding back. Knowing this was more terrifying than the mysterious pain itself. He reckoned he hadn't felt so frightened since the day he saw Billie die.

He remembered that day clearly. The sky had been blue and cloud-less above Serena, another piping hot day in the summer of '75. Michael was playing backyard cricket with Jude, who lived two blocks around the corner and often came over to the house to play, especially during the school holidays. They were both in their swimming trunks (Jude's red, his yellow) and their eight-year old bodies were tanned and supple. Michael was holding the bat, a new Slazenger he had just got for his birthday, and Jude was tossing and catching the tennis ball, readying himself to pitch it down. Michael knew all Jude wanted to do was hit him in the head with the tennis ball. All he wanted to do was hit the ball over the fence with his new cricket bat. That's the way it always was that summer.

Jude's end was the clothesline. Michael's end was the back wall of the house, where he was tapping the bat on the ground and waiting for Jude to deliver the ball. They were separated by no more than fifteen yards. They were also as far as they could get from his mum's precious vegetable garden in the bottom corner of the yard. Hitting the ball into the vegetable garden was instantly out, no questions asked, followed by an immediate change of innings. Michael really wasn't too concerned about that. He was going to hit Jude a lot further than the tomatoes and the cucumbers—he was going to hit him over the fence and out of the yard.

Michael tapped the bat on the ground and watched his cousin. Jude had a knowing grin on his face. He was wandering near the edge of the vegetable garden at the top of his run-up, which Michael thought was ridiculously long. It was obvious Jude wanted to cause some serious harm with the ball. Michael wasn't worried. He tapped his Slazenger on the grass again and waited.

Jude wasted no time. He ran in and delivered the ball as hard as he could. Michael watched it hit the grass and take a nasty kick, jumping straight for his head. There was no time to take a swipe with the bat. He jerked his head backward, but the ball seemed to follow him, chasing him like a large demented wasp. It shot barely an inch past his nose and clattered into the wooden boards of the back wall. He had escaped instant humiliation by the barest of margins.

Michael picked up the tennis ball and threw it back to Jude. After a brief flurry of words, something to the effect that Michael couldn't hit the ball if he tried, Jude went back to the top of his run-up. Michael tapped the Slazenger on the ground, talking to himself and making sure he concentrated properly this time. The last thing he wanted was to be brained by a bouncer from Jude; he'd never hear the end of it. Jude ran in again and sent down another fast delivery, which Michael swung at and missed. The ball passed just over the top of the rubbish bin and thumped into the wall again, much to Jude's obvious delight.

Jude mocked him once again. Michael threw the ball back and

gritted his teeth, saying nothing, hoping to wipe the cocky smile off his cousin's face. Jude ambled to the top of his run-up for a third time, strutting with confidence. Michael wiped the sweat off his brow with his forearm and tapped the Slazenger on the ground, thinking that if Jude bowled another bouncer he was going to hit it so far Jude was going to get a sun burnt palate watching it pass over his head. Jude steamed in and fired down his fastest ball yet, thundering it straight for the spot between Michael's eyes. This time Michael saw it coming, and he got into position early. He stepped back, lifting the bat high, and then connected beautifully with a perfect pull shot. He watched the ball sail in a high arc over the backyard fence and out of sight. In baseball terms, it was a homer. In backyard cricket terms, it was six-and-out. But he didn't care; the stunned look on Jude's face made it all worthwhile.

Jude mumbled something Michael couldn't quite hear and stormed over to the corrugated iron fence, pressing his eye against a rusty hole to search for the ball on the other side. The next-door neighbour's house belonged to an old man in his seventies who lived with his wife and retarded son. They had a Great Dane called Belvedere, which roamed their back garden like a sentry but was as harmless as a mouse. Sometimes he escaped by digging a hole beneath the fence and then went charging around the streets of Serena scaring the willies out of little old grannies until his owner managed to recapture him. Michael liked Belvedere. He threw biscuits and chunks of meat over the fence for him whenever he could, but for reasons he never knew, Jude always seemed wary of him.

Over by the fence, Jude was visibly excited by something he could see through the hole. Gesticulating wildly, he shouted for Michael to come over. Michael dropped the bat and rushed over to join him, eager to see what was happening on the other side. Jude peered through the hole again, and then took his eye away from it, looking directly at Michael with an expression of utter disbelief.

"Someth'ns wrong with Billie," he said, hushed and afraid. Billie was what he called the Great Dane because he couldn't quite manage to say Belvedere without tripping over his tongue. "I think he's dyin', Mikey."

Not knowing what to expect, Michael quickly peeked through another rusty hole. The midday sun had heated everything it touched like a devilish King Midas, so the act of pressing his cheek to the fence was like laying his face onto a barbeque hotplate. He ignored the pain to see what Jude was raving on about. What he saw made his skin crawl. Belvedere was lying on the ground writhing in agony, foam drooling out of his mouth like washing suds, eyes rolled back and his legs and tail and body shaking feverishly. Billie was dying, that was for sure.

Five minutes later, Michael pulled his eye away from the hole, the skin of his right cheek and eyebrow scalding red. Billie was twitching no more. If this was death, he thought, it was horrible. He suddenly felt dizzy and he had to suppress the violent urge to vomit. His breathing was short and shallow and he desperately needed to sit down.

Jude, on the other hand, was positively joyous. His blue eyes were gleaming and the smile on his face was as broad as the fence. He was jabbering excitedly, as if it were the best thing he had ever seen.

Michael was suddenly furious. With every word Jude uttered, he could feel his head begin to throb. Hitting him over the head with the Slazenger would have had the same result. He clenched his fists and swallowed hard, then did something he had never done before—he punched Jude flush in the face, a right hook that connected with his cousin's jaw as well as his bat had connected with the ball. He immediately regretted what he'd done. His hand now hurt like hell.

Michael braced himself for the expected retaliation. They were going to have their first punch up and he was not looking forward to it. To his surprise, Jude did nothing at first, just gaped in shock, then gently rubbed his jaw and glared at him. Coldness washed over his face. Michael was about to say something, maybe even apologise, but he saw something in his cousin's eyes that was as frightening as watching the death of Belvedere—seething hatred. His voice suddenly evaporated like sweat in the midday sun.

"You'll regret you ever did that," Jude said, then turned around and sulked away.

Michael watched him disappear around the side of the house, rubbing his jaw. Later that night, Michael lay in his bed tucked beneath the faded yellow sheet, feeling quite lost, feeling quite ashamed at witnessing the agonising death of an innocent animal. The skin on his scalded cheek had formed into an ugly blister, but at least his hand had stopped throbbing. In fact, he didn't seem to feel any pain at all, only sadness, horrible sadness.

His dad was sitting at the end of the bed, seemingly at a loss for the right words to say. Billie had apparently been fed a steak laced with rat poison, something called warfarin, but which Michael initially heard as wafin. It had caused a massive bleed inside Billie's brain called a stroke. That's why he'd been fitting and drooling.

Whatever the reason, Michael hoped he'd never have to see such a horrible thing in his life again. He recalled the chilling words Jude had said earlier that day: Someth'ns wrong with Billie, I think he's dyin', Mikey.

Seeing the Great Dane die wasn't the only thing that was worrying him, though. He knew Jude wasn't going to forget this incident. Not for a long while. Not ever.

The school bell sounded the end of the final period, shaking him from his memories. Michael jumped, and for some reason absently rubbed his fist. He turned and faced the class. They were patiently waiting for him to say something, their faces staring up at him like sunflowers tilted toward the sun. He knew what they wanted to hear, so he quickly gave them permission to leave.

The volume in the room immediately turned to full. The children gathered their bags and packed their books away, then began streaming out of the classroom into the corridor and merging with the children exiting the other classrooms. A little girl in a bright floral dress ambled up to him. Her name, for some reason, eluded him. She was a cute kid, a real daddy's girl—blonde hair, blue eyes, perfect lips. Pointing to the blackboard, she asked him what he'd written.

He turned around, at first quizzical, then wide-eyed and incredulous. On the blackboard, in large white letters, was a message that seemed to have come from beyond the grave, as if it had been spelled out on a ouija board:

*Something's wrong with Angie.*
*I think she's dying, Mikey*

35

Michael staggered back, grabbing a steadying hold of his desktop. He read it again, his mind stumbling over the words like a dyslexic. The little girl asked him another question, but he was still too stunned to answer.

Suddenly, a mental image flashed before his eyes, of Angie drooling and twitching on the ground in a foetal position, writhing in agony, one hand clasping her belly, the other her head.

"Just like Billie," he whispered, horrified at the idea.

He kept staring at the blackboard, running his hand through his hair. He'd never had a premonition before, he didn't even believe in them, but this felt very much like one now, like déjà vu in reverse, as if he could sense something bad was going to happen before it did.

He heard the little girl's footsteps running out of the classroom. She was obviously bored with receiving no answer to her questions and wanted to catch up with her friends before it was too late. He watched her leave and waited until she was out of sight before rubbing the offending sentence off the blackboard. As the duster wiped away the words, he caught himself smirking. The stress of the past few months was affecting him a lot more than he realised. He needed to relax. He needed a nice long holiday sitting on the beach reading a good book and drinking beer. Lots of beer.

He finished cleaning the blackboard and glanced outside the dirty windows. The sky was drizzly grey and the light was already fading. Some kids were shooting baskets on the basketball court, which also doubled as the school quadrangle. Others in parkas and raincoats were saying farewell to each other beneath the two large eucalypts over on the far side of the court. He figured it was time he stopped dawdling and got going as well. Removing his leather jacket from over the back of his chair, he looked up at the clock above the lockers on the back wall. It was showing ten to four, though he knew it was five minutes slow. He hadn't bothered to set it to the proper time because he liked the thought of having five minutes less to go before the end of school. Nevertheless, time was ticking and Angie would be waiting. In slow, exaggerated movements, he made his way to the door. He felt like a man twice his age; his bones felt achy and his feet hurt. That holiday couldn't come too soon.

He stepped out into the corridor, what he thought of as the highway of the building, and was surprised to find himself its sole occupant. To his right was the reception and principal's office at the main entrance. To his left, the staff room and emergency fire exit at the rear. The classrooms abutting the corridor reminded him of prison cells lining death row. He couldn't wait to get out of here quick enough.

After locking the door, he hastened as fast as his tired body would allow toward the main entrance. Halfway there, he heard the click of a shutting door from behind. He turned around to see the rotund figure of his friend, Norman Page, exiting his classroom. As well as the cream cardigan and beige trousers he was wearing, he carried a grey tatty coat over the crook of one arm and a taupe leather briefcase under the armpit of the other. Michael had once seen inside that briefcase. It was filled with nothing apart from nudie magazines and candy bars. Norman locked his classroom and looked up at Michael. There was a frown deeply embedded in his brow, which Michael reckoned was as permanent as his stubby nose and double chin.

"You look wonderful, my friend," Michael said, smiling.

Norman grabbed his belt and hoisted his trousers over his over-hanging belly. "And you're a very handsome woman," he replied in his best Elvis Presley impersonation.

Michael thought the lip-curl lingered on his face like a poorly reconstructed harelip. He watched Norman turn and waddle towards the staff room. After a few steps the large man halted, sensing that Michael wasn't following, and turned around to confront him.

"Are you coming to the staff meeting or not?" he asked.

Michael kept smiling as he had. "Not today, Mr. Page. I've got a get-out-of-jail-free card."

Norman's shoulders slumped and he almost dropped his briefcase. Michael could see he was having problems figuring out how he could get away once again whilst everyone else had to stay behind. Norman was always complaining that Michael was the headmistress's pet. It drove Norman mad. He was always late in the mornings and missing meetings, while Norman was never late and yet was forever under the watchful eye of his superiors. Norman felt that no matter what he did, everything always went pear-shaped. Michael, he was forever grumbling, was luckier. Everything always seemed to work out for him, as if the gods were always on his side. Michael had to disagree. Norman didn't know the problems he was facing at home.

"But, but how can you?" Norman said, still obviously flummoxed. "It's out of the question. You can't leave before Frau Hitler gives her orders for the month." He clicked his heals together, dropped his coat, and gave a Nazi salute. "Vee must obey! Resistance is futile!" His fake German accent echoed around the corridor and Michael hoped no one else had heard, especially the headmistress. It would just be Norman's luck if she had.

"Then call me nobody, mein Kommidant," Michael said, looking at his watch. "I've got an important rendezvous in an hour. Angie won't let me get out of it."

Norman lowered his arm. "Sure, you're off to enjoy yourselves while your poor friend suffers at the hands of a sadist. Don't desert me like this Mikey, you know I can't cope alone. I'm always the sacrificial lamb. Why can't it be someone else for a change?"

The look on Norman's face was almost pitiful. If Norman knew what he was about to do, Michael thought, then he probably wouldn't complain so vociferously. If he himself had a choice, he would gladly exchange places with Norman right now.

Michael bade farewell and left his friend to pick up his coat and attend the meeting. "Mikey, I almost forgot," he heard Norman say before he exited through the main doors. "Bridget's cooking for Thanksgiving tonight. She asked if you and Angie would be interested in coming over later."

"Thanksgiving? Who celebrates that?" Michael said with his hand on the door.

Norman shrugged. "We do. Bridget's father was a US Marine. He settled in Sydney after the war and we've kind of kept up the family tradition."

Michael took a moment to consider the offer. "I don't know, Norman. I'm not sure how long this thing's going to take. Can I call you later?"

"Sure, if I'm still alive to take your call."

Rolling his eyes, Michael waved goodbye and strode outside. The main entrance opened onto the basketball court-cum-quadrangle. Beyond and to the left was the teachers' parking lot. The threatened drizzle he had seen from the classroom had materialised into light rain and he was forced to break into a trot. He cursed. This incessant weather was beginning to really get on his nerves of late. He was beginning to feel permanently damp, as though his clothes were always wet.

As he reached the parking lot, the sky visibly darkened and the rain began to fall in heavy drops. He cursed again. He spied the faded yellow paintwork of the VW parked between two other cars and began running to it. He jumped in and slotted the key in the ignition, grateful to get out of the rain. Annoyingly, the steam lifting from his soggy clothes fogged the windows almost straight away, and when he turned the key he felt a sudden chill, more than he expected wet clothes should, like he had just sat down inside a freezer. He began to shiver and his teeth chattered uncontrollably, and right at the moment the engine sputtered into life the image of Angie twitching and drooling on the ground flashed before him.

Once again the unnerving premonition of dread washed over him. A voice suddenly popped into his head, hushed and frightened, as if narrating the image: *Someth'ns wrong with Angie. I think she's dyin', Mikey.*

He slammed the gear stick in reverse and accelerated back. "Please don't let anything be wrong with her," he mumbled. Except, to his dismay, no matter how hard he tried he couldn't erase that image of her from his mind.

He sped through the gates out of the school grounds. The idea of going to the hospital suddenly didn't seem so bad.

## CHAPTER 3

MICHAEL DROVE EAST in the fast lane along ANZAC Highway, heading toward the city from the coast and pretty much against the flow of rush hour traffic. The windscreen wipers swayed back and forth, sweeping away the drizzle that blurred his vision. The streetlights were already on and every car was driving with their headlights blazing.

Out of habit, he glanced at the dashboard clock. It hadn't worked since Angie passed the car on to him when she inherited the Corolla from her parents, permanently stuck at three seventeen, but he didn't need to know the time to know that he was running late. Hoping he wouldn't encounter any speed traps, he pushed the throttle and weaved in and out of the traffic until, elbow-like, the road kinked northeast and he came to a halt at a red light.

The opposite side of the intersection was a vista of green. Michael had read in a guidebook that one of the charms of Adelaide were the vast parklands that completely framed the city, enabling the visitor to escape the bustle of the city centre and experience the serenity of the countryside. ANZAC Highway forged its way through this sylvan rim like a grey river slicing through a forest. Lining both sides were imposing eucalypts, which were now swaying haphazardly in the gusty, drizzly wind. About a kilometre or so further on, the road abruptly terminated at a jagged wall of glass and cement. Of all the city buildings, the State Bank Building where Angie worked on the nineteenth floor was by far the tallest. It reminded him of a jutting middle finger on a hand in which all others were bent at the knuckle, that petulant one-finger gesture favoured by most teenagers when the teacher's back was turned.

The traffic arrow turned green and Michael turned off the highway.

For ten minutes he drove east, keeping the south parklands and the cityscape to his left. Until now he had made reasonable time, but slow moving traffic merging from the city centre and uncooperative traffic lights were combining to make the journey all the more frustrating. When he finally arrived at the fourth major intersection, which formed the southeast corner of the parklands, he turned left and progressed northward, once again against the rush hour flow.

As expected, on the opposite side of the road, St. Mary's Hospital rose into the bleak sky out of the serrated horizon of suburban rooftops. Its twin, eight-story buildings reminded him of two giant tombstones rising out of a cemetery. He stared at them as he waited for a break in the traffic to cross over. How on earth had he let himself be talked into this? he mused, running a hand through his hair. Angie knew how much he hated hospitals.

*You know damn well why you're here*, he answered himself. *Because of what happened this morning. Someth'ns wrong with Angie.*

The outward-bound traffic slowed and he crossed into a side street toward the main gates. An unsmiling security guard waved him beneath an upright boom and into the visitor's parking lot, which, to his chagrin, was looking quite full. He passed a sign welcoming him to St. Mary's Hospital, yet the very thought of walking inside was making him suddenly apprehensive. The hospital complex was the third largest in Adelaide, though never once had he stepped foot inside its gold-brick walls. Thousands of times he had passed this hospital, and thousands of times he had wished he would never have to pass through its doors. He was not relishing the prospect of doing so now.

Three rows from the gate he found a space, parked the car, and got out. Head down, he began to trot through the drizzle toward the eastern building until he realised it was the nurses' residence. He halted, momentarily disorientated, then saw a sign above the sliding glass doors of the western building: ST. MARY'S HOSPITAL MAIN ENTRANCE. He hastened there now.

Inside, the lobby was busy with patients and staff. He immediately felt irked and crowded. A woman was speaking animatedly on a payphone in the far corner near the florist and the news agency. A man was struggling on a set of crutches with his leg in plaster. A young child with a scabrous rash all over her face was holding a woman's hand, crying. Closer, an old lady in a nightgown was wandering this way and that with a note pinned to her back: PLEASE RETURN ME TO WARD 1C. I AM LOST. It was just as he imagined a battlefield in the First World War, hectic with the traffic of wounded humanity. But it was the smell he disliked most. The lobby reeked of disinfectant and foreboding.

He eyed the clock above the entrance. Five minutes past five. Not as late as he originally thought, but late nonetheless. He quickly scanned for his wife. She was nowhere to be seen. He tried to look behind two stern looking women with white coats and black stethoscopes heading in his direction, but as he stepped back to let them pass, he inadvertently bumped into a nurse carrying several patient files, some of which dropped from her arms and spilled onto the floor. Feeling culpable and a little foolish, Michael at once bent down to help her pick them up, but in his haste he accidentally banged his head with her elbow, causing her to lose grip of the remaining folders. This only furthered his embarrassment. Resting on his hunches, he gathered some of the loose pages together and handed them back to her, apologising for his carelessness.

She too gathered up the sprawled files. Like many in the room, she was stern and unsmiling. Michael briefly wondered what it would be like to work in such an environment where people were perpetually angry and depressed, and then figured he would probably end up with a long and dour face before too long. Picking up a loose leaf of paper that had slipped from a file, Michael wasn't sure whether her brusqueness was due to frustration of being delayed or plain arrogance, but when she took the paper and looked at him he froze. She was stunningly pretty. He hadn't been struck by a woman's beauty since he saw Angie in her little black dress standing at the front door of her house on the night of their first date. That was over six years ago and a lot of women had passed before his eyes, but none that could match this woman. Her almond shaped eyes, deeply dark and seductive; her shoulder-length hair, as black and shiny as a still lake on a starry night; her smile, full and wide, with perfect white teeth, like petals of a daisy. She reminded him, for some unknown reason, of a young Egyptian princess, like he imagined Cleopatra would have once looked, including her delicate olive skin and the dark beauty spot above her left lip. Their eyes met briefly, then quickly away.

He handed the last file to her. She thanked him for his help and stood up. Michael stared, unmoved from his hunched position as she walked toward the elevators with brisk strides, adjusting the white uniform on her curvaceous backside as she went. Standing slowly, he heard his name being shouted. It was Angie.

He searched the direction of her voice and saw her waiting near the reception beneath an information sign that hung on chains from the ceiling. Like this morning, she had her hair pulled into a bun and she was wearing her blue, two-piece work suit. The suitcase, however, had been swapped for a matching handbag. Her rimless glasses were also nowhere to be seen, probably replaced with contact lenses. She seemed relieved that he was here.

With a smile he waved and she waved in return. He was immeasurably glad to see that she was well, even more so that his earlier concerns about her well-being were probably nothing more than the result of an over-enthusiastic imagination. He quickly crossed the lobby to where she was standing and pecked a kiss on her red lips.

"Are you feeling better?" he asked.

For a brief moment she stared blankly into his eyes, misunderstanding the question, and then said, "Yeah, no more pain." She seemed unaware that she was running her hand over the lower part of her belly. "I told you it wasn't anything to worry about."

He scrutinised her face, trying to ascertain whether she was telling the complete truth or not. He decided to let it pass and took her by the elbow. "Come on, then," he said, eager for this to be over and done with. "Let's not hang around in here. Let's do it."

They passed the shops toward a set of white double doors marking the west wing of the hospital: TO MATERNITY, NEONATAL AND PEDIATRIC WARDS, OUT PATIENTS AND ACCIDENT & EMERGENCY DEPARTMENT. Just as they passed beneath the sign, Angie stopped.

"Are you sure you want to go through with this?" she asked. There was hesitation in her voice. "I mean, I don't want you—us—to do anything we might regret."

Michael could sense her anxiety. He had the feeling that he if just said the word, she would be more than willing to leave with him right now. The idea was appealing, but he remembered what his father had said about women blaming themselves for being unable to conceive. The last thing he wanted was for Angie to spend the rest of her life mired in guilt. "I'm not going to pull out at this stage," he said, smiling lopsidedly, "not unless you want me to."

She bit her bottom lip, like someone given the opportunity to finally do something they had always desired but were struggling with the reality that it was actually happening, frightened by it coming true. He could see the ambivalence in her caramel eyes. Then she shook her head, and said, "No, Mikey. I want to make sure we have done everything we can before we give up hope."

Five minutes later, they arrived at the outpatient department on the second floor. A plump, middle-aged nurse ushered them into a side door marked "Fertility Clinic". Her hair, predominantly grey and streaked with black and white strands, was tied into a ponytail with a rubber band. Forty years ago, Michael thought, it would have been a pink ribbon. She had sad eyes, and thanking her with a smile and a nod he followed Angie into the waiting room. The clatter of fingers over a keyboard alerted them to a secretary with a blonde bob sitting behind the reception desk. They walked up to the desk and patiently waited for her to acknowledge their presence. She didn't. From where he stood, peering down onto her, Michael could see dark roots sprouting out of her head like unwanted weeds. An appointment book was lying face up next to the keyboard.

The secretary continued to type, deliberately ignoring them, so Michael surveyed the waiting room. Around its perimeter, empty green-grey seats backed the white walls. A glass coffee table bedecked with a fern pot plant and a scattering of women's magazines occupied the centre of the room. At the far end, next to a large print of an aerial photograph of Adelaide, was a closed door, on which his gaze fell upon a gold plaque with black etching he could only just read: DR. B. ROUBEN. It was a name he wasn't familiar with, and he pondered on its origins, whether it was French, or maybe some other European country.

In the meantime, the ingénue behind the reception desk was still typing on the computer. Angie absolutely hated rudeness and Michael could tell that her already thinning patience was being stretched to its limits. She cleared her throat, deliberately loud, and the keyboard fell silent, though several seconds passed before the secretary raised her eyes above the computer screen.

"Can I help you?" she asked, her brow gouged into a severe frown. On her right cheek was a large pimple that throbbed like a recent bee sting.

"Hello," Angie said, sweetly, her lips twitching into a cynical grin. "My name is Angie Joseph. I believe I have an appointment to see the doctor at five."

The secretary glanced at the clock above the entrance. "You're late," she said, and reached for the appointment book. "The doctor is a very busy man. He can't be expected to wait for patients to arrive whenever they want."

To Michael, it was clear this secretary felt 'the doctor' was her private property. He had an idea she dreamed of jumping beneath the sheets with him and screwing his brains out, and for a brief moment he felt pity for this woman with the dark roots. She sighed loudly and flicked through her appointment book.

"What did you say your name was?"

"Angie Joseph."

"Hmm. Yes, here it is." She took a pencil and slashed through Angie's name, almost, Michael thought, like an executioner. "Go and take a seat. I'll call you when the doctor is ready." Pointing with the pencil to the empty seats, she closed the book with a snap.

Michael followed his wife to a seat at the far wall beneath the aerial print of Adelaide. She snatched from the sprawl of magazines atop the coffee table a ragged copy of *Woman's World*, on the cover of which a model smiled with an exotic beauty that reminded him of the nurse he had accidentally collided with in the lobby. He spied a glossy pamphlet lying on the seat to Angie's left and picked it up as he sat down. At first he thought it was a package holiday brochure, but soon realised upon closer inspection it was, in fact, a brochure for the hospital briefly describing its facilities.

Angie flipped through the pages of the magazine while he read about the "impressive" services of St. Mary's Hospital. No sooner had he finished, the door to the doctor's office opened. Some cheery voices said goodbye to each other and then a woman and her husband walked out. Given the bulge of her stomach, Michael guessed she was almost ready to give birth. The moment the couple passed the secretary on their way out, Michael heard a muffled, static voice from the intercom behind the reception desk asking for the next patient to be brought in.

Unhappy and unsmiling, the secretary picked up a wafer thin medical file. As she walked toward them, Michael saw that it was marked ANGIE JOSEPH HT950765P in thick black marking pen, and that beneath her décolleté dress she also had a pair of surprisingly long and shapely legs. When she asked them to follow, it was not so much a question as an order. He took Angie's hand and they followed the secretary into the doctor's office.

The doctor was sitting with deep concentration behind his desk in a plush, red-leather chair writing in the notes of the previous patient. Behind him, the solitary window framed his upper torso like a painting, through which the last remaining rays of the day shrouded his head and shoulders in a glowing tippet. His pristine white shirt was probably designer label, Michael guessed, as most likely was the navy-blue suit and maroon and white striped tie he was wearing. He oozed cash, and Michael now had a clear understanding why the secretary was so protective of him. He felt a prick of jealously and briefly wondered what Angie was thinking.

The secretary gestured for them to take a seat in the leather chairs facing the doctor. Then she put Angie's file on top of the desk and slipped quietly out of the room. While the doctor busied himself with the previous patient's notes, Michael quickly scanned the room. Like the doctor, the office was immaculately decked out. The desk, something antique and mahogany by the look of it, dominated the room and engendered an air of iatric importance. On the wood-panelled walls to his left were the doctor's many certificates and diplomas, hanging like captured standards. The breakfront bookcase to his right was filled with leather-bound medical books. Michael could imagine what Angie was thinking. The décor was what she would call "tastefully expensive," everything from the gold plated fountain pen the doctor was scrawling with to the plush crimson carpet beneath their feet. It was not his type of décor at all, too garrulous, too pretentious. He felt distinctly ill at ease.

The doctor closed the file he had been writing in and reached for the new one. An awkward silence had fallen upon the room. "Hi, I'm Dr. Benjamin Rouben," he said, clearing his throat and smiling broadly. Michael figured this was his "welcome" smile to first comers, one that was supposed to make them feel relaxed, but it looked forced and overly cheesy. "But please call me Billy, that's what my friends call me." He turned to each one in turn and acknowledged who they were.

Angie's returning smile was anxiously thin and Michael saw her tighten her grip on her handbag. Michael flicked his eyes back to the doctor, nodded once, rigidly, and then lowered his gaze to his hands. The doctor reminded him of a Sicilian Godfather. His dislike for him was immediate and surprisingly visceral. He disliked his slick black hair that clung like fresh paint to his scalp. He disliked the perfect whiteness of his teeth. He even disliked his olive skin, and he especially disliked his dark brown eyes that crawled all over Angie and mentally undressed her. True, he disliked most doctors, except his dad. They were all no-good arrogant sons of bitches who thought they were god, especially this one. Who was he trying to impress with his why-don't-you-call-me-Billy routine and smiling like a cat that just ate the canary?

Michael shifted in his chair, decidedly uncomfortable with this whole thing. He looked at Angie, almost pleading with his eyes. He wanted to tell this guy thanks, but no thanks, that coming here was an unfortunate mistake, and then go and find another doctor who didn't look so smarmy.

"Welcome to my clinic," Dr. Rouben said, directing himself mainly to Angie. "I know you must be nervous. Everyone is on the first visit. But don't worry, soon this place will be like your second home, and I hope just as comfortable."

Angie kept returning his smile, and Michael kept shifting in his seat like one of his boys in his class desperately holding on to a full bladder. He really didn't want to hear all this. He just wanted to get up and leave, but he knew the chances of that were not very good.

Dr. Rouben glanced down at the open file on the desk. "I have a little information about you both here," he said, "from the preliminary medical form you sent to my secretary. Do you mind if I run through it with you to make sure everything is in order?"

Michael saw Angie nod out of the corner of his eye. It was obvious that she wasn't having the same doubts he was. He resigned himself to staying. That's okay, he thought. He'd hear him out and then tell Angie what he thought of him when they were at home.

"How often do you get migraines?" Dr. Rouben asked Angie.

"Not often, maybe three or four times a year," she said.

"Do you take any medication for it?"

"Only paracetamol. Nothing really works, just rest and a dark room."

Dr. Rouben picked up his gold fountain pen, scrawled a brief note in her file and then flipped over to the last page of the questionnaire. "It says here that you had your first period when you were twelve." Angie nodded again. "Have there been any problems?" he asked, to which she shook her head.

Michael looked at her, cocking his eyebrow. Had she not mentioned anything about the pain in her stomach? When did she plan on telling him? Or was she going to keep quiet about it?

"It seems everything is in order," Dr. Rouben said. "There doesn't seem to be any obvious medical concerns that would preclude you from conceiving a child, so now we need to get to the bottom of why it's not happening. I believe you've been trying to have a baby for nearly three years."

Angie nodded, gripping her handbag even tighter than she had. "Over three and a half, actually."

Dr. Rouben cleared his throat again. "Before I go into the details of what this clinic is all about, and what we would like to do over the next few months, I want to be frank with you both. Ten percent of adults in the western world, male and female, are infertile. That means for every ten of your friends one of them cannot conceive a child. Either of you may be that one. This means that anywhere between ten to twenty percent of couples are going to be childless." The room was silent. To Michael, it was as if the doctor was deliberately letting this piece of information sink in for several seconds before he went on. "Before we go any further, it is imperative you wash away all your feelings of guilt—both of you—for not being able to have a child the so-called normal way. Do you understand what I'm saying?"

Michael crossed his right leg over his left, feeling uncomfortable with the direction this was going. It was opening up too many fresh wounds in his and Angie's relationship, wounds that he'd rather have let heal in their own time without someone else intervening, especially someone like this guy. "We know it's not our fault," he began to reply.

Dr. Rouben held up his hand. "Of course, but it's something that I like to address straight away."

"Okay, thank you, Dr Rou… Dr. Billy, but Angie and I are still a bit uncomfortable with this whole thing. We need a little more time before this will start to feel like a normal thing to do."

Angie shot him a glance, but said nothing. There was an impatient look in her eye, as if the last thing she wanted was to wait any longer for something to be done.

"I understand, but it may help to extinguish all concepts you may harbour of what you consider normal or natural," Dr. Rouben said, twitching the first two fingers of both hands in the air, like rabbit ears, Michael thought, to emphasise the word "natural". "This clinic specialises in assisting couples who are experiencing difficulties procreating, that's all. We are not producing babies in factories. The pregnancy still takes nine months, the mother still gives birth, and the baby still needs feeding and its diaper changed. What can be more normal or natural than that?"

Michael switched legs. Angie remained silent.

"Look, Angie and Michael," he said, directing himself mainly at Michael, sensing his unease. "I don't want to do anything that you're not comfortable with. That means both of you. If either of you are having doubts about going through with this, then it's not going to work. I need full cooperation, no halfway efforts, and if you need more time to consider alternative opportunities, then please, go home and think about it some more. There's no shame in having doubts."

Michael certainly had doubts. About seeking help, about this guy, this room, this hospital, about everything really. If it were his decision, he would get up and leave straight away, check out before he had the chance to check in. He turned to Angie in the hope that she'd grab this opportunity to make a graceful exit. Their eyes met and he was immediately disheartened. She'd been sold. There was no way they were going to leave. She had already checked in while he wasn't looking and there was only one real eventuality from now on.

"No," he said with a sigh, turning back to the doctor, "we don't need to think about it anymore. We've been doing that for too long." He paused, almost unable to say what was on his mind. "You have our full support."

The tension in Dr. Rouben's face seemed to fade away like the light shining through the window behind him. He relaxed into his chair, and said, "Excellent. We're here to help you start a family, and that makes us extended family, does it not?"

Angie glanced at Michael and then at the doctor. "Well, then," she said, in what Michael recognised as her professional tone of voice, "let's get down to business."

TONIGHT MICHAEL IS dreaming of the black shadow again. As before, everything is in black and white, the trees, the houses, the street, and there are no other people. It's like time is nonexistent—all the cars are stationary, the birds aren't flying—everything is at a standstill, except him, he is running. His chest feels like exploding and his heart is galloping. Suddenly, he realises that he's on a street he recognises. It's not his street, Christopher Street, but it's a street somewhere in the neighbourhood. His legs feel heavy, like two logs, but he must run faster than ever before. He wonders why.

A mysterious voice answers his thoughts. From where it's coming, he doesn't know: *You have what they want. You have what they need.*

He is confused as to who they are and what they want. He begins to slow. Turning, he sees the black shadow, huge and dark and menacing, not too far behind. He is terrified. He tries to run but his legs are too weak to carry him further. Now he feels as if he's not moving at all, as if the pavement has turned into a treadmill: his legs are moving, but he is going nowhere.

Then he hears the whispering voice again, warning him: *Quickly! They're after you. Run, Michael.* RUN!

It fades, like a child's cry as it is being carried away… slipping away… into silence, as if abducted by the shadow. He feels alone and scared. He must run. He must, because now he knows the chase is on. *They* are after him

—*they*, and the black shadow.

AROUND NOON THE following day, Michael stirred from his thoughts of last night's nightmare. The whole morning had passed in a blur. He couldn't stop thinking of the black shadow, and only now in the open air could he clear his head and focus on what he was doing. It was Friday, November 24th. It was lunchtime. He and Norman were on teacher's duty, and they had even managed one complete circuit of the oval before he had snapped out of his daydreaming, before he returned to the land of the living, as Angie often said. He figured they would have to do at least another two more laps until the bell signalled the end of lunchtime.

All around him children cavorted on the grass, shrieking with delight. One girl was doing summersaults, her yellow dress flipping over her head revealing a pair of white knickers each time she rolled over. Few, mainly girls, were sitting cross-legged on the ground in groups of three or four, chatting animatedly, but for the most part kids were running and squealing in one game of chase or another, for no particular reason it seemed except to run.

Norman asked him a question, which he didn't completely hear. Michael slowly turned to him with blurred, half-dazed eyes. Norman was wearing a pair of brown corduroy trousers and a tan, V-necked sweater with large, mustard-yellow squares, raiments Michael associated with retired executives dawdling on the golf course. Norman clutched his belt and hoisted his trousers over his belly, looking somewhat impatient, as if he was envisaging slapping Michael in the face or throwing a bucket of ice over his head to wake him up.

"Are you going to tell me how it went last night, or not?" His voice had risen to a low squeal. "You told me this morning you went to the fertility clinic at St. Mary's with Angie after work," he said. "That's why you didn't make it around for dinner, which, by the way, you missed out big time. Bridget cooked up a gorgeous feast."

Michael only now remembered that he was supposed to have phoned Norman after the clinic appointment. He had simply forgotten when he and Angie got home. They had flopped in front of the telly for a while and then went to bed, too exhausted to do anything else. He apologised to Norman for not ringing.

Norman shrugged, seemingly not too upset by his forgetfulness "Anyway, you were telling me about last night," he said.

Michael glanced to his right, pondering his reply. A small creek ran past the oval's southern most edge, lying just beyond the wire-mesh fence that encircled the school. Its bed was sandy and dry, barely visible through the wattle shrubs and eucalypt trees lining its banks, and he wondered if Angie felt that way about her body, dry and barren. From the treetops a galah squawked and took off in flight, momentarily startling him. Within seconds, the sky was filled with a maddened flurry of grey and pink as fifty or so of its feathered companions joined it in flight. They seemed without a care in the world, and he briefly thought, if he had wings, would he bother with all the earthly problems of human existence?

"It went quite well, I guess," he said, watching the birds fly overhead. "Dr. Billy told us not to feel guilty about our situation. He said lots of couples have difficulty conceiving," and then he lowered his head, sighing. "We're not the first, I guess, and we won't be the last."

Norman's neck was craned to the sky as he too watched the parrots fly by. "What's this Dr. Billy like then, you know, apart from being the god of fertility?" he asked, now looking at Michael.

Michael quietly grunted, as he would if Norman had trodden on his toes. He let his thoughts return to the previous evening and the initial reaction he had to the doctor and his plush office. "Angie likes him," he said, running his hand through his hair. "She thinks he's charming."

"But you don't?"

"I don't know," and now Michael was feeling as awkward as when he was sitting in the doctor's office. He took several deep breaths with his head to the light-grey heavens. The last of the noisy birds flew over. "I just get a strange feeling from him. It's like he's got an ulterior motive to be so pleasant."

"Of course he has," Norman said. "He wants to make money. Isn't that what every doctor wants? It's how he pays for his three cars and five houses. He has to be charming and nice so you'll give him money and tell all your friends what a lovely guy he is and how he solved all your problems. He's also thinking about your second and third kids as well. Money, money, money, that's what it's all about." Norman rolled his thumb and fingers together, pretending to feel the wads of cash in his hands. "Anyway, what's wrong with that?"

"That's not what's bothering me," Michael said, now running a hand through his hair and returning his gaze to the children running on the oval. "I know he has to make his money, but it's, well, I don't think I like my wife calling other men charming and nice."

"Ha!" Norman said, gleaming. "So that's it. You're jealous. You're as green as your jumper. Look at you. You're not concerned with how good a doctor he is. All you're worried about is that Angie finds him charming."

"Okay, okay. I admit it. I'm a little insecure about it."

Norman chuckled, as though in recognition of his dilemma. Michael was silent for a while. Another lap was completed and he reckoned it wouldn't be long before the bell would ring to end the lunch period. The galahs, too, he saw, had returned to the treetops overlooking the dry creek bed, squawking loudly. Norman wanted to know what else had happened and Michael knew he wouldn't relent until he had heard every last detail, so he told him about the blood tests Angie had to have and the abdominal scans she was booked in for later in the week. Even he had to give a sample of sperm to be examined, which brought a chuckle from Norman. The doctor was hoping these preliminary investigations would give some clue as to why they couldn't conceive.

"Kids," Norman said, shaking his head and sighing. "One's enough to drive me up the wall, and I've got five! Take my advice, Mikey. Pull out now while you still can. It'll be the death of me to see you throw your life away like this." Michael watched Norman put his forearm to his brow, like a ham Shakespearian actor in sorrow. "I can't bear to watch you do it. I'd rather die than let you make the same mistakes I did."

"Stop being so melodramatic," Michael said, smiling lopsidedly. Norman had a way of lightening any situation, and he was glad for his company. "It's going to be okay. I've always wanted to have my own children. Look," and he spread his arm to the kids on the oval, "see how happy they are. I want what they have."

"There's no need to be so pathetic." Norman rolled his eyes and sighed exaggeratingly loud, feigning disappointment. "Let it be said that Norman Page tried his best, but not even he could do anything to save his friend."

Michael said nothing, just smiled

Norman threw his arms outstretched, lamenting, "Am I the only sane man left in the world?"

The ringing of the bell drowned his words. Normally, Michael would have been happy to end another thankless lunch hour of teacher's duty, but he had been enjoying his time with Norman and was sad that it had to come to an end. They waited until all the children had left the oval before following them to the rear entrance of the building. The bricks of the school façade were the deep rusty colour of the central Australian desert soil, and from his angle the kids looked like multi-coloured ants returning to the safety of the anthill after gathering supplies for the nest.

They wandered slowly into the school corridor after the kids. The noise was incredible. The children were shouting and screaming and stomping, and as Michael and Norman approached their respective classrooms they had to shout to each other to be heard. They bade goodbye and agreed to meet each other after the final bell for a quick drink at the local tavern. It was Friday night, after all, it had been a busy week and Michael reckoned he deserved a drink or two. Norman was about to step into his classroom, when he abruptly stopped and turned around.

"When will the test results be available?" he asked.

"December 22nd," Michael said. "Hopefully it'll be a nice Christmas present for Angie."

He smiled and walked on towards his classroom, but he wasn't thinking about the results of the fertility tests. He was thinking of nightmares and running and whispering voices.

# CHAPTER 4

THE WEEKS PASSED slowly; four drawn out weeks spent in purgatory, Michael reckoned, pending the results of the fertility tests. Life continued much as before, except for the occasional bouts of insomnia playing havoc with his sleeping patterns. Angie was still getting up early and working late, whilst he himself was whiling away the time at school writing report cards for the class and getting them ready for the summer break. One of the enjoyable perquisites of teaching were the number of holidays he had, except he probably wasn't going to do much with his time off other than mow the gardens and watch the cricket, perhaps even re-paint the ghastly yellow walls in the kitchen or strip the wallpaper in the hallway. Heaven knew, he'd have a lot of time on his hands. He and Angie weren't going to bother with a vacation this Christmas. It just didn't seem as if either of them had the energy to spend a week at the beach house in Serena or visit friends in Sydney or Melbourne. They didn't even attend either of their work's Christmas parties, something they did every year without fail. They just weren't in a celebratory frame of mind. He knew there was only one thing occupying both their thoughts, and the torment of waiting for the test results was almost unbearable, as though he was doing penance for previous sins, of this life and others.

Almost a month after the appointment at the fertility clinic, Michael was alone at home watching a movie, the kind of boring re-run the TV channels always air in the week leading up to Christmas. He was about to flick channels when the telephone rang. It was Angie calling from the office to say that her car wouldn't start and she'd be even later coming home than usual. She sounded annoyed and frustrated. The battery was flat again, the second time that month, and the mechanic from the RAA wouldn't be able to attend to her car for at least another hour. Michael offered to pick her up. She objected, but he insisted, maintaining that he had nothing better to do. So she agreed to cancel the callout for the RAA and wait for him to arrive.

Twenty-five minutes later, the security guard swiped him through the front doors of the State Bank Building and activated the elevator, which rushed him straight to the nineteenth floor. The clock on the wall behind the reception desk said it was half past nine when Michael walked in. Angie still had some photocopying to do, so he sat down at her tidy desk while she busied herself at the Xerox machine. Whenever he had visited her in the past, there was usually a constant background murmur of office chatter, phones ringing, and fingers on keyboards that he found mildly comforting, but not tonight. Of the fifty or so lawyers, accountants, secretaries and receptionists she shared the office with, Angie was the sole remaining employee at that time of the night. Even the cleaners, he saw, had already left.

He turned to gaze out through the window. The view from up here was probably one of the finest in Adelaide. On the horizon, the ocean was turning dusky following the sun's spectacular splashdown of orange, red and yellow, and several stars were twinkling in the darkening sky. At that moment, an approaching Qantas 737 roared over the city, not too much higher than the building. It swooped down toward the airport, which was lit up like Las Vegas, stirring a brief fantasy of flying somewhere exotic—Jamaica, Bali, The Maldives, Zanzibar—anywhere he could just put his feet up and forget about life for a week. How he yearned for the peace of mind it would bring.

The whir of the Xerox machine brought his attention back inside the office. He caught sight of a small calendar pinned to the grey partition behind Angie's computer screen. Tomorrow's date, the 22nd of December, was ringed in red, and he knew it wasn't because it was the last opportunity for late night Friday shopping before Christmas.

Angie's voice from behind suddenly startled him. Michael spun around in the chair and saw her standing at the end of the desk looking flustered. "Shall we go?" she asked, rubbing her temples. "I think I need to get home soon. I'm coming down with another migraine."

They duly left, leaving the reception light on behind them, and took the elevator to the basement. With a minimum of fuss, Michael jumpstarted Angie's car in the parking lot. He made a mental note to take it to a mechanic in the upcoming holidays to find out why the battery was always going flat. Then he followed her home, fearing that the car might give her more troubles on the way.

He needn't have worried. They arrived home without any further hiccups, but to his disappointment Angie went immediately to bed, saying she wasn't interested in the fricassee that he had cooked and was keeping warm in the oven for her. Michael returned to watching the TV in the lounge room. He figured that there was nothing he could do to help when she had a migraine as bad as this. As he sat down on the couch and grabbed the remote control, he heard Angie head down the hallway to the bathroom. He could hear her rummaging through the cabinet for some paracetamol and, moments later, the sound of brushing teeth. Then he heard her returning footsteps treading lightly on the hallway carpet. She mumbled goodnight and went to lie down in the dark bedroom with a cool, damp facecloth over her brow.

After the movie finished, he switched off the TV and tiptoed quietly into the bedroom, hoping that he wouldn't be up all night worrying about tomorrow. He silently undressed and then snuggled beneath the sheets. Angie had managed to fall asleep. He could hear her light breaths, like peaceful whispers, and was glad for her. He knew how terrible these migraines knocked her around, but he was still slightly envious of her ability to drop so easily into sleep, even with a throbbing headache. He himself would probably have no such luck tonight. These past four weeks had been a trial of worsening insomnia he was finding increasingly difficult to overcome.

Staring at the ceiling, he heard the grandfather clock in the hallway chime twelve. Tomorrow he and Angie would be going to the fertility clinic to see Dr. Rouben, to sort things out once and for all, to find out the results of the tests they did last month. Despite his best intentions not to be, he was immediately wracked with worry. What if Dr. Rouben had discovered something incurable? Would he tell them? Of course he would, that was his job, but would he tell them everything, would he hold something back? Or would he actually come right out and say it?

Michael was suddenly distracted from his thoughts by something outside the window. "Come on Jack, old boy, come on!" said a whispery male voice.

Michael had heard this voice a dozen times or more over the past four weeks; it was the old man he called gramps taking his dog for a walk on their nightly round. He could hear the jingling of Jack's dog collar and the patter-patter of his paws on the cement path as he hurried to catch up with his master. Their routine seemed somehow normal, safe, and like Angie's ability to fall asleep at the drop of a hat, he was envious of gramps and Jack and their normality.

"Good boy, Jack," said gramps in his whispery tone. "Good boy." Then they were gone.

By the time gramps and Jack returned twenty or so minutes later, although it felt more like twenty hours, Michael was still wide awake. Time was passing unbearably slowly. Seconds were hours. Minutes were days.

At twelve thirty, he heard the familiar chugga-chugga-chugga of a VW Beetle passing by, just like his, its headlights sweeping along the ceiling through the crack in the curtain. Like gramps and Jack, it was a regular at this time of night. Half an hour later, he heard the scurry of a woman's high heels, at first faint, then louder. Her heels scuffed, then faded away. The Grandfather clock chimed one.

Time passed. It was impossible to tell how much. Another car swept its headlights across the ceiling. Then at some point the grandfather clock chimed two. Michael was just feeling he might be able to doze off when he suddenly heard another noise. He quickly faced the window. It wasn't one of the usual noises he had become familiar with. It was something odd, something that sounded like a rolling pin crunching over broken glass. Probably slowly moving tyres flattening twigs and leaves on the street, he figured. There was no sweep of light over the ceiling, though. No headlights. Whoever was outside didn't want their presence to be known.

The wheels stopped. The engine idled. Then silence.

He sat up, staring at the closed curtains, expecting Angie to complain in her sleep at his sudden movements, but she didn't wake. He cocked his ears. There was no further sound outside. He decided to take a look to see who was out there. Before he peeked behind the curtain, something instinctive caused him to hesitate, something primal that was telling him he shouldn't, it was better he stayed in bed and forgot all about it. Curiosity, after all, killed the cat.

He looked anyway. A cop car was parked across the road, sitting in the shadow between two streetlights. In the darkness, he couldn't see much apart from someone smoking in the driver's seat, the red tip of the cigarette glowing like a firefly. The face was a formless black mask, reminding him of the dark shadow in his nightmares. Suddenly, the cop turned in his direction, sensing the flicker of the curtain. Michael quickly stepped back toward the bed, holding his breath. He wanted to look again, but what was the point? It was just a cop taking a smoko break.

Careful not to wake Angie, he tiptoed back to bed and somehow got to sleep. He didn't dream and he didn't hear any more noises outside.

The next morning, Michael roused himself out of bed after eight. After breakfast and waiting for Angie to finish in the bathroom, he showered and then got dressed in front of the large mirrored doors of the bedroom closet. His jeans felt snug around his waist, and he let his blue shirt, a tad faded and old, hang loose over the belt. He considered brushing his hair and then decided it looked fine as it was. In the reflection, he watched Angie slipping into a black, shoulderless dress and smooth it over her waist, liking the way she wiggled her hips. He saw the backwards time on the bedside alarm clock next to her. It was almost nine and the appointment was just over an hour away.

"Why are you taking so long?" he asked, glancing over his shoulder. "Don't you want to get the results of our tests?"

"Of course I do," she said. Her gold crucifix was dangling on the outside of her dress as she rolled up her stockings. "I just don't see why we have to go so soon. It's too early."

"We were late for him last time. It's polite to be punctual."

She glared at him, her caramel eyes steely hard. "Sure, okay, why don't we take a packed lunch and have a picnic in his office? We'll have plenty of time."

Unable to pacify the surge of frustration, he threw the brush onto the bed. The purple sheets and quilt, he barely noticed, were crumpled and unmade.

"You've been trying to avoid this whole issue for a month," he said. "You're trying to stall."

Angie suddenly ran out of the bedroom crying. Michael hung his head in the air and ran a hand through his long locks. He stared outside through the open curtains, looking for inspiration. Here we go again, he thought. How much longer was this going to go on for? His gloom deepened to match that of Angie's. The prospect of spending the rest of his life like this filled him with despair. What could he do if the remainder of their marriage was going to be as fraught with angst such as now? Perhaps it would be better for all concerned if he tried to make light of it, as Norman would, but somehow this didn't seem the answer. It made him think for the first time of leaving her.

He drew a deep breath, then reluctantly followed her down the hallway to the bathroom. Unlike previous times, the door wasn't locked. Angie was sobbing, perched on the closed lid of the toilet, elbows on her knees and her head held in her hands. Her fingers were massaging her temples and he tentatively apologised, holding out his arms for an embrace.

She looked up at him through teary eyes and stood up. He hugged her and when she hugged him back he was surprised to feel the bony protuberances of her shoulder blades through her dress. As her face pressed to his chest, he could feel her tears leaving damp spots on his shirt. They stood this way for several minutes. Then he lifted her chin with his finger and kissed her gently on her lips. They tasted salty and sweet, like strawberries dipped in the sea. They pulled apart and Angie wiped away a tear with the back of her hand.

Michael went to the kitchen to make some coffee, relieved that a major crisis had been averted. Angie stayed in the bathroom to freshen up. After a minute or so, while he was putting the kettle on to boil, he heard a muffled cry, like someone in pain covering their mouth with their hand so that nobody else could hear. He spun around and yelled out to Angie to see if she was all right, but didn't receive an answer. He left the kettle on and rushed to the bathroom. The door was locked, so he pressed his ear to listen through it. His shoulders swiftly tensed at the sound of her muffled cries.

"What's going on in there?" he said, raising his voice. He banged on the door when she still didn't reply. "Angie! Talk to me. Are you all right?"

It was several seconds before she answered, several seconds in which he seriously considered breaking down the door. "It's okay," she said, and yet her voice sounded weak and strained, very much as if everything was not okay. "I just stubbed my toe on the bath."

"Come on then," he said, his shoulders relaxing. The kettle in the kitchen was now whistling. "Let's have a coffee and get going."

The bathroom door unlocked and Angie stepped into the corridor, averting his inquisitive gaze. She was wiping her eyes with the back of one hand and rubbing her lower belly with the other. She was also walking without a limp, he noticed.

WHEN THEY ARRIVED in his office, Dr. Rouben was seated behind his imposing pedestal desk reading from Angie's medical file. His black hair was slicked back, his tanned face cleanly shaved, and he was dressed immaculately as ever in a suit and tie. His expression, however, was stern and serious, which, for Michael, didn't augur well. Michael had to suppress the pressing urge to ask what the investigation reports said.

Instead, he busied his attention around the office. Like the doctor, the room had barely changed, except, of course, for the Christmas decorations; green and silver tinsel draped over the graduation certificates on the wall, and up and around the breakfront bookcase; Christmas cards that hung on a piece of string tacked across the window; and, like an afterthought, a small, plastic Christmas tree perched on his mahogany desk. All things considered, he was ready for Monday, Michael thought with a cynical grin. The only thing missing was a white beard and a sack of presents.

"I have the results of all the tests we did last month," Dr. Rouben said, immediately engaging Michael's attention. "Ask any questions you want as I go through them."

Angie was sitting rigidly, her back as erect as a flagpole, her hands tightly clutching the handbag on her lap. Michael swallowed a hard lump that had been collecting in his throat since he walked into the office. They listened as Dr. Rouben began explaining the reports one by one, neither daring to say a word and both, seemingly, holding their breath. Michael's mouth felt dry and he wondered if Angie's felt the same.

"First, Michael," Dr. Rouben said, glancing in his direction, then back down at the pathology report. "Here are the results of your test. Sperm count: ninety million per millilitre. Seventy five percent normal active motility; eighty-three percent normal morphology." Dr. Rouben looked up from the file with a reassuring nod. "That means you're able to have children, Michael. You have what it takes to be a father."

Michael didn't know whether to be grateful or not. Now they knew the problem was definitely with Angie, which caused him to have mixed feelings. On the one hand, he knew she would be devastated, and in a way he wished he were the one with the fertility problems so that it would relieve her suffering. Yet, on the other hand, had he not also entertained, in his weakest moments in the dead of night, the hope that it wasn't him? Didn't every man deep down hope that his boys could swim? Being fertile was what defined a man, wasn't it?

He nodded, saying nothing and trying not to look too overwhelmed with all the medical jargon.

"Now, Angie's tests." Dr. Rouben smiled reassuringly and Michael reached over to take her hand. She didn't face him, instead continued to sit rigidly in the leather chair and stare straight ahead at Dr. Rouben. He glanced once again at the pink pathology reports. "Your FBC, full blood count, is normal," he said, "which means you are not anaemic, and your white cells that fight off infections are at healthy levels. Your ESR, the rate at which your blood cells settle to the bottom of a test tube, is normal too, which is what I was expecting from a young, fit woman such as yourself," at which Angie seemed to find her voice.

"Then why do you test for it?" she asked.

It was exactly what Michael was thinking. What was the point in doing a test that was so non-specific? It only complicated the issue. He felt Dr. Rouben was giving them the good news—bad news routine, giving all the results of all the normal investigations, even the ones that were apparently as esoteric as an ESR or whatever it was, and deliberately delaying the results of the really important tests, the ones that Michael knew were going to come back negative.

"It's a useful indicator to an underlying disease, such as SLE, that may not be exhibiting symptoms or signs at present, and if we can detect it early, it may save your pregnancy." Angie nodded stiffly, seemingly satisfied with the explanation, and Dr. Rouben continued. "Your U's and E's, urea and electrolytes, the blood chemistry in other words, is all normal. Your growth hormone, follicular hormone, luteinizing hormone, and thyroid hormone levels are normal. The hormones produced by your ovaries, oestrogen and progesterone, are also normal."

He paused, and for a ghastly moment Michael thought he was going to give every detail and explanation of each hormone. Listening to him drone on was driving drive him mad. He just wanted him to hurry up and get to the results that really mattered. Then Dr. Rouben said, "Every blood test we have done is absolutely fine. You are a prime example of womanhood."

"Then why can't I get pregnant?" Angie said. "I'm not such a prime example of womanhood if I can't get pregnant am I?" She put her hands to her face and began to sob.

"Angel," Michael said, putting his arm around her shoulder. Again he was stuck by how easily he could feel her bones. She seemed to have lost weight in the past few months almost as easily as she shed her clothes before getting into bed. "That's not true."

"Your husband's right," Dr. Rouben said, handing Michael a box of tissues to give to Angie. She took several, then wiped her eyes and blew her nose. "What did I say when we first met? Nobody is to blame. Get all these thoughts out of your head. You're no help to me when you're full of guilt, and I'm sure you're no help to Michael this way either."

"I'm sorry," she said, dabbing her tears. "What have you found? What can we do about our situation?"

"That's better, a fighting spirit. That's how we'll get you a family. Now, let me finish reading the results." He returned to the pathology reports and read aloud. "PAP smear: normal cell differentiation, normal cell growth," he said. "No evidence of neisseria gonorrhoea, chlamydia trachomatis, group B streptococci, herpes simplex, or human papilloma viruses." Again he looked up. "Which means there's no evidence of any sexually transmitted disease causing your infertility."

Angie's posture seemed to relax slightly. She cast Michael a quick, almost guilty glance. He briefly wondered what it meant, but let it pass, still thinking that Dr. Rouben was employing delaying tactics, that there was something he wasn't telling them. Even if it was bad news, he wanted to know right now and for Dr. Rouben to stop beating about the bush. He and Angie had waited weeks for these results. He had lost god-knows how many hours of sleep over them (and Angie god-knows how many kilos). The waiting was driving him crazy.

It was Angie who spoke next, and he figured she must have been thinking along similar lines. Sitting up straight in her chair, she said, "Dr. Rouben, I don't want to know what's normal. I need to know what's abnormal."

"I understand," Dr. Rouben said, his tone calm and placatory.

He pushed his chair back and stood, a serious expression across his face. Then he headed to the light box fixed to the wood-panelled wall on which his certificates of academic achievement were hanging, and Michael was suddenly filled with that same sense of foreboding as when he first entered and saw the doctor reading the reports in Angie's medical file. He figured that the time for delaying was over and that this was the moment when Dr. Rouben was going to deliver the bad news. Dr. Rouben flicked a switch on the light box and its fluorescent tube flickered on and off several times before remaining permanently on. Out of a packet of x-rays he removed two large films and placed them on the light box, then signalled for Michael and Angie to join him.

They obeyed, albeit hesitantly at first. It was the first time they'd stood side-by-side with their obstetrician. He wasn't a tall man, about the same height as Norman Page, and slightly stockier than Michael had first surmised by his face. His eyes were at the same level as Angie's and he was standing so close that Michael could smell his expensive cologne, though it was not one he was familiar with. They all stared at the films on the light box, on each of which were printed sixteen multi-coloured still-frames in four rows of four. Michael tried to interpret the images, but they were just a swirl of colour with no discernable shape or form and he could make neither head nor tail of what they were supposed to represent.

"These are the MRI scans we did of your uterus and ovaries, Angie," Dr. Rouben said, after a brief moment. "Sometimes a woman may have problems conceiving because there is something abnormal with her ovaries, for example polycystic ovarian disease, except that's not the problem for you." He paused, and Michael could see he was trying to formulate the correct sentence in his head. "Do you remember telling me about the pain you feel in your lower abdomen halfway through your menstrual cycle?"

Michael's eyes flared with alarm. He saw Angie unconsciously rub her lower belly and nod, saying nothing, as if the memory of the pain had cowed her voice. Michael too remembered when he was standing in the doorframe of the bedroom just over a month ago, Angie doubled over, agony etched on her face, her skin horridly pale. He remembered her muffled cries in the bathroom this very morning, and he remembered the flash of an image in the teachers' parking lot as he prepared to leave school for the first appointment here, of Angie twitching and drooling on the ground. It washed over him in icy waves then as it did now. There was something wrong with Angie, something bad. He knew it.

"The reason you get pain is the same reason you cannot conceive," he heard Dr. Rouben say. Then he saw him put his hand gently on Angie's back to get her to move closer to the scans. Michael shuffled closer too. Pointing to two pictures in the centre of each MRI film, Dr. Rouben said, "These are your ovaries, your left and your right."

Now that they had been pointed out, Michael could easily identify them. "But you said her ovaries were normal," he said.

Dr. Rouben dropped his hand to his side and stepped back. "They are, they're just not allowed to do their job."

Michael ran a hand through his long hair. It made no sense. What was preventing Angie's ovaries from doing what nature had created them to do? He now wished he'd paid more attention to his biology teacher at high school.

The tip of Dr. Rouben's forefinger now rested on his chin. "How can I put it?" he said. He pointed back to the MRI scans. "The ovaries are in perfect working order. That is, they produce the right hormones at the right time, oestrogen and progesterone, and they release an ovum, an egg, at the appropriate time of the month. But they're being prevented from doing it in the right place."

Angie, Michael saw, was staring directly ahead at the MRI scans and biting her bottom lip. One hand was also grasping her crucifix. Dr. Rouben directed himself at her. "Normally at the time of ovulation, which happens to be exactly in the middle of your menstrual cycle, the fallopian tubes reach up like a hand for the ovary on both sides of your body to catch the ovum that is about to be released. Look here." He went to his desk and grabbed a pen. Michael watched him remove the lid and put the pen back down. He closed his left hand around the lid and outstretched his arm so that his fist was held at shoulder height, beneath which he placed his right hand in position to catch the lid, like a claw. "Let me explain. My fist is your ovary and the pen inside it is the ovum, the egg. My open hand, my right, is the distal end of your fallopian tube. When the ovary is ready to ovulate it signals with certain hormones for the tube to get closer so that it can catch the egg like this," and he moved his open, clawed hand closer beneath his fist. "Hopefully, when the ovary releases its egg, the tube is close enough to catch it." He opened his fist and out dropped the pen lid into the palm of his other hand. "The egg can then move down the fallopian tube to be fertilised. The ovary and fallopian tube then move apart. If the egg is not fertilised this particular cycle, it's ejected out of the body when you have a period and the whole process is repeated in one month's time."

"All right," Angie said, shrugging. Michael had to marvel at how well she was seemingly coping with all this, far better than he. Maybe this was the kind of language she understood. She was a lawyer, after all, she was used to coming to grips with difficult concepts. "But what does this have to do with me?"

Dr. Rouben transferred the pen lid to his other hand, preparing to repeat the whole exercise. "In your case, Angie, what happens is this," and he demonstrated by opening his fist and allowing the lid to drop to the floor. "Your fallopian tube is stuck and unable to move closer to your ovary and catch the egg when it's released. When this happens, the egg falls into another part of the abdomen, usually towards the posterior aspect of the uterus in a place called the lesser sac. Therefore, it's unable to be fertilised and can sometimes cause pain in mid cycle, like you've been experiencing. This is why you cannot conceive."

Michael watched Angie out of the corner of his eye. She was holding the crucifix as she had, her face a blank mask. He could only begin to imagine what she was going through and could only guess at the questions that were racing through her head. What could possible be the cause of such a thing? Was it something she was born with, or something she acquired later in life? Could it have been prevented? There seemed too many questions and too few answers.

Dr. Rouben looked at each one in turn. He was silent again, and Michael could sense he was about to give them the answer they had spent so long waiting to hear. Michael was suddenly wracked with uncertainty. He wasn't sure he wanted to know.

"It's usually caused by a sexually acquired infection," Dr. Rouben said, finally, "with a bug called chlamydia. We call the disorder, Pelvic Inflammatory Disease—PID."

Michael was shocked. He looked at Dr. Rouben, then at Angie, and then back at Dr. Rouben. It seemed implausible. Angie had never complained of such a problem, either recently or in the past. He himself had never had a sexually transmitted disease to pass on to her, so how could she get it? Then he stopped his line of reasoning. The answer had been staring at him in the face; he'd just been too cowardly to admit it. The late nights after work, the pregnancy kit in the bin beneath the bathroom sink, the guilty glance when Dr. Rouben had given the results of the PAP smear, it all added up to one thing, didn't it?

Angie glanced at him. There was definitely guilt in that look. His hands clenched tightly, but he kept his thoughts to himself, gritting his molars and contemplating how he was going to approach the issue with her after the appointment had finished. However he put it to her, it was going to be heated and messy.

Angie faced Dr. Rouben, and said, "But my PAP smear was normal."

"It was… is normal, but that doesn't mean you didn't have an infection some time in the past."

Again that glance. Michael could feel himself flushing with anger and confusion. "How long ago? Before I met Michael? Is it possible that…" Angie didn't finish. The words trailed off into silence and her eyes stared distantly at the MRI scans.

Michael could sense she was reliving some horrible torment she'd suffered in the past, a torment she had tried suppress for a long, long time that had now revealed itself in all its ghastly forms. He felt his initial anger turn to sympathy. He'd been too quick to judge, too quick to lay the blame for their problems at her feet. Now it was his turn to glance at her with guilt etched in his eyes. She was still grasping the crucifix around her neck, a sure sign that something was bothering her terribly. He wanted to ask her what had happened, he wanted to know it all, but this was neither the time nor the place.

"So how do we fix the problem?" he asked Dr. Rouben. "How do we unstick her tubes so that they can catch her eggs?"

Dr. Rouben was solemn. "I'm sorry," he said, shaking his head. "We can't do anything. Medicine has no cure for this type of problem."

To Michael, the news was devastating. It was the news neither he nor Angie wanted to hear. He could see she was crushed. She kept staring at the MRI scans and grasping her crucifix to her chest. "Can't you do something?" he asked, running a hand through his hair. "What about surgery? What about medication? Surely there's something you can do."

Dr. Rouben turned aside, gesturing for them to take their seats. "Why don't we sit down and discuss what options we have at this particular point in time?" he said, planting himself down behind his desk.

"There's nothing you can do?" Michael asked.

"Michael, darling, why don't you sit down and hear what Dr. Rouben has to offer first?" Angie patted the chair next to her. She seemed to have recovered quickly from her initial shock. "Please."

Dr. Rouben waited for Michael to be seated before continuing. "There is no medicine that can help and surgery may make things worse. As I said, she has PID, but she has an unusual case. Normally, women with the disease don't get pain; it's usually indolent. By that I mean it's silent, the woman is unaware she has a problem. When we make a decision on how to treat it, we have to think of the woman's… Angie's, immediate and long term future."

"Does this mean we can't have children?" Michael asked.

Dr. Rouben clasped his hands together and leant forward, his elbows resting on his desk. His smile, Michael thought, was like his father's when he was about to deliver good news. "Do you believe in immaculate conception?" he asked.

Michael initially thought he hadn't heard the question correctly. He scratched his head, and stared at him. Was he joking? Mary and Jesus and all that stuff? He turned to Angie, who was sitting as rigidly as before, then back at Dr. Rouben. "Are you saying that the only chance for us to have a baby is to wait for God to descend from the sky and make love to my wife? You must be crazy." He felt himself getting worked up, just like the time he punched Jude in the face when they were kids. His face was flushing. "I don't believe Mary immaculately conceived Jesus," he said. "I don't even believe in God, and so if that's all you are offering us, we'll go and take our money to someone who can help us."

"I believe," whispered Angie, staring over Dr. Rouben's shoulder. Her expression was glazed, Michael saw, and she was continuing to press the gold crucifix to her heart, now with the flat palm of her hand. Michael was dumbstruck. She turned slowly to him, and when she spoke her voice was choked and husk. "Why are you staring at me like that? Is it such a strange thing for a Catholic to believe Jesus was born of the Virgin Mary? I have always believed in the Immaculate Conception and I always will."

Michael threw his hands in the air, exasperated.

Angie ignored him. "You are not God," she said to Dr. Rouben. "How do you propose to conceive our child?"

Dr. Rouben eased slightly into his chair. "If you define God as a being that is able to create life without the need for sexual intercourse, then I am God," he said. "At least in that limited definition of the term. I have participated in over one thousand successful immaculate conceptions in the past fifteen years, and I wish to add your baby to my list. Have you heard of *in-vitro* fertilisation?"

"Of course. Is that what you have in mind for Michael and me?"

"Indeed. I think it's your best chance to have a baby."

Michael caught Angie looking at him, seeking his approval. He shrugged his shoulders. She looked back at Dr. Rouben. "What's involved?" she asked, eventually.

"It's relatively simple nowadays." Dr. Rouben glanced at the only photo in the room and Michael followed his gaze. The picture sat on the break of the bookcase to his right. In it, Dr. Rouben was dressed in fisherman's garb. He held a rod in one hand and a trout in the other, beaming proudly at the camera. "I stimulate your ovaries to increase its ovulating capacity with a special hormone called clomiphene," he said, turning back to Angie, "to produce lots of eggs. I collect them by inserting a needle and then sucking them out. It's a very safe procedure and only minimally painful. After I've done that, I fertilise some of them in a test tube with Michael's sperm and then place three or four into your uterus two days later. Hopefully, one will take hold and produce a viable pregnancy. Sometimes, two or three, or even more, successfully embed. Who knows, within a year you may be the proud mother of twins or triplets."

He paused. There was complete silence.

"Now, tell me," he said finally, leaning back in his chair and clasping his hands behind his head. "Is that not an immaculate conception?"

Michael stared at him. This whole thing was turning into a farce.

# CHAPTER 5

TWO DAYS LATER, Michael and Angie were coming home from an afternoon spent at the arcade in nearby Norwood. Angie's car wouldn't start again this morning and so they had taken the Beetle. It was Sunday evening, the day before Christmas, and the backseat was full of groceries and last minute presents. Michael pulled into the driveway and parked behind Angie's car. Angie gazed pensively out of the passenger window holding the crucifix to her chest, and as he killed the engine Michael had an idea he knew what was bothering her.

"You haven't said a word for ages. Is it what Dr. Billy said on Friday?" he asked. Angie said nothing. "I thought you'd be happy we can finally do something about starting a family."

Rubbing her temple, she sighed, then faced her husband. "I am happy," she said. Michael wasn't convinced; there was no smile on her face or cheer in her voice. Even the flowers printed on her spaghetti-strapped dress seemed sad. "It's just that, well, you know, it's not every day you're told that your body is decrepit and you can't have kids."

"But you can."

"Not naturally I can't, not without the help of modern science. You know what my mother thinks of all this, don't you? She thinks IVF is like playing God, like the people of Babel who tried to build a tower to heaven. She doesn't think we should be doing this, especially when Dr. Billy comes out and says he thinks we can have an immaculate conception. He definitely thinks he's playing God. He openly brags about it."

Michael looked at her with a puzzled expression, not sure he had heard her correctly. "Angie, your mother is dead. She doesn't *think* anything anymore."

"You know what I mean. Maybe someone who can't have children naturally shouldn't have them at all."

Michael ran a hand through his hair. "Angie, don't do this to yourself," he said. "It's not good and it's not right. If Dr. Billy can help us, then why shouldn't we let him? You've said as much yourself in the past."

She hesitated, and Michael could tell she was consternating whether or not to tell him what was really occupying her thoughts. She glanced at him, then quickly away; the same look she had given him in the fertility clinic two days ago. He felt a lump rise in his throat.

"That's not the worst part," she said, finally. Her voice sounded abrasive, like fine sandpaper. "I… I feel guilty."

He hoped she meant not being able to conceive and nothing else. He hoped she wasn't about to divulge anything other than remorse at disappointing her husband. "You know Dr. Billy said that this is an extremely common problem," he said. "You know it's not your fault. You have nothing to feel guilty about."

"That's not what I mean. I don't feel guilty about that anymore."

Michael saw her stare out of the passenger window at the next-door neighbour's front lawn. She turned back to him, opened her mouth, then shut it again, and he was suddenly awash with the dreadful knowledge that she was about to reveal she had been having a secret affair with her boss and ex-fiancé, Stephen Pickering, and that they had decided to get back together again. That's what she had really been doing all these late nights, he imagined her saying, the marriage was a sham and she couldn't live with him anymore. It was over.

She opened her mouth again and he braced himself for the worst. "I haven't been totally honest with you," she said, after another slight hesitation, "and I want to put some things straight."

His jeans suddenly felt tight around his thighs and he could feel damp patches down the back of his denim shirt. Michael closed his eyes, wishing she wouldn't go on any further. He didn't want to hear any more. It was denial, pure and simple. If he didn't hear it, it didn't happen. He guessed this was how someone felt immediately after they'd been told they had cancer, or some other incurable disease. It was not the Christmas present that he was expecting to receive this year.

"You know that as a Catholic, my parents expected me to remain a virgin until I married," and Michael nodded, wondering why she needed to reiterate what he already knew. She had told him on several occasions that he was the fist man she had ever made love to, and then only on the night of their wedding. Even though her parents had been dead for some time, she had remained faithful to their wishes. He could now hear the uncertainty in her voice as she continued. "I never told you the complete truth. You're not the only man I've had sex with."

He opened his eyes. Angie was sitting rigidly still, holding the crucifix to her chest and staring straight ahead, unable to look him in the eye. In the past, he had supposed that there would come a time when he'd have to confront a partner's infidelity. It was inevitable, something he figured every man would have to do at some point in his life, and preparing for its eventuality was the best way he knew how to deal with it. He often imagined the scene: there would be tears and accusations of blame; he'd feel angry and start shouting and screaming; he'd threaten divorce and storm out of the house, probably back to his parents' or to Norman's. There might come a time a little later when he would find forgiveness, but he suspected not. Unfaithfulness was the highest form of betrayal. It was unforgivable.

Except, that's not what was happening. He felt unexpectedly calm, almost to the point of peacefulness. He felt like shouting and threatening divorce no more than he felt he wanted to give up trying to have a baby. Perhaps, and this was the least expectant of all, Angie's honest remorse was dousing the flames of anger and bitterness before it exploded into uncontrollable rage and he said things that would cause irreconcilable damage. His mind was surprisingly lucid. It was as clear as the window through which Angie was staring and he discovered that he could empathise with what she had been suffering, that he could see the reasoning behind her actions as clearly as he could see the neighbour's flowers and shrubs. She needed love. She needed security. She needed to feel accepted as a woman once again. These were things she had probably decided she couldn't receive from her husband. Uncomfortable as it was, he prepared himself to listen to what she had to impart. He owed her that much, at least.

Angie began by saying that it was a distasteful memory, a memory she had tried to erase from her mind, but simply couldn't. It happened when she and Stephen Pickering were still going steady, sometime in the autumn of 1989 while she was still at college, at least six months before a mutual friend had introduced her to Michael at the cinema. She disclosed every detail, every emotion and every thought of that night.

She and Stephen had gone to the restaurant at Eagle-on-the-Hill. It was supposed to have been a romantic affair; a candlelit dinner for two, a window table overlooking the glimmering lights of Adelaide, champagne and oysters, the whole works. She even wore the long black evening dress she only pulled out of the closet for special occasions. She had a feeling that that was the night he was finally going to propose. Stephen was handsome, his family was rich, and she knew that life as a Pickering would be a life of privilege. It all seemed perfect.

The dinner was sublime and he eventually did propose. Of course, she immediately said yes. They smiled and laughed and celebrated with a bottle of champagne. By the end of the dinner, a third bottle lay upturned in the bucket of ice. Stephen paid the bill, but when she stood to leave the city lights twinkling up from the plain below began to merge kaleidoscopically together, a swirl of glimmering orange and sparkling white. She had let herself get too carried away with the celebrations. After a moment to wait for everything to come back into focus, she walked tentatively and slowly out of the restaurant, Stephen's arm firmly around her waist.

Stepping outside, she hung her head back, soaking up as much of the fresh night air as she could. She hoped she'd be able to make it to the car before she collapsed on the doorstep of the restaurant. That would have been embarrassing, especially when her new fiancé was a high-flying partner in one of Adelaide's premier law firms. They crossed the parking lot, her ankle twisting once or twice in her high heels. Finally, he opened the door of the car, but such was her relief that she failed to notice she'd been ushered into the rear passenger seat.

Like a rapist, he was on her in a flash, kissing her neck, groping her breasts and tearing at the straps of her dress. She felt instantly suffocated, claustrophobic almost, and she wondered if this was what it was like to be attacked by a dog. She felt like vomiting. He was now half naked on top of her. She was on her back, her dress up around her waist like a whore. The windows quickly fogged and she opened her mouth to try to speak, when suddenly her panties were jerked to her ankles. His breath was like a wounded bull in her ear, the prandial smell of champagne heavy on his breath, and his hips pressed roughly onto hers. All of a sudden, he was inside her. There was a sharp jolt of pain, a twinge, and then before she knew it, it was over.

They got dressed in awkward silence with barely a glance at one another. Her lace panties, she saw, were ripped and useless and she absently tossed them back to the floor where she had found them.

"I'm sorry," he said, finally. "I've defiled your purity."

Perhaps it was nervousness, she wasn't sure, but laughter rushed out of her mouth like the many champagne corks that had been popped throughout the evening. She immediately regretted it. Stephen's face went hard, as if she'd personally insulted him.

"Do you think this is something to laugh about? This is serious! We're going to have to get married as soon as possible, next week maybe. My dad's got contacts. He can arrange it."

There was more than just a trace of contempt in his voice and it triggered something deep inside her, something primal, atavistic. She was only partially able to restrain the anger bursting from inside. He'd been organising her whole life since they'd started dating and now she thought that because they'd had sex for less than a minute they had to get married next week. It was contemptible. She wasn't going to be told what to do with her life, not by him, not by anyone. Her parents had done it all her life, her friends at school had done it, and now he wanted to continue where they'd left off. She was sick and tired of it and she wasn't going to let it happen.

"Don't you tell me what to do!" she said, glaring at him.

He grabbed her wrist. "Watch what you're saying," he said. "You know it's for the best."

"There you go again!" she said, snatching her hand away. She was almost screaming. "Always trying to control me. I don't need to be told what to do or say, and I certainly don't need you to make decisions for me, especially when it comes to marriage! I'm a woman and I have a right to determine my own future. You don't want a wife, you want someone like your mother, to behave like a well-trained dog, and you've been trying to turn me into her since day one. Well, I'm not her, I'm *me* and if you don't like who I am then… then you can go and shove your marriage where the sun don't shine!"

"If that's the way you want it, then that's the way you'll get it," Stephen said, almost snarling. "But you're throwing away the best opportunity you'll ever get of having everything you ever wanted. I'm the best goddamn thing that's ever happened to you and you know it. I can give you everything you ever dreamed of, money, power, status. You should count your lucky stars I even considered you worthy to have sex with."

Her eyes widened with venom. Her whole body was trembling. She placed her hand on the door handle and told him that she never wanted to see him again, that if he even so much as telephoned her she would go to the police and file a rape charge. He sniffed contemptuously. They both knew nothing would ever come of it. He had contacts that would quash the charge before it was even printed on paper. She stepped out of the car, removed the ring and threw it at him. Then she slammed the door in his face and walked away. From behind, she heard his muffled voice say, "You weren't even that good!"

She snorted in disgust and headed straight back to the restaurant. After waiting an hour for a taxi she got home and went straight to the shower. She felt ashamedly dirty. He was right about one thing; he *had* defiled her, but not physically… *psychologically.* That was worse. Then the tears started. She cried all night, for many reasons, guilt, shame, anger, sadness, but mainly guilt. She had walked into the lion's den wide eyed and willingly. It was her own fault and she couldn't blame anyone else, not even the champagne.

"So now you know why I feel so guilty," she said to Michael. Her eyes, he saw, were brimming with tears and streaked with lines of red. She hadn't let go of the crucifix the entire time she'd been speaking. "That bastard stole my virginity and infected me with chlamydia. He's the reason why we can't have children. I wish I'd never met him."

She buried her face in her hands. Michael breathed easy and leant over to kiss Angie on the temple. His relief upon learning that she hadn't been unfaithful was as seemingly immeasurable as her grief, but there was pity in his heart for what she had endured. Like many victims of such a despicable betrayal, she had obviously been reliving that moment over and over and over again, in her dreams, when she woke in the morning, while she drove to work, as though she was made to suffer this outrage every minute of the day. Worse, she was made to face it every time she walked though the doors of Sugarman, Klein & Pickering, every time she saw him at the water cooler. She was made to feel it every time she went to a meeting in his office, every time she received an email from him. It was a never-ending nightmare.

He now realised that he had seen only of a fraction of the suffering that was tormenting her soul.

ANGIE WENT TO lie down on the bed for an hour when they got inside the house. She told him she could feel another throbbing headache coming on. Michael understood. He took the groceries to the kitchen, unpacked them, rolled up his shirtsleeves and carried on with the dinner preparations. The previous night he had marinated a shoulder of lamb in half a bottle of cheap red wine and let it sit in the refrigerator for twenty-four hours. He set the oven to preheat, then took the meat tray out of the fridge and placed it on the dividing bench.

Cooking was his passion. If he had had it his way he would have become a chef and studied in Paris instead of becoming a primary school teacher. His parents had believed otherwise, that he was better off going to the university and getting a "proper education." He recalled his dad saying, "Get an education first and then you can go and do what you want. It's folly to throw away the opportunity to go to university. Believe me, if you don't do it now, you'll live to regret it when you're older. I don't want to see my only son throwing his life away on a fanciful dream."

Dreams were for those who could afford to have them. Michael knew that as well as anybody. So the kitchen became a theatre of dreams where he could fantasise serving the finest dishes to the rich and famous. Tonight's menu was roast lamb, medium rare, marinated in Australia's finest claret, seasoned with rare spices from the East, and complemented with *vegetables du jour*. He chuckled to himself, thinking he was going to make this the best Christmas meal Angie had ever had.

He slid the meat tray into the oven and began to prepare the vegetables. As he did, he thought about the last two days. The results of the fertility tests were bittersweet. He didn't like seeing Angie going through this torment; he could tell this whole ordeal was taking its toll. At least they knew it wasn't life threatening. That was one good thing to come out of the appointment. Norman was always saying things only got worse before they got worse, but he hoped he was wrong. He hoped the worst was now over, that the problem was identified and that they could begin to deal with it. He thought again of Angie. Having a child might even help to resolve some of the pain that was still lingering from that episode with Stephen Pickering.

Thinking about it as he was, the situation actually wasn't so bad. From his perspective, he could see a faint flicker of light at the end of the tunnel. Angie couldn't conceive naturally, but so what? Dr. Rouben had provided them with a lifeline—IVF—and if that's what they had to do, then so be it. He certainly didn't have a problem with playing God. Angie was having a few doubts, but that was normal, especially for someone with a Catholic upbringing. As far as he was concerned, God didn't exist, so it didn't matter. Now they could start to plan for the future.

That was a new concept. Since his days at the university, planning for the future meant planning which pub to get drunk in with his buddies on a Saturday night. The future was now something to embrace, not run away from. Albeit with the help of a little medical science, Angie was going to have a baby. She wasn't having an affair. That was just his imagination taking him for a fool. Furthermore, Dr. Rouben wasn't so bad; he only wanted to help. Who cared how much he charged? Angie's medical insurance was paying for it all. They had certainly been through hell over the past few months, Michael thought as he peeled the carrots. Now they could look forward to a brighter future, one in which there was the sound of little feet running up the hallway, of laughing, of crying, of being a happy family. For once, things seemed to be heading in the right direction. Their destiny was in their own hands thanks to the miracles of modern science. Norman was wrong. Things always got better no matter how bad it seemed.

Michael felt sweat bead on his forehead. It had got surprisingly hot. Wiping his brow with a tea towel, he went to the back door and slid it open. Almost immediately, a cool evening breeze fluttered into the kitchen. Outside, the setting sun had cast mountainous shadows over the messy backyard and plastered rose-pink wallpaper over the sky. The hills to the east were the only things still bathed in late sunlight. Michael went back to the chopping board and set to work slicing the carrots into slivers and the onions into quarters. He adorned a pair of oven gloves and pulled the meat tray out of the oven. Like he was on autopilot, he placed the vegetables in a neat circle around the shoulder of lamb, braised the meat and vegetables, and slid the tray back in.

After cleaning the mess he'd made, he ventured into the lounge room to relax while the meal slowly cooked. He saw the telephone sitting on the little table next to the Steinway and thought of giving Norman a quick ring to say Merry Christmas. Instead, he slumped into the sofa and sank into its deep cushions, thinking he would call him later.

At some point he dozed off and then woke up. He figured it hadn't been for too long; there were still remnants of daylight filtering through the window onto the angel sitting atop the Christmas tree. The fake tree was bought at the local hardware store, he recalled, for their first Christmas together as husband and wife in 1992. He had taken it out of its box four weeks ago and put it together as Angie had asked him to do, setting it up in the gap between the television and the window. He remembered Angie coming home that night, taking one look at the tree and shaking her head. Saying something beneath her breath he didn't quite catch, she promptly relocated it into the corner, where it stayed. Since then, presents had stacked up beneath it. There were presents for everyone, including the cleaner at Angie's office. Angie had done most of the shopping, as usual, though there were some he'd bought himself—lapis lazuli earrings for his mum; a pair of golf shoes for his dad; and, for Angie, a new automatic camera, one year's subscription to *Woman's World*, her favourite perfume, Kenzo, and some sexy black underwear (ostensibly for himself). He began imagining what she'd be like in her new lingerie, smiling lewdly at the thought.

"What are you reminiscing about?" Angie asked from the doorway. "You look like you've just played a trick on someone."

Michael flicked his head around. He hadn't heard her approach at all. "My angel has risen and is as beautiful as the star of Venus," he said, beaming.

He watched as she ran her fingers through her dishevelled hair and frowned. Her floral dress was slightly crumpled, one of the straps now hanging loose off her shoulder. "I look like someone who's been asleep for ten years, but thank you anyway." She lifted the loose strap up onto her shoulder. "When's dinner ready?"

Michael stood from the couch, still smiling. He glanced at the Elvis clock. The meat had now been roasting for over an hour and a quarter. It was only another ten to twenty minutes away from being ready. "Soon, my darling, my gorgeous one, the light of my life."

"Are you drunk?" Her face brightened into what Michael thought of as her wedding day smile.

"Only on life," he said and ran over to hug her.

"Stop it," she said with a laugh, and playfully pushed him away. "What's got into you?"

"I've rediscovered what I'd forgotten—that I married an angel," he said, "and that we're going to have a baby." He tried to tickle her tummy, but she pulled away and turned around, upset. His heart sank into the blue carpet and he opened his mouth to try to console her, to raise her spirits, but his voice went AWOL. He wanted to embrace her and tell her he would always be there for her, that no matter how bad things seemed at the moment they were going to come through it, that things were going to get better. Something prevented him from doing so, some kind of internal emotional anchor men threw overboard whenever the going got rough, he reckoned. She sniffled, wiping a tear from her eye with a scrunched tissue she had been holding, and Michael felt all the positive thoughts and emotions he'd had over the past hour being wiped away too. He moved cautiously around her and headed to the kitchen to see how the roast was going.

She followed him down the hallway, keeping her distance. He peered into the oven through its greasy window. The fat of the lamb was splattering against the oven's inner walls and the meat and vegetables had browned nicely. He told Angie that he thought it was almost done.

She didn't answer, lost in a world of her own, silent and withdrawn. Like a mute robot, she grabbed some cutlery from the kitchen drawer and began setting the dinner table.

Michael was worried. She had returned to the distant and evasive patterns of behaviour she had exhibited over the past year. He decided to try another tact, asking her how long she thought it would be before she was able to request maternity leave.

Still preoccupied, Angie laid the rest of the knives and forks on the table and smoothed out the terracotta-red tablecloth. The table wobbled slightly as she ran her hands over the cloth. "You mean, how long will it be before I ask Stephen?" she said, after a moment.

That's not what Michael had meant. He hadn't wanted to mention her ex at all, given what she'd just told him in the car. Angie appeared indifferent. It seemed that in her attempts to deal with what had taken place that night in the parking lot of Eagle-on-the-Hill, Angie had built an impregnable emotional wall around herself, a wall as high as the tower of Babel, which probably enabled her to talk about him as if nothing had happened at all. Michael wasn't sure that was a good thing. Suppressing feelings, especially feelings as powerfully emotive as those she was dealing with, never resulted in anything good, just like that fabled tower. That was Angie's way, though; had been since the day he met her.

He shrugged his shoulders, and said, "I guess. What's he going to say when you tell him you're pregnant and want some time off?"

"I'm not sure. I've begun to realise that he doesn't like women very much," she said, and went to the cupboards above the sink to remove two plates, her mother's best china.

"What do you mean he doesn't like women? Is he gay?"

Angie laughed, nearly dropping the plates. "No, definitely not," she said. "He's just a misogynist, that's all. I wish I knew that before I dated him."

"It sounds like he and Norman would get along just fine."

"I agree, but at least Norman has a heart. That bastard was born without one." She took the plates to the table, stopping to get two green candles and a box of matches from the pantry. "He thinks he owns everyone," she said. "He thinks he can use people just as he sees fit. He gives me the creeps. I have no idea what I saw in him."

Michael raised his eyebrows, crossed his arms and leant against the sink. He figured it was good therapy to let her release her tension. Besides, he kind of liked hearing the sound of her voice. It had been too long since they'd had a discussion, and even if the only topic of conversation was that son-of-bitch boss of hers, he wasn't going to stop her now.

"He's like every man walking on the planet," Angie continued, shaking her head as she laid the plates and arranged the candles, "a testosterone fuelled Neanderthal whose only emotional responses are either to fuck or kill." Michael cleared his throat. Angie ignored him, but he didn't mind; he was actually amused to hear her talk this way. "He treats his women like TV sets. He thinks he can just flick through the channels until he finds the one to suit his mood." She was now pretending to use a make-believe remote control, clicking its imaginary buttons with her thumb. "He wants to flick between personalities like he's surfing the channels. He's unbelievable. If he doesn't find the channel he likes, he thinks all he has to do is press the off button, or even worse, *mute*, and get her to shut up." Her eyes were now fuming. "He's so pathetic it's beyond a joke. He's a control freak. He wants every woman to be a proper lady in public and a whore in bed, switching between the two when he demands it, and when they don't conform to what he wants he gets angry. I'm seriously considering resigning and going to another firm."

This was news to Michael. Apart from the odd grumble about working too hard and inefficient bureaucracy, Angie had never once mentioned anything about quitting her job. He didn't think it was such a wise thing to do considering all the time and energy she had invested in the firm, but he didn't say it. As a sop, he said, "I know you don't like the way Stephen treats you and other women, but will it be any different in another firm? As you said, men are just testosterone fuelled Neanderthals."

Her hands were now on her hips, and as her eyes glazed over in thought, pondering what he had said, Michael saw the opportunity to change the topic to something else, quickly telling her that he'd been having thoughts along those lines as well. He looked at Angie and she looked back. Her eyebrow was cocked, a sure sign she didn't think that both of them should be unemployed and searching for a new job at the same time, especially if a baby was on the way. "Why haven't you ever said anything?" she asked.

He ran a hand though his hair, averting her gaze, and said, "I've been there for over five years and I'm still doing the same job. Don't get me wrong, I love teaching the kids, but the promotions don't seem to be coming my way like they are for you and Jude. I want to see what happens with the baby first, though. I'm not going to make a decision of finding another job until we're more certain it's for the better." The stove timer rang and he bent down to peer into the oven once more. "The food's almost ready," he said, standing erect.

Angie rubbed her bare forearms and Michael glanced behind her through the open door. Like a caravan of gypsies, the cold darkness had silently arrived outside. He had been standing so close to the oven that he hadn't noticed. She slid the door closed, locking it with the small skeleton key that always remained in the lock, then sat at the table and lit the candles. Michael grabbed a corkscrew from the cutlery drawer and selected a bottle of wine from the wine rack at the foot of the wall that separated the kitchen from the laundry room. He put the bottle of wine between his thighs and tried unsuccessfully to prize the cork out with both hands.

"Here, give me that. You're going to break the cork," Angie said, holding out her hand across the table for the bottle. Michael duly obliged and the cork popped effortlessly in her grasp. She flashed him a "see-that's-how-you-do-it" smile and wiped the top of the bottle with her finger. It was an extremely provocative gesture and Michael felt the urge to make love to her right there and then across the dining table. "Why are you looking at me like that?" Angie said, glancing up.

A lopsided smile adorned his face. "Looking at you like what?"

"I don't know," Angie said, "but it looks sordid." He could see that she was trying not to smile, as if she had sensed his intentions; the edges of her mouth were turned slightly up as she looked at him. She raised the bottle of wine. "Would you like a glass?"

He knew what he would've preferred, but a glass of wine was an adequate substitute. Angie held her glass aloft, ready to make a toast. She was as free from any troubles as he had ever seen her, even when they were on their honeymoon at the Gold Coast sunbathing on the beach or drinking cocktails at the hotel pool. He joined her at the table and they toasted to a Merry Christmas. Michael reckoned he too hadn't felt this good since those days immediately following the wedding. It had been a long time, but things were finally getting back to normal.

MICHAEL WASTED NO time in serving the meat and vegetables. As they ate, they small talked. Michael was glad the weather appeared to be getting better; the winter had dragged out far too long. Angie agreed. He was looking forward to spending some time with his parents and family tomorrow for Christmas lunch. Angie agreed with that too. The conversation was getting awkward and he glanced over at her as he took a sip of wine, knowing that they were both deliberately avoiding any discussion about Angie's infertility. It was as though neither of them wanted to inflict unnecessary hurt on the other.

"I've decided we should try this IVF thing," she said after a moment of silence, guessing what was on Michael's mind. "I know my mother would disagree, but I've thought about it and I think we should at least give it a try."

Michael looked up from his plate, grateful that the air was now cleared. He knew he wouldn't have had the courage to broach the subject himself. "Good. I think that's the right decision."

"I'm worried, though." Michael just nodded and finished off the wine in his glass. "I'm worried that it won't work," she said. "I'm nearly thirty and time is running out. This may be our only shot at it."

Michael took a bite of roast lamb. He supposed her concerns were justified to some extent, but he really didn't think she needed to be too worried about it. "Women in their forties are having test-tube babies all the time," he said, glancing up. "Now that medicine and science is so good, it's perfectly feasible to have children whenever you want to. Anyway, Dr. Billy knows what he's doing. We'll have a baby before you can think of a name for it."

Angie seemed to have stopped eating for the moment, prodding her meat with the knife. "Do you really think what he said is true?"

Half standing, Michael reached over the table and grabbed the bottle of wine, careful not to burn his sleeve on the candle flame. He topped up Angie's glass, then filled his own. The bottle was two-thirds empty, he noticed. Angie would have said it was one third full, like his dad would too. He just couldn't see it that way, no matter how hard he tried. He figured the world was split into those who saw what they had left, the ostriches, and those who saw how much they didn't, the eagles. The ostriches stuck their heads in the sand and pretended everything was rosy when it wasn't. The eagles, like he and Norman, were realists, those who didn't pretend that life was full of roses when it was really full of thorns. He guessed it came down to genetics whether you were born an ostrich or an eagle.

"Which bit do you mean?" he asked, putting the bottle down.

"That IVF is an immaculate conception."

"I don't believe in all that claptrap, you know that." Michael lifted his knife and fork off the plate, paused, and then put the knife and fork back down, rather more forcefully than he'd intended. The china clinked loudly, and Angie flinched at the sound. "But if you think about what he said, I guess it makes some sort of sense. All around the world, every day, women are becoming pregnant with IVF. Norman was right," he said, recalling a hitherto forgotten conversation with him about the recent trend of role reversal with men and women in the western world, "society doesn't need men any more. Science has made God obsolete, especially with *in-vitro* fertilisation, and it's also making men obsolete in the process. You're going to be another Mary."

Angie reached up and touched the crucifix hanging atop her breast. "Seriously, though," she said, gazing deeply at him, "don't you think we'll be playing God if we go through with this? If my mother was alive, she would never allow me to have a child this way. You know how strongly she felt about this sort of thing."

Before answering, he glanced down at the knife and fork resting on his half finished plate. They were crossed, reminding him of duelling epees, and he could feel his frustration stir at the mention of her mother. He had only met her two or three times before the accident, and in a way he was glad that she wasn't around anymore, glad that he wasn't forced to put up with her religious nonsense, though he would never contemplate ever mentioning such a thing to Angie. Much in the same way as he had with Dr. Rouben, Michael had taken an instant dislike to his would-be mother-in-law. The feelings, he assumed, were mutual. As an atheist, he was no better than the devil in Shirley Potter's eyes. Probably worse. At least the devil believed in God! She was ludicrously fanatical in her beliefs, which irked him no end, and a domineering busybody more interested in the opinion of the priest or members of the congregation at St. Paul's than the wishes and emotions of her own daughter. It was something Michael found hard to fathom, that other people were seemingly held in higher esteem than those of her own family. Worse, her influence over Angie was still as strong now as it was when she held dominion within these walls. The memory of Shirley Potter haunted everything they did.

"This *sort of thing*, as you put it," he said, now drawing a breath, "is what puts food on your table every night. This *sort of thing* keeps your house warm in the winter, it keeps the lights on when it's dark outside, and it drives you to work so that you can earn money and have a life. Science is the god of the Twentieth Century. Your god has been dead a long time, a myth mankind has out grown just as we outgrew Father Christmas when we were kids."

"Science is not God," Angie said. Her stare was as fanatical as her mother's faith. "Science cannot create life."

"Then tell me what it is we're doing with Dr. Billy? Does life not start at conception when sperm meets egg? Is creating life in his test-tube not like a god?"

"I don't know. It's not the same thing as God crating Adam and Eve, or giving Mary the Immaculate Conception of baby Jesus."

"Oh, isn't it?" he said. "The only difference is that your god had a bigger test tube to play with, that's all. Other than that, it's the same thing."

Angie put her hands in her lap and looked down at the table, silent and thoughtful. Realising that he had once again upset her, Michael flushed. Why do you keep doing this to her, he thought, staring down at his plate and the crossed knife and fork. Hadn't she had enough of late to worry about? She certainly didn't need her own husband piling up more misery for her. Lifting his gaze, he apologised for upsetting her yet again. She smiled, except it was with as much as warmth as the refrigerator on which those annoying Jesus magnets were placed. They ate the rest of the meal, much of it in silence, and then went early to bed.

That night they made love for the first time in over a month and Michael dreamt of running down an empty street in panic, a black shadow in pursuit. He woke with a start and sat up in bed, putting his hand to his brow. It was damp. The clock said 2:47 a.m. and Angie was hushed in her sleep next to him. His throat felt raw and raspy and his heart was thumping. The dream seemed to know no limits of terror. It was getting worse each successive occasion, which was now almost every night. He tried to immediately forget it.

Suddenly, outside the window, he heard a car engine start and he jumped, still buzzing with nervous energy. Then he heard the crunch of rolling tyres over twigs and leaves as the car slowly pulled away. When he got up and peered behind the curtains to investigate, he thought he saw the rear taillights of a cop car disappearing down the dark street. As the curtain fell back into place, he shrugged and went back to bed, letting the thought disappear, just like his dream.

# CHAPTER 6

JUST AFTER THE New Year, Dr. Rouben rang to set a date for the insemination procedure. He was going on holiday, he said, and when he returned there was going to be a backlog of about six weeks before he could fit them into his schedule. If they didn't mind, would they possibly consider a date sometime around mid-February? It was Angie who had spoken to him, and although Michael could tell she was disappointed that it wasn't earlier, she gave him her approval. "Insemination Day", or I-Day, as they now began calling it, was pencilled in for the 14th of next month. The wheels of destiny, Michael mused, were now well and truly turning.

Somehow, the next six weeks just disappeared, swallowed by the hot summer sun. He didn't re-paint the kitchen or strip the wallpaper in the hallway; he didn't do anything he'd planned at all. He didn't even mow the lawns or get the battery in Angie's car fixed. All he seemed to have energy for was to watch a lot of sport—cricket and tennis and golf during the day, English soccer and American football at night. The time difference between Australia and the northern continents, he reckoned, made 24-hour sport-viewing a real feasibility.

It helped being an insomniac, too. He was just unable to get to sleep before three or four in the morning, and when he did the nightmares woke him up in a cold sweat. They were getting worse. To compound matters, the school term was about to begin. Another year was soon to start, another class to organise and prepare for, and he just didn't feel up to it. Despite the break, it felt as if last year had finished only yesterday. There seemed to have been no time to recover from one class to the next, no time to recuperate his energy.

Angie didn't seem to notice that he had done none of his household chores. She was immersed in her own sea of thoughts for most of the time. He saw her little, yet when he did he was pleased to see that she was less edgy, less quick to snap at something he said or burst into tears. She wasn't quite back to the woman he once knew, the carefree woman he got down before on one knee and asked to marry, but there were signs that that woman was slowly returning from her long period of voluntary exile. Warmth was returning to her smile. Her caramel eyes, though often dreamy and distant, looked less careworn and burdensome, and her voice was losing its demanding bitterness. Work was still occupying most of her day, yet significantly less than before. She now began leaving for work as late as eight or half past eight, and was even arriving home before seven o'clock some nights. He figured it was the imminent prospect of becoming pregnant that was soothing her troubled mind.

Before he knew it, I-Day had rushed upon them. Michael walked into the maternity unit on the fifth level of St. Mary's Hospital in search of Angie, reflecting on what was about to happen. Considering all that had gone before, he should have been happier, but the prospect of watching Angie having a surgical procedure sat sour, like lukewarm milk, in his stomach. There was nothing he could do about it now, however. The wheels were in motion. He just had to put his doubts to the back of his mind and support his wife. It was she, after all, who had to suffer all the pain, like the woman in the room to his left screaming a chilling, high-pitched wail that echoed off the walls and made him flinch and spin around. She screamed again. It sounded like torture. Ignoring it as best he could, he walked up to the deserted nurses' station. Two red helium balloons in the shape of large hearts were drifting towards the ceiling like kites in a windless sky, each attached by silver ribbons to the computer keyboard at the desk and embellished with the words: BE MY VALENTINE. A dozen white roses were sitting on the desk, carefully arranged in a glass vase, and as he arrived the telephone next to the computer started ringing.

The door behind the nurses' station opened after several rings. A midwife harried out to answer the phone, but just as she picked it up it fell silent. A stream of dusty sunlight fell through the window upon her long, greying hair. Michael guessed she was in her late forties and, by the look of resignation on her face, either desperate to leave her job or leave the man she had married.

"Can I help you?" she asked, flicking her eyes to the clock above the door.

Michael didn't need to follow her gaze. It was quarter past two and he knew he was running late to meet Angie, late for I-Day. Angie was going to be furious. She was probably going to scream at him like the woman in labour screaming at the top of her voice behind him. "I was told by the reception lady in the lobby to come here to look for my wife," he said, half apologetically. "Her name's Angie Joseph."

The woman was still screaming in the room behind. The midwife turned and looked at the large whiteboard hanging on the back wall. Michael saw a list of women's names in blue felt pen, their designated bed number, treating obstetrician (either Dr. Rouben or Dr. Foley), and attending midwife.

"Your wife's name doesn't seem to be here," the midwife said, facing him. She seemed to take it personally. "Have you checked next door?"

Michael expressed his thanks and hurried off, grateful to get away from that god-awful screaming. He trotted down the corridor, past the elevators and several single-bedded cubicles, and into the second of the hospital's two maternity wards. Angie's name, he quickly discovered, wasn't written on the whiteboard there either. Now he was starting to worry. If he had already missed the insemination procedure, it would be years before Angie forgave him.

"How many weeks pregnant is she?" asked another midwife. Perched behind the nurses' station as though it were her private property, she was large and fat and sweaty, with a double chin that engulfed her neck. A box of variety chocolates was sitting open and half empty in front of her.

"She's not pregnant," Michael said, to which the fat midwife cocked her bushy eyebrows in cynical surprise. At least, he thought, running a hand through his hair, not yet, not as far as he knew. "She's due to have *in-vitro* fertilisation this afternoon. I was told to come to the maternity unit."

The fat midwife harrumphed that he was told wrong. All insemination procedures took place in the operating suite on the second floor.

Michael's eyes widened and his heart skipped a beat. He spun around and ran back down the corridor to the elevators, thinking Angie was going to kill him. The only thing he had to get right this summer break was to ensure he was at her side when Dr. Rouben inserted the fertilised eggs into her womb, and he couldn't even do that properly. He pushed the elevator call button once, twice, and then continuously, tapping his foot and running his hand through his hair. They were taking an eternity to arrive, so he darted for the emergency exit and harried three levels down to the second floor, taking two steps at a time.

He exited into the elevator alcove, bursting through the door immediately opposite the entrance to the operating suite. The doors were security locked and he had to buzz the intercom to be allowed in. Behind the reception desk was a whiteboard, as he'd now come to expect. On it was Angie's name. She was due to have her procedure at 2:30 p.m. in Operating Room 3. He breathed a sigh of relief.

The nurse behind the desk seemed too busy to notice his presence, and only when she glanced up did he feel a flicker of recognition. Eyeing her without trying to stare, he wondered where he had seen her before. Then he realised that she was the same nurse who he had bumped into in the lobby last year and caused to spill the medical files she was carrying. Her beauty had bewitched him then, just as it did now—her supple olive skin, the little mole above her sensual lips, her dark, provocative eyes—though there was more than just a hint of tiredness on her pretty face to suggest she had been up all night, and he wondered if she'd been moonlighting to earn some extra cash. Like almost every single person around them, she was wearing operating livery—blue gown, pink hair-cap—and pinned above her right breast was a photograph identity tag. Her name was Maria Sanchez.

Maria showed him to the men's changing room and instructed him to change into theatre attire. She would wait for him outside OR3 with Angie, who was currently in the patient bay receiving an epidural anaesthetic for the insemination procedure.

It took Michael just over five minutes to get changed. He now looked like all the doctors, nurses, orderlies and cleaners he'd seen, though rather embarrassingly, like a boy who had outgrown his clothes, his blue trousers were too short to cover his lime-green socks. He stepped outside the changing rooms, trying to slide a number of loose hair strands that were falling out back beneath his hair-cap. He looked around, slightly disorientated, not knowing were to go to next. He asked another nurse where to find OR3. She quickly pointed down the corridor before disappearing into an adjacent room filled with cigarette smoke and voices from some TV soapy, marked STAFF ONLY.

Michael eyed the corridor. The operating suite had a certain tenseness about it he didn't like. It was as though everybody was in a minor state of panic, just as he had been ten minutes before when he realised he was in the wrong place. He saw doctors and nurses rushing in all directions. He saw orderlies pushing patients on gurneys. He saw an anxious family crowding around an unconscious patient in the post-operative bay. The sense of trepidation was as strong as the smell of disinfectant wafting up from the linoleum floor. If purgatory existed, this was it.

He continued down the corridor, stepping back once or twice to allow a patient on a gurney to be pushed hurriedly by. As she said she would, Maria was waiting outside OR3. She was holding a set of patient files and looking impatiently at her watch pinned above her left breast. Behind her was a heavy-set medical orderly, the only one in the corridor with a smile on his face. Michael wondered where Angie was, and only when he neared and Maria took a step back did he see her lying on the gurney the orderly was pushing. She was wearing only a flimsy patient gown and her hair was covered with a white hair-cap. She seemed scared. Her face was pale, her lips twitched every so often, and her eyes darted around the room. He called out to her and she immediately propped herself on one elbow and waved. He hastened to the gurney and embraced his wife, apologising profusely for being late, yet again.

"I was afraid you'd forgotten the big event," Angie said, hugging him tighter. Then her tone of voice softened, becoming more relaxed. "You know I would never have forgiven you if you weren't here for I-Day."

Michael hugged her back, pressing his cheek next to hers. "I know," he said.

Out of the corner of his eye he saw Maria glance at her watch again. "Excuse me, Mr. Joseph," she said, "but we must take your wife inside. We're running a little late and Dr. Rouben has a long list this morning."

Michael pulled away from Angie's embrace. It was happening. It was really happening.

"If you wouldn't mind just waiting here while we get ready," Maria said. "I'll call you as soon as we're about to start."

Michael nodded and told Angie he would see her in a minute. As she was pushed past, he caught sight of an epidural syringe-pump lying on the coarse white blanket between her feet. A bright, fluorescent-yellow label with Angie's name and hospital number was stuck to the syringe, from which a thin tube coursed like a colourless asp over her left knee and beneath her back. He couldn't see any further, but he had seen enough medical programs to know it was attached to a needle inserted between the vertebrae of Angie's lower spine, paralysing her legs more powerfully than the venom of a brown snake. The double doors to the operating room then shut in his face.

He tried running a hand through his hair, but he had forgotten he was wearing a hair-cap. He could hear a woman wailing from the direction of the reception. Nurses and doctors hurried past pushing an unconscious patient on a gurney into an adjacent operating room. It made him worry even more about Angie. He tried not to think about the things that could go wrong, the gruesome horror stories of medical negligence that always seemed to make it onto one or other current affairs program or the front page of the *Adelaide Sun*. He tried not to think of the scalpels and needles and other instruments of pain that were being prepared behind these closed double doors. Despite his best efforts not to, that was all he did while he waited.

Nearly ten minutes passed before the doors to OR3 opened again. The orderly exited and told Michael that he could now go inside, then he disappeared down the corridor toward the reception.

The powerful smell of bleach inflamed Michael's nostrils the second he entered and made him slightly light headed, but what struck him the most about the room was its brightness. It was like something out of a science fiction movie, stark white with a dash of shiny silver. Maria gestured for him to take a seat on a small stool she had placed next to Angie, who was lying on the operating table draped in green surgical sheets, her legs strapped in stirrups and splayed in the air like a frog. A large, disk-shaped light was pouring light over her naked inner thighs and pubic area, which Dr. Rouben, in green surgical attire, was swabbing with rusty-coloured iodine. As Michael approached, Angie turned and smiled, seemingly okay with what was happening.

"Good morning, Michael," Dr. Rouben said, his voice slightly muffled behind the mask covering his mouth and nose. "How are you feeling? Ready for the big event?"

"A bit nervous," he said, sitting on the stool. He took Angie's hand and squeezed it. "But as ready as I can be, I guess."

"This will probably be the best Valentine present you have ever had, your first baby." Michael silently agreed. He felt Angie squeeze his hand. "They say babies conceived on St Valentine's Day are always lucky in love."

Angie remained unusually quiet. Michael wondered if she was thinking about that night with Stephen Pickering, if she had any idea back then of the consequences that she would have to endure six years down the line. He also wondered what her priggish mother would have made of her daughter exhibiting her vagina like a museum art piece to a stranger.

Dr. Rouben finished sterilising Angie's groin and tossed the dirty swab into a yellow bin liner attached to a surgical tray next to him. The tray was on wheels and had two shelves, like a small metal bookcase. On the top shelf was a pile of green towels and several kidney-shaped bowls stacked one inside another. Within the top dish were small white square swabs and a range of different sized needles and syringes that gave Michael the creeps. There was also an array of surgical equipment—scalpels and pincer-like instruments and other things—that he imagined wouldn't look too out of place in a torture chamber. At the thought of what Dr. Rouben was going to do with them, Michael felt his stomach churn a little.

He averted his gaze. Above Dr. Rouben's head, fixed to the corner of the ceiling, Michael saw a small video camera. Dr. Rouben caught him staring up at it. "Don't worry about that," he said. "We video every procedure. It's hospital policy, for medicolegal reasons. It's the way of the world nowadays. Everybody wants to sue." Dr. Rouben then took a sharp needle from the tray and pricked Angie several times on the area of the upper thigh he had covered in iodine. "Can you feel pain when I do this?" he asked, to which Angie shook her head in reply. "Excellent," Dr. Rouben said, putting the needle back. "We should be able to start soon."

Michael shuffled in his seat. Angie squeezed his hand again and bit her bottom lip. He figured she was feeling as completely powerless and overwhelmed with this whole situation as much as he was. It was all rather intimidating, actually. He was glad he could now sit; his legs were feeling wobbly and he didn't know how long they would hold out.

Dr. Rouben reached for a long, thin, straw-like metal tube and placed it into Angie's vagina. Michael gulped, wide eyed, and began to sweat a little. The heat under that operating light was more powerful than it looked.

"I'm about to dilate the cervix so that it will accommodate my introducer," Dr. Rouben said to Angie. "Then I'm going to place the eggs I took from your ovaries two days ago and fertilised with Michael's sperm into the uterus."

Angie nodded and Michael wiped the sweat from his forehead with the back of his hand. He suddenly felt quite steamy. He also felt weak and dizzy. He could feel his heart racing fast and furious beneath his blue surgical gown. It was like being trapped in a white box, as if the room was suddenly a vacuum devoid of oxygen, as if he was suffocating, and he knew he had to get out of there to breathe. What helped to keep his dignity intact was the numbness of his legs. Thankfully, they were feeling as paralysed as his wife's because he knew that if they were fully functional he would have been up and out through the doors in a flash, screaming like a madman.

Hoping this feeling of suffocation would wash over soon, Michael concentrated on watching Dr. Rouben position himself between Angie's splayed legs. One hand was fully immersed into her vagina, guiding the probe into its proper place, the other now reaching up to the array of surgical equipment for a syringe. Michael kept staring. The syringe was huge, and tipped with an even bigger needle. He had never seen anything so grotesquely enormous, not even when he was a kid and everything seemed gigantic and overwhelmingly massive. He heard Angie ask if he was all right, her voice distant and stifled, coming to him as if from an adjacent room. He just nodded, his mouth too dry to speak. He felt appalling. He didn't need a mirror to know that he had turned as white as the operating room.

Then, as Dr. Rouben put the syringe inside Angie, something snapped inside him. Suffocating waves of nausea flooded his body. The ceiling and walls began to spin wildly and his stomach churned, threatening to release its lunchtime contents in one retching surge. With the hand he was gripping Angie's, he squeezed even tighter, and with the other hand clung to the edge of the stool. Another wave of nausea flooded his body. He hung his head back to try and ease the sensation of spinning and saw the video camera staring down at him, like a single mocking eye.

It was the last thing he remembered before his eyes rolled back into his sockets and his body slumped to the floor.

# CHAPTER 7

MICHAEL SPENT THE next month and a half in a state of minor apprehension. The insemination procedure had done nothing to allay his troubled mind. In fact, if he really thought about it, it seemed he had only swapped one set of concerns for another. He no longer worried about the reasons why Angie couldn't conceive or if she was having an affair with her ex-fiancé. Now his worries were different. He worried for the health and safety of both Angie and the baby they hoped had taken seed in her womb. He worried that they might not have the finances to send the child to a good school or university. He also worried that he might not have what it took to be a good father, someone like his dad, for instance, someone who could provide the joy and security and acceptance a child needed to be a confident and balanced person. Was this what parenthood was all about, non-stop worrying?

His sleepy mind was running through these thoughts when Angie gently slapped his face to wake him. His mouth was thick with the taste of sleep, his head was groggy and his eyelids were lead, the aftermath of a wretched night. It was like a bad hangover, only worse. He had been dreaming again.

Her voice took on a more urgent appeal when he didn't rouse the first time. His eyelids creaked half-open, protesting as though held on rusty hinges, and through the slits he watched Angie grab the radio-alarm clock from atop the bedside drawers and put it in front of his face. "It's half past nine," she said. "Come on! Hurry up! We have to leave. The appointment's in less than an hour."

Michael now opened his eyes fully. The room was dim and Angie was sitting on the edge of the bed, dressed in faded jeans and a lilac long-sleeved shirt. It was Saturday morning; all he wanted was to lie in. He attempted to lift his head off the pillow, then let it flop back into the soft down. Angie put the clock back on top of the set of drawers and tossed the quilt off his naked body, after which she went to the window and flung aside the purple curtains. Sunrays streamed onto Michael's face and he blinked, adjusting to the sudden brightness. What he saw rendered him speechless. The mid morning sun draped her slender shoulders in a stole of liquid white, like an angel. She was simply stunning.

Something good had happened to Angie in the past six weeks. There were no more long drawn out days at the office, no more childish moues or sullen moods, no more doubts or misgivings; there was a lambent aura emanating from her body, a golden light that shone from her very core. She was reborn, it seemed, vivacious, poised, and incredibly alluring. She had even regained most of the weight she lost leading up to Christmas. It was a change he approved of, and he suspected it was not just because their sex life had taken off like a rally on the stock market.

With a reluctant sigh he staggered out of bed to go to the bathroom. She handed him the purple towel draped over the end of the bed, which he wrapped around his waist as he ambled past the open window. Even though his eyes had now fully adjusted, the outside morning had lost none of its brightness. Summer had seemingly hijacked the month of April, holding autumn at ransom, and the stunning blue sky heralded yet another hot day. It pleased him. He wasn't looking forward to the winter again and every warm day was an opportunity to embrace with open arms.

He looked back at Angie. He was about to comment on how gorgeous she and the morning were, when suddenly the sound of crunching tyres distracted him. He spun around to see a cop car driving slowly past the front of the house. Although obscured by the brims of their caps, the faces of the driver and passenger were turned in his direction and staring silently, like vacant mannequins. He should have felt comfortable and safe, but as always when he saw cops he was filled with an irrational sense of foreboding, as if they were going to arrest him for something he'd never done, or worse, for all the misdemeanours he'd gotten away with. The cop car rolled by and sped up when it reached the far end of the house.

Angie told him to stop daydreaming and get in the shower. He stopped staring outside and made his way to the bathroom while Angie tidied the bed and went to the kitchen to make some coffee. As he turned on the faucets, he could hear her humming to herself, a happy, melodic tune that sounded like a nursery rhyme. He hung the towel behind the bathroom door and stepped into the shower. He quickly washed his hair, not wanting to waste any more time than he already had and thereby avoid the sting of Angie's wrath. For some reason, a vision of an Italian restaurant flashed before his closed eyes. He was initially perplexed, but after thinking about it for a moment he understood the connection between that and the forthcoming appointment. He rinsed the suds from his hair and face, and over the noise of splattering water shouted to Angie, "I had a dream last night about the baby."

He knew that would pique her interest. Sure enough, Angie came to the bathroom. Michael saw her blurred lineaments through the plastic shower curtain as she leant against the doorframe holding her happy mug. "We don't know if we're going to have a baby yet," she said, sipping her coffee. "That's why we're going to the clinic to have the ultrasound scan, to see if I'm pregnant or not."

"I don't need an ultrasound. I already know. It's going to be a girl."

He turned off the shower faucets. The sound of running water ceased and he brushed aside the shower curtain. As he stepped out of the shower, she handed him the purple towel that he had hung behind the door. Her eyes were curious, waiting for him to continue, straining, as if she were tied to a leash. He dried himself off, saying nothing, deliberately teasing her. It was like dangling a woollen ball in front of a kitten—he dangled and she snatched a claw at it. He wrapped the towel around his waist and then squeezed past Angie out of the bathroom, patting her on the bum.

Angie followed him back to the bedroom. "And just how is a dream supposed to predict the sex of our child?" she asked, sitting on the edge of the bed.

Still saying nothing, he found a pair of red boxer shorts in the bedside drawers and put them on. Then he tossed the bath towel onto the purple quilt and slid open the mirrored closet door. Sifting through the layers of clothes that were piled neatly on the inner shelves, he finally found the pair of black jeans he wanted to wear.

"Michael! Answer me."

He decided not to tease her any longer. "You have to promise not to laugh, okay?" he said to her reflection in the mirror, slipping his feet into the jean legs.

Angie took a sip from her mug and nodded. He pulled the jeans up and zipped the fly. With a wry grin, he slid the mirrored door closed and faced his wife. "You remember the nightmares I've been having?" he said, running a hand through his damp hair. Angie nodded again. "Last night I had it again, except it was different from all the others. It's never exactly the same, but it always starts off the same way. I'm running down a street somewhere around here. The weird thing is, it's always quiet—no birds are singing, no dogs are barking, nobody's shouting—and it's always in black and white. My legs feel heavy and my chest is about to explode. Sometimes I wake up at this point, there's sweat on my brow and I'm breathing hard and fast like I've done a marathon or something. That's always been the problem. I'm running like I'm being chased, but I don't know who's behind me, except there's this black shadow with no face and I'm really frightened, as if it wants to kill me."

Michael looked away, distant, like he figured a writer would at his desk, searching for inspiration. He scratched his head and took a deep breath. "Anyway, the past few times I've been able to see who's chasing me," he said, eventually. "It's a man in a white cloak, like the one's the boxers wear, you know, with the hood, and it's almost down to his ankles. It's like the robes the monks wear, too, only this guy's no monk. He has a gun in his hand and he's pointing it at me and shouting like a crazy man. He keeps yelling at me to give it back, but I don't have any idea what he wants, only that he thinks I must have stolen something from him and he's really mad."

Angie stroked her hand upon the purple quilt next to her thigh, smoothing out the wrinkles. "You've never been this worried about your dreams before," she said.

Michael nodded in agreement. This dream had shaken him more

than any time previously. The memory of that black shadow was truly terrifying. It was fear beyond anything he had experienced during the waking day, fear, he hoped, that would remain securely immured within the confines of his imagination. He was reminded of something he had read several years ago: you have nothing to fear but fear itself. It was of little consolation to him now.

"What worries me now, though," he said, "is how *real* it seemed. I know how ridiculous it sounds, except the more I try not to let it worry me, the more it does. Does that seem strange?"

She shook her head. "There's a message you have to learn from your dream," she said. "Just be patient and it will reveal itself."

Michael figured she was probably right. "I think I already know what it is," he said, and ran a hand through his hair. He saw Angie reach for her crucifix, seemingly unaware that she was doing so. He smiled lopsidedly. "As I said before, we're going to have a baby girl."

Saying it out loud hadn't sounded as ridiculous as he'd been worried about, and Angie hadn't laughed at him as he'd expected. In fact, she seemed to have taken it as seriously as gospel. Michael turned back to the wardrobe and slid open the second mirrored door. He sorted through the hanging shirts and jackets until he found what he was looking for, a black shirt with short sleeves. Slipping it on, he saw Angie's reflection stand up and put her now empty happy mug down on top of the dressing table, next to which were her cosmetics and creams and perfumes. She sat down and began applying foundation to her face. Michael grabbed a pair of black shoes from the shoe rack and socks from the drawer, then went to the bed, perching on the edge where Angie had just been.

For a while, Angie was lost in thought. "How can you come to the conclusion that we're going to have a baby girl from a dream in which you're being chased by a gun wielding monk in a white robe?" she asked as Michael slipped on his socks and shoes. "I can't see the connection."

Michael laughed, knowing full well how completely obscure it sounded. It hadn't made much sense to him at first, either. "You know how dreams chop and change," he said, tying up the shoelace on his right foot, "one minute you're walking along the street and then the next you're sitting in a plane or on the beach?" Angie nodded, continuing to apply her foundation. "Well, anyway, the next thing I know I'm standing at the entrance of an Italian restaurant, lost and confused. Everything's changed from black and white to colour now. One good thing, though, the guy in the white robe is no longer chasing me. He seems to have disappeared somewhere. I look to my left and right, and then behind me, just to make sure of where I am."

He looked up from tying his left shoelace, watching her deftly caress her upper and lower lids with a black eyeliner pencil, captivated once again by the glow of the sunlight as it draped around her shoulders and hair. The sun, too, was doing special things to the bedroom. It flooded the room, lending its interior a soft hue, like purple mist. For a brief moment he was reminded of the story of Alice in Wonderland—Angie was Alice and this room was the magical land into which she had fallen down the rabbit hole. It was as fanciful as his dream.

He shook himself out of his reverie and finished tying his laces. "Anyway, I saw that I was standing on the pavement outside Piccolo Diavolo, can you believe it, our favourite, of all restaurants? I was looking around, slightly confused as to how I got here, and then I saw my reflection in the window. I got a bit of a shock. It was me, but not really me—my hair was shorter and I had a crescent scar on my cheek—and then I suddenly realised that this was all a dream. I don't know if you've ever had that happen, when it suddenly dawns that nothing is real, you're dreaming everything, the place, the people, the cars, even yourself."

He caught her eye in the dressing table mirror. Holding the eyeliner from her face, she shook her head and shrugged her shoulders.

"Well, it's kind of freaky," he said. "You feel you can do anything, like you're god or something," and he saw her cock an eyebrow, as if he had just committed an unforgivable sin.

He realised that perhaps he shouldn't have said that. Angie had always reprimanded him for blaspheming and it was something he rarely did in her presence. Slightly flustered, he grabbed the hairbrush from her cosmetic bag, and continued from where he had left off. "Then a waiter came to the door and asked if my name was Michael Joseph. I said it was and he said that there was someone here waiting for me. I remember thinking it was kind of weird because I hadn't arranged to meet anyone, not that I could recall anyway." He manoeuvred around the bed to the mirrored closet doors and began vigorously brushing his hair. "So I followed the waiter through the restaurant to a table at the back and that's when I saw who was sitting there—you, and a strange man with a briefcase."

After a few more brushes, his hair was almost free of tangles. He stopped and looked over his shoulder. Angie packed her lipstick and foundation cream into the cosmetic bag, motioning with a nod of her head for Michael to continue. Her face was impassive and it was difficult to read what she was making of all this. He wondered if she thought he was going crazy, that the pressure of trying to have a baby had suddenly taken its toll and he had lost his mind. He certainly didn't feel crazy. In fact, he probably hadn't felt this sane in his entire life. After the turbulence of the past twelve months, he now felt as if his life was back on track. Everything was running as smooth as a well-oiled engine, as if all the parts in the machinery of his life fitted neatly together and there was nothing out of place to seize it up. He took a fleeting look at himself in the mirror. Maybe he was going insane. The world didn't work like that for guys like him.

Angie asked what the guy in his dream looked like. Brushing his hair again, he glanced at her reflection sitting patiently on the stool in front of the dressing table, her expression still unreadable. "The guy was strikingly handsome," he said, smirking a little at the memory. "I was a bit jealous at first, I guess. He was dressed in a suit and tie, like a lawyer, and smiling as if there were no cares in the whole wide world. You looked beautiful, too. You were wearing a red cape and had your hair up in pigtails, like Little Red Riding Hood on her way to visit her grandma. You were even wearing the red lipstick I like.

"When I arrived at the table I saw you reading a document, or contract, kind of like the ones I've seen you bring home from work sometimes. As I sat down, you borrowed his pen and signed your name at the bottom of the page. You looked happy, as if you'd just won a million dollars or a trip to Disney Land, but I was frightened. I thought you'd just signed away your soul to the devil or something. You seemed to realise my concerns and leant across the table and kissed me on the cheek. You told me that there was no need to worry any more, that it's all been arranged."

He turned around, splaying his arms with his elbows tucked into the sides of his waist and shrugging his shoulders, welcoming an opinion from Angie. She just stared at him, her eyes now as curious as when she had been leaning against the bathroom door, and probably as curious as he remembered feeling in the dream. She said nothing, however.

"I asked you what had been arranged," he said, tossing the brush onto the bed, "but you didn't reply, you just kept smiling and handed the guy the document. He locked it away in his briefcase and when he looked up I saw his eyes, piercing blue, as if I was looking straight into his soul. They were kind and gently reassuring in a strange way, and I asked him what the document was you'd just signed. He told me that he had sorted everything out, that me and you were going to be just fine, we weren't to worry if things became a little confusing in the next few months or so, it was all going to work out in the end. I demanded to know more, but all he did was repeat what both of you had already said, that everything was fine. I was getting pretty spooked by all this, as you can imagine. I'm not someone who deals well with weird shit like this. The instant I'm told not to worry about something, I worry about it. It didn't matter how much I raised my voice or demanded some explanation, the guy wouldn't budge."

Michael paused and his eyes turned up and to the right toward the ceiling, deep in thought. "But he did say one thing," he said, straightening his back and looking Angie in the eye. She stared back at him, gripping her crucifix. "The guy leant forward across the table and whispered in my ear, 'You're going to have a baby girl, Mikey. An immaculate conception, a miracle of life.'"

Pursing his lips, Michael scratched his head. He had come to the part of the dream that conflicted most with his sense of reality. Which, he thought, was exactly what dreams were, non-real, except this dream was not like any other. He had been lucid throughout the whole event. He was aware of everything, his thoughts, his emotions, his past memories, just as he was now, in the waking day. The distinction between real and non-real had been blurred. It was hard to dismiss what had happened as just a dream, just as it would have been hard to dismiss the insemination procedure as a figment of his imagination. He wasn't quite sure whether he could believe what he had witnessed in his dream or not.

"After he said that he sat back and smiled," Michael said after a while, running his hand through his hair and frowning, "content, like a pussycat after it's just polished off a bowl of milk. Then I looked at you. You were just as happy and suddenly all my worries fell away. I felt as if the weight of the world had somehow been resting on my shoulders and had now been lifted. It was as if this guy had waved a magic wand and solved all our problems in one stroke. I believed him completely, not only because I wanted to, but because there was no choice—he spoke the truth and I *knew* it. We were going to have a baby and it was going to be a girl.

"I didn't know what to say other than thank you. The guy smiled and said he was only a messenger, and that he was happy we were happy. I asked him what he meant by only being a messenger and he said I had a lot to learn about the ways of the universe, that there was always something bigger than what we see, a greater plan, and that I must learn to open my eyes and embrace the larger world. I said he was beginning to sound like a bible-bashing evangelist, and do you know what he said?" Michael was now staring at Angie with deeply worrisome eyes, searching desperately for some meaning in what he was about to say. Then he spoke, hushed and almost reverent. "I am not the man you think I am. I am a messenger, an angel, and my name is Gabriel."

Angie gasped, gripping her crucifix even more tightly than he thought possible. Michael looked at her quizzically. She was blinking rapidly, mouthing the name of the archangel. A long time passed before she spoke. "God wants us to have this baby," she said, suddenly looking up at Michael. She wiped a tear from her eye with the tip of her finger. "I know it."

"You know I don't believe that," he said.

Angie was about to retort, but instead kept her thoughts to herself, as if she knew there was no point in arguing with him. He figured she was right. No matter what she said, he was going to see what he wanted to see, believe what he wanted to believe. This was one thing they would never agree on; it was better left alone.

He moved around the bed and offered his hand to help her stand, thinking that if he'd known from the start the dream was going to cause such a reaction he would never have mentioned it. He looked at the bedside alarm clock. Time was fast running out if they wanted to get to the fertility clinic on time and avoid Dr. Billy's bitch of a secretary giving them the third degree again.

Picking up her purse from the dressing table, Angie mumbled something beneath her breath that sounded like a challenge, something like now they would see if his dream really would come true. Michael suspected not. Without doubt he'd had a powerful dream. Hell, he still felt shaken and dazed by the whole ordeal, but as the morning slowly passed and his head began to clear, he could feel his mind recovering somewhat, enough to realise the folly of confusing dreams with everyday reality.

Dreams were just dreams. Nothing more.

THEY WERE LATE, five minutes, and the secretary, as Michael had predicted, growled at them when they arrived. They were the only patients. They sat silently in the waiting room, watching the seconds tick slowly, slowly by. Angie's hands were crossed in her lap one minute, by her side the next, then back in her lap soon after. She was far too anxious to read any of the women's magazines piled beneath the glass-topped coffee table.

Somehow, Michael's confidence that Angie was going to have a baby girl had vanished on the way to the hospital. Like he imagined the anxiety going on inside her mind, his thoughts were now turning and twisting and convoluting like contortionists at the circus, over and over, round and round, inside and out. The questions always began with, what if? What if the insemination didn't work? What if Angie had a miscarriage? What if it were twins? He began wringing his hands, like his wife.

Dr. Rouben must have heard all the commotion going on inside his head, Michael reckoned, because his voice crackled on the intercom behind the secretary's desk that very second and asked her to bring in the last patients. They were ushered immediately into a cramped examination room attached to the main office. In a cream shirt, russet trousers, dark leather shoes, and a paisley silk tie, Dr. Rouben was sitting on a stool in front of an ultrasound machine that looked to Michael like a portable computer perched atop a large, grey audio system. He greeted them as they entered and took Angie's medical file from the secretary, who he then dismissed for the day. She immediately exited the room. It was the first time Michael had seen a smile on her face.

Dr. Rouben instructed Angie to pop herself on the examination bed and unfasten her jeans. Michael was asked to stand behind and watch the ultrasound screen over Dr. Rouben's shoulder. Michael stood back as Angie nervously laid herself on the bed, undid her buttons and lifted up her lilac top to reveal her slim, naked belly. Dr. Rouben flicked a switch and the ultrasound machine blipped on. It began humming quietly, monotonous and drone-like. He began typing in Angie's name and medical number into the machine's database and, once done, asked Michael to switch off the lights.

Dr. Rouben, Michael saw, when his eyes adjusted to the darkness, smothered the ultrasound probe in a jelly-like substance squeezed from a tube of gel and placed the probe against Angie's naked belly. Bright and distinctive white shadows darted across the monitor screen, reminding Michael of raindrops caught in the headlights at night. He heard Angie complain with a laugh that the jelly was cold.

"Let me just move the probe around and see what we can," Dr. Rouben said. There was hopeful expectation in his voice, which Michael found mildly comforting. "Normally at six or seven weeks gestation we don't see very much, but we'll try."

As he slid the probe over her exposed belly and fiddled with more knobs, Michael stared at the screen in anticipation. Dr. Rouben was silent. His wife was silent. There was no other sound except his heart drumming a crazy rhythmic beat in his ears and the monotonous drone of the ultrasound machine. He remembered what Angie had said in the bedroom this morning, that god wanted them to have a baby and had sent his trusted archangel, Gabriel, as a harbinger. He didn't believe a word of it, but he did believe that he wanted Angie to be pregnant, more than he could find words to express it.

Dr. Rouben abruptly cut short his thoughts. "There! Do you see it?" he asked.

Michael's heart began to beat faster. Lifting up on tiptoes to get a better view over the doctor's shoulder, his attention was focused entirely on the screen, but he saw only fuzzy snow flicking over it. There was nothing to get excited about. Instead, he wanted to scream in anger and frustration. It had all been a waste of time, all of it; he was a fool to have believed Dr. Billy could help them. He glanced at Angie, wondering what she was thinking. In the darkness, he could just make out her hand grasping the crucifix. She was deathly still. At least, he figured, she couldn't see the grimness of his despair. He hoped she wasn't as low as he was feeling, except that was just wishful thinking. If Dr. Rouben couldn't locate any signs of a foetus inside her uterus, he knew she'd be more devastated than when they were told the reasons for her infertility.

Dr. Rouben kept moving the probe over Angie's belly, telling her not to move and mumbling that he thought he saw something, but Michael knew there was nothing to see. Whatever had flashed across the screen was only the ghost of what could have been. He felt dejected.

"There it is! I've got it!" Dr. Rouben suddenly exclaimed.

Michael held his breath and stood on tiptoes again. There, on the screen in front of Dr. Rouben, something fluttered fast. It was small, tiny in fact, a tiny white butterfly that flickered its wings in a rapid quiver. Although most of the snow still flurried in distracting gusts, there was no mistaking the beginnings of life that had taken seed in Angie's womb. "A heartbeat," Michael whispered.

Dr. Rouben seemed momentarily distracted, but he spun the monitor to the side so that Angie could see. "Here it is," he said. "Your little baby."

Angie stared in wonder, her jaw dropping silently ajar. "It's a miracle," she whispered, and squeezed her crucifix.

"That it is my dear," Dr. Rouben said. "Now, lie still for another minute please while I do one more thing." He spun the monitor back so that it was directly facing him, leant forward and flicked a switch on the consol. All at once, the unmistakeable sound of life filled the room: WHOOSH-WHOOSH-WHOOSH-WOOSH-WHOOSH.

"Can you hear it, Mikey?" Angie asked, her voice choking with tears of joy. "Do you hear our baby's heartbeat?"

Michael, too, could barely talk. "I hear it, Angel," he managed to say.

Dr. Rouben took some measurements and then flicked the switch. The WOOSH-WOOSH stopped, but in his ears Michael could still hear it echo around the room. Dr. Rouben's hands worked quickly across the consol as he took more measurements and recorded data. "Let me check the rest of the uterus," he said after a minute, "and see if we don't have a brother or sister in there as well."

He squished more of the jelly onto the tip of the probe and moved it over the skin of Angie's belly. Several times he moved the probe to a new location, mumbled something beneath his breath, and fiddled with the dials on the ultrasound machine. Michael kept staring wide-eyed at the screen, barely able to contain the joy bubbling inside him. He could feel his cheeks straining, so large was the smile on his face.

Not too long after, Dr. Rouben declared that he had finished scanning. He wasn't sure if there was another baby, but there was definitely one viable foetus in Angie's uterus. He congratulated them both. In November they were going to be the proud parents of at least one baby, maybe two.

Dr. Ruben asked Michael to flick on the light switch. The brightness caused everyone in the room to blink for several seconds. Dr. Rouben took a tissue from a box before handing it to Angie to clean the jelly off her stomach, and after cleaning the tip of the probe, clipped it back onto the side of the monitor. Then he switched the machine off and its low, humming whirr faded away, like a satisfied sigh, unlike the smile on Michael's face, which remained as permanent as a tattoo. Angie wiped the tissue over her belly, plonking it in the bin beside the bed. She thanked Dr. Rouben and faced Michael, her eyes gleaming like radiant moons.

"You were right," she said. "We're going to have a baby."

Dr. Rouben gestured for Michael and Angie to make their way out of the examination room. "Of course you are," he said, following them into his office. "Was there any doubt?"

"I'm afraid we were quite doubtful," Michael said. As he and Angie took their seats, he reached for and squeezed her hand. They glanced fleetingly into each other's eyes. "Not now. We're going to have a baby. It's everything we've ever wanted."

"It's just like you dreamed it would be," Angie said, and Michael laughed quietly. Dr. Ruben made his way to the chair behind his desk. "Michael had a visit from the Archangel Gabriel in his dream last night," she said to him. "He told Michael that we're going to have a baby girl."

Michael immediately reddened and lowered his eyes to his shoes. He hated to think that the doctor thought he was a religious crackpot. He couldn't believe Angie had come out and said that. What was she thinking? A doctor wouldn't be interested in such nonsense. Despite reddening even more, he glanced up. Dr. Rouben opened Angie's medical file, a slight smirk on his face. It confirmed everything Michael thought. He reddened further.

"I'm beginning to believe this really is an immaculate conception," Angie added, and Michael wished he could crawl into a dark hole and pretend this wasn't happening.

## CHAPTER 8

LATER THAT AFTERNOON, Michael and Angie wandered out of the local supermarket in Burnside. The sun was sitting low on the horizon, just above the houses and trees of the inner suburbs, and the sky was beginning to turn the colour of navy blue. They were heading vaguely in the direction of where they thought they had parked the car, their weekly groceries in hand. Somehow, its exact location had slipped Michael's mind, and for the time being it was lost in a hodgepodge of assorted blues, greens and reds. It was like searching for a single yellow jellybean in a bag of hundreds. They were in no hurry though, and as they walked his thoughts began to turn to other things.

An awful lot had happened in the space of a few hours, quite a lot in fact. Michael was pinching himself with delight at the prospect of becoming a father. He had to admit he had had his doubts about Dr. Billy at the start. Too good looking, too arrogant, too smarmy, he recalled thinking on their first meeting. He had to take it all back and eat his words. Dr. Billy really *had* performed a miracle of science, and he and Angie really *were* going to have a baby, the foetal heartbeat on the ultrasound scan was proof enough of that. He felt a lightness of being, as if every cell in his body was lifted with the thought of siring a child, of watching his baby grow, its first words, its first steps, of teaching it how to read and write and count, and so much more.

A young mother with a toddler walked passed them into the supermarket. A year ago he probably wouldn't have noticed the child, but now he was seeing them everywhere. The new car syndrome, he guessed; once you were thinking of buying one, you saw every model that drove by. Angie kept walking toward the parking lot, head down and keeping her thoughts to herself. Michael quickly caught up. Despite the joy in his heart, there was something nagging him, something that resisted his best efforts to assuage.

"I don't think you should have said what you did to Dr. Billy this morning," he said, scanning the parking lot for the car. "He probably thinks we're religious nutcases now."

Angie kept walking, but turned to speak to him over her shoulder. "If you're ashamed of me, then don't be," she said, and Michael immediately wished he hadn't broached the subject. He could sense by her tone of voice she was ready to have another argument, in the supermarket parking lot of all places. "It's not important what Dr. Billy thinks about my faith," she said. "What's important is that the Archangel Gabriel visited you in your dream and that we're going to have a baby girl."

Michael spied the domed roof of the Beetle amid a collection of motor vehicles two rows back from the pavement, about a hundred yards or so up ahead. He remembered an old trick Norman used on his wife. When he got into the car he was going to turn the volume of the radio up high and pretend he couldn't hear. Then he wouldn't have to listen to Angie harp on again about religion and God and crap like that. "Will you cut out all this nonsense about angels, please?" he said. "Let's just get home. I don't want to talk about it."

"Nonsense?" she said, spinning around. "What about the fact that I'm pregnant, huh? Is that nonsense?"

Michael hesitated before he spoke, knowing that when Angie was as inflammable as she was now he had to carefully watch what he said. "What I was trying to say, is," and he paused, searching through his mental thesaurus for the right words, ones that he hoped wouldn't spark an explosion.

"Is that you're embarrassed about what's happened," she finished for him, and her eyes were now beginning to glow hot with frustration. "You're embarrassed about your wife, and you're embarrassed about your dream."

In a way, he guessed he was, except that wasn't entirely all. He was finding it difficult to confront the glaring truth that, whether he wanted to believe it or not, he had had a premonition that came true and was now too frightened to admit it because it went against everything he believed in. A dream was supposed to be nothing more than a creation of all the anxieties and problems festering in our brain, a state of the mind. He had majored in psychology, for crying out loud, he knew all about it. Dreams were a figment of an overactive imagination that had its roots deep in our subconscious, not a conduit for predictions of the future. As Freud said, all we were meant to do was analyse them logically. He and Angie had been trying to have a baby for nearly four years, it was only natural that it affected his mind, and what affected his mind affected the way he dreamed, whether he liked it or not. He wanted to have a baby therefore he dreamed they were going to have one. It was that simple.

Nevertheless, he knew it wasn't as simple as that. It didn't explain why he, an atheist, dreamt about one of God's angels. "I'm only saying that Dr. Billy is a man of science," he said. Angie was now several yards ahead. "We shouldn't bother him with our religious beliefs. It's not relevant."

Angie stopped in the middle of the pavement and spun around. Her eyes reflected the fiery orange light of the setting sun, and to Michael they actually appeared to be burning with fury. "Science and religion are not incompatible bed partners," she said. "Only in your mind they are."

Michael wasn't budging. His jaw was set. All his life he had considered faith in a super being nothing more than a sustained psychotic episode, no better than a schizophrenic who lived each day in a constant state of delusion. Except, having faith was more socially acceptable than the poor bastard with a mental illness. It really wasn't much different. They had gone through hell and high water over the past year or so to have this baby, and he'd be damned if he was going to start trusting in a god who had only created misery and pain for them. He told her as much.

"Let me tell you something," she said. Though calm and low, there was a forceful demand in her voice. He imagined this was the way she spoke to clients who she felt were withholding vital pieces of evidence. "You may not like to hear this because it goes against the grain of everything you have ever believed in, but you have to listen to me because what I say will affect the way our child is brought up. I believe things happen for a reason. I also believe you had a remarkable experience last night—heaven's above, one of God's angels visited you, Mikey—and yet you refuse to believe it. What more will it take?"

He averted her gaze and eyed the parking lot. He had been so absorbed in the argument that he hadn't, until this moment, noticed the strange looks on the faces of shoppers passing them to and from the supermarket. He felt a little foolish, hoping no one had overheard them. "What you ask of me is impossible," he said, facing Angie and keeping his voice deliberately low. "This conception is not miracle of God. I think you've taken this completely way over the top."

Angie thrust her jaw and was silent, momentarily thrown off guard. Her eyes glazed and he could almost read her thoughts etched into her frowning brow. Was she taking it too seriously? Had the strain of having a baby really pushed her over the edge? Was she now closely, if not totally, delusional? Because that was exactly what he was inferring, was he not?

Then she snapped herself out of it. Her eyes refocused and her brow smoothed over, losing their lines. "You either believe miracles happen every day or not at all," she said, steady and sure. "Albert Einstein, one of your so-called *science gods*, said that. If he believed in God, then why can't you?"

"Because God isn't *real*. You can't see God." He grabbed an apple from the bag of groceries he held in his left hand. "This is real," he said. "I can see it. I can touch it. I can smell it, and I can taste it. That's what makes it real." He spread his arms toward the parking lot. "Show me where God is and I might believe you."

Angie put her bags down next to her feet on the cement pavement. "Put your bags down." Wavering at first, Michael reluctantly obeyed. Angie grabbed his other hand, putting it on her belly, and said, "Do you feel this, Mikey? There's a child growing inside because it was conceived in a test-tube. This is as real as your apple although you can't see it. Thirty years ago this child would have been classified as a miracle. Do you stop believing it's a miracle because it's now an everyday event?"

Michael certainly did. The simple fact remained that she was pregnant, not because of the will of any god, but because of the incredible technological feats of IVF. It was yet one more thing to support

115

his conviction that science, given enough time and resources, could disprove any so-called miracle, past, present or future.

He was about to say this to Angie when he suddenly noticed the pupils in her eyes dilate and her hands rush to cover her lower belly, as if she'd just seen something to cause her to instinctively protect the unborn child in her womb, as if someone had just ambled into the parking lot with a gun and was about to start randomly shooting at people. Just as he turned around to see what Angie was gaping at, he felt a tremendous blow to his ribs, just above his left kidney. His neck whipped back and he was thrown off balance. He lurched forward, and Angie's arms reflexively embraced him, catching his fall.

Quickly regaining his balance, he peered around to see what had hit him. All he saw was the back of a petit woman in a black dress and white sandshoes, now more than fifty paces distant, sprinting away from them. It was difficult to believe a woman so little could have hit him with so much force; it felt like he'd been collected by a runaway shopping-cart full of groceries. She was running toward an old brown Chrysler Valiant, very similar to the one Jude owned, pulling out of a parking space beneath the floodlit supermarket sign. He heard her call out to the driver, who Michael couldn't see, and the car stopped.

"You know who that woman looked like," Angie said, briefly glancing over her shoulder, then returning to Michael. "Dr. Billy's assistant. You know, the one who was in the operating room when you fainted."

Michael scanned once more in the direction he had seen the woman run. The car pulled out onto the main road and disappeared in the sea of traffic. Several people leaving the supermarket had stopped to watch what had happened and were staring at him and Angie, though no one offered any assistance. He stretched his back, rubbing the painful spot where he had just been collected, then picked up the groceries at his feet. There was a faint glimmer of recollection in his mind. If only he had seen the woman's face. Then he could've been more certain. As it was, she just had to remain anonymous.

Angie also picked up her grocery bags. "She seemed to be in an awful hurry to deliver that package," she said. "I thought it was a shotgun covered in crimson rags when I first saw her."

Michael was thankful that it wasn't. He joined his wife, who had already started wandering toward the Beetle. As he got to the car and unlocked the door, he let the incident slide from his thoughts, and by the time they arrived back home he had completely forgotten about it.

THE FOLLOWING TUESDAY at 6:55 a.m., Michael woke in the darkened bedroom to the annoying buzz of the alarm clock. He slammed the snooze button. Angie stirred next to him, mumbled something inaudible, then fell immediately back to sleep. The sun shone through the crack in the curtains, a thin sliver of light that pried his eyelids open like a crowbar levering the cover to a manhole. Squinting, he nudged Angie with his elbow. He was desperate for more sleep. He wanted Angie to have the first shower so that he could have a few more minutes to close his eyes. Just ten minutes would be enough. For some reason, he was feeling particularly under the weather this morning, his mouth was thick with sleep and his stomach was queasy, as if he had just ingested ten cups of double-strength coffee. He nudged Angie again. To his immediate disappointment, she rolled away from him, grumbling that she didn't want to get up just yet.

Suddenly, the slight uneasiness in his upper belly rapidly worsened, threatening to expulse in a huge surging gush. Saliva filled his mouth and sweat droplets condensed on his brow. In panic, Michael flung back the quilt, jumped out of bed and sprinted to the bathroom, holding his hand over his mouth. He flung himself down on hands and knees, scraping the skin on his kneecaps on the bathroom tiles, and retched into the toilet bowl. Wave after nauseous wave it came. With each vomit his skull echoed with the tormented screams of his body, as if every single cell was drowning in whatever toxin had flooded his system. He felt as though he was going to die puking up, not exactly how he had envisaged his last moments on earth would be at all. He didn't know he could feel so bad. It was certainly far worse than the fainting episode in the operating room.

Finally, after a minute or two, it stopped, much to his relief. It seemed he wasn't going to die after all. He straightened his back and wiped his mouth with the back of his trembling hand, wondering what had caused this horrendous sickness. Maybe it was something bad he had eaten yesterday. He took some deep breaths, which slowly helped his stomach to settle. He started to relax and breathe easier, but just when he thought it was over, it began again. He retched hard into the toilet bowl, so hard in fact he barely heard Angie's footsteps hurry down the corridor. She burst naked into the bathroom and, likewise, emptied the contents of her stomach into the sink next to him. The sound and smell of her retching made him vomit even harder, this time so forcefully he feared he'd tear the lining of his stomach.

After however long, he wasn't sure, they managed to catch their breath. Wiping their mouths with the back of their hand, they laughed nervously at one another, not really knowing what to say. They showered and hastily got ready for work, both agreeing that they must have caught a bug from the roast chicken they'd had for dinner. Angie managed only a bite of dry toast for breakfast, forgoing her usual cup of coffee, and Michael only a few mouthfuls of cornflakes. With every spoonful, he could feel his stomach spasm in protest. He decided not to tempt fate any longer and pushed the bowl away from him. He went to work hoping that whatever it was that was causing this would settle by the time he got there.

It proved to be a forlorn hope, and, to his unending dismay, the pattern of vomiting repeated itself over the next three mornings. By Friday, during yet another ten minutes of throwing up in the bathroom, Michael was beginning to worry that it was something other than just a stomach bug. He hated being unwell. He hated feeling under the weather and useless. It was as though his very masculinity was being challenged, and he wished he could be as stoical about the ordeal as Angie was. His dad often joked that doctors were the worst patients, except Michael knew otherwise; doctor's children were the worst.

Before he shaved, he glanced into the cabinet mirror. He looked pale and wan, all vestige of colour seemingly washed out of his face. Even at the best of times, he knew he wasn't an oil painting, but these last few days were beginning to make their mark and make matters worse—he reckoned his appearance was not too unlike that of a gargoyle carved in marble. If he still felt and looked this bad after school had finished today, he was going to ring his dad and ask him to prescribe some anti-sickness medication. Angie was going to need some too, even though he was now sure she was suffering from morning sickness, something that would presumably improve as the pregnancy progressed into the second trimester. His problems, however, were going to need some sorting out.

Less than an hour later, still weak and tremulous, Michael wandered into the staff room at Wattle Gardens. He was desperate to get through the day without any further episodes of vomiting. Most of the teachers had already arrived and the room was buzzing with gossip of one form or another. In the far corner, he spied Norman sitting on the sofa drinking coffee and eating a chocolate bar. Michael crossed the room and they greeted each other. At that moment, before he could rush outside to the staff toilets, he vomited cornflakes all over Norman's ankles and shoes. The room immediately quietened. Every set of eyes turned upon him. He apologised profusely to Norman and to the rest of the staff, maintaining that he had food poising from something he ate the other day. Norman looked shocked, but he laughed if off. So did Michael, although he knew there'd be an inquisition from his friend and headmistress later in the day regarding his current state of health.

That evening, back at home in the lounge room, Michael rang his dad, still feeling moderately ashamed at what he'd done in the staff room earlier. The situation was getting out of control, he mused. His body was breaking down. His muscles constantly quivered and his legs were getting feebler, now barely able to support his weight for more than a few minutes at a time. Telephone to his ear, he punched in the number and leant against the Steinway to help ease some of the strain. The bump jangled the piano keys and caused his and Angie's wedding photo on top to flop onto its face, giving him a startle. With his remaining free hand, he awkwardly set it back upright.

After the sixth ring, Robert finally answered. Michael quickly told him his concerns over what had been happening during the past few days. His voice quivered slightly, like his hands and legs. He loathed sounding so weak and pathetic.

"Look, Mikey," Robert said, "it's normal for you to feel this way.

I don't think you realise how common it is for husbands to feel a little under the weather when their wife is in the first trimester. What you're going through is most likely psychosomatic. At worst, it's a gastrointestinal virus. There's a lot of it going around at the moment. Try not to worry."

"I'll try not to," Michael said, but he was secretly concerned that his dad might somehow be wrong. This seemed more than just a stomach bug or a psychological reaction to Angie's morning sickness.

Thankfully, as his dad had assured, the vomiting and retching didn't last too long. It just seemed to fade away on its own accord over the next few days, allowing him and Angie to return to their usual routine, biding their time until the baby arrived.

The months went by quicker than he had anticipated. Winter arrived with force, and, before he knew it, some time around the nineteenth week of the pregnancy, Angie had a little bump, which seemed to enlarge daily. The twenty-week ultrasound scan showed that the baby was healthy and growing well. Dr. Rouben informed them that he could determine the sex of the child, if they wanted to know. They did, and it came as no surprise to Angie. She had already told all her friends and Michael's parents many weeks before that she knew that it was going to be a girl, and, to his mortification, about the dream in which an angel had told them the news. She had even begun to decorate her old bedroom pink for the baby.

"I kind of like the name, Jessica Lee," Angie said one day in a baby shop, eyeing a cot she liked the look of. "It's got a nice ring to it. And Jessica was my mother's middle name."

Michael shuddered at the thought of his deceased mother-in-law. At least Angie hadn't insisted on the name Shirley. They bought the cot, and some pink linen, and said no more.

To Michael's delight, the first signs of spring arrived soon after. Notwithstanding her earlier pronouncements at Christmas to search for another firm, Angie continued her employment at Sugarman Klein & Pickering. Now that she was of a more delicate disposition, Angie made more of an effort not to overwork herself, staying at the office only as long as necessary to fulfil her duties and refusing to take on extra workloads, much to Stephen Pickering's unmitigated chagrin.

Somehow, she even managed to persuade him to allow her a full six weeks maternity leave. According to Angie, he had initially refused her request, stating that she hadn't been employed long enough at the firm to entitle her to anything other than holiday leave. Angie wasn't perturbed. She had prepared herself for this deliberate obstructionism and had downloaded from the Internet the most recent amendments to the law regarding her rights as an imminent mother-to-be.

She and Michael chatted about it over dinner that night. He laughed when she described the look on Stephen's face as he read the printout and realised that he had no choice other than to accept, a look she said was rather like a snarling hyena. Stuck in a corner, her boss begrudgingly relented, though only on the proviso she worked until the day she gave birth. It was a petty rebuke. Angie had wanted to take four weeks maternity leave prior to her due date, the 11th of November, to rest her rapidly enlarging body and settle her mind, and then take some holiday leave after the baby was born. Stephen, it seemed, was deliberately caustic. Maternity leave, he told her, was postnatal, not antenatal, and as her boss he was fully within his rights to determine when his staff could take their holidays.

Angie confessed to Michael that there was nothing legally she could do about it. Stephen's parsimoniousness didn't stop there, either. He had begun harping on about the firm's sacrifice to her, allowing her far more time off than any other woman employed by them. He wanted to know what Angie's sacrifice was in return. She told Michael later that she had wanted to ask him if her virginity wasn't enough, but she bit her lip and prudently remained silent. She also told Michael that while she had been standing in front of his desk, she could feel Stephen mentally undressing her, removing her clothes piece-by-piece until she felt she was as naked as the day she'd been inseminated by Dr. Rouben, and, although she couldn't say for any real degree of certainty, she thought she had seen him play with his cock through his trousers while he ogled her breasts.

The news of Stephen's outrageous behaviour sent Michael into a silent fury. He could feel his face glowing redder than a hotplate on the stove, infuriated with Stephen's treatment of his pregnant wife. The guy had no shame. He wanted Angie to make a formal complaint to the other partners in the firm. Stephen's conduct was completely unacceptable.

Angie shook her head and reminded Michael that the firm was paying for all the costs of the IVF and obstetric care. If all she had to do was endure a few lascivious glances across the office from her ex-fiancé in order for them to have this baby, then that was a sacrifice she was willing to make. "Besides," she said, "you know he's treated me far worse in the past."

Her apparent tolerance of the situation didn't appease Michael. He wondered if there existed a bigger prick in the entire world than Stephen Pickering. The guy's arrogance was beyond belief. How could someone like him become a partner in one of the top law firms in Adelaide, if not Australia? Was egotism and pigheadedness really the only qualities that determined success in the corporate world? Did everyone at the top abuse power so blatantly? Angie was right. Her boss was nothing more than a testosterone-fuelled Neanderthal whose primitive emotions went no further than fucking or fighting. The only differences between him and these ancient cave dwellers was that he wore designer suits instead of animal furs and carried out his day-to-day activities in a plusher cave.

Michael's contempt for Angie's boss was gut wrenching. It took some while for his temper to calm and for his mind to settle. The best therapy, he found, was to fantasise inflicting grievous bodily harm upon the guy. It gave him immense pleasure to imagine punching Stephen in the face whenever next he bumped into him. He imagined grabbing him in a headlock and ramming his skull through the windows of his nineteenth story office. He imagined kicking him in the testicles, pulling his trousers down around his ankles and humiliating him in front of all the staff. He would take glee in doing all these things and more, though he knew better than anyone he would do no such thing. He hadn't raised his fists in anger since he hit Jude, way back in 1975. Still, it felt good to fantasise about it, and his anger went the same way as the vomiting episode.

One Saturday afternoon in the lounge room, not long after, a front-page headline in the *Adelaide Sun* caught Michael's attention. It was about a sheep called Dolly. Below it, there was a lesser item of news he fleetingly noticed, that yet another baby had been kidnapped, this time from St. Mary's Hospital, and that his cousin, Jude, was heading the investigation, but his concentration was fully captured on the main article. Dolly, it said, was your average, everyday ewe, apart from one small difference—she was a clone. Scientists in Scotland had performed the remarkable feat of cloning a sheep for the first time, a modern day miracle. To Michael, it was simply more evidence to confirm his belief in the inevitable triumph of science fact over religious dogma.

Angie was not impressed. She was reading the article over his shoulder as they sat on the couch. "It's unethical. They won't stop until they have cloned a human being," she said. "Thank goodness my mother isn't alive to see this. She would have a heart attack," and Michael barely suppressed a gleeful chuckle.

The last trimester of the pregnancy meant for Angie weight gain, bad backs, occasional urinary incontinence, and any number of aches and pains. The whole pregnancy was an alien experience to Michael, and a few times he openly stated to Norman his gratitude of being a male. He couldn't imagine what it must be like to have something else growing inside of him. Aside from the psychological aspects of it, the physical discomfort was something he was glad he didn't have to endure. Angie was now so big she couldn't lie on her stomach when she went to sleep, if she could get any sleep at all. She tossed and turned most of the night, and to Michael every time she moved it was like a gorilla jumping up and down on the bed.

Not that he minded. It was a joy to spend most of the nights in a state of semi-consciousness cuddled up to Angie with his hand on her belly feeling the baby kick and punch. He figured he was in training for the expected deprivation of sleep when the baby was born. What's more, it helped him from dreaming too often of the black shadow and the men in white hooded robes. He'd had about as much of those nightmares as he could stand.

ONE OCTOBER WEDNESDAY during the spring break, when Angie

was about thirty-seven weeks pregnant, Michael was sitting around the house in his jeans and T-shirt, not doing too much other than wondering what he could do today. He was eating a sandwich when the telephone rang. It was Angie, asking whether he'd like to accompany her to the antenatal clinic for a routine check-up. He thought, why not? There was nothing else he particularly had in mind to do. There was no schoolwork to worry about, only the impending birth to occupy his thoughts. Angie said he should call past her work and pick her up. He agreed, though declined to meet her in the office; he didn't know if he could control his anger if he saw Stephen Pickering. Angie laughed and told him she'd meet him on the pavement outside the main entrance instead.

After locking the house, he reversed the Beetle onto the street and headed toward the city. Less than ten minutes later, he spied Angie in a matching brown cardigan and knee-length skirt waiting near the bus stop in front of the State Bank Building. Her hair was pulled into a bun and she dangled her handbag in front of her slender legs. Somehow, even with the size of her nearly full-term belly, she continued to maintain an outward show of professionalism. She simply refused to buy anything that resembled a maternity dress. It seemed she would rather be seen naked in court than wearing what she called "over-priced, out of fashion garbage." Instead, she preferred to buy skirts and tops two sizes bigger than she normally would. Her bra size, too, Michael had noted with some approval, had ballooned from a B to a C cup.

Angie wasn't the only one to have enlarged in the past eight months. His stomach, too, was annoyingly bigger. It was now like a little beer belly. This past month he had started to fasten his belt two buckle holes wider than in previous years and his shirts were starting to hug appreciably tighter. Perhaps his sedentary lifestyle was slowly catching up on him. Norman was forever joking that he'd never managed to lose the weight he gained from the first pregnancy, and now Michael understood that it perhaps wasn't so much a joke as a cynical snipe at the cruel reality of life. Was it common for husbands to also put on weight with their expectant spouse? Was it psychosomatic, like the vomiting episode? He hoped not. At this rate, if he didn't watch himself, he would be a fat forty-year old heading for his first heart attack before he knew what had happened.

Angie saw him in the car from a distance and waved. Michael pulled up alongside the curb and she hopped in as quickly as she could, plonking heavily into the passenger seat and pecking a kiss on his cheek. He did a quick U-turn and headed back toward the eastern suburbs. It took less than fifteen minutes to drive to St. Mary's hospital, Adelaide's wide grid-patterned streets making it easy for them to cross the city through the lunchtime traffic, and at quarter past one they walked into Dr. Rouben's private outpatient's clinic.

"I'm afraid Dr. Rouben has been called urgently to the operating room for an emergency caesarean section," said his secretary from behind her desk.

It was a bit of a shock to both of them. Michael feared for the poor woman who had to undergo the operation. He dreaded to think what necessitated such drastic action and he tried to imagine what the woman's husband must be going through, wondering how he himself would feel if he was told his wife had no other option than to have the baby delivered that way. After all the issues involved in conceiving this baby, he knew Angie wanted to give birth naturally. He knew she wanted as little medical input into the delivery as possible. It was her way of saying, "This baby is truly mine." He wanted that too, except if either she or the baby was in imminent danger, then he guessed there would be no hesitation in allowing the doctors to do what they had to do. Yet, he still hoped Angie would never have to go through that.

"Will he be back soon?" he now heard Angie ask.

The secretary filed her nails and rolled her eyes. "Dr. Rouben won't be attending this afternoon's clinic at all," she said, splaying her fingers and examining her nails. "He asked me to reschedule all appointments." Reluctantly, she put her nail file down and opened the appointment book. "Is tomorrow afternoon good for you?"

Angie shook her head. Michael knew that she'd had to fight tooth and nail to get Stephen Pickering to allow her to take this afternoon off. There was no way he was going to let her have time away again tomorrow. "I can't take any more time off work this week," Angie said. "Are you sure Dr. Rouben is unavailable for the rest of the day."

"I'm sure," the secretary said, rather contemptuously, Michael thought, and closed the appointment book with a snap. "The only option is for you to go down to the antenatal clinic on the ground floor and wait to be seen by a midwife."

They eventually found the antenatal clinic near the ER department, asking twice for directions from busy nurses. The waiting room was bland, with several grubby plastic chairs backed against three of its grey-white walls. There were no windows, just four numbered white doors along one side of the room. Six other pregnant women sat silently around the room, all at roughly the same gestation as Angie, Michael guessed, and all trying to while away the time reading out-of-date women's magazines. Angie gave her name to the receptionist, who handed her a urine bottle and asked her to give a sample. Michael sat down on the chairs by the far wall and waited for Angie to return.

Yesterday's newspaper had been left folded on the seat on which he sat. SERIAL KIDNAPPER LOOSE IN HOSPITAL, the headlines read. *Three babies abducted from St. Mary's in nine months.* Michael picked up the paper, immediately captivated, not to mention a trifle concerned. The report suggested a strong link with the abductions to someone on the inside, perhaps a member of the staff, someone who knew the system and the ins and outs of the hospital well enough to avoid detection. There was no substantive proof at all, it seemed, just conjecture, and the police were neither confirming nor denying it. There was a quote, "No comment," from Chief Inspector Joseph. He wasn't letting anything out of the bag.

Michael could only hazard a guess as to what had happened to the baby. He remembered Jude once telling him that, statistically, seventy-five percent of all abducted children were murdered within the first three hours. He felt pity for what the young women must have gone through—nine months of pregnancy, their hopes and expectations, the trauma and pain of childbirth—only to have their child snatched away, never knowing what had happened to them. His heart went out to them. It was terrible, truly terrible.

Angie returned five minutes later, but after an hour they were still waiting to be seen. By that time, there was only one other woman in the waiting room. Then the door to room 2 opened and out stepped a nurse holding a medical file with a stethoscope draped around her neck. Michael was surprised to see that it was Maria, the midwife who had been present during the insemination procedure in February. Smiling, Maria called them in.

Angie stood slowly, holding the crook of her back. Michael could almost feel her reliving all the aches and pains over the past eight months. If it wasn't the persistent backache, it was bloated constipation, or itching vaginal thrush, or an incessant headache. Just when one niggling ache went, another took its place. Today, it seemed, it was the back, again. She held onto his arm and they followed Maria into the examination room.

It was perversely small and cramped, not much bigger than the ultrasound room, Michael recalled, attached to Dr. Rouben's office. An aging chair and wood-veneered table cringed in the far corner of the room. An examination bed propped precariously against the opposite wall and a naked light bulb shed weak, wan rays from its tungsten filament. Like the waiting room, there was no window. If there was one word for this room, Michael thought, it was disillusionment. He silently thanked his lucky stars for Angie's private medical insurance.

After removing her shoes, Angie hopped onto the bed, laid flat on her back and scrunched up her cardigan and shirt to expose her weighty belly. Michael remained standing near the door. The room was silent as Maria palpated Angie's abdomen, feeling the shoulders and head of the baby and listening for its heartbeat with an odd looking instrument she called a Pinnard auscultator, a white plastic instrument that flared out like a trumpet at one end and tapered into a small earpiece at the other. Satisfied that all was fine, Maria pulled Angie's cardigan back over her exposed belly and put a thermometer under her tongue. While she waited, she took Angie's pulse.

After a minute or so, Maria released Angie's arm and removed the thermometer from her mouth. Holding it up to her eyes to read the mercury level, she said, "Are you looking forward to the big day, Mrs. Joseph? Dr. Rouben tells me this is a very special pregnancy."

"It's a miracle, really," Angie said, and she flashed Michael a glorious smile. "We've been trying for a baby ever since we got married and, well, you know how it can be when you really want something and then you suddenly realise it can never be. We were beginning to give up hope. We're so happy Dr. Rouben could help us with our dream. He's such a great doctor."

"He certainly has a charming way with his patients," Maria said, lowering the thermometer. "I bet you can't wait."

"Michael and I are very excited," she said with a nod. Maria sat at the table to write in Angie's medical file, which, like her belly, seemed to have grown larger and fuller with the pregnancy. "We're thinking of having more children after this one." Michael cocked his eyebrows, wondering if all women divulged personal information so readily to complete strangers, or if it was just his wife. "Do you have any yourself?"

Maria put the pen down and stood up. "No, Mrs. Joseph," she said, moving to the side of the bed. "I don't even have a husband."

She removed a blood pressure cuff from a hook on the wall above the bed and slid it around Angie's upper right arm, inflating it with several quick squeezes of the hand pump. With the other hand, she removed the stethoscope from around her neck, put the earpieces into her ears and placed the diaphragm onto the crook of Angie's elbow. Then she twisted the cuff's release valve, keeping one eye on the sphygmometer. Air hissed out, but no sooner had the cuff deflated, she repeated the whole procedure, and then once more.

Finally, Maria removed the cuff from Angie's arm, now frowning. "It's nothing to be alarmed about, Mrs. Joseph," she said, fixing the cuff back onto the hook, "but your blood pressure is slightly up today."

Michael immediately began fearing the worst. He didn't like the sound of that any more than he liked the hissing of the cuff. He suddenly felt his own blood pressure shoot up, an immediate throb behind his eyeballs. "Is it serious?" he asked.

"Not at these levels," she said, glancing up at him, then back at Angie. "It's only one forty-five over ninety, but I think we need to keep an eye on it." Michael felt some of the tension release from his body and the disconcerting feeling behind his eyes began to ease. Maria moved back to the table and sat down. "I want you to come back to Dr. Rouben's clinic tomorrow, Mrs. Joseph," she said, writing in Angie's medical file again, "and have your blood pressure and temperature taken again, just as a precaution. If it gets higher, I'm worried you could get pre-eclampsia."

Angie was struggling to sit and so Michael went over to help. Taking her by the hand, he gently pulled her up. Once sitting, Angie slid her legs over the edge of the bed. "Pre what?" she asked, grabbing the hem of her cardigan and straightening the creases.

"Pre-eclampsia—uncontrolled blood pressure brought on by the pregnancy," Maria said over her shoulder. "At the least, it can be nothing more than a slight rise in blood pressure with no physical symptoms, but at the other extreme," and she paused, like someone hesitant to say more than what they felt was necessary. Eventually, she said, "At the other extreme you could suffer from extreme headaches, blurred vision, nausea, and you could fit, like an epileptic. If a pregnant woman has a severe seizure the baby can abort. It's usually catastrophic for the mother... and fatal for the baby."

Michael didn't need reminding how fatal a seizure could be. Why had no one mentioned before now that something as serious as this could happen? Why hadn't Dr. Rouben said anything, or his dad for that matter? Out of the corner of his eye he saw Angie palming her crucifix to her chest through her cardigan. "What are the chances of Angie getting pre-eclipsia?" he asked Maria.

"You mean, pre-*eclampsia*," she said, putting down her pen. "The urine sample Angie gave earlier didn't show any traces of protein, so I don't think the chances are very high, but we don't want even the slightest chance to go unheeded. That's why I want Angie to come back for regular checkups until the baby is born, starting tomorrow. I'll let Dr. Rouben's secretary know you'll be paying him a visit."

Angie looked at Michael. "Stephen will just have to bear my absence, whether he likes it or not," she said with a sardonic smile, and hopped down off the examination bed. Her shoes were standing neatly beneath it where she had placed them. Slipping her feet into them, she thanked Maria and said goodbye, promising to return to the clinic tomorrow afternoon.

As they walked out of the main entrance into the sunshine, Michael's head was filled with worry. He always knew that there were complications of pregnancy, but he had always pushed those thoughts to the back of his mind when they surfaced to bother him. Not any more. With this most recent hospital visit the fretful, almost hysterical, voice of doubt now gained a degree of legitimacy it hadn't previously deserved, and trying to push it away was like trying to ram a fat man through a hole in the fence. He now wished Angie had never had her blood pressure checked. He wished the doubts and worries would go away and leave him alone. Except, he knew the chances of that were slim. He knew they would continue to torment him until the baby was born and they were both well and truly out of danger.

The next three weeks, he mused, were going to be hell on earth.

PART TWO


THE
MONTH OF
THANKSGIVING
1996

# CHAPTER 9

ALWAYS RUNNING, MICHAEL thinks, always running. He knows this dream well. He knows the street but cannot remember its exact location. Part of the problem, he reckons, is that he sees only black and white; the lack of colour defamiliarises the locality. It is deathly quiet, too—it's always quiet—no birds are singing, no dogs are barking, no cars pass him by. It's like a hot summer's day in which not even the bees can spare the energy to buzz. His legs are weak and feel like lead. It hurts to lift them but he must run. His heart beats painfully and his chest is on fire. He looks over his shoulder and they are there, not far behind: three men in white hooded robes, faceless ghosts, and they're closing fast. Suffused with fear, he spurs on, confused as to why they are chasing him.

The reply to his thoughts is an unknown whisper, a soft lute: *You have what they want. You have what they need.*

Feeling something heavy, he looks down and for the first time sees the answer to the riddle. In his arms sleeps a baby girl. He now knows what they want—his unborn child—but he is careless. He trips and sprawls, the baby spills. The hooded men swoop and steal the child away. He screams, but no sound emerges. There is only the silent stillness. He tries to stand, but his legs buckle beneath him. Again he cries out, and again there is no sound.

The white men disappear into the distance with his baby. In the still air their voices easily carry, taunting: *We have the baby! We have the baby!*

Michael woke with a start. His mouth was dry and the back of his throat was in flames. Had he been screaming? At least he hoped not. His eyelids were loaded with lead but he managed to keep them from falling closed and look around, reorientating himself. He was sitting alone behind his classroom desk; he figured he must have accidentally fallen asleep and been dreaming again. Out through the window to his right, the children gambolled noisily in the school quadrangle, frolicking blurs of colour against the grey sky. Now he remembered. It was lunch break, Wednesday, the 6th of November.

A red plastic lunchbox lay open on his desk. He unenthusiastically spied its contents: a Granny Smith apple, two cream biscuits, and a sandwich wrapped in plastic wrap. Slowly and awkwardly, he snapped the lid back into place, sighing. He was extremely tired and lacklustre, languorous, like a little death, and he hated not having any energy, especially this feeling of being churned through a log mill and spat out the other side. The last time he felt this fragile and pathetic was during that week of vomiting last April. Even his blue sweater and jeans felt listless, like loose skin. He stared at the lunchbox in front of him, wishing the day would end soon, wishing he could just close his eyes and go to sleep. Sleep would be divine, if only the nightmares would stay away.

Out of nowhere, the door to the classroom flung open, hitting the wall with a bang. Michael was almost too tired to be startled. Slowly, he turned his gaze from his lunchbox to the grinning face of his friend. Norman was dressed in a white shirt, crimson cardigan, brown cotton trousers, and Michael knew his chance of catching a breather before the children returned from lunch just ran out the door Norman had just opened. His shoulders slumped. The effort to smile was considerable. In fact, the effort to even breathe was considerable. All he managed in returning a greeting was a half-hearted twitch of the lips.

Norman took one look at him and frowned with worry. Then he scanned down the corridor, for what Michael wasn't sure, before closing the door behind him. "What's up, buddy?" he asked, taking a spare child's chair to the desk and sitting to Michael's left. "Is there anything wrong? You look like a bucket of shit."

Michael wanted to laugh at the lack of tact, but it hurt, especially his stomach. He knew he looked as bad, if not worse, than Norman's eloquent appraisal of him. This morning in the parking lot, before he got out of the car, he had glimpsed himself in the rear-view mirror and had had a minor shock. His face was pasty and his eyes had lost their sheen, dull and lifeless like a pair of blown light bulbs. He had wondered if corpses looked as bad. Now, removing a handkerchief from the front of his jeans, he proceeded to slowly dab his brow. His skin felt clammy and friable, like paper soaked in water, and he had to stop himself from recoiling in horror, frightened that it might peel off his face if he touched any further.

"Yeah, I don't feel so good," he said, finally, struggling to keep his eyelids open.

Norman shook his large head and said in no uncertain terms, "You've got to get yourself to the hospital, my friend. You need to get this sorted out."

"I've already spoken to dad. He said it was probably a virus and I should get some blood tests." Michael could hear his voice stretching like a worn elastic band into a long drawl, barely audible above the squealing of the children outside. "I went to St. Mary's ER last night after school," he said. "It's just the flu, anyway. I'll get over it."

"Like hell it's the flu!" Norman said. "I'm no doctor, but I know the flu doesn't make your face go as puffy as a giant marshmallow or make you put on as much weight as your good friend Norman Page."

Through droopy eyes, Michael caught Norman's gaze and held it briefly, contemplating whether or not to tell him the truth. It wasn't the flu. Norman was right, but he also knew Norman couldn't keep a secret even if there was a million dollar reward attached to it; he had a way of wearing classified information like a badge on his cardigan. Michael, sighed, "Please don't tell Angie if I tell you."

Norman nodded, though Michael knew he was making a mistake. He had a feeling the news would somehow filter back to Angie. She didn't need to know what the problem was, not yet anyway. What with the everyday problems of pregnancy and the recent concerns about her blood pressure, which thankfully was still all right and needing nothing more than to be checked every two days or so at the clinic, she had enough to worry about without him making things worse. Then again, Norman was his best friend and he had to trust him sometimes.

"It's not the flu, you're right," Michael said, eventually. "I've got kidney problems. The doctor said they weren't working as well as they should. I probably caught an infection sometime ago which may have damaged them, something like tonsillitis or food poisoning, most likely that stomach bug I had that time I vomited on your shoes."

Michael quickly pondered the absurdity of that whole week. Norman was grinning, he saw, and his eyes were momentarily distant, presumably remembering the same incident. It was funny now, but not at the time, and Michael was immeasurably glad that it hadn't recurred. He started back up. "It's affected my kidneys somehow and that's why my face is all puffy and why I've put on over thirty-five pounds in the past three months."

"Thirty-five pounds? My God, what are you eating?"

Michael's eyes flicked to the lunchbox. It bordered on the ridiculous really. All his life he'd been slim. He was one of the lucky ones, like Jude, who could eat what they liked and not put on an ounce of weight. He didn't even exercise, which drove Norman mad. Now, though, he was putting on weight like a fat kid who ate nothing but donuts. "I've hardly eaten anything at all lately," he said, pushing the lunchbox away from him across the desk with the tip of his forefinger. "I don't have any appetite."

Norman's shoulders shrugged and his hands splayed, palms up, like a waiter holding two pots of tea. "How can you put on that much weight if you're not eating? It's impossible."

"Not if you have kidney problems, apparently. It's got something to do with retaining water." Then he burped, long and loud. "It's also affecting my gut. I seem to have so much wind. I can even feel it move down my bowel sometimes. It's really weird."

Norman relaxed his shoulders and hands, and nodded, as if he knew exactly how Michael felt. "So what's the doc doing about it?"

"I'm booked for an ultrasound scan of my kidneys next week to see what's going on." Michael reached into the top drawer of his desk and pulled out a small plastic bottle of pills. When he shook them they rattled. "I have to take two of these a day and they make me piss like a trooper," he said. "I've been to the toilet six times already today and last night I got out of bed three times."

Norman stared at the plastic bottle, transfixed like a child watching a magician pull a rabbit out of a hat. "That can't be good," he said.

"Well, if I don't take them the doc says my blood pressure will go through the roof and I'll blow a hole in my brains so big they'll be picking up the pieces for a week." Norman, Michael saw, was still staring at the bottle. "If my blood pressure comes down in the next month or so I can stop taking them," he said, "providing the ultrasound scan is normal, that is. He thinks it's just a temporary thing and I'll get over it. I have to, the baby will be popping out in five days and the last thing I need is to be sick." Michael replaced the pills in the top drawer. "Angie's having a check up at the fertility clinic later today to make sure she's okay and to have her blood pressure checked again. We're supposed to go to an antenatal class this evening after she's finished, but I'm too exhausted. I'll barely make it through the teachers' meeting."

Michael's shoulders slumped again. He desperately wanted to leave straight after class, except Frau Schmetterling was on one of her power trips and not even if he died could he get out of it. The bell rang the second he glanced at the clock on the back wall above the children's lockers. Lunchtime was over and he could already hear some of the more eager kids tromping down the corridor. He ran a tired hand through his hair and told Norman that he would see him later in the staff room. Just as Norman stepped out of the classroom, the first of Michael's kids wriggled past his large round frame. Behind them, he could hear the noise in the corridor getting louder, reminding him of an approaching stampede. He sighed deeply; it was going to be a long afternoon, but he would make it. Then he would go home, have dinner, go to bed early and have a sick day tomorrow. He would be refreshed and ready to tackle the class once more the following day.

THE TEACHERS' MEETING went on and on. To Michael, it felt like one of those interminable Catholic services Angie had dragged him along to in the early days of their courtship. To make matters worse, his bladder was squealing. The pain was incredible, and he hoped he was going to make it through without pissing his pants. Finally, just after six, Miss Schmetterling dismissed the teachers and Michael immediately hauled his heavy frame to the toilet to relieve himself. It was as close to heaven as he thought he'd ever get.

By the time he returned to the staff room, almost everyone had gone. Norman was chatting to a couple of younger teachers about some particularly troublesome kids they had in their class and moaning about the lack of discipline or respect or whatever with today's youth. Michael waved goodbye and ambled with heavy strides down the corridor. As he passed the payphone in the reception area he decided to give Angie a quick call. He wanted to ask how the appointment went this afternoon and if he needed to pick up any groceries on the way home. He also wanted to tell her that he wasn't up to going to the antenatal class this evening.

Angie picked up the phone on the seventh ring. The connection was bad, typical of these payphones, with an annoying hum in the background. Her voice sounded as tired as he was feeling and when she hesitated after he inquired about how things went at the clinic, he knew things weren't good. He pressed her again.

"Really, Mikey," she said. "I just wish you wouldn't worry so much. My blood pressure is just a little higher than normal, that's all. It's nothing to get worked up about." She paused again, and Michael could envisage her scrunching her eyes and rubbing her temples. "I've also got a little bit of a headache coming on. I just need to lie down in the dark and put a damp towel over my brow. By the time you come home, it'll be better, you'll see."

They said goodbye and he replaced the handset on the receiver. He stepped out of the school building and began crossing the asphalt to the parking lot. This afternoon's clouds had blown away, leaving a spectacularly clear vernal sky, though he knew it would be pretty much dark within three quarters of an hour. Halfway to the car, his eyes suddenly caught a flash of orange light in the heavens, and then another, like a shooting star. As he craned his neck to inspect the sky more closely, he realised that he'd forgotten to ask Angie whether or not she wanted him to get some groceries for dinner. For a brief moment he stood motionless, deciding whether to go back inside and make another quick call to Angie, or to get in his car and drive home as fast as he could. After watching another orange light flash by, he hung his chin to his chest, contemplating. The day had been too long. He felt terrible and sapped of energy. All he wanted was to get home and fall asleep in Angie's arms.

Finally, he decided that it was better to be safe than sorry. He spun around and trotted back to the main entrance into the reception area to the payphone. He rummaged his jean pocket for loose coins and then dialled home. The phone rang out to the answering machine. It beeped and his wife's taped voice told him he could now leave a message. He frowned, looked quizzically at the black handset, and then hung up. Staring at his trainers, he ran a hand through his hair, perplexed as to what had happened to Angie in the five minutes since he last spoke to her. Maybe she was already lying down on the bed with a damp towel over her brow and didn't want to answer the phone, he figured. Probably the best thing to do would be to wait for a couple of minutes and then call her again.

At that moment, Michael heard footsteps echoing down the corridor and glanced up to see Norman holding his briefcase and smiling like a cheeky cat. "You should be home in bed," Norman said. "You look terrible."

"I know, I know," Michael said. "I'm just trying to get hold of Angie before I go."

For a minute they small talked about the teachers' meeting, but Michael's mind kept wandering back to his wife. Unable to wait any longer, he rummaged through his pocket for some loose change and pressed the redial button. The phone rang out to the answering machine again. He banged the receiver back in its cradle and ran a hand through his hair. He could feel something was terribly wrong. Suddenly, he recalled the words he had written on the classroom blackboard nearly a year ago to the day: SOMETHING'S WRONG WITH ANGIE. I THINK SHE'S DYING, MIKEY.

Placing a hand on his hip, and the other through his hair, he stared at the floor, anxious, pensive, trying to shake the image of that message from his head. After a few seconds, Michael grabbed another coin out of his pocket and began redialling again.

As it rang, Michael banged his fist against the payphone, yelling into the handset for Angie to pick it up. Frustration was setting in with every second he didn't hear Angie's voice. What had happened? Why wasn't she picking up the phone? He knew he was over reacting, but what if something was wrong? If something had happened to Angie, there was practically nothing that he could do here. That was the plain simple truth of the matter; he could do absolutely nothing, and that made things worse. His stomach began to churn. He felt like a parent watching his daughter drown in the middle of the lake, unable to swim out and save her because he had never learned to swim himself. Michael banged the payphone again.

"PICK UP THE DAMN PHONE, ANGIE! PICK IT UP!"

Looking a little taken aback at his outburst, Norman tried to convince him that everything was all right, but Michael wasn't listening. Eyes blazing, he cut short his friend. Norman made to say something else, then closed his mouth and began biting his nails. Michael pressed his ear to the earpiece. Suddenly, it stopped ringing and he heard Angie's cheery voice on the other end, but it was only the answering machine again. Michael cursed and fisted the payphone. He took the phone away from his ear and was about to hang up when Norman grabbed his arm and told him to leave a message.

Michael took a second to think about it. They had no idea whether or not she was in trouble. It may be nothing at all, they just didn't know. It could be something as simple as Angie accidentally locking herself out of the house. For all he knew, she was now waiting for him to come home and let her back inside. He glanced at his arm held by Norman, then at the phone. What the hell, he thought. He had nothing to lose. Michael wrestled the receiver back off Norman, agreeing to leave a message.

Her taped voice stopped speaking and there was a momentary silence before the answering machine beeped for the caller to leave their name and number. "Hi, Angel, it's me," he said as calmly as he could, though he knew his voice signalled all the troubles he was feeling. "If you can hear me I just want you to pick up the phone. Please pick it up, Angel." He paused, waiting for her to answer. Once again he was overcome with the memory of that message written on the blackboard. He ran a hand through his hair. Out of the corner of his eyes, he saw Norman return to biting his nails. "Come on Angie! Pick up the phone!"

The answering machine clicked off.

Michael slammed the telephone receiver back into the cradle. He kept staring at it, running a hand slowly through his hair, lost in a storm of worry. He had to get home at all costs. Nothing else mattered. Angie was in trouble. "Someth'ns wrong with Angie," he said under his breath, hushed and afraid. "I think she's dying, Norman."

Norman momentarily paused from biting his nails. He had gone pasty white, something Michael didn't like the look of, and his eyes were wide with alarm. "What, what do you mean you think she's dying?" he said. "What are you going to do?"

Michael figured he had two options. He could ring the emergency number and get an ambulance to take Angie to the hospital, or he could rush home and find out what the problem was first. The initial option didn't seem plausible. How could he tell the emergency operator what was wrong with his wife when he wasn't even there? He couldn't just say it was a hunch, or a premonition, no matter how real it felt. The operator would treat it as a hoax and hang up. He really had only one choice.

"I have to get home and see what's happened," Michael said. "That's all I know."

Michael heard some faint voices and footsteps echoing down the corridor. He and Norman both looked, but saw nobody.

Norman returned to biting his nails, watching Michael. "What do you want me to do?" he asked, eventually.

"Why don't you keep ringing until she answers?" Michael sighed, nodding to the payphone. "Just press the redial button. If she's okay, just tell her I'm on my way back, but don't say anything to upset her, okay?"

Norman patted his trouser pockets and a new look of concern passed over his face. Michael quickly scrounged his back jean pocket and gave him a handful of change. Then he hastened to the main entrance. He was just in the process of opening the door when he heard Norman say, "Hey, Mikey, don't drive too fast, okay? Don't kill yourself getting home."

"I won't," he said, and quickly left the building.

He stepped outside into the early night and began jogging across the school basketball court toward his car, the lassitude of earlier today seemingly washed away with the flood of adrenaline flowing through his body, now a distant memory. Just ahead, four security lights bathed the teachers' parking lot in white mist. It was practically empty except for five remaining vehicles, of which his Beetle was one. A little more than halfway, he fumbled the car keys from his front pocket and they fell to the asphalt with a jink. Cursing, he picked them up and, as he stood, caught a flash of light in the darkened sky. Mouth agape, he stared at the maelstrom of firelights shooting across the heavens, like he could remember as a boy watching fireworks on Bonfire Night for the first time at Serena, and for a moment his mind was devoid of any coherent thought.

He woke out of his fleeting daze with a jolt, catching himself staring at the sky and the zipping orange lights. He began to jog again towards the parking lot. He jumped into the car, not bothering with the seatbelt, and sped out of the school grounds.

Fifteen minutes later he was racing up ANZAC Highway, slicing through the traffic, weaving between the trucks and cars and buses that seemed to be almost at a standstill. Michael's palms felt sweaty on the steering wheel and he constantly wiped them on his jeans and through his hair. He kept on thinking about Angie. What had happened? Why wouldn't she answer the telephone? It just wasn't like her to ignore it, even if she did have a headache.

A billboard with the picture of a mother and her newborn baby advertising diapers flashed past. It reminded him of Angie's impending birth, and the recent concerns over her blood pressure. A series of images suddenly raced through his mind as fast as the car was racing through the traffic, filling him with dread, of Angie, lying on the floor, her eyes rolled back, her legs and arms shaking and saliva drooling from her mouth, as if he were watching Billie the Great Dane dying in his neighbour's backyard all over again. It was his precognition, his *reverse déjà vu*, forewarning him. The vision was too real to be ignored.

Maybe she had been fed some *wafin*, he thought, and had suffered a massive bleed in her head. It spurred him on even faster.

Just then, a dark blue sedan swerved in front of him from the slow lane. He braked, almost shunting it from behind. Cursing, he darted over to the inner side, but a motorbike pulled out from nowhere and he jerked the Beetle back into the fast lane, narrowly missing the sedan with his rear end. He heard the driver honk angrily. Michael gave him the bird, then cursed the motorcyclist, who also gave him the bird, twice. Michael returned the compliment and sped on.

Not too far up ahead, stationary cars were now blocking his way across three lanes. Michael shook his head in frustration and gritted his teeth. ANZAC Highway had become a gigantic parking lot. Forced to pull to a halt behind a yellow mini, he opened the door and stepped out, thinking there must be a bad accident up ahead. Splashes of light from the sky splattered like raindrops on top of the stationary car roofs, over which he could see the jam stretching as far as the next major intersection. Many motorists had got out of their cars to see what was happening too, curious shadows with hands on their hips or scratching their heads, reminding him of mannequins posing in a department store window. He also began absently scratching his head. Further on, past the intersection, large dark silhouettes of eucalypts lined the perimeter of the parklands, beyond which the city buildings reached toward the streaking skylights with their windows illuminated, like giant advent calendars.

Michael heard a chopper flying over and looked up. There were actually about half a dozen of them hovering with their spotlights on. He wondered what the hell was going on. Then his thoughts returned to Angie and whether Norman had managed to get through to her. It was looking as if that was his only hope now.

Michael got back into the car and slammed the door. He figured there was no way he could get through the jam ahead, and he banged the steering wheel with the palm of his hand. The image of Angie lying on the floor unconscious and fitting was growing steadily brighter, like the swarm of lights flashing overhead. He honked his horn, holding it down for several seconds, then wound down the window and stuck his head outside.

"Hey!" he said to the driver leaning against his mini and smoking a cigarette. "Get a move on! Get out of the way! This isn't a picnic!"

The driver turned around and gave him the finger.

"My wife's sick!" Michael shouted, almost hysterically. "I've got to get her to the hospital! Get out of my way!"

"Tell your sob story to someone else, mate," the driver said. "I'm not moving!"

Michael retracted his head and honked his horn again. The mini driver didn't bother to turn around, instead stared into the heavens and watched the lightshow. Michael hung his head back and screamed, to no one in particular, maybe to all the bastards that had ever crossed his path, like the immovable mini driver ahead of him, or maybe to all the helpless situations he had ever experienced, like now. He reached down and turned on the radio, hoping to get some information about this traffic jam and a possible route around it.

"*… and in the skies above us we can just make out the meteorite shower that has stunned scientists,*" said a female reporter in a voice that Michael thought was as chirpy as a little girl discovering jewellery for the first time, "*and if you look outside, you can see it's quite a spectacular show.*"

He glanced up through the windshield to the night sky. The tiny shooting lights of deep ginger continued to flash across the heavens, which he now likened to an interstellar plague of fireflies. Michael kept looking. He could already feel himself hating these lights. They weren't spectacular at all. They were the cause of this infuriating traffic jam and were keeping him from getting to his house and Angie.

The reporter continued. "*I have with me here, the Professor of Astronomy at Adelaide University who can explain what's happening. Professor.*"

"Uh, yes," said a nervous, squeaky voice, which reminded Michael of a timid lapdog, the kind that yapped and attacked your ankles, but as soon as you glared at them they scampered away with their tails between their legs. He hated those dogs almost as much as he hated these lights in the sky. "*The earth, in its position in the outer reaches of the Milky Way,*" said the professor, clearing his voice, "*often comes into contact with intergalactic clouds of debris that, say, planets closer to the centre of the galaxy wouldn't normally encounter. These dazzling lights are caused when the minute interstellar dust particles entering the earth's atmosphere burn up into little fireballs. The last time something like this happened, according to some astronomers, a certain famous baby was born in a manger in Bethlehem.*"

Michael had had enough of listening to this crap. He flicked through the various channels in the hope of getting some information on the traffic chaos. To his dismay, every channel was talking about the lights and had their own panel of experts to describe what was happening. He flicked off the radio and thumped the steering wheel in frustration. He reversed the car, almost backing into the stationary blue sedan behind. The driver hooted and Michael gave him the bird, quickly scanning the road on the opposite side. Unlike the inward lanes, the lanes heading out of the city were virtually clear of traffic, giving him an idea.

No sooner had he made the decision to bypass the traffic jam via the smaller side streets, the Beetle was clunking off the grassy median strip and cutting across the sparse outbound lanes of ANZAC Highway.

For the next ten frustrating minutes he weaved in and out of the suburban streets, backtracking several times when blocked by traffic or confronted with a cul-de-sac. He recalled the rat experiments in his psychology class at university, in particular the rat-in-the-maze experiment in his final year. He recalled how the rat ran back and forth in the maze, running into the same high walls, the same dead-end alleys, never once finding the piece of cheese he had placed in the centre for its reward. Michael now knew how that poor rat felt. It seemed that every road around the city had come to a standstill, as if he were in a gigantic maze trying to find the piece of cheese, his house, as if the whole world was against him. He felt as if his every move to get home was being hampered deliberately, and it barely registered that he had weaved his way through the suburbs and was now just south of the main road not too far from St. Mary's Hospital.

At another intersection blocked by traffic, he came to a screeching halt. Two pedestrians, a young couple holding hands, walked in front of his car staring at the sky. Michael honked for them to get out of his way and ran his hand through his hair. The guy glared at Michael and gave him the double finger. The woman glared too. Michael reversed quickly into somebody's driveway, then sped back along the street from which he had just come. He again thought of the rat and wondered if it ever considered giving him the double finger and telling him to find his own piece of cheese.

Michael eventually managed to bypass the mayhem around the

blocked intersection by backtracking almost a mile and crossing over the main road through a Red Sea-like gap that had opened up in the traffic. He fortuitously remembered a shortcut that his father had shown him through the grounds of the psychiatric hospital and spent the next few minutes cutting through it, thereby circumnavigating the final major blockage to his house. Just as he did, Michael was again overwhelmed with the image of his wife, fitting and drooling, and he pushed the accelerator to the floor.

The car sped on through the dark streets. Not too long after, he unexpectedly found himself on the road that bordered the eastern edge of St. Mary's Hospital. As he passed the twin buildings, he was once again reminded of two tombstones rising out of a deserted cemetery. At the T-intersection he turned right, in the direction of home, and as he accelerated away from the hospital he was struck by the street's uncanny familiarity. He'd been here before; he knew it.

In a flash of sudden understanding, he realised where he had seen this vision before—his recurring nightmare. Coldness entered him, rising from the floor of the car through his feet, up his legs to his chest and head. He began to shiver all over and his teeth chattered uncontrollably. It was the same street on which he is always running, always being chased by the men in white hooded robes. Just like the dream, it was eerily silent. Several cars were parked on either side of the street. There were no pedestrians walking along the pavement, no dogs were barking from the gardens, no birds were singing in the treetops. Even the hue was eerily the same. Though illuminated a little more than expected because of the meteorite shower above, the street was tinted with a kind of sullen orange. He now realised that he had mistakenly thought the dream was in black and white, but it was actually in *sepia*, like the old photographs he had seen of the city taken in the mid-1800s. It felt surreal, as if he was driving in a snapshot of history that had come alive, as if he had somehow encountered a live re-enactment of his dream.

He blurted with laughter. The similarities were just too uncanny to be believed. Always in that dream he recognised the street, yet was unable to pinpoint its exact whereabouts, like a word that sat frustratingly on the tip of his tongue. Now he knew. John Street. The very same street he had taken many times on his visits to St. Mary's with Angie.

He shook his head, pushing the throttle even harder. This was just getting too weird. He wanted to get away from here as quickly as he could. To make matters worse, he recalled how the dream ended, with the hooded and faceless trio taunting him as he lay sprawled on the ground: *We have the baby*! *We have the baby*! He also recalled all too well the feeling of utter helplessness as he watched them disappear with his only child.

A parked car flashed by on the passenger side. He glanced down at the dashboard and saw the speedometer needle move past 50 mph, just as an ambulance turned into John Street up ahead. He barely registered its siren, too absorbed in his own dream-like world and the pressing need to get away from here. When he looked back at the road, the ambulance was so close he could clearly see the paramedic in the driving seat. He was seconds away from a head-on collision. Screaming involuntarily, he swerved to the left, just missing the ambulance as it roared past, only to see the shadow of a eucalypt spring out from the side of the road like a black panther pouncing on its prey. He swerved the other way, but he was going too fast. The wheels squealed in protest, unable to turn in time, and he heard a loud *thud*! as the car sideswiped the bow of the tree.

The Beetle flipped on impact and Michael was spat out the door like a piece of chewing gum. For some reason, as he was flying through the air, just before his body crunched into the road, he thought of the rat in his psychology experiments, how he had never found his piece of cheese, and how his life had ended gruesomely in the dissecting laboratory of the biology students. Then he hit the asphalt. It all happened in the space of seconds, but to Michael it was an eternity, frame by frame in slow motion. A stab of pain tore through his right shoulder, followed by a sound like the pop of a champagne cork. As his head scraped along the road, he felt the skin of his cheek peeling back and his right ear tearing almost completely off. His hips then collided with the cement guttering and he bounced like a dead cat, coming to rest in a semi-lifeless heap.

In the darkness he saw stars flashing across the sky. He began staring at them, fixated and dazed. Then the street briefly flashed orange, like a solar flare, quickly settling back into its sepia tinge. A soft boom was followed by a warm blast of air through his bloodied hair, which he confusedly associated with the lighting of a bonfire and not with the explosion of his car.

The ambulance continued on, sirens blaring, then the air seemed to still, like in his dream. Blood seeped into his eyes, blurring his vision, and he tried to wipe it away, but a wrench of pain gripped his right shoulder like the jaws of a bear trap and he cried out in agony. Moments later, he heard the hurried footsteps of someone approaching. He thought he heard a male voice ask if he was all right. It seemed such a stupid question. Michael was about to answer, but he heard the guy say something else that filled him with horror: *We have the baby!*

Michael tried to say something and get up. Unbelievably, he couldn't move. He couldn't talk either. It was all happening exactly as he had dreamed, and as he began to lose consciousness he found to his alarm that it was increasingly difficult to distinguish the nightmare from reality. There were now more footsteps. More voices and faces. Michael could only peer at them through the slits of his bloodied eyelids. There were three of them now. They were wearing white hooded robes and were smiling at him.

Michael again tried to reply. He tried to tell them that his pregnant wife was unconscious at home and that they had to call an ambulance for her.

The men weren't listening to him. They were discussing something amongst themselves. After a moment, one of them turned and said: *We have the baby!*

Michael watched with despair as the guy disappeared. He felt a chill rise through his body, like before when he suddenly recalled the scene of his recurring nightmare, and his jaw began to chatter. He was so cold. Soon, his whole body was racked with shivering. The coldness was doing something to him he didn't like, sucking the life out of him. He felt completely numb. His mind was beginning to fog, he knew he was slipping into a coma, and the last thing he heard was the last thing he wanted to hear:

*We have the baby!*

# CHAPTER 10

IT WAS DARK, very dark, and in the confusion Michael grasped for any sense of reality, for any fragment of normality. For some reason he couldn't see, not even a speck of light, he was completely cocooned in blackness. He wondered if he had suddenly gone blind, or whether he was somewhere in a darkened room. It was difficult to tell, and the lack of vision was extremely disconcerting. He could hear, though. That was one saving grace. There were odd sounds filtering through to his consciousness. He could hear a babble of voices, like whispering mourners at a funeral, and for a horrid moment he thought he was inside a coffin, listening to the congregation of friends and family gathered to pay their last respects. He was trapped and they were going to bury him alive, or worse, cremate him. He tried to shout. He tried to tell them that he wasn't dead, except something was stuck in his throat and was preventing him from making a sound.

The sudden surge of panic didn't last long. He quickly realised that he couldn't be in his death casket. There were deep monotonous sighs and inhalations to his right. It sounded like he reckoned a robot would breathe, or someone having a bad asthma attack, noises that he wouldn't really expect to hear inside a church or crematorium. Furthermore, there were odd beeping noises at regular intervals, like alarm clocks that had been set every few minutes. Wherever he was, he could confidently eliminate the notion that he was about to hear his own eulogy from his father.

He relaxed a little. Suddenly, as if the act of calming down had lowered his guard, his body was racked with pain. It felt like he had been pegged to the ground and every child and teacher at Wattle Gardens had taken their turn to sink their boot in. His stomach squealed, like it had been ripped apart and sewn haphazardly back together. His head pounded with every beat of his heart. His hips felt bruised and shattered. His right ear throbbed. What's more, something was shoved up his right nostril. It was hard and irritating and he wanted it out. He tried to pull it, but he was so exhausted his hand got no further than an inch or two into the air before it slumped back down.

Now even more curious as to where he was, he tried to open his eyes. Frustratingly, they were locked as tight as shutters in a storm. He wondered, perhaps, now that he knew he wasn't dead or dying, whether this was a dream or hallucination of some kind. He'd certainly had dreams as nightmarishly realistic as this one in the past. It was certainly possible that this was all a figment of his mind. He tried turning his head toward whatever was making the harsh breathing noises and immediately got his answer—deep slashing pain, as if something was trying to rip his arm from his body, as if someone was hacking at his shoulder with a machete. It wasn't a dream. The pain was too real. Far too real.

Then where the hell was he? What had happened? Why couldn't he remember?

A brief flash of memory illuminated the darkness. He remembered an ambulance and shooting lights in the sky. He remembered three white hooded figures hovering over him like impatient vultures. How long ago was that? A day? An hour? A minute? He didn't know. The darkness had erased time, like his memory.

Though it wasn't a complete void. There was something else, another memory he was uncertain of. He remembered bright white lights and flashes of silver. He remembered, bizarrely, a Scottish accent, and screaming, horrible, horrible screaming. Were they more dreams, or had they happened? What did they mean? Without some form of perspective, these half-erased images were just as vague as a few nouns and adjectives plucked at random from a sentence, words that made no particular sense without the context in which they'd been written.

Just then, something alarmed and he heard hurried footsteps shuffling toward the noise. He heard a female voice mention something about low blood pressure. Then the beeping stopped. What the hell was going on? He caught a pungent whiff of bleach through the one nostril that wasn't plugged. He grimaced, suddenly realising in horror where he had encountered that smell before. He was in a hospital.

"I think he moved," said another female voice.

"Angie? Is that you?" he asked. The lump in his throat had partially shifted, though it burned agonisingly when he spoke and his voice sounded raspy.

"What did he say?" said a male voice.

Did he recognise that one too? "Who's there?" Michael asked. "I can't see you."

"I can't understand him," the man said. "He's mumbling too much."

The asthmatic robot kept breathing and wheezing to his right. Another alarm beeped and there was more scuffled footsteps. The beeping was silenced. He tried to clear his throat again, but it was like swallowing a hot coal. He had to open his eyes, had to get out of the darkness and see who they were, see where he was. With all his strength, he managed to pry his sticky eyelids apart and peer through the thin crack. The figures were still there, they hadn't left, but he was unable to focus clearly and make out their identity.

"Who are you," he asked again. "Where am I?"

"What did he say?" the man asked.

The voice seemed to come from the figure on the left. He was sure he recognised it, could almost put a face to it, it was so close, like the name of the street in his dream, and just as exasperating.

"I think he wants the baby," the female said.

Michael quickly turned his eyes to her. He thought her voice was also familiar, but attributing a name and face to it was beyond his capability at this particular time. The blurred figure took several steps towards him holding a bundle of blankets, a small face partially hidden amongst them. He tried to lift his head off the pillow, but couldn't; the pain in his shoulder and stomach was too great. When she spoke to him, he stared at the woman in shock. It was his nightmare all over again. *We have your baby!* he heard.

Despite the pain, he struggled once again to lift his head off the pillow, but the gravitating pull of the black abyss from which he had just emerged tugged at his consciousness and he gave up. He began to slide into the blackness, slipping further and further away from the unknown figures and his baby. He tried to shout. He tried to scramble and claw his way back to the surface, but was dragged back down, as if something in the abyss had hold of his ankles. He tried to fight it. His fingers dug into the surrounding darkness as if it were mud. He hung on with all his strength, but it did no good.

He slid further down, into the blackness and beyond.

AN INDETERMINATE TIME passed before an alarm beeped nearby, waking him with a jolt. Michael moaned and sought to open his eyelids. He was confused and disorientated again. Desperate to get his bearings, he groped for any semblance of familiarity. He heard the harsh mechanical breaths to his right. That was something he could remember. It was somehow comforting, a frame of reference that he could cling to like a man stuck on top of a burning building would cling to a propped ladder.

His disorientation slowly diminished as more faint tendrils of re-collection rose from the ashes of his memory, smoky images of a recently forgotten past. There was a babble of softly spoken voices in the background. He remembered thinking that they were like murmurs at a funeral the last time he stirred from his deep unconsciousness, but unlike then he didn't panic; he no longer assumed he was trapped inside a coffin. He inhaled and grimaced at the smell of bleach and disinfectant. Despite the revulsion, it was something familiar to cling to, like the harsh breathing and the voices. It was all starting to come back to him.

"How's our patient doing, Sister?" he heard a man ask. It wasn't the same voice as yesterday (or was it earlier today?), different somehow, yet familiar too. Like before, his eyelids resisted his efforts to pry them open, barely moving apart, yet through the half-open slits he saw a man with dark hair in a blue suit standing at the foot of the bed. The room was also dim, making it difficult to see.

Michael slowly put the pieces of the puzzle together. The guy had called her Sister, so she must be a nurse, or a nun. Therefore, he figured, his initial assumption that he was in a hospital was probably right, and the guy was most likely a doctor because he had asked her how the patient (him?) was doing. It could only mean one thing—something bad must have happened. Something so bad, in fact, that he couldn't remember a thing about it.

Michael turned to catch a glimpse of the nurse. He was racked with a piercing pain that tore through his right shoulder. Something *very* bad had happened, he thought, moaning, something that nearly tore his right arm off.

He was at a loss to explain what could have happened. Had he been suddenly struck ill and fallen unconscious? He doubted it. The pain he was feeling now was different than what he would expect if he'd just been laid low with a mystery illness. He would feel more nauseous and lethargic, like a bad case of influenza, if that's what had happened. What he was feeling now—his aching right shoulder, the stabbing contractions in his belly, his throbbing right ear—all indicated something worse, something more life threatening. Had he been involved in some kind of natural disaster, like an earthquake, or flood? That was unlikely. Perhaps it was something much simpler than that. Perhaps he had gotten himself involved in a fight and had taken a severe beating from someone. He struggled to remember the chain of events leading up to now. Then he gave up, brushing the thought aside.

He could hear the nurse and doctor chatting about some medical stuff, something about decreased urine output and the need to increase his fluid intake by ten percent. He didn't understand most of it, though it did help to confirm his suspicion that he was somewhere in a hospital. Michael then heard the nurse refer to the man as Dr. Rouben.

"Dr. Rouben?" Michael asked aloud, snatching at a familiar name. The back of his mouth was like a dry lakebed and it stung in needles when he spoke. He coughed and tried to clear his throat, but it only made it worse.

"Michael?" the man in the blue suit asked, his voice full of surprise. "Are you awake?"

Michael tried to sit up. He was struck again by a tearing slash in his right shoulder, and then an agonising stab in his belly. He stifled a scream and his head flopped back down onto the pillow. Dr. Rouben told him not to move, that he had been in a bad accident and had suffered a lot of internal injuries. He was now in St. Mary's Hospital, in the intensive care unit, and that he must try to relax and conserve his energy.

At least it explained why he felt like he'd been sawn in half and then stitched back together like Frankenstein's monster, Michael thought. Although the doctor's words helped to partially assuage his disorientated state of mind, relaxing was the last thing he could do. He desperately needed to know more.

"Where's Angie?" he asked. "Is she all right?"

He saw Dr. Rouben glance toward the sound of the wheezing robot. "She's, uh, she's doing fine," he said, turning back to Michael. "We'll let you know what happened in a couple of days. When you're better."

Michael knew he wasn't going to get any more information out of him at this point in time. He also wasn't in any fit state to argue or demand that Dr. Rouben tell him immediately, so he had to be satisfied with what he was told. "How long have I been in here?" he asked.

Once again, Dr. Rouben wavered. "It's been three days since the accident."

*Three* days? Could he really have been unconscious for so long? He wanted to discuss what had happened, but he was so tired it was an effort to even think. As his eyelids began to droop, the artificial light from the fluorescent tubes on the ceiling shimmied in hazy white mist around Dr. Rouben and the Sister, like an aura, like white hooded robes. Michael felt himself being sucked into the black abyss once more. He tried to cling to the rapidly diminishing state of consciousness as though it was his last moments on this earth.

"What happened to my baby?" he said, choking on the words, an inarticulate smudge of vowels and consonants even to his own ears. He knew he was barely incomprehensible, but he kept trying. He had to know. "Where is she?"

Dr. Rouben turned to the nurse. "Did he say something about his baby?"

"I think so," she said.

"It's okay," he said to Michael. "We have the baby. She's in the NICU. She's fine."

To Michael, the words were just faint echoes through the dark void into which he was powerless to prevent himself falling: *We have the baby! We have the baby!* As he spiralled deeper and deeper into the abyss, the words reverberated off the dark walls, taunting and teasing until he was enveloped completely and he heard no more.

THE SILENCE WAS blissful. He was surprised by the degree of comfort to be found in nothingness. Silence was peace. Silence was still. Silence was calm, and it was in the silence that he could feel himself being revitalised. He figured he was probably dead, probably died some time ago, in fact, in the hospital, the last place he ever wanted to die, but he wasn't alone. There were others. He could hear angels talking.

"I don't think he knows," said a male voice. "I don't think he's been told."

"Does she have a name yet?" It was a different voice, female.

As Michael listened, the darkness became lighter, grey, like the colour of clouds recently spent of rain. It was the reverse of what he felt slipping into the black abyss; he was being lifted toward a light, freely, like a balloon slipping from a child's grasp and drifting toward the sun. He blinked several times, opening his eyes to the white surroundings.

He was in a small hospital room. His vision cleared sufficiently to make out his friend Norman and his wife, Bridget, though they hadn't noticed that he was awake yet. They were standing at the foot of the bed paying attention to a bundle of blankets that Bridget was holding in the crook of her arm. Norman was wearing a brown cardigan and trousers. His wife, almost as portly as Norman, was wearing a loose fitting dark blue dress with long sleeves and had her long dark hair braided into a ponytail.

"How can it have a name, woman?" Norman said, exasperated. "Its parents have been in a coma for nearly four days!"

"She's not an *it*," Bridget said, cradling the bundle of blankets back and forth. "She's a sweet little girl who needs a name."

"It's Jessica," Michael said with a chuckle.

Norman and Bridget suddenly looked up. The surprised expression on their faces made Michael laugh a little more, but he had to stop because of the pain it was causing in his belly.

"Mikey!" Norman said, his eyes big and startled like a child caught in the act of stealing cookies from the jar. "You're awake!"

"So it seems." He tried to sit up, but his shoulder protested with a squeal of pain, as did his stomach. "Looks like I've woken up into the real world again," he said, wincing, and sank back into the mattress.

"Here, would you like to see your baby?" Norman asked, reaching for the bundle of blankets from his wife. He moved around the side of the bed and, after helping Michael to sit, handed her to him. "Here she is. Look, she's even got a cute little birthmark on her cheek," he said with a chuckle. "She's gorgeous. Can't say she got that from your side of the family, though."

Michael chuckled as Norman rested the baby in the crook of his left shoulder, splaying the blankets so that her face was showing openly. Despite the pain flaring in his right shoulder he lifted his arm and caressed Jessica's face with his finger. She was as beautiful as her mother and the joy he felt in holding her for the first time dulled the pain better than any analgesic the doctors could prescribe. She had inherited Angie's cute nose and full lips. Her eyes were large and blue, though he hoped they would change to brown, like her mother's, as she grew older. He was relieved to see that she hadn't inherited his hooked nose or pronounced brow and chin. Though maybe, he hoped, she might have his thick brown hair.

"Hello, my little girl," he said softly. He tried to position her slightly better in his arms, but when he moved his entire body squealed in pain. Scrunching his eyes, he bit his bottom lip to prevent himself from crying out, and waited for the pain to abate. Eventually, after several seconds, it did. "I think I know what Humpty Dumpty must have felt like when he fell off the wall," he said after a moment.

"At least they could put you back together again," Norman said, moving back to the end of the bed. "You had a pretty nasty fall."

"I gathered that much." Michael groaned again with another flash of pain in his shoulder. "What have they done to me?"

"Well, your shoulder's heavily strapped," Norman said. "The

doctors said it was dislocated and badly bruised. You've also torn a few ligaments around the joint and broken your collarbone as well."

Michael continued to cradle the bundle of blankets and stroke the baby's face. He listened with an air of detachment, kind of glad that it was his friend telling him the extent of his injuries and not the doctors. Norman made it more bearable, somehow, like sprinkling sugar on something bitter, like grape-fruit. The doctors would have tried to confuse him with a lot of medical jargon, thinking the less he knew the better he would feel. Not Norman; he went straight for the jugular.

"Your right ear had to be sown back on and you also have a nasty scar on your cheek with a dozen stitches," Norman continued. "Oh, and your hip's broken, too, so don't try and get out of bed by yourself. And I see they've also given you a free haircut. That's one good thing to come out of all this."

Michael tried to feel his hair and grimaced when his shoulder scream-ed in protest again. "Where am I now?" he asked, after a second. "This room is different. I remember being somewhere else for a while."

Norman informed him that he was in a single-bedded cubicle just down the corridor from the ICU on the top floor. He had recovered sufficiently enough not to require any further intensive medical treatment. The worst was over. Now all he needed was bed rest and rehabilitation.

Michael looked around. The room was clean, although he didn't like the sterile bleach smell wafting in his nose. It was also extremely white, almost as white as an operating room, and there was a square black box fixed to the ceiling directly in front, above Norman and his wife. Despite the protestations of his shoulder and stomach, Michael turned his head to the right, catching sight of a small portable crib beneath the window. He glanced outside over the top of several get-well cards standing on the windowsill. The bright blue sky was spotted with large cumulus clouds as white as the walls of his room, and he could just make out what he thought were the eastern parklands in the distance. He figured, though it was purely a guess because his mind still wasn't thinking as straight as he would have liked, that he was somewhere in the south-western sector of the hospital.

He returned his gaze to the baby in his arms. She was truly as gorgeous as her mother, which suddenly reminded him. "Where's your mummy, hey?" he asked, and then looked up at Norman and Bridget. They quickly averted their eyes. Michael repeated himself, but neither answered, both waiting for the other to say something. He asked again more demandingly. Norman still didn't say anything, keeping his eyes trained to the floor. Michael faced Bridget, who briefly met his gaze, then looked outside, her eyes brimming with tears. The silence was deeper than the void from which he had been immersed for the past four days and he suddenly found himself wishing he were back there. The abyss seemed to have swallowed them all. No one spoke. Michael turned from Norman to Bridget to Norman to Bridget, back and forth, waiting for one of them to say something. The baby smacked her lips and yawned.

"What's happened to Angie?" he asked, almost pleading. He could only imagine the worst possible outcome. "Is she…?"

Norman and Bridget blurted "No!" together. They looked at each another, like two guilty criminals who had just been caught red handed robbing the bank, waiting uncomfortably for the other to speak. It was Norman who finally spoke. "She's unwell, Mikey," he said.

Michael tried to sit further up, but he was clamped to the bed by the weight of the baby in the nook of his armpit and the searing jag of pain from his stomach and shoulder. "What do you mean? Where is she?" he asked, gritting his teeth through the discomfort. "What happened? Was she in the accident?"

"Angie wasn't in the accident, only you. She had a seizure and…" Norman started.

"A seizure?" Michael said, nearly shouting. A sudden vision played in his head, like a rerun of an old movie. In it, Angie was lying on the lounge room floor. Her eyes were rolled so far back into her skull just the whites were showing. Her legs and arms were twitching and thrashing about. Spittle was drooling out of her mouth. "Why? What happened?" he asked, shoving the image out of his mind. "Is she going to be okay?"

Norman held out both hands, gesturing for Michael to calm down. To Michael, it looked as though he was patting a large, invisible dog. "It wasn't anybody's fault," Norman said. "It was all so… *unexpected.*"

Michael stared out of the window in a daze. He felt emotionally dead as Norman recounted what the doctors had told him about Angie's condition. The pregnancy had caused her blood pressure to rise extremely high. No one was to blame. No one could have foreseen how bad it was. It was just one of those things, though that was of little consolation to Michael. All his fears over the past few weeks had become reality. He felt an illogical sense of guilt, as if his constant worrying had somehow been the cause of Angie's misfortune.

Norman told him that someone had called the paramedics to the house. Whoever the mystery caller was, they'd saved Angie's and the baby's life. The paramedics had found Angie lying on the lounge room floor. She had been unconscious, partially aborting the baby, and they had rushed her to the hospital. Michael found himself wondering if it was the same ambulance that he had nearly collided with, the same ambulance that caused him to swerve into the tree on the side of the road. If it were true, the irony was truly incredible. As Norman continued, Michael kept staring out of the window, watching the clouds drift across the sky. Angie had suffered a seizure on arrival and was taken straight to the operating room for an emergency C-section, he heard. It was the only thing that would stop the seizure and save the baby. The baby came out fine, though she initially needed a little bit of oxygen to help her breathe. Unfortunately, and Norman hesitated before he went on, Angie suffered a massive internal haemorrhage and had to have her uterus removed to prevent further blood loss. She could no longer have any more children.

Michael closed his eyes and let his head sink into the pillow. The news was as painful as his stomach and shoulder, even worse. He knew his body would recover from its wounds, but this was something neither he nor Angie would recover from. The only consolation was the little baby cradled in his arms. At least she was safe. Michael opened his eyes and glanced at her, then lifted his face to his friend. Norman appeared to falter again, glimpsing briefly at his wife. It seemed that there was more to tell.

Norman cleared his throat, then looked back at Michael. Sighing, he dropped his arms to his side. "I, I didn't want to be the one to give you the bad news," he said, and glanced at his wife again. An unspoken taboo quickly passed between them, something, Michael could tell, neither could bring themselves to say. Bridget turned away and looked outside through the window, dabbing her eyes with a scrunched tissue she had removed from the sleeve of her dress.

Finally, Norman said, "Angie... she... she hasn't recovered from the operation. She's still in a coma." Then, almost as an after thought, he added, "The doctors said it was a miracle she survived, so who knows what may happen? She's come this far. They're not giving up on her. It's still early days."

Michael drew a deep breath and stared at the stark white ceiling, wondering how much worse it could get. The baby had now found its thumb and was making contented sucking noises in his left ear. Norman and Bridget glanced awkwardly at one another again, and Michael braced himself for more terrible news, but it didn't come. They just stood there in silence, staring at him.

Michael felt a tear drop from his right eye and course slowly down his cheek. He needed to be alone. He asked them to go and they left, heads down and solemn. Just as Norman was about to follow his wife through the door, Michael lifted his head off the pillow and called out to him. "Thanks for being so honest," he said. "I appreciate it."

"No problems, buddy," Norman said, and Michael thought he had never seen him so emotionally drained. "Get well soon. Your kid needs you."

## CHAPTER 11

MICHAEL WASN'T ALLOWED to eat anything for the next two days except crushed ice and the occasional sip of water. His bowels, according to the nurses, weren't working properly yet. They weren't working, he grumbled, because there was nothing in there. He hadn't eaten since he was in hospital, almost a week ago. The nurses were unimpressed. They ignored his pleas for food and gave him his ice chips in a Styrofoam cup. Staring at them every morning at breakfast time, he reckoned he had never wished for a bowel movement so much in his life.

Getting out of bed was an impossibility, too. Anyway, that's what he told the physiotherapist, a six-foot ash blonde that could have been Hitler's grandchild. Like the nurses, she didn't pay his protestations much heed. On the fifth day, she came waltzing into the room with a Zimmer frame, the kind of walker he had only ever seen old people use. She threw back the sheets and pulled him into a sitting position. His broken hip screamed and his stomach squealed, but before he knew it he was standing behind the Zimmer frame like an octogenarian with dodgy knees.

For the next ten days she forced him out of bed morning and afternoon and ordered him to walk as far as he could with the frame. The first two days were the worst. He could barely get to the toilet. It was as if he was learning to walk all over again. After five days of physiotherapy, nine days since the accident, he finally had the strength and coordination to visit Angie in the ICU for the first time.

Sitting in his room, Michael waited for Maria Sanchez to bring Jessica up from the neonatal intensive care unit where she was being cared for while he recuperated. It was the one part of the day he really looked forward to. From the very start, Maria had taught him how to bottle-feed and how to bath her. She had even taught him how to change her diapers, something he didn't find as revolting as he had imagined. He was immeasurably glad for Maria's help. It was difficult to even hold the baby with his injuries, let alone do anything else, but he was greatly pleased to be able to do even these minor tasks. It even helped to take his mind off his recent trials and tribulations, especially those concerning his wife. Jessica was simply a joy.

Maria, on the other hand, was an enigma. She was always polite and softly spoken, never in a hurry, unlike so many of the other medical staff he had come to meet, and yet he had a gut sense that she was always holding something back. She rarely spoke about herself when he tentatively broached the subject of her past, except to say that she had emigrated from Colombia with her mother in the mid-80s when her father, a policeman, was shot dead on the streets of Bogotá. The assailants were unknown, presumably members of a drug cartel. When she told him the news, her face was stern and unsmiling, just as he remembered her the first time they accidentally bumped into each other in the lobby last November. Michael pressed her no further.

Around midday, after the physio had wrung him through the mill again, Maria pushed a portable crib into the room, just as she had done every day since he had been stuck in this god-forsaken place. Michael glanced inside the crib. Jessica was sleeping peacefully, wrapped in a white hospital blanket and wearing a pink bonnet. He thought her more gorgeous every day.

"Where to today, Mr. Joseph?" Maria asked.

"I thought we might go and see her mummy," Michael said. "I've been avoiding it for too long."

Maria accompanied him down the corridor towards the ICU, pushing the crib just behind and to his right as he plodded along with the Zimmer frame. It was slow going, but he was determined to get there. Once they finally arrived at the doors, Maria buzzed the intercom to be let in. Michael drew a deep breath. Since he had regained consciousness after the accident, he had been waiting for this moment. Only twice could he recall being so nervous; waiting at the altar for Angie to walk down the aisle, and three years before that, walking up the steps of the front porch on the night of their very first date. A woman's voice answered Maria's call and asked who she was. She spoke into the intercom microphone and a second later Michael heard the click of the security latch being electronically released. Maria then held the doors open for Michael to pass through.

Three nurses were writing in medical files behind the nurses' station as he and Maria entered. Only one of them looked up, proffering a quick smile of recognition to both of them. Michael returned her welcome and continued forward with the walker into the ICU. He immediately disliked the feeling of controlled mania, of beeping ECG monitors and gasping artificial respirators, of doctors and nurses in surgical gowns who neither ran nor walked, but harried, and who spoke in hushed undertones without meeting anyone's eye. He also disliked the feeling that death visited this place on a regular basis.

To compound matters, the room was incredibly dim. Every blind was drawn and not one ray of sunlight filtered through the windows. The bank of fluorescent tubes barely shed enough light to see the beds along the far wall. He could imagine crematoriums less grim. As he lifted the frame and stepped behind it, a nurse hurried across the room and began writing on a large flowchart at the end of the first bed. A man in a navy blue suit was reading the charts over her shoulder. His back was turned and he was shaking his head, presumably unhappy with the patient's progress. Michael's gaze went to the prostrated woman in question. He immediately recognised her, and gasped.

From the day Norman had told him of Angie's plight, Michael had received very little information on her progress. The medical staff had only drip fed him with what they thought he could handle, ice chip equivalents for his constipated emotional state. It was yet another point of grievance he had toward the doctors and nurses, but upon looking at her now he understood why they had been so reluctant to give him too much information at once. Even from a distance, he could tell she was on death's door. If he had been told the true extent of her condition, he doubted that his own recovery would have been so rapid and problem free.

Michael took a moment to take it all in. He stopped in his tracks, just staring at his wife, the enormity of the situation now only starting to sink in. Angie was in a coma, breathing with the aid of a ventilator. Her skin was pale and lifeless, and her once beautiful hair was now tossed haphazardly, like a wig left to knot and tangle in the wind. She was hooked up to an array of monitoring equipment, one of which was beeping annoyingly, and like some lifeless robot undergoing a tune-up, several tubes entered and exited her body. One came out of her mouth. One came out of her abdomen. One was even inserted into her right nostril, attached to a bag of milky fluid that hung from a T-bar above her untidy scalp. Yet another coursed from somewhere beneath the blankets, emptying its amber contents into a bag hooked to the nearside bed leg.

Michael kept staring, too shaken to even blink. Although he had prepared himself for the worst, the shock of seeing her like this was still too much to bear in his weakened state. He suddenly couldn't think straight. Was no one else bothered by the beeping alarm? It was driving him mad. He wanted to scream to someone to do something about it, anything, just get rid of that god-awful noise. To his relief, the nurse went to the head of the bed and pushed a button on the monitor, instantly silencing it.

Michael gripped the Zimmer frame, steadying himself. As he took a deep breath, he heard Maria ask him if he was all right. He nodded in reply. The last time he had seen Angie she was dressed and ready for work, vibrant and full of expectancy with the upcoming birth. This woman on the bed was but a pale reflection of what he had seen. He found it difficult to believe that minutes after he had spoken to her on the telephone that day, she had suffered a seizure and ended up like this, a hair's breadth away from meeting her maker. The greatest tragedy was that she hadn't even set eyes on the baby she had sacrificed her womb for. It wasn't fair. If this was the price of worshipping God, then he was glad he didn't believe.

Keeping his eye on her, Michael imagined that he himself must have looked like death warmed up this same time last week. He could only hope that she recovered as quickly as he had. As he crossed the room to her bed, he could hear the man in the suit discussing Angie's prognosis with the nurse. His back was still turned, but Michael immediately recognised the voice.

It was Dr. Rouben, and neither he nor the nurse was aware that Michael was approaching from behind. "She's not so good, I'm afraid," the nurse said to him, somewhat sombre. "We've taken down the dobutamine and dopamine infusion yesterday but the anaesthetist still doesn't think she'll pull through. He's worried about her neurological status."

Dr. Rouben muttered something just out of earshot, eyeing the medical charts at the end of the bed. Michael clunked the Zimmer frame forward. Suddenly, like a cat caught stealing across the neighbour's yard, Dr. Rouben spun around to see what had made the noise. Michael stopped, struck by the degree of surprise on the doctor's face. Then, almost instantly, in the time between alarm beeps, his face changed into a welcoming smile.

"Michael, good to see you," he said. "You've made a fine recovery."

With Maria pushing the crib close behind, Michael trundled with the Zimmer frame toward the bed and nodded a weak return greeting. His eyes returned to Angie. She was motionless, except for the mechanical rise and fall of her chest, to which the nurse was now listening intently with a stethoscope. Her gold crucifix, he noted, was no longer around her neck. The ventilator wheezed, forcing air into Angie's lungs, and Michael suddenly remembered where he'd heard that inhuman sound before. He figured that after the accident he must have been stationed in the bed next to Angie. Unbeknown to him at the time, it was her ventilator that he could hear in the lurking darkness of his semi-comatose state.

"So, is this our special little girl?" Michael now heard Dr. Rouben ask.

Michael looked over and saw Dr. Rouben peering into the cot. Another nurse had joined them at Angie's bedside. Michael remembered her as the Nurse Unit Manager, the matron of the ward, or the NUM, as the junior nurses called her. She was a likeable woman barely an inch over five feet tall with large voluminous breasts that seemed as wide as she was tall. She and Maria were also staring at the baby.

"I hope you don't mind her here," Michael said, still gripping the handles of the walker. "I thought it might be good if she laid next to her mum for a while."

"Of course not," the NUM said, bending over the cot and tickling the baby under the chin. The baby turned its head reflexively to the side and smacked its lips in anticipation of a feed.

"I see she has a little strawberry nevus," Dr. Rouben said, caressing the red, circular birthmark on Jessica's left cheek. His dark brown eyes moved slowly from the baby to Michael. "She's adorable. You must be proud."

Michael's eyes seemed to glaze as he nodded in agreement. He glanced at Angie. "Tell me though, Dr. Rouben," he said, "do you think Angie will pull through?"

Dr. Rouben turned his attention to Angie. His face seemed full of thoughts as the ventilator inhaled and exhaled noisily. The nurse listening to Angie's chest moved wordlessly to the foot of the bed and wrote down her observations on the flowchart. "I think we must take it one day at a time," he said, after a while. Then he inhaled deeply, almost as loud as the ventilator breathing air into his patient. "She's had a stroke, Michael."

Michael wobbled on his heels and staggered back a step. He grabbed the Zimmer frame more tightly, giving himself a moment to compose himself. He remembered once again the day he and Jude witnessed the death of the Great Dane. He remembered his dad informing him that Billy had been fed a steak laced with poison, *wafin*, causing a massive bleed inside the dog's head, a stroke. Michael stared at his knuckles gripping the handles of the walker. They were starting to go white. "How bad?" he now asked.

"The CT scan shows a small hematoma in the region of the left parietofrontal lobe," Dr. Rouben said, tapping his left forehead with his forefinger to show Michael the approximate position of the brain that had been damaged. "Hopefully it will resolve spontaneously. Repeat scans show that it hasn't increased in size since the initial event," and he glanced at Angie, then back at Michael. "I've asked the neurologists to review her on a daily basis. They think she's got a fifty-fifty chance of suffering no adverse effects at all and about a one in three chance of mild symptoms that could effect her for life."

Michael stared at his wife, desperately wishing that he had done something to prevent what had happened. He wished that he had excused himself from the teachers' meeting. That's what he should have done. He should have insisted on leaving. Then he could have avoided those damned celestial lights before they had a chance to block the highway like some clogged coronary artery and gotten home in plenty of time to rescue Angie.

But, he hadn't. He had stayed because he dreaded the repercussions from the headmistress if he left straight after the final bell had rung. It was the worst decision he'd ever made, infinitely more than the decision to follow his dad's advice and to attend teachers' college rather than follow his dream of flying to Paris and becoming a chef. Both those decisions had been made out of fear, he now understood. He was a coward, a pathetic, cringing rat too scared to stand up for himself and do what he knew was right. It hurt deeper than the pain in his hips to know that the decisions he'd made were directly responsible for Angie's current condition. He kept staring at her, hating himself for his weaknesses. He wished he could take her place so that she could see and hold the little girl she had carried for almost nine months. He was the one that deserved to still be in a coma. He was the one that should be suffering, not her.

It wasn't the first time he had castigated himself over his ineptness since he had regained consciousness and learnt of Angie's predicament. Lying in bed for twenty-four hours of the day, unable to move, there hadn't been much else that occupied his thoughts. He had gone over and over all the possible things he could or should have done that day, like a chess player reviewing the moves of a game he should have won. Should he have taken another route home? Should he have driven slower, or even faster? Should he have telephoned the ambulance when he and Norman were standing in the school reception and waiting for Angie to answer the phone?

As usual, these thoughts only led in circles. In the end, someone had called the paramedics and Angie and the baby were saved, so it was doubtful anything he could have done would've made much of a difference. That's what bothered him the most. As with all the moves that he could have made, other than the ones he ultimately had, they probably wouldn't have altered the course of events at all; the final result was always the same—checkmate. It left a bitter taste in his mouth, more so than any of the medicines the nurses had forced down his gullet recently. This was Angie's destiny.

Michael now tore his eyes away from her. "What are the sorts of things we can expect as a result of the stroke?" he asked the doctor, sighing.

Dr. Rouben waited a moment before replying. His expression was still solemn. "Personality changes, short-term memory loss, maybe epilepsy," he said. "We won't know until she wakes."

Michael saw that everyone's attention was focused on Angie. He sensed that they knew what Dr. Rouben really meant was, *if* she wakes. Michael closed his eyes and tried not to think of the worst possible outcomes. He thought of his father, a man who had delivered bad news to his patients for many, many years, and what he would say if he was now on the receiving end of it. He would tell him to think of the positives, Michael mused, to think of the recovery she's already made, and to think of the little girl lying in the cot that needed him to be strong and brave at this time. Michael reached into the cot and caressed the baby's scalp. It seemed to ignite a spark in his tired face. Then he glanced at Angie, shifting awkwardly on his feet. This nightmare, he knew, was far from over.

Dr. Rouben took the opportunity to excuse himself, saying that he had to attend to another patient. Michael shuffled behind the Zimmer frame to a chair at Angie's bedside. Maria pushed the crib between him and Angie, then followed the NUM to the nurses' station, leaving Michael to spend some time alone with his wife.

He took Angie's hand, sandwiching it above and below with his. The ventilator wheezed and an alarm beeped from another patient's monitor. Michael turned his attention to Angie's puffy face. Her eyelids flickered, as if she somehow felt his presence, but it seemed they were too heavy to open fully. He knew the abyss into which she had fallen. He knew the fears that she was experiencing, the utter horror of that dark place, and he hoped and he prayed for a miracle of science to save her. For the first time, he could now imagine what it would be like without her.

He kissed her hand and began to cry.

IT WASN'T UNITL three days later that he actually felt confident enough to take his first steps without the assistance of a nurse or (Nazi) physiotherapist. Struggling through the pain of his hips and stomach and shoulder, he slowly swung his legs out of bed and stood behind the Zimmer frame. His legs were incredibly wobbly, but he stuck to his task and managed to get halfway to the en-suite bathroom before he needed to stop and rest for a minute The patient gown flapped open at the rear like a coat that had been put on backward, and he hoped no one was about to walk into the room and see his bare ass.

Michael clunked the walker forward again. He could not believe how exhausting it was. It was going to be good when he no longer needed to use it. He dreaded to think what it was going to be like when he got old, and he could now appreciate how lucky he had been up to this moment simply to walk. How many times had he taken it for granted? How many other things, like his health, his job, his wife, had he been oblivious to, or less than grateful for, in the past?

He was about to take another step when Norman breezed into the room. Michael gripped the Zimmer frame, steadied himself on his wobbly legs and peered over his shoulder. Norman, in a crimson cardigan, white shirt and navy blue trousers, was holding aloft a black gym bag, presumably containing the spare clothes Michael had asked him to bring. Michael figured that he must have come straight from school, which was confusing because he had assumed that it was the middle of the mid-semester break.

"What's the date today?" Michael asked.

"The 21st," Norman said, putting the gym bag on the bed.

"Wednesday or Thursday?"

"Thursday."

Michael took another laborious step with the Zimmer frame. He placed the walker forward, shuffled behind it, and opened the door to the en-suite bathroom. Before he entered, Norman grabbed the gym bag off the bed and fished out a set of keys from inside.

"I've got some bad news for you," he said, handing the keys to

Michael. "When I went to your house to get your clothes, your front door was open."

"Open? What do you mean?" Michael asked, glancing at the keys in his hand.

"The lock was broken."

"Broken? Who broke it?"

Norman shrugged. "There was nothing taken. The place seemed neat and tidy, so I don't think it was anyone thieving your stuff. It must have been the paramedics when they had to get Angie. I guess they had to break the door down to get in."

Norman then told him that he had arranged for a locksmith to come by later that evening. Michael was grateful. The last thing he wanted was an opportunistic thief to empty the house before he was discharged. He handed the keys back to Norman to keep until the lock was fixed and took the gym bag, threading his left arm through its handles. He told Norman to wait a minute while he changed. Despite the pain of his right shoulder, Michael managed to remove the ridiculous patient gown and slip on a pair of jeans. Packed inside the bag was also a black, short-sleeved shirt. It was going to take too long to button it, so he left it open at the front, gathered his things and struggled out of the bathroom.

Norman was staring out the window, absently leaning over Jessica's crib with his hands clasped behind his back. Michael clunked the frame forward, accidentally banging into the door. Norman turned around. His eyes, Michael saw, were immediately attracted to the massive raw scar that ran the entire length of his abdomen. Coursing like a dry riverbed, it ran down from the pit of his stomach, around his bellybutton and then disappeared into the sea of blue denim. Norman kept staring at the scar, mesmerised. "How many stitches?" he asked.

"None," Michael said, and smiled lopsidedly, "but I do have twenty-three staples."

Norman moved around the side of the bed to get a better view. He bent down to peer at Michael's stomach, hands on knees. Large metal staples pinched together the edges of the scar, running the length of it and giving the impression of rungs on a rope ladder. Norman had a look of utter amazement. He straightened his back and Michael saw his eyes move to the crescent scar on his right cheek, then to the side of his head.

"They did a good job on your ear," he said, stepping out of the way to let Michael shuffle toward the bed. "It doesn't look as if it's about to drop off anymore."

Michael reached up and felt his right ear, immediately struck by a twinge of shooting pain in his right shoulder. "The nurse said it was almost ripped right off," he said, grimacing. "It still feels a bit swollen and numb."

"At least it's lost that horrible gangrenous colour. Bridget thought you were going to lose it," Norman added.

Michael smirked. While Angie remained critical in the ICU, he considered his own state of health the least of his problems. He took a concerned glance at Jessica over by the window, dreading to think how he would cope if Angie didn't pull through. It was something he didn't like to think about, so he concentrated on the laborious task of getting to his bed. He dumped the gym bag onto the bed, then, almost in slow motion, rested the Zimmer frame against the wall near the bedside cabinet and sat down on the edge of the mattress.

If only his stomach and shoulder didn't hurt so much, Michael mused, he'd be able to get out of this place and take his daughter home. Remembering some exercises the physio had taught him to help with his shoulder, he bent his right elbow and began lifting it up and down into the air, like a slowly flapping wing, grimacing every time he did it. In spite of the discomfort, it was still much better than it was, he told Norman, but he still couldn't lift much with it yet. Norman asked when the doctors thought he might be able to check out.

"About another seven or ten days." Michael stopped the exercises and began buttoning up his shirt. "If all goes well."

At the top of his vision, he saw Norman hesitate before asking his next question. Norman shuffled on his feet, glancing up at the blank TV screen, then at Jessica, and finally back at him. "And Angie, how is she doing?"

"Okay, I guess… considering." Michael stopped midway through slipping a button through an eyelet and stared out of the window at the sun, now beginning to set over the parklands. "She's off the ventilator now," he said, recommencing with his buttons. Then he added, "But she still hasn't regained consciousness," and stopped again, staring distantly outside.

When Norman eventually departed for home, Michael went to visit Angie, this time alone. A nurse was taking her blood pressure when he arrived. They wordlessly greeted one another as he took a seat on the opposite side of the bed and took hold of Angie's free hand. Although she had greatly improved, and although she no longer required the ventilator to breathe, she was still receiving her daily nutrients through a tube inserted into her nose, and her bladder was still draining via a catheter into a urinary bag hooked to the nearside bed leg. Nonetheless, she was looking infinitely better than the day he first laid eyes on her. Her face had lost a lot of the puffiness and her skin, though still pale, had recovered a significant degree of colour. The hand he was holding, too, seemed less limp. It was as if life's vital force had returned from whatever dark place it had disappeared to, but Michael wasn't letting his hopes get away from him; she was a long way from recovery yet.

Michael kept holding her hand. The nurse finished taking Angie's blood pressure and returned to the end of the bed to write the results on the medical chart. "Do the neurologists know when she might regain consciousness?" he asked.

The nurse glanced at Angie and shook her head. "We just don't know, Mr. Joseph," she said. "It could be today. It could be a month. It all depends on how severe the stroke was."

Michael wondered how, with all the modern technology at their disposal, the doctors couldn't calculate the extent to which the stroke had affected her. It seemed a simple task, unless they knew a lot less about the brain than they pretended to. He was about to ask another question, when he suddenly felt his hand being squeezed. It was faint, like a brief twitch, but he was so alert to any movement that he would have felt a butterfly land on his skin. He spun back to face Angie. Her eyelids were flickering, briefly and faintly, like the twitching of her hand, as if she was trying to open them.

"Angie, it's me," he said, leaning closer. "Can you hear me?"

Her eyelids flickered again and he could have sworn that she tried to turn her head to face him, but the effort seemed too great. He felt his heart lurch. The nurse went to the other side of the bed, removing a penlight from her top pocket. With her thumb and forefinger, in a kind of reverse pinching motion, she gently pried Angie's right eyelid open and flashed the light into her eyes. Angie's pupils immediately contracted and she moaned, a soft little whimper that was more like a mewing kitten than the irritated complaint of a mature, seven and a half stone lawyer. The nurse repeated the procedure with the other eye. Angie moaned again.

Michael was now as excited as the day he and Angie discovered that they were finally going to be parents. Like the fluttering heartbeat they'd seen on the ultrasound in Dr. Rouben's examination room, Angie's soft whimpers were a distinct and undeniable sign of life. He leaned forward even more, perching so far on the edge of the seat that he almost slipped off, and called out to her once again.

This time, Angie definitely moaned in reply. There was no doubt about it. It sounded just as she sometimes did when he nudged her awake in the morning after a late or sleepless night—petulant and mildly cantankerous, like a cat told to move from its cosy position in front of the fire. The nurse went back to the end of the bed to write down the new observations on the chart, saying to Michael that Angie was making a considerable step towards recovery. Inside, he was chortling with joy. He brought Angie's fingers to his lips and kissed them. He felt a faint, twitch-like squeeze of her hand in reply.

MICHAEL NOW SPENT almost every waking minute of the day at Angie's bedside. He refused the physiotherapist's advice to attend rehabilitation classes in the gymnasium on the ground floor, preferring to hobble to and from the ICU with his Zimmer frame as his only exercise. He knew that he wouldn't need it for much longer, or so he told her; he could feel the strength returning to his legs almost hourly.

Likewise, Angie's progress was remarkably rapid. Given what she'd gone through (the doctors, true to the manner in which they'd drip fed him information over the course of his admission, told him that she had almost died twice on the operating table and needed to be revived with emergency CPR), she had astounded most of the medical staff with the speed in which her condition improved, including the phlegmatic Dr. Rouben, who Michael thought had seen it all and was never surprised at anything.

Michael was still worried, however. He wanted Angie to get better even quicker. As long as she was in hospital, he was always going to be concerned that something unforeseen and untoward would happen. Bad luck seemed to be following him around like a bad smell of late. He wanted Angie out of the ICU and back home as soon as possible where they could put this whole episode behind them. Home meant normality. Home meant all this shit was over and done with and they could finally get their lives back on track and get to the task of raising Jessica, their little angel.

Four days after Angie had made those tentative signs of recovery, Michael trundled with the walker into the ICU to see her sitting in a bedside chair talking to Maria. Cradling Jessica, she had a blanket over her upper legs and abdomen and a pillow behind her head. All the tubes had been removed from her body, including the nasogastric tube, which Michael figured could only mean she was well enough to eat solid food again. She had also adorned the gold crucifix that the nursing staff must have removed when she was rushed to the operating room that fateful night. It dangled over the top of her patient gown, nestling in the gap of her upper cleavage.

Maria heard the Zimmer frame approaching from behind and turned and smiled. Like Angie, who was smiling at Jessica, her face added warmth and light to an otherwise dim room. As Michael perched his backside on the edge of the bed, Maria excused herself and left.

They chatted about this and that, about the hospital food, about the doctors and nurses, and, of course, about when they hoped to be getting home. He could tell, however, that she wanted to get something off her chest. During the course of the last few days, the medical staff had informed Angie of most of the details of her operation and subsequent admission to the ICU. Michael filled her in on whatever detail she was missing, which wasn't much, then proceeded to tell her about his accident and recovery. When he finished, Angie began to tell him what she remembered of the evening before she collapsed and was rushed to hospital. He tried to tell her it wasn't necessary, but she was determined to recount everything that she possibly could. Michael relented, sensing that it was important for her. He figured it was probably as much for her benefit as for his.

Angie's memory hadn't been affected at all, unlike Michael, who was still having minor black spots of recollection of the immediate moments leading up to the accident. She remembered everything prior to the seizure. She had come home from the supermarket with a horrid headache, assuming at first that it wasn't anything more than the beginnings of another migraine. Michael nodded, recalling the conversation on the telephone about it. Then, Angie said, just after she'd put the phone down and turned on the television, she was struck blind. One second she could see the news report of flashing lights in the sky, and the next it was total blackness, as if the power had suddenly been switched off inside the house. She had known immediately that she and the baby were in serious trouble.

Michael asked if it was her that had called the ambulance, but she shook her head and shrugged her shoulders, unable to think whom the mystery caller might have been. She had heard the telephone ring several times, but the first contractions had gripped her stomach like an iron claw; the pain had been inconceivable, the blindness completely disabling, the pressure inside her skull greater than ever, and she had collapsed to the floor. Lying in the foetal position, she had screamed for help for what seemed like forever. The phone kept ringing and she had tried to get up, but all her strength had gone. Then the answering machine cut in and she had heard Michael asking her to pick up the phone. Knowing it was her only hope of saving the baby, with one final effort, she managed to somehow get on her knees and crawl to the telephone, banging her head on the piano leg and grazing her knuckles as she went. But just as she fumbled for the phone, Michael hung up. At that moment she was paralysed with pain, the most terrible contraction of them all having seized her, draining every ounce of her strength, and she collapsed again, this time face first, onto the carpet. Seconds later, she felt blood oozing between her legs—the baby had begun aborting—and she fell back on the only thing she knew what to do, pray to God that Michael could get back home in time. That was when she fell unconscious.

Michael estimated that she must have blacked out around the time he was running to his car in the teachers' parking lot and saw the lights in the sky. Angie now squeezed the gold crucifix. "The next thing I remember was hearing your voice," she said, looking up at him, "and then waking up in here."

He heard shuffling footsteps approach from behind and then a polite clearing of someone's throat. It was the NUM. She was holding a pair of white cotton stockings in her hand, which, she explained, Angie needed to wear to maintain a good circulation in her legs, otherwise the blood would clot and cause a deep vein thrombosis, a DVT. She also explained that Angie was unable to receive injections of heparin to thin her blood, as Michael had, because of the stroke; the risks of causing another bleed inside her brain were too high to take any chances. It was yet one more reason why Michael wanted Angie out of this place and back at home as soon as possible.

"Now, if you don't mind, Mr. Joseph," the NUM said. "Angie's due for her physio appointment in five minutes. She has to keep mobilising, you know."

Michael could sense how exhausted Angie was feeling. He could see the tiredness in her caramel eyes—reliving the incident was seemingly almost as painful as the real event, as he himself could attest from his own experience—and he knew all she wanted was to be left to alone to rest, but what had to be had to be.

He went back to his room as soon as the NUM had rolled the stockings onto Angie's legs, reflecting on what Angie had told him. Her ordeal had been more harrowing than he'd imagined. She'd also been extremely lucky, the extent of which he hadn't fully realised until now. If the paramedics hadn't arrived when they did, she probably wouldn't be here to talk about it. It gave him pause for thought.

# CHAPTER 12

BY THE DAY of his discharge, Michael no longer needed the walker to mobilise, much to his delight. Angie, by contrast, was just beginning to take her first steps with one of her own. The physiotherapist was no more concerned with her condition, Michael noticed, than she had been with his. She had Angie up and out of bed before she could even think of complaining, which, Michael mused, was a minor miracle. Perhaps Angie had met her match. Perhaps, like him, she quickly realised that there was no point in arguing with the physio; she was just going to have to walk. Michael, though, could barely contain himself. He was finally leaving.

The doctors had given him the final okay to discharge earlier in the afternoon. Michael sat on the edge of the bed in jeans and a white T-shirt, the black gym bag between his feet, waiting and thinking anxiously about returning home with Jessica. Running a hand through his now shortened hair, he glanced over his shoulder to see if Norman, his promised transport, was anywhere in sight. From where he sat he could make out the elevators in the empty corridor, their silver doors lined side by side like four mysterious portals into the netherworld. He was beginning to wonder, however, whether he was ever going to step inside one of them and leave this god-forsaken place.

He turned back. Clothed in a pink cotton jump suit, Jessica was lying in the crib near the window, the soft orange rays of the late evening sun stroking her face like a painter's brush, her cherubic cheeks glowing. She was motionless except for the faint rise and fall of her chest beneath the hospital blankets. Like a gathering of guardian angels, get-well cards from family and friends sat on the windowsill above her. To the left of them was a bunch of native Australian flowers arranged in a small wicker basket, which had arrived earlier today for Angie. A small white card dangled from the rim of the basket and he opened it.

> *Dear Angie,*
> *Hope you are regaining strength and good health. We eagerly await your return to work and hope to be introduced to your special little girl.*

Michael wondered why the word "special" was underlined. His face flushed when he saw whose signature it was at the bottom of the card: Stephen Pickering, on behalf of all the staff at Sugarman Klein & Pickering. He was bemused to discover that there was no mention of him, and flicked the card over to see if anymore was written. There was nothing. He thought immediately of throwing the card in the bin, along with the flowers, and then stopped himself. They weren't his gift. Angie would have to decide their fate.

Bored with waiting, he absently perused several other cards. Three were from his parents, one from his uncle and aunty, one from his cousin, Jude, two from Angie's friends, and one from the staff at Wattle Gardens. One card grabbed his attention the most. It had a cartoon picture of a buxom woman standing naked in a doctor's surgery with a thermometer in her mouth, a caption beneath it reading: *But doctor, I only wanted to have my eyes checked.* It was from Norman, almost surely without the knowledge of his wife. Michael chuckled.

Putting the card back onto the windowsill, he glanced outside. On the opposite side of the main road, on which rush hour traffic was still zooming past, eucalypts in the parklands swayed to and fro, as if trying to attract his attention to the shadows reaching across from the cityscape like black reedy fingers snatching at his baby. Michael ran a hand through his short hair, still trying to come to terms with how it felt, and just as uncomfortable with this unusual sense of gloomy paranoia. Even the distant sun sitting atop the tall State Bank Building was like a large orange eye staring at him from behind the lens of a giant magnifying glass. Why was he feeling as if he was being watched? He wasn't normally the suspicious or cagey type. Maybe, he figured, it was these walls; he felt like a canary in a birdcage. It was time he left.

Michael stretched his arms and brought his attention back inside. On the television mounted near the ceiling, the anchorman for Channel 5's five o'clock news was reading the headlines. Michael really wasn't interested in the goings on of the outside world. It was too depressing. As far as he was concerned, he had had enough bad news over the past three weeks to last a lifetime, and in his present frame of mind he didn't care if he missed another news broadcast or a daily tabloid until the day his epitaph was chiselled onto his headstone. The idea appeased him. From this moment on, he was happy to live in ignorance. No news was good news. Perhaps, he half joked, he should take his family to go and live in a monastery, or convent, anywhere secluded where they could shut themselves off from the cruelty of the outside world.

He heard heavy footsteps echo in the corridor behind and he turned just in time to see two policemen hurry past his room. Turning back, he caught a breaking news story on the television cutting to the face of a pretty news reporter. Her shoulder-length blonde hair and large brown eyes reminded him of his own wife recovering in the ICU at the end of the corridor, and in her two-piece suit the resemblance was even more striking. In the background, the yellow-brick façade and the sliding glass doors at the front entrance of St. Mary's Hospital were immediately recognisable. Michael's interest was suddenly perked, despite his recent denunciation of the woes of the outside world.

Following her cue from the anchorman, the reporter stared into the camera and spoke into her microphone. "Less than two hours ago, another baby was abducted from the neonatal intensive care unit here at St. Mary's Hospital."

Michael cast an anxious glance at Jessica. Her eyes were closed and her right thumb was firmly implanted inside her mouth, sleeping peacefully, and he wondered what he would have done had the crib been empty. Fortunately, she'd been with him most of the day, away from the NICU when the other baby was taken. It could easily have been Jessica, though, something that was too horrid to even contemplate. He briefly considered turning the television off; the last thing he needed to hear was news of a kidnapper loose in the hospital. Instead, he continued to watch, transfixed.

A gust of breeze ruffled the reporter's hair and a few loose strands fell onto her face, which she flicked quickly behind her ear. "That makes a total of four newborn babies to have been abducted from this hospital in the past twelve months," she said.

The television screen then split in two, the left half showing an anxious, middle-aged anchorman leaning with his elbows onto the desk in front of him, and the right half showing an attractive blonde standing in front of the hospital, her hair slightly buffeted by a mild evening breeze. "I have with me, Chief Inspector Joseph," she said, "who is in charge of the investigation."

As she turned to her left, the camera panned slightly back and Michael saw his cousin, Jude, resplendent in full police uniform, standing next to her. Jude's face was calm and professional, and his piercing blue eyes seemed to have lost none of their sharpness. Michael tried to recall the last time they'd spoken to each other. Jude certainly hadn't been in to see him at the hospital since the accident, which he thought a little odd; the get-well card standing on the windowsill was the meagre extent to which their communications had amounted to since last Christmas.

"What have you learnt so far about the abductions occurring at this hospital?" the reporter asked, offering Jude the microphone so that he could reply into it.

Jude cleared his throat, as if about to give the speech of his lifetime, and Michael knew by his expression that he was revelling in the opportunity to appear on the news. He always did love the attention, Michael thought with a wry grin. He was forever seeking the adoration of others, especially women, and what better way to get it than on television? He really should have been an actor; Hollywood was just the kind of place where he would have thrived.

"We have some information on the baby abducted today," Jude said. "She is a little girl only three weeks old. Her mother, we believe, is a young woman who had given her up for adoption immediately after birth. The baby was residing in the hospital awaiting the legal papers to be filed before she could be placed into another family, and we have so far been unable to contact her natural parents to tell them the news."

The reporter flicked another loose strand behind her ear. "Is there a possibility that they are connected with the abduction?"

"It's one possibility we need to eliminate." Jude stared directly at the camera. "We don't know if the mother of the child has had second thoughts and decided to reclaim her baby. If this is the case, I would like to assure her that we do not want to prosecute her, only to ask her to come forward so that we can discuss what has happened."

Then the reporter asked a question that Michael presumed was on every viewer's mind. "Do you think there is any connection with the other abductions earlier this year?"

Michael thought he detected a slight smirk grace Jude's face, but it was gone in an instant. It left him feeling disconcerted, though he had no idea why. "At this point in time we believe them to be separate incidents," Jude said, quickly glancing at the reporter, then back at the camera, "and we are treating them as such."

"But what kind of guarantee can you give to mothers who are about to have their baby here at St. Mary's that something like this will not happen again?"

Jude scratched his nose and shifted his weight from one foot to the other. "We are working closely with the security department of St. Mary's Hospital to ensure that something as terrible and distressing as this cannot and does not happen again," he said, and Michael recalled the two policemen he had just seen hurry past in the corridor a few minutes ago.

"And how are you doing that?"

Again Michael detected a smirk on Jude's face. It was gone in a flash, and maybe only someone who had known him since childhood, someone who was acquainted with his facial expressions better than most, would have noticed it. Michael knew that look. He knew Jude was absolutely revelling in all the attention. He hadn't changed. This was not about the abducted baby. It was about getting his face on television and getting another promotion. This was just a stunt. Jude's flagrant opportunism was appalling and Michael was revolted at the depths to which his cousin would delve to further his own cause. He clenched his fists, suddenly feeling the urge to run downstairs and flatten him in front of the camera. He wondered if Jude would sulk away, like the time he hit him in the summer of '75, or if he would have him arrested on the spot and thrown in jail.

"The security department is providing us with all the security footage they have captured on CCTV cameras," Jude said, "and we will be sifting through them over the next 48-hours, or so. Hopefully, we will get a positive ID on the man or woman who took this baby."

Michael reckoned he had seen enough of Jude's showmanship. Just as the camera panned from Jude to the reporter, he picked up the remote control that was resting on the bedside cabinet and pressed the standby button. The TV screen went blank.

At that moment, Norman suddenly bowled in through the open door. His cheeks and brow were flushed with a shiny film of sweat, as if he had spent the whole day in the sun and just realised he'd forgotten to use sunscreen lotion. He told Michael that he'd heard the news on the radio and seen the police and TV crew outside. "It wasn't Jessica, was it?" he asked, panting.

Michael tossed the remote onto the bed covers and told Norman to relax. Jessica was safe and there was no reason to get so worked up. Norman eyed the crib beneath the window, and breathed a loud sigh of relief. Michael followed his gaze. Oblivious to all the commotion, Jessica was peacefully and contentedly sucking her thumb, her eyes closed. As Norman patted the sweat off his brow with a handkerchief, Michael picked the gym bag off the floor and gathered the get-well cards and flowers from the windowsill, almost throwing them into the bag in his haste to leave. Then he gently lifted Jessica out of the cot and cradled her in his arm.

"Let's go say bye-bye to mummy before we go," he said to her.

Norman followed him into the corridor, just as one of the elevators in the alcove announced its arrival with a *ding!* A female cop hurried past, smiling at the baby. Michael smiled back and Jessica yawned and smacked her lips.

"When do the docs think they'll let Angie go home?" he heard Norman ask from behind.

"Ten days, maybe seven at the earliest," he said over his shoulder, thinking how glad he'll be when all this shit was over and they could all be home as one big happy family. "They're waiting for me to leave so they can give her my room. She doesn't need to be in ICU any longer."

Barely a moment after he finished speaking, a suavely dressed man in suit and tie called out to him. He had just emerged from the elevator and was carrying a bunch of white roses. Michael glanced over at him but didn't reply, assuming he was yelling out to someone else down the corridor. The guy called out again. This time, Michael and Norman stopped and turned around.

"Excuse me, sorry, but are you Angie Joseph's husband?" the guy asked, catching up with them.

Michael hesitated, trying to figure out where he had seen this man before. The blonde hair was immaculately cut, not a strand out of place, reminding him of Dr. Rouben in a certain kind of way, though a little younger, somewhere between thirty-five and forty. The man in the suit quickly proffered his hand. It was firm and a little too eager, Michael mused, like an over excited vicar welcoming a new believer into his rapidly declining flock.

"I'm Stephen Pickering," the guy said, smiling broadly. "I thought I recognised you. We met several years ago at a staff and partners evening. I'm Angie's boss."

Michael was unsmiling. He recalled the same night when he had been introduced to Angie's ex-fiancé for the first time. He also recalled every bad thing Angie had ever said about him. His anger quickly flared. The guy had some nerve, didn't he? He knew as well as anyone Angie couldn't stand the sight of him. Why was he here? What was suddenly so important that he had to leave his office and come to the hospital?

Stephen immediately turned his attention to the baby in Michael's arms. "And this must be your *special* little girl," he said, smiling at her. "She's very cute," and he looked up at Michael. "You and Angie must be very happy."

Michael shuffled awkwardly, and said, deliberately pithy, "Yes. We are."

Stephen suddenly picked up on Michael's increasing antagonism. He held out the roses and took a step back. "I, uh, I just wanted to give these to Angie and to wish her good health and all that, and see that she and the baby were recovering from their ordeal."

Michael took the flowers, holding them uncomfortably with the hand in which he was also holding the gym bag. He thought of the card and flowers that had arrived earlier and his smile was thin and without meaning, not trying very hard at all to mask his disdain. "I'll let her know," he said.

There was a brief moment of hesitancy before Stephen spoke. "Well, okay, it was nice to see you, and especially nice to see your baby. I guess I'll see you soon, I hope."

Michael nodded, still smiling as he had, and watched Stephen turn around and walk back to the elevator-well.

When Stephen was out of earshot, Norman asked, "What's the story between you and Angie's boss?" He was also watching Stephen leave. Then he faced Michael. "If looks could kill, he'd be lying on the floor in a pool of blood."

Michael turned to him, suppressing his anger. "It's just that he's got a nerve coming here to see Angie when he knows just as well as anyone she can't stand being within shouting distance of him," he said. "Did you know that she used to date him before she met me? She was even engaged to him, but they had a big falling out. He's a lecherous creep."

"Maybe he's just trying to make it up to her, you know, with her nearly dying and all that."

Michael shook his head, squinting, as if trying to see into the back of Stephen's head and figure out his real motives. He didn't trust Stephen Pickering as far as he could throw him. "There's something else on his mind," he said. "I don't know what, but I could see it in his eyes."

Michael let it go and began heading toward the ICU. The double doors were only another fifty or sixty paces ahead and he put the roses in a bin as he walked past. Norman was lagging behind, taking his time looking over his shoulder at Angie's boss as he disappeared around the corner. Michael hurried him along, not wanting to spend a minute longer than was necessary in this place.

He suddenly felt quite chilly.

THE SUN HAD all but set when Norman's car turned onto Christopher Street. Venus was twinkling and the moon was rising above the hills and rooftops to the east. Michael glanced at the redbrick letterbox at the top of the driveway as they pulled in and idled past. It was empty, which was odd; there should've been at least a couple of weeks' worth of letters and junk mail spilling out of it. Did it really matter, though? Why was he concerning himself over such mundane matters? He thought no more of it, happy just to be out of the hospital, and he turned his attention back to the driveway ahead of him. The headlights were reflecting brilliantly from the rear of Angie's red Corolla until Norman flicked them off and killed the engine. He sighed with relief. He was home at last.

Michael peered down at Jessica and caressed her cheek. She blinked awake in his arms and stared up at him, as if instinctively sensing his change of mood. All day he had been dreaming of this moment. He was going to go inside, feed Jessica, put her to sleep in her new cot, maybe grab a beer with Norman, maybe even sit down at the telly and order a takeout pizza. Then he was going to go to bed, early, and get as much sleep as he could before Jessica's four o'clock morning feed.

Before he opened the door, Michael caught a reflection of himself in the passenger side window. He studied it for a brief moment, the nose that hooked slightly, the firm jaw line, the high brow now more evident with the shortened hair. The stitches had been removed some days ago from his ear and face, and the remaining scar on his cheek was a fine, pink crescent, like a backwards C. All in all, he figured his face was about as normal as it could have been considering the events of the past three weeks.

As he opened the passenger door and swung his feet out, grimacing and grunting like a wounded bull trying to get to its feet, Michael struggled to stand with the baby. Norman offered to take Jessica, but Michael refused his help, finally getting out. His stomach was still less than one hundred percent, and still a wee bit sore; it felt kind of like someone stabbing him in the gut whenever he tried to stand from a sitting position or whenever he wanted to sit up in bed. His hip still wasn't totally pain free, either, but it was really only a minor inconvenience and he wasn't going to let it hamper his progress. He grabbed the gym bag from the back seat and wandered to the top of the driveway to check the letterbox, just to make sure it really was empty, which it was.

Norman, meanwhile, went to the rear of the car, the shadow from the neighbour's maple tree on the opposite side of the street partially covering his face as he opened the trunk. To Michael's surprise and gratefulness, Norman removed several plastic supermarket bags bursting with groceries. Beaming, he held the bags aloft. "I looked in your refrigerator the other day and it smelled worse than a rubbish truck," he said. "I couldn't let you come home on Thanksgiving Day to mouldy food in the house, now could I?"

As Norman shut the trunk, Michael mused at the speed in which time had passed. Was it really a year since Norman invited him around to his place for a Thanksgiving meal his wife had cooked? He closed the flap of the letterbox and headed across the overgrown front lawn toward the porch, full of thought. A lot of things had happened in that year, things he was still having trouble remembering with any clarity. The accident had jumbled his memories a bit, shaken them around like pieces of a jigsaw puzzle in a box and leaving him now to fit them back into sequential order, fill in the missing gaps so to speak. Most of the pieces were there, except for a memory blackout of the three days he was in ICU and a hazy recollection of the immediate hour preceding the accident. He just hoped, that with time, the missing memories would come back.

Almost immediately, it occurred to him that he had missed his ultrasound appointment, and he exclaimed his anguish out loud. "The doctor I saw in the ER wanted me to have my kidneys checked," he said to Norman, who was several steps behind. "Remember I told you that the day I had the accident? He wanted to see why my blood pressure was so high and find out why I was retaining water."

Norman just shrugged in reply. Michael headed slowly toward the front porch with Jessica and the gym bag in hand, thinking that he probably had a good excuse for missing the appointment. Then he recalled his father complaining on numerous occasions about the number of ungracious patients who never cancelled their appointments, how they cost him thousands and thousands in lost revenue each year, and he figured he ought to ring the ER department in the next few days or so and apologise out of politeness. As he rummaged his pocket for his keys, a yellow Renault drove past the house from the direction of the city, its headlights momentarily blinding both he and Norman, and also flashing onto a white transit van shrouded in the orange glow of the streetlight beneath which it was parked. On the van's side, Michael was able to read a sign: MAD HATTER'S LAWN MOWING SERVICE— MAD SERVICE AT A MAD PRICE! He thought of giving them a call, too. The back garden was probably a complete jungle by now, if the grass on the front lawn was anything to go by, and, like most things to do with the house, he couldn't see where he was going to find the time in the next few weeks to do it himself.

Stepping up onto the front porch, he let the gym bag fall onto the welcome mat and removed the house keys from his front pocket. The jingle unlocked a memory of last Thanksgiving Day and the first time he entered the fertility clinic. Had he known that day what he knew now, knowing what he and Angie would have to go through over the ensuing twelve months—the anxiety, the heated arguments, the aches and pains, the vomiting, the pre-eclampsia, the emergency caesarean section and, of course, the accident—he probably would have had second thoughts about doing it again. He peered down at Jessica, and immediately thought otherwise. There really wasn't any doubt. He would do it all again tomorrow if he could.

Norman stepped up to the porch laden with groceries. To Michael, he seemed more anxious than normal. "Are you going to open the door," Norman said, "or are we going to stand outside all night?"

Michael slid the key into the lock, taking note of how new and shiny it looked against the chipped and splintered doorframe around its edges; the paramedics must have given the door an almighty kick to get it open. He picked up the gym bag and pushed the door open, somewhat anxious at what state the house would be in. He flicked the light switch and saw that nothing had changed: the faded yellow and white striped wallpaper, the thin blue carpet, and the black hole past the grandfather clock at the end of the hallway—the kitchen—was just as he remembered. If Angie had told him a month ago that he would be glad to walk in and see these walls and floors one day, he would never have believed her. Yet, it was true. Even the familiarity of something he almost detested was now remarkably soothing.

As Norman waddled to the kitchen with the grocery bags, Michael tossed the gym bag through the open bedroom door. It looped into the darkness and landed with a soft thud. Then he went to the baby's bedroom and switched on the light. Jessica's layette was just as he had left it three weeks ago. His gaze moved from the wallpaper, mainly white with large pink flowers, to her wooden cot in the middle of the room. Several toy animals looked out between its bars like imprisoned beasts in a zoo, arranged around the pillow, which, like the sheets, was as pink as the jumpsuit Jessica was wearing. As he laid Jessica in the cot, she made some smacking sounds with her lips. His eye caught a little red light flashing on and off near one of the toys. It was the voice-activated baby monitor. He drew the curtains closed and switched the baby lamp on, then flicked off the main light and went to the kitchen to get Jessica a bottle.

Norman, he saw, had dumped the grocery bags on top of the divider and had already stored most of the groceries away. Norman was now opening the refrigerator, on which Michael read the words of the magnets: GOD GIVES WHAT'S RIGHT—NOT WHAT'S LEFT! and: JESUS LOVES YOU!

Sure, he thought, shaking his head. That's why his wife nearly died giving birth and had a small haemorrhage in her brain. That's why he nearly died in a car accident and had a scar as long as the River Murray running down his stomach. One of the first things he was going to do, he decided, was throw those goddamn happy-clappy fridge magnets in the bin before Angie arrived home. He was going to rid himself of everything that annoyed him, starting tonight.

He wandered around the divider to the dining table, bypassing Norman as he put a carton of milk into the refrigerator. On the table was a pile of about a dozen letters or so, mainly bills and bank statements. The world stops for no man, he mused. "You think of everything, don't you?" he said, recalling the empty letterbox outside.

Norman glanced over. "Oh, that wasn't me," he said. "I didn't bring in the mail."

"Then who did?" Michael asked, beginning to sort through them. He happened upon the telephone bill, went to open it, then decided he didn't want to worry about bills tonight.

Norman shrugged and went back to the divider. "Maybe your

mum and dad. Who else has keys to your house?" he said, and Michael thought that he was more or less right, that they had probably come over at least once or twice whilst he and Angie were in the hospital to check out the house and make sure everything was okay.

Michael tossed the letter he was holding on top of the rest of them. Norman's hands were now inside one of the grocery bags. Next to him, on top of the microwave, was a grey box no bigger than a cigarette packet, the speaker for the baby intercom. Through it, Michael could hear Jessica smacking her lips and sucking hungrily on something, presumably her thumb. He slapped his forehead with the palm of his hand, momentarily disappointed with his forgetfulness. He had left her bottle in the gym bag.

Michael hurried to the bedroom whilst Norman stacked away the remaining groceries. When he returned with the bottle, Norman offered him a beer. They drank to their friendship, and then Michael told Norman to go and put his feet up on the couch and relax. He would come and join him after he had quickly fed the baby. While he fixed Jessica's feed, Michael heard the television switching on in the lounge and Norman flicking through its channels. He took another sip of beer and wiped his mouth with the back of his hand.

"It's good to be back," he said to the kitchen. "No more shit and no more bad news. From now on it's going to be plain sailing. It can't get any worse than it has."

FEEDING THE BABY and getting her dressed in clean pyjamas took longer than Michael had anticipated. While he was burping her, Jessica vomited on his T-shirt, and when he changed her diaper she urinated on his hand. He could have sworn there was a cheeky glint in her eyes when she did. Finally, after rocking and singing her a lullaby, she was sleeping peacefully.

He quickly showered and put on some warmer clothes—jeans, long-sleeve shirt, blue sweater—then joined Norman in the lounge room. Neither of them could be bothered cooking, so they ordered a takeout pizza to eat while they watched the highlights of the cricket.

At some stage, slouched with Norman on the couch, Michael glanced lazily over his shoulder at the Elvis clock on the wall. Elvis swung his hips from side-to-side and sung into his microphone. It was already nine o'clock. It was surprising at how time just disappeared with a baby, as if she swallowed seconds and minutes with every bottle he put into her mouth. Unbelievably, it was almost time for a feed again.

Norman belched, a can of beer in one hand, the other patting his belly. Michael wiggled himself into a sitting position and picked up the now empty pizza box lying on the carpet between the television and his feet.

"I hope you tipped the delivery boy," Norman said, and Michael scoffed, as if what he had just heard was anathema to everything Norman stood for. "I wouldn't want to upset someone who looked like a member of the Hell's Angels if I were you."

"He did look pretty mean," Michael said, recalling the goatee beard and tattoos on the guy's forearms when he handed him the money for the pizza. "He wasn't riding a Harley though, just a scooter. I saw it parked behind that white van outside."

"Yeah, but did you tip him?"

"Are you joking?" Michael stood with a little discomfort and made his way toward the hallway. "I learnt everything I know from the Norman Page School of Misers."

"Don't say I didn't warn you," Norman said, belching again. "That guy looked as if he had some pretty mean friends. You don't want to piss him off by not tipping him, do you? When he finishes his shift, he might just be angry enough to get them all together and pay you another visit with some sawn-off shotguns and baseball bats."

Michael rolled his eyes. Norman's melodramatics were the last thing he needed to hear right now. He had enough on his plate without having to worry about a deranged pizza delivery boy returning to collect his tip. Sipping his beer, Norman picked up the remote control and flicked the channel, claiming that he wanted to see what was happening with the baby abducted from St. Mary's earlier today. Michael exited into the hallway. He heard the familiar theme music heralding the nine o'clock news on Channel 5 drifting toward him as he passed the door to Jessica's layette. The baby lamp in the corner of her room cast a soft glow, like a full moon veiled with wispy clouds, and he could just make out her tiny, shadowy shape as she slept on her back in her new cot.

The grandfather clock chimed the new hour when he entered the kitchen. He hastily folded the pizza box in half and shoved it into the rubbish bin beneath the kitchen sink. He smirked, thinking how Angie would have chided him for all the calories he had just ingested. Then again, it wasn't as if he needed to go on a diet for a while, was it? He had lost enough weight in the past three weeks without having to worry about that.

Just as he was about to return to the lounge room, his eye caught on something to his left. He checked his stride, moved to the refrigerator and peeled off the magnets, throwing them into the bin with the pizza box. There was immense satisfaction in that simple act, as if he had finally rid himself of some oppressive weight around his neck.

Suddenly, Norman shouted to Michael. It was something about an update on the kidnapping. Michael hastened to the lounge just in time to see the familiar, weather-beaten face of the anchorman, Max Cessini, introducing the news flash. He turned to face a television monitor on which the reporter could be seen standing outside the main entrance to St. Mary's Hospital. Michael rounded the couch and sat back down. It was the same woman, he noticed, that he had seen earlier interviewing Jude. The hospital's façade was almost lost in the darkness behind her, but the entrance was brightly lit and it illuminated her blonde hair like a golden fleece. She held a microphone to her parted lips, which, he noted, were painted fiery red.

Norman was about to say something, but Michael silenced him, holding up his hand. It seemed that the reporter had some dramatic news on the identity of the person responsible for the abduction. Michael leant forward in his seat and put his elbows on his knees. Norman crossed his legs, left over right.

"The police have just released this photograph taken by the CCTV security cameras in the hospital earlier today," the reporter said. A black and white photo flashed onto the screen. "It shows the woman the police are trying to contact for questioning about the abduction."

Michael stared at the photograph. He could suddenly feel the hairs on the back of his neck beginning to stand. He could also feel his face losing its colour, as if that damn tube was still stuck up his nostril and draining all the blood from his face. The shot was taken in one of the hospital corridors from an angle looking down. It showed a woman with a blonde bob who wore a pair of black-rimmed glasses and a dress that came down to her knees, which Michael instantly recognised as a cleaner's uniform. Over her shoulder was slung a large white laundry sac, almost certainly inside which was the unfortunate kidnap victim. Although her pretty face was staring down at her sandshoes, a dark beauty spot could clearly be discerned above her left upper lip. Despite the blonde wig, she was immediately recognisable—Maria Sanchez, Dr. Rouben's assistant, the midwife who had been helping him and Angie over the past year.

The photo was replaced by the live image of the reporter standing in front of the hospital. "The police aren't saying much, but they have stated that they believe the woman in the photograph is an employee of the hospital. She is only wanted for questioning and they have refused to divulge her identity. They say that at this moment she is not a suspect and they have not issued a warrant for her arrest."

Once again the photograph flashed onto the television screen. Michael shook his head in disbelief and shifted uneasily in his chair. Notwithstanding the clever disguise, there was no mistaking who it was. As with any truth that was unpleasant, he didn't want to believe it; but it was definitely Maria. His mouth was feeling quite dry and his brow, like his palms, was suddenly quite moist, as the camera now focused on the anchorman. Max Cessini's face was lined with professional concern and his elbows were resting on the news desk in front of him.

"Are the police giving us their thoughts on a motive?" he asked.

The screen switched once again to the reporter. She nodded and smiled and kept holding the microphone to her mouth. "The police aren't willing to come out and directly say what they believe just yet," she said, staring at the camera. "There are lots of theories floating around at the moment, from a lonely woman desperate to have a child of her own, to kidnapping for ransom. But the most bizarre one of all going around, and I have to say it's just a theory, not fact, is that she is a member of a satanic cult who sacrifice human babies and children to the devil."

Michael swallowed a lump in his throat. "I… I know that woman."

Norman glanced at him, then back at the television. Michael, too, kept staring at the screen, unable to tear his eyes from it. The reporter was standing before the camera listening to another question the anchorman was asking, but he wasn't paying attention to it. "That woman who abducted the baby," Michael said, running his hand through his hair, "was one of the midwives who helped us with the pregnancy."

He suddenly stopped. This whole thing was too creepy. He couldn't watch any more. He turned slowly to Norman, who was staring at him with vicarious angst, and told him to turn off the telly. Norman quickly searched for the remote control and found it in the crack of the cushions between he and Michael. He fumbled it and, after three attempts at pressing the standby button, the TV went blank.

Michael kept shaking his head and running his hand through his hair. He had now entered the realms of the unbelievable, that place of incredulity where tragedy had been avoided only by the barest of margins. That place where executives were late for planes that crashed on takeoff, where tourists checked out of hotels minutes before the walls and ceiling collapsed, where skydivers whose parachutes failed to open fell into haystacks and survived. Except now he was there. He was now that fortunate executive, that disbelieving tourist, that fluky skydiver. Maria could have abducted Jessica any moment she chose. She could have done anything she wanted. The impact of this realisation was truly sickening. Worse, the reporter had said that Maria was a member of a satanic cult that made human sacrifices to the devil. He shuddered to think what she was doing right now with the abducted baby, the baby that could just as easily have been Jessica.

Suddenly, the telephone rang on the foot table behind the couch. Norman visibly jumped and Michael felt his heart skip a beat. "Who could that be?" Michael said, as he and Norman stared at each other. "No one knows I'm out of the hospital yet."

Norman shrugged, but Michael thought his eyes were telling a different story. The phone kept shrilling. "Maybe it's your dad," Norman said, diverting his gaze to the telephone. "Maybe he phoned the hospital and they told him you checked out."

It sounded plausible, but Michael still didn't want to answer it. "I'll get it for you," Norman said, quickly getting up. He picked it up before it cut to the answering machine. "Hello… yes, this is Michael Joseph's house… I'm a friend. He's busy at the moment. Can I take a message? … Uh ha… yes… okay." There was a pause and Michael could hear the muffled voice of a woman speaking on the other end. "Really? When?" Norman asked. Then, "Oh God… okay… uh ha," and Norman seemed to wobble slightly. He steadied himself, putting his free hand on top of the piano. Michael couldn't see his face because his back was turned, but from the sound of his voice he could tell he was close to tears. "Uh ha… okay… I'll tell him. He'll be there as soon as possible."

Norman slowly replaced the handset, as if it was an expensive piece of fragile China, and started to bite his nails. When he turned, Michael saw that his assumption had been right—Norman's eyes were brimming with tears. Michael's head was now a swirl of emotions and thoughts of impending doom.

Norman wiped his eye with a knuckle, then said, "That was the hospital, Mikey." He seemed unable to say what was bothering him. He kept biting his nails, and wiped another tear that had fallen down his cheek, this time with the palm of his hand.

Eventually he spoke, choking on words that were barely audible. "Angie… She… she's dead."

# CHAPTER 13

MICHAEL STRUGGLED TO gain any semblance of normality. He now understood what people meant when they said their world had turned upside down. The walls of the room seemed to be spinning. The floor was rising and falling beneath his feet, as if in the process of exchanging places with the ceiling. It was as if the entire house was being tipped over on its roof. In fact, it was rather reminiscent of the time he and Angie went to a theme park on their honeymoon and ridden on a roller coaster with a double loop. Sitting on the couch now, it felt like he was turning up and around and inside out, a white-knuckle ride inside his own lounge room. He felt neither despair, nor grief, nor anything he normally associated with the death of a loved one. It seemed he had no time to feel anything apart from mind-numbing fear, like those two, nerve-jangling minutes at the theme park. He grabbed hold of the armrest and hoped to ride out this uneasy sensation.

It seemed to help. Within a few seconds, the whirling, spinning motion slowed to a halt, giving him time to settle.

As quickly as his mind returned to normal, despair caught up with him. A tear dropped onto his cheek and coursed down to the corner of his mouth. He wiped it away with a flick of his finger and glanced at the clock on the yellow and white striped wall. Elvis sang into his microphone and swung his hips one way then the other, back and forth, in a mournfully hypnotic rhythm. To Michael, every fraction of its arc seemed arthritic and unbearably slow. Only three minutes had passed since the phone call; it seemed like three eternities in purgatory. Finally, after taking a deep breath, he stood and asked Norman to repeat what had been said on the telephone.

Norman was staring distantly at something on the carpet, mouth agape. Then, like a dormant robot jolted into action, he looked up, and said, "It was one of the nurses in the ICU."

Michael wondered whose job it was to deliver the bad news to grieving relatives, whether it was the NUM or whether she delegated it to someone more junior. He took another deep breath and ran his hand through his hair again. "What did she say, exactly?"

"She Angie said had a clot in her leg, a DVT or something that they didn't know about. It was a complication of her surgery."

Michael glanced at the clock once more. It was almost a quarter after nine. He recalled the NUM mentioning something about DVT's a few days ago when he had paid Angie a visit to her bedside, and he tried to remember more details of what she said, but couldn't. One thing he knew, she certainly didn't mention the fact that Angie was in danger of dying from it.

Norman looked suddenly exasperated. "But how can a clot in the leg kill anyone?" He spoke so fast that the words merged almost unintelligibly. "It doesn't make sense."

Michael shrugged, a defeated gesture, like someone who had survived a devastating illness and was told it would take a lifetime to pay off the medical costs. "Does anything in life make sense? The fact is, Angie's dead." He ran a hand through his hair, and sighed. "I have to get to the hospital. I guess they'll want me to sign some papers."

Norman continued to stare at him, surveying Michael's morose face. "Are you sure you're okay to drive?" he asked. "Do you want me to give you a lift? I don't mind and you could use the company, I think."

Michael shook his head. "No, mate, I need you to stay here and look after Jessica."

"You sure? I mean, you know what I'm like with kids."

Michael patted him on the shoulder, and said, "You'll be fine. I trust you. She won't be a problem and, besides, the last thing I want to do is take her back to that place. I don't want her to see... well, you know..."

Michael slowly picked up a set of car keys lying on top of the telephone directory next to the phone, head bowed. Every flexion and extension of his joints was an apotheosis of pain. He slowly exited into the hallway and stepped out onto the porch, listening to the crickets and the efficient click of the new lock as the front door closed. His mind was a fog of emotion. He probably wasn't in any fit state to drive, despite what he had said to Norman. He really didn't care, though. He didn't care if he drove into another tree and killed himself. At least he wouldn't suffer anymore. The idea was incredibly seductive. He'd get in the car without putting on his seatbelt, reverse out of the driveway, accelerate away fast and aim directly for the eucalypt at the end of the street. It would all be over in a matter of seconds. There'd be no more grief, no more pain, just nothing, blissful nothing.

At Angie's car, he glanced into the rear and saw the baby seat they'd installed in preparation for bringing her home. It jerked him out from the mire of despair in which he'd been wallowing. Jessica needed her father; she was dependent on him for everything. He couldn't just leave her to grow up an orphan. He had responsibilities. Even if everything threatened to pull him under, he would stay strong and keep his head above the waves for Jessica. She would be his purpose in continuing to live. They would get through this horrid time together. It was the way it had to be.

With newfound resolve, he unlocked the driver's door and jumped in behind the wheel. He turned the keys in the ignition, but it didn't start. The starter engine didn't even click in. There was nothing, no sound, no life, as if the car had died with its owner. He tried again with the same result.

Two minutes after he had left the house, Michael was back at the front door and unlocking it. "I think the battery's dead," he said to Norman when he entered the lounge room. Norman was sitting on the couch and had turned the TV back on. "Angie must have accidentally left the lights on. Anyway, your car's parked behind. Do you mind if I borrow it?"

Norman reached into his trouser pocket and removed his car keys, exchanging them with the set Michael was holding. Michael told Norman that he would see him in about an hour. Then he turned and made his way out of the house again to Norman's car. The engine growled awake, whining as he reversed out of the driveway.

197

IT TOOK LONGER than Michael expected to return from the hospital. According to the dashboard clock, it was now 10:24 p.m. It was the end of a day he knew he would never forget. Hurrying across the front lawn to the porch, he winced a little from the stab of pain in his belly. The partial moon had drifted higher and further westward, now floating like a luminous Christmas tree angel above a tall eucalypt at the city end of the street. He gave it only a fleeting glance.

At first he wasn't aware of anything untoward, but as he neared the porch a strange, irrational feeling of dread overcame him. He stopped in his tracks and looked at the house, expecting to see the luminescent flicker of light from the TV shine through the lounge room window. It was just dark. In fact, the whole house was drowning in darkness. It had an atavistic, silent feel to it, like an old farmhouse that had been vacant for several years. Worse, like a cemetery on Halloween.

On any other night, the darkness would not have concerned him too much. Not tonight. This was one Thanksgiving Day that could become a chapter in a book on the weird and the bizarre. He could feel that something about the house was odd, very odd, something that defied any rational explanation, and he hoped that this feeling of anxiety was just an echo of all the problems of the past three weeks. He could feel that his subconscious was trying to courier an important message, but his mind was as jammed as the highway had been that night he had the accident and the message simply wasn't getting through.

Stepping onto the porch, he rapped on the front door for Norman to let him in. Without warning, the door creaked slightly ajar. He took a surprised step backward. Then tentatively, as if not sure what he was seeing was real, he pushed the door with the tip of his index finger. It swung open.

Inside was pitch black. All the lights seemed to have been switched off. As he cautiously stepped forward, avid silence greeted him like a growling black dog. No sound came from the lounge room, and the atavistic feeling he had just had a moment ago returned with sudden force. His hackles were suddenly rising. He called out to Norman, but there was no answer.

He stepped into the hallway and groped for the light switch. Although the darkness disappeared instantly, the silence remained, if not exaggerated. His senses felt sharp, as if flicking on the light switch had turned on an amplifying mechanism in his brain, like turning the volume up on a stereo system. The brightness in the hallway seemed preternatural in its intensity, as did the musty aroma of the old blue carpet lining the floorboards. Even the tic, tic, tic of the grandfather clock at the end of the hall was louder than normal, like clicking fingers in his ears, but it was the vacuous silence between the seconds that disconcerted him the most.

He hoped Norman hadn't left Jessica alone by herself. He had trusted him to stay and look after her. He called out again, now finding it difficult to swallow. There was no answer.

His heart began to beat a steady double tempo. At the end of the illuminated hallway the kitchen was a chasm of darkness, like a burnt head at the end of a matchstick. He continued to call for Norman, this time softer, more uncertain, but still with no response, only the rhythmical tic, tic, tic of the old grandfather clock. To his right, the lounge room was as dark as the kitchen, likewise the bedroom to his left. He turned on the bedroom light and peered in. At first he thought everything was in order, but then he saw that several shirts and underpants and socks were flung haphazardly over the purple quilt, some even sprawled on the floor, thrown there in haste. He figured Norman had been searching for something and came up short. But what could he have wanted? Why was he in such a rush?

He backed out of the bedroom, taking one final look before venturing further down the hallway. He glanced over his shoulder, sensing something behind him. There was nothing untoward; he was just scaring himself. His hesitant, creeping footsteps creaked down the hallway. He couldn't recall the floorboards ever creaking so loudly, nor could he recall ever being in a situation that was beginning to scare him as much as this. The nightmare of the three hooded strangers stealing his baby was comparable, but that was just a dream, it wasn't real, and...

And then he stopped in his tracks. "Jessica!" he whispered, and rushed to her room.

As he entered, he trod on something hard in the doorway, twisting his ankle with a painful twang. For some reason, the baby lamp in the corner of the room was off. He groped for the light switch near the doorframe and felt his foot land on something else, something soft. The light flicked on and he peered down. The head of a toy hippopotamus was poking out from beneath his foot like a squashed beetle. He held back a choked, nervous laugh and lifted his gaze to the cot in the middle of the room, blinking twice before his mind could record the reality of what he was seeing. The pink linen sheets and blanket were thrown back like a large, gaping wound. A toy lion was lying at the foot of the cot upside down, its head caught between the bars on the opposite side and its legs in the air like a dead carcass. Jessica was gone.

Michael hurried forward. His right foot was smarting with its recent twist, but he ignored it. He reached the cot and caressed the linen, as if trying to feel her presence, as if trying to convince himself she wasn't really gone, that his baby was still lying between the sheet.

"Norman! What have you done with my baby?" he screamed. "Where have you taken her?"

Michael heard a noise from behind and whirled around. There was nothing there, just the vacant doorway framing the faded yellow and white striped wallpaper on the hallway wall opposite the room, empty and devoid of meaning, without soul, like he felt right now.

Then he heard it again—a shuffle, as if a heavy trunk was being dragged along the carpet. The doorframe remained vacant, except it wasn't as completely vacant as he had first thought. The solid object he had twisted his foot on when he rushed into the room was on the ground there, the baby monitor. The shuffling continued, bringing his attention back to the hallway. He tried to guess what could be making that noise.

Suddenly, he remembered the savage-looking pizza delivery guy, his tattoos, his goatee beard, and he remembered what Norman had said earlier in the lounge about him returning with his friends. Was this what had happened? Had they come and exacted their revenge on Norman while he was at the hospital?

The shuffling noise stopped just outside the door. He called for Norman once again.

Still no answer, but he heard a creak, slow and stretched, like a door on rusty hinges swinging in the breeze. The soft booms of his heartbeat sounded like distant cannon fire and he could feel their recoiling blows beneath his blue woollen jumper.

All of a sudden the doorframe was filled with a man staggering toward him, his face contorted with rage and his hand held high into a fist. Michael yelped in fright and the cannon booms were replaced with the rat-a-tat of machine gun fire. He reflexively shielded his face with his arms, waiting for the blow, but as the bellowing madman rushed in, Michael noticed the crimson cardigan he was wearing. "Norman?" he blurted.

Just as surprised Norman lowered his fist, but wasn't able to stop his lumbering momentum forward, and for a horrid second the picture of himself being flattened beneath the heavy frame of his good friend flashed in Michael's mind. Norman, however, surprisingly nimble on his feet, quickly sidestepped and altered direction, brushing Michael's damaged shoulder. Michael grunted with the pain of the collision and quickly dropped his defences to rub the injured joint, but as Norman lurched to a halt and steadied himself, Michael's eyes widened with alarm.

"What the hell happened to you?" Michael said, examining the mess of bloodied hair behind Norman's right ear. It had clotted into a dark crimson paste, reminding Michael of tomato base on a pizza, and several large spots of blood had dripped onto the collar of his white shirt. It looked like he had been hit from behind with a baseball bat.

Norman lifted his hand to feel the tender lump behind his ear, wincing. For several seconds he kept feeling his head, cautiously, then lowered his hand. His fingers were covered in blood. "I'm gonna kill that bitch," he said.

Deep furrows immediately gouged across Michael's brow. "Who are you talking about?" he asked. Norman didn't seem to hear, continuing to stare at his bloodied fingers. With both hands, Michael grabbed his friend's shoulders and shook him. "Who are you talking about?" Michael asked again, still shaking him. "Who was here while I was gone? Who did this to you? Was it the pizza guy?"

Norman looked up at Michael, his eyes fraught with alarm. He broke free of Michael's shoulder hold and rushed to the cot, spying the flung back sheets and the empty space between them. "Oh, God. I'm sorry Mikey. I'm so sorry."

Michael felt a coolness rise up through the floor and slowly ascend to the crown of his head, like a cold winter wind that had wormed its way through the floorboards and wrapped itself tightly around him. Since the moment he realised it was Norman staggering into the room, he had clung to the hope that Jessica was safe, somewhere in the house. Now, all his hopes were blown away with those words.

"What do you mean, Norman?" he said, his voice as light and cool as the draft he felt rising through him. "Where's Jessica?"

Norman remained silent. Michael asked the question again, hoping he wasn't going to get the answer he thought he already knew. Norman shrugged once more, looked away and then timidly met Michael's gaze. "I'm sorry Mikey," he said, and he spoke with such helplessness that Michael was almost moved to tears. "I didn't realise it was her. She took me by surprise."

Michael felt a change come over him. He glared at Norman with the steely guise of the last man standing in a bar room brawl still hankering for more. He had rarely felt so angry, so fearsome. He could feel the thin crescent scar on his face begin to throb, and from Norman's expression he realised that he was looking as threatening as Norman did when he came barging into the room a moment ago.

"Who?" Michael said, taking a step forward. "Who didn't you realise it was?"

Norman began biting his nails, his only source of comfort and security at this moment. "The woman who has been taking all the babies from the hospital," he said over the knuckles of his hand.

The answer was not what Michael had been expecting. It was like a thump to the head from behind, like Norman had recently received. Then again, he thought, somehow he knew she would come, somehow he knew she would take his baby. He had been expecting it, hadn't he? He ran his hand through his hair and swallowed a dry lump that had collected in his throat.

Norman stopped biting his nails and lowered his hand to his side. Michael could feel the full force of his despair. A little guilty that he had caused Norman to feel so bad, Michael stepped back and for the second time in minutes accidentally trod on the baby monitor. He bent down and picked it up. "Why don't we go and sit in the lounge," he said, absently examining the transmitter. He was surprised at his calmness, in view of what he had just heard. "You can quickly run me through what happened before I call the cops."

Norman cleared his throat like a guilty boy unexpectedly receiving a reprieve from his father, and followed him up the hallway. After switching on the lounge room light, Michael put the transmitter on top of the piano next to his and Angie's wedding photo. He apologised for shouting at Norman and sat down on the couch; he was out of order, he shouldn't have raised his voice at his friend. Norman replied with a shrug, as if he had heard worse, which, Michael mused, he probably had, especially from his wife. Michael, however, felt the need to explain his behaviour in spite of Norman's deference.

"When I saw her empty cot," he said, "I thought it was you that'd taken her. I feel guilty. I shouldn't have jumped to conclusions."

Norman threw his arms out wide, somehow managing to smile broadly. "I forgive you. I would have been much worse. You're coping remarkably well."

Michael tried to smile. Norman had that infectious jovial quality about him that made it impossible not to, but smiling was almost as painful as his belly whenever he made a sudden movement, and it felt more like a cringe. "Why don't you just tell me what happened?" he said. "Then I'll know what to tell the police."

Norman was suddenly serious again. He ambled around the couch to a position in front of the television, rubbing his forehead with the palm of his hand as if trying to knead the memory back into shape. Michael sat back and waited for him to begin. Norman moved his hand to the back of his head, gently feeling the lump that had formed behind his ear. When he eventually started, the words left his mouth with the speed of a swimmer leaping out of the blocks.

"I remember waving goodbye and shutting the front door," he said, the words splashing out with spittle drops. "I heard the car start up and reverse out of the driveway. I remember thinking that you should take your time because I didn't want you to rush to the hospital and have another accident. I came back in here and rang my wife and told her not to expect me till late because something had happened at the hospital."

Norman now began pacing back and forth, pausing momentarily in his commentary. "Then I sat down where you're sitting and watched the end of the news," he said. "First the sports results and then the weather. I finished off the beer I'd been drinking." He pointed to the empty beer can on the carpet. "And that's when I heard a knock on the door. I thought it was you again. Maybe you'd forgotten something or were having trouble with the car. Needless to say, when I answered the door it wasn't you, it was, you know, that woman."

Norman paused for a moment, as if trying to remember something important, and brought his fingernails back to his mouth. Michael saw his gaze return to the swinging Elvis on the wall. "That was about five minutes after you left," he said, eventually.

Michael nodded. He had been well on his way to the hospital by then. "But why did you let her inside?" he asked.

"I didn't know it was *her*," Norman said, obviously distressed at what he'd done. His face was ruddy and he was gesticulating wildly. "Do you think I would've let her in if I knew who she was? Her hair was black, and on the TV it was blonde. Besides, in the dark I couldn't see her face that well, and she said she was your midwife from the hospital and had come to check on the baby and make sure you were coping."

"At twenty past nine at night?" Michael said. "Who makes house calls at that time? Doctors don't even do that anymore."

Norman bowed his head. "I'm sorry, Mikey. I didn't know."

"No, it's okay," Michael said, immediately contrite. "I'm not blaming you for what she's done. You didn't know who she was. She's obviously well adept at deceit and lies; she probably would've fooled me. Anyway, what happened next?"

Norman shook his head. "I don't know. She said she wanted to see Jessica and when I turned around to show her the baby's room, I blacked out. She must have hit me over the head with something hidden in her dress." He reached up absently and touched the large lump on his scalp. "Anyway, when I woke up I was lying face down on the carpet in here," he said, taking a deep breath and rubbing his cheek.

"She must have dragged me by my feet because I've got carpet burns on my face and elbows. The bitch is tiny, but she's strong."

"She's insane," Michael said, pursing his lips. "Do you remember anything else before I call the police? They'll want to take a statement from you."

"Just waking up and hearing noises in Jessica's room," he said. "I thought it was Maria and I wanted to catch her by surprise. I didn't realise I'd been unconscious for so long."

Michael recalled how Norman's face had been contorted with anger when he barged into Jessica's room and figured he must have been mightily pissed off at being clunked over the head. "You weren't the quietest stalker in town," he said, with a morose chuckle. "I thought you were the pizza delivery guy. I thought he'd come back just like you said he would."

Norman's eyes suddenly widened, as if he had just seen Maria walk past the doorway in the hall. "What happened with Angie?"

"Angie? Oh, she's fine." Michael could see that his calm, almost offhanded reply had surprised Norman. "She's excellent, in fact."

"But, I thought…"

Michael waved him away with a flick of the wrist. "Nah, she's alive and well," he said. "When I got to the hospital and asked the nurses in the ICU who had phoned me, they just looked at me blankly and said no one had. I asked if I could see her and they said it was after visiting hours, but I told them I wasn't going to leave until I saw that she was fine for myself. They'd already moved her from the main ICU to my cubicle and when I got there she was sitting up in bed eating yoghurt. She was just as surprised to see me as I was to see her."

"Then who called to say she'd died?"

"Well, it's obvious now, isn't it?"

Norman looked pensive, shaking his head. "You're right. But how did she know you weren't here?"

"She must have been sitting outside the house and watching us." As soon as he said it, Michael suddenly recalled the yellow Renault parked on the opposite of the street when he reversed Norman's car out of the driveway earlier. "She must have called from a mobile," he said, "watching us through the window."

Both he and Norman turned to the large picture window that opened out onto the front lawn. Beyond that, beneath the streetlight, they saw the white transit van still parked outside the house. Norman went over and drew the curtains, snapping them together, as if he could feel more prying eyes peeping in.

Michael stared at the drawn curtains with a glaze in his eyes. Was all this really happening? Was Jessica really gone? He remembered thinking earlier tonight that he was one of the fortunate few who had somehow avoided disaster, just like an executive who had missed a flight that crashed on takeoff, as if the hand of providence had guided him and Jessica to safety. Not anymore. Somewhere between then and now he had boarded that plane and gone down with all the passengers and crew. He had crossed the line. He was now on the *other side*, that place humans found so morbidly fascinating, where onlookers gasped and pointed and thanked their lucky stars they weren't there. It was a place from which you couldn't return. Once tragedy struck, it was with you for the rest of your life. He wished he hadn't boarded that doomed flight. He wished he was dreaming in bed and that he would wake up with his pregnant wife by his side.

It wasn't to be. Over by the window, he could see Norman's blurred face staring at him, a tad sheepish. He wasn't dreaming. Destiny, that cruellest of vixens, had him by the balls. This shit was happening for real and he had to stop denying it. He had to pull himself together and find out what happened to Jessica.

Michael ran a hand through his hair. The first thing he was going to do was call the cops. In fact, he was going to do better than that. He was going to call his cousin. Jude was in charge of the investigation of the other baby. If anyone knew what to do about getting his baby back, it was him.

# CHAPTER 14

MICHAEL'S FINGERS HAD just touched the telephone when it started ringing. His hand jerked back, as if the phone had just tried to bite him, but after the second ring it fell silent. Michael clenched his fists, eyeing the phone the way he would look at a dog that had just mistaken his hand for a pork chop. Then he ran one of them through his short hair and looked over his shoulder at Norman.

"Who do you think that might have been?" Michael asked.

Norman shrugged and bit his nails, returning his gaze with large open eyes. "Maybe it was her again."

Michael absently scratched the crescent scar on his cheek, wondering just what the hell he should do. Call the cops? Call his dad? What about Angie? Surely she had a right to know what had been happening. He would certainly want to know if the shoes were on the other feet, if it was himself lying in the hospital and Angie was here trying to deal with this mess.

The phone started ringing again. Michael recoiled as if it had made another snap at his hand and Norman jumped. It rang again. Neither of them moved. Michael stared at the phone and then at Norman, but Norman wasn't going to do anything apart from bite his nails.

The phone kept ringing. Michael wondered what he should say to her if it was Maria calling. She'd probably demand something in return for Jessica, but what could she possibly want? They weren't millionaires. He could barely scrounge together two thousand dollars if she wanted a ransom. It had to be something else. He reached out for the phone, then stopped. Perhaps he should just pretend that no one was home and let it ring out to the answering machine. Except, that probably wouldn't work. She knew he would have discovered her hoax at the hospital and made his way back by now. In any case, she knew Norman was still here; she would probably keep ringing until someone answered. There was no avoiding the issue. He was going to have to speak to her at some point in time.

The phone rang again just as he picked it up. There was a moment of silence on the other end, a moment that seemed more like a year, before he heard a female say, "Your phone's being tapped."

"What?" Michael said, to which the woman repeated what she had just said. It was the most ludicrous thing he'd heard all night, even more than what Norman had said about the pizza delivery guy returning to collect his tip with a baseball bat. "What are you on about?"

"I'll tell you in a minute. First of all, go to the window and tell me what you see."

"Who is this?" Michael said, and yet he already knew. He recognised her voice and didn't need to be told her name. "It's *you*, isn't it? What have you done with Jessica?"

Maria cut him short and repeated her instructions. Michael could tell by the tone of her voice that she wasn't in any mood to compromise; he figured the most sensible course of action was to do as she asked. Reluctantly, he went to the window and cupped his face against the glass. After looking around and seeing nothing untoward, he drew the curtains closed and returned to the phone. Norman was standing motionless between the TV and the couch with an expression of bewildered consternation. His fingers were hooked into his mouth and his wide eyes were following everything Michael did.

Michael put the telephone to his ear. "Did you see a white van?" he heard her ask.

What on earth she was going on about? He didn't care if there were a thousand white vans out there. He only cared that she brought Jessica back home, unharmed. "Yeah," he said, snorting. "So what? They've been there for weeks."

"If I'm not mistaken, it said: MAD HATTER'S LAWN MOWING SERVICE—MAD SERVICE AT A MAD PRICE." Michael frowned, trying to remember, and ran a hand through his hair. He hadn't paid it much attention. "It's not a lawn mowing van," she said. "It's the police. They've got your house under surveillance."

He choked back a laugh. She wasn't serious, was she? Why on earth would the police bug his house? He wasn't a gangster or drug dealer. He didn't have a crop of marijuana plants growing in his back yard, or a kilo of cocaine stashed beneath the kitchen floorboards. He had been a law-abiding citizen all his life. The worse thing he had ever done was pinch a road sign as a prank during orientation week at college.

"The police are doing what?" he said. "You've got to be joking."

"I'm not joking. They've been watching you for months. Unscrew the speaker end of the handset."

He pictured Maria's pretty face holding the telephone to her ear, probably a mobile because it was cutting in and out, like someone driving while she talked. He also tried to picture how a nurse from Colombia could get herself mixed up in kidnapping and Satanism. Was it for money? Was it for power? Or simply for kicks? He looked at the speaker end of the phone and thought of telling her to fuck off on the next plane back to her native homeland, but he could hear the rising tension in her voice and thought it wasn't such a good idea. She sounded angry and flustered. The last thing he wanted was to upset the woman who was in direct control of his daughter's life.

"Just do as I say," she said, somehow sensing that he was in two minds. "I haven't got time to waste."

He hesitated no longer, twisting the speaker until it came away easily in his hands. Michael peered in. Two wires, red and green, ran behind what he assumed was a small black speaker and into the coiled telephone wire connecting the handset to the telephone proper. Between the red and green wires, where they connected to the speaker, was a small silver button as shiny as chrome. It was no bigger than a five-cent piece, though roughly twice as thick, like a watch battery, and it had no markings. It was obviously alien.

He suddenly felt the temperature rising. He felt his brow break out in a mild sweat and his heart skip a beat. There was also an uncomfortable burning sensation now spreading over his body, an itch that felt as if an army of ants with hot needles for feet was marching from the floor, up his legs and abdomen to the top of his head. The itch was everywhere. Even his eyeballs and testicles weren't spared. He glanced over at Norman, who was biting his nails and watching him intently. He didn't seem to be feeling the heat like he was. Michael hooked his finger into the neck of his blue sweater to release some of the hotness and peered back at the dismantled handset.

"I, I don't believe it," Michael said, mainly to himself. His voice echoed in his ears, as if he was listening to someone else over a bad, long-distance line. He picked out the alien object between his thumb and forefinger, and gestured for Norman to move closer. "What do you make of this?" he asked, holding it up in front of his face.

Norman shrugged. "I've never seen anything like it before. What do you think it is?"

"I have an idea." Michael quickly reassembled the handset, but his hands were sweaty and the silver object nearly slipped from his grasp. Jeez, he was hot. Perhaps he should take off his sweater, but glancing up at Norman he saw that the heat was causing him no affect at all. Didn't he feel anything? Michael armed the sweat off his brow.

"You're right," he said to Maria, as Norman rested his backside on the ridge of the couch. "What should I do with it?"

"It's a miniature transmitting device," she replied. In the background, he thought he could hear the sound of a car engine slowing down and then accelerate, as if she had just made a turn. "A bug in other words. It has a radius of about one hundred metres. Flush it down the toilet and then tell me if the van is still outside."

"But if it's the police bugging my phone, why should I listen to you?" he asked.

"Because I have your baby."

Michael thought about hanging up on her right there and then, but decided against it. He had no idea how she'd react. What could he do? There just seemed nowhere to turn. He was becoming more confused and hot, like he imagined someone lost in the desert would feel, staggering from dune to dune in search of water, knowing that if they stumbled and fell they would die beneath the burning sun. He ran his hand through his hair, then scratched the side of his face. The itch was getting worse. He wondered if he had ever had anything so bad.

"Just do as I say," he heard Maria say, picking up on his uncertainty. "Flush the bug down the toilet and then tell me what the van is doing outside."

"Why have you taken my baby?" he said, trying to sound defiant and in control despite this feeling that he was burning up inside. "If you bring her back I won't call the cops." He heard her laugh, as if what he had just said was the funniest thing she had ever heard, a mocking kind of laugh that made him feel two inches tall. He quickly came up with a different tact. "Your face is all over the TV. They know it's you who's been abducting all the babies. You won't get away with it."

"I know," Maria said, distantly. Then, more firmly, "So if you ever want to see your baby, you'll do exactly as I say…"

"No, goddamn it!" Michael shouted into the handset, clenching it tightly. "You're gonna bring Jessica back to my house right now, and if one hair on her head is so much as out of place, you're gonna wish you were never born. Do you understand me?"

Out of the corner of his eye, he saw Norman take a step back. He flicked his hands up at the wrist and shook them, trying to say that it might not be such a good idea to yell at the woman who had just kidnapped his baby. Michael ignored him. All his fears, all his anxieties, of the preceding weeks had been built up into a storm of unspent fury. The red mist had him in its shroud. He imagined that this was what some soldiers felt like when they flipped and went on a murderous rampage, venting their fury on innocent civilians. Maria was lucky she wasn't standing in front of him at this moment because he knew he could easily kill. He knew he could wrap his hands around her throat and strangle her until she went blue in the face and stopped breathing. It would be as simple as baking a cake, and infinitely more satisfying.

"You're in no position to give me orders!" Maria shouted back. Michael took the phone away from his ear, waiting a moment before putting it back. He gulped, hoping he hadn't gone too far. "I have your baby and if you want to see her again you're going to follow my instructions to the letter. Do I make *myself* clear?"

Michael was at a loss at what to do. He was beginning to fear that he was losing control of the situation. Far worse, he was beginning to fear that he was losing control of his mind. Often, when he was a teenager learning to drive, he'd had nightmares of driving down the highway in a runaway car. In the nightmares, he'd come to a stoplight and put his foot on the brake, but the car would continue to drive forward

211

and smash into the side of a truck. This was exactly the same state of affairs, only this time he was driving with his daughter in the back seat. He had to somehow get control of himself and the situation. He couldn't just let Maria dictate terms to him.

"I'm gonna call the police," Michael said, staring at the silver bugging device in his hand. "In fact, I don't have to. I can just talk into this thing." He raised it to his lips. "Is someone listening? Will someone help me? There's a crazy woman on the telephone and she's kidnapped my daughter. I need help!"

"Don't be stupid," Maria said. "The bug only picks up the frequency waves of the speaker in your phone. Talking into it won't do a thing. Now throw it away and tell me if the van is still outside."

The burning itch was driving him crazy. Michael glared disdainfully at the coin-like transmitter and then threw it against the wall. He watched it hit just beneath the swaying black hips of the Elvis clock and tear a small strip of wallpaper. "You're out of your sick little mind if you think I'm gonna follow your orders," he said, scratching the hand that was holding the receiver to his ear.

"You have no idea what you're dealing with Mr. Joseph," and her voice faded for a second before coming back. "There are powers beyond your control. I advise you not to fight against them. The police will not be able to protect your baby, believe me."

Out of the blue, like a welcome sea breeze on a hot afternoon, Michael felt his rage cooling, slowly. It blew away the red mist and cleared his mind. From where it came from, he couldn't say, but he was infinitely glad for it. He'd almost lost control there for a minute, and he now realised that he had better watch what he was saying; Maria was like a Doberman, tempered and playful one minute, viscous killer the next.

"What are you talking about?" he asked, his voice matching his new temperament. "Why can't the police help?"

"Your baby is special, Mr. Joseph," she said. She sounded calmer, too. "She's more special that you'll ever believe. There are people, evil people, who want to get their hands on her. If you want her to live, you'll do exactly as I ask."

Michael was silent for a while, scratching his brow. Here it was, the kidnapper's demands. It was time for negotiation. Now he'd find out what was going on inside her sick little head. "I'm listening," he said.

"Good. First, look outside your window and tell me if the van is still there."

Michael turned to Norman, who was still biting his nails, and relayed Maria's request. Norman hurried to the window, flicked the curtains slightly open, cupped his face against the glass and peered out onto the dark street. He faced Michael, shaking his head in acknowledgement that it was gone.

Michael passed on this information to Maria. "Good," she said. "They know their cover's blown." She continued with her demands. "Second, if you call the police, your baby is dead. Am I clear on that?"

Michael cleared his throat. He hated the way he was being manipulated, knowing that there was nothing, absolutely nothing, he could do about it. He scratched the side of his head, still tingling from the hot itch. It felt like sunburn, the type of all-over sunburn that made you glow like a red light at night and didn't let you sleep because even the touch of the cotton sheet on your skin made you flinch in pain. Only this was worse; this was internal.

"Yes," he said. "You've made yourself very clear."

There was still more, it seemed. Maria wasn't finished. "Lastly, pack your bags for a long trip." The sound of her voice faded briefly before coming back. "We're leaving Adelaide."

"I'm not leaving without Angie," he said. "If we're going anywhere, then she has to come too."

"Your wife's not relevant," Maria said. "It's you that's important."

Michael ground his molars and felt the flush of heat surge through his body once again. The temperature soared back to where it had been a moment ago. He had to calm himself otherwise he was going to lose his temper again. "Not relevant?" he said between gritted teeth, doing all in his power not to scream into the telephone. "If you're as heartless as that, then you're sicker than I thought you were."

"Mr. Joseph, be quiet!" Maria spoke with such force that Michael thought he had blown his chances of ever seeing his daughter again. He immediately wished he could take back what he had just said. "If you want your wife to come along, she can, but I don't advise it," she said. "It's dangerous enough as it is and we don't want to jeopardise ourselves if we can help it. Wait by the phone. Don't go anywhere and don't call the cops. Don't call anybody, okay? I'll get back to you in an hour."

Michael heard the line go dead and for a brief second contemplated ringing the police straight away. Then he remembered what she had said and, though it went against his better judgment, decided not to take the risk.

"What the hell was that all about?" he heard Norman ask.

Michael ran his hand through his hair and slowly faced his best friend. Norman was still standing by the front window and biting his nails, the orange glow of the streetlight falling onto his bloodied scalp through the slit between the frayed edges of the curtains.

"That was Maria," Michael said, the sentence coming out as sluggishly as he had turned. "She has Jessica."

"I figured that much out myself." Norman stepped forward into the space between the television and the couch. "What are you going to do, call the cops?"

"No, if we do that, she'll kill Jessica. She made that plain enough."

"Then what do we do?"

"We wait," Michael said.

FOR OVER AN hour, Michael paced back and forth in front of the TV, shaking his head, occasionally running his hand through his hair, every so often pausing to gather his thoughts, and once or twice rubbing the thin crescent scar on his cheek. A few times he caught his reflection on the blank television screen, thinking that on school trips to the Adelaide zoo he had seen bears pace back and forth in their cage not to dissimilarly. Waiting for Maria to phone back was unbearable.

Michael eyed the Elvis clock on the wall for about the thousandth time since Maria had called. The big hand was now exactly overlaying the small hand and both were pointing directly at the ceiling. Beneath Elvis's swaying hips there was a small, torn strip of wallpaper. The silver telephone bug had made that mark when he threw it against the wall earlier. It then ricocheted somewhere beneath the couch, and now, for some reason, he had the sudden desire to find it and crush it beneath the heel of his sandshoe.

Norman shuffled his backside on the couch, distracting Michael. Norman brought his hand to his face to bite his nails again, and Michael saw that he had chewed every nail to the quick. Michael had given him one of his clean white shirts to replace the one sporting bloodstains on its collar, though the crimson cardigan and brown corduroys he had refused to change. His freshly shampooed hair was now free of blood clots and his skin had a scrubbed-up rosy pink sheen. Norman examined his hand for a brief second, then, disappointed, let his arm fall to the armrest.

A small bell jingled from behind the closed curtains. "Come on Jack, old boy, keep up," Michael heard someone say. The bell jingled quicker and Michael went to investigate. He cautiously opened a small crack between the curtains and peered outside. It was gramps, taking his black Labrador for a stroll. Jack, it seemed, was a good deal older than his master.

Michael closed the curtain and glanced back at the clock. "Where is she? She's thirty minutes late," he said to Norman, running a hand through his hair. "She lied to give herself an extra hour to get away. I'm a fool. I should have called the police straight away."

The ring of the telephone cut him short. Michael rushed over and picked it up, resting his back against the piano. "It's me," he heard Maria say. Her voice sounded flustered, like someone racing against time, or being chased. "Have you packed your bags?"

Michael eyed the black suitcase resting against the wall beneath the Elvis clock. He had packed it mostly with Angie's clothes and stuff he knew she couldn't do without. As he listened to Maria, he thought he could hear the rumble of car tyres over an unpaved road in the background. He figured she was now driving back to the city from wherever she had been, presumably where she was keeping Jessica hidden with whatever accomplices she was involved with.

"Yes," he said. "Where are you? Where's my baby?"

"Be ready in thirty minutes," she said. "Don't move. I'll pick you up at your house."

Michael was left holding a dead line. He put the phone back down and told Norman what he had just heard. Maria's behaviour was becoming more baffling by the hour. Either she was really stupid, or something else was going down. Not that he had ever experienced a kidnapping before, but it went against anybody's definition of common sense to return to the scene of the crime. The only explanation he could think of was that she was going to take him to where she was keeping Jessica. "I've got no choice. I have to go along with it."

"Don't be a fool," Norman said, standing. "Call the cops. They can arrest her when she gets here. It's the only sensible thing to do."

Michael ran a hand through his hair. On the surface, what Norman said was true; it probably was the only sensible course of action. Except, that was not what he was going to do. He had heard tyres driving on a dirt road when he just spoke to her, and there weren't any dirt roads in the city, so it was distinctly plausible that Maria had hidden Jessica somewhere miles away, somewhere in the countryside. If the police arrested her, he feared she might not tell them where Jessica was; she might just decide to let his baby die of starvation if the cops didn't release her, something he simply wasn't willing to risk happening. He was caught between the devil and the deep blue see. At least he knew Jessica was still alive. Whatever Maria's game plan was, it wasn't in her best interests to harm her, and he wasn't going to call the police until he found out what she wanted.

"You can't just let that crazy bitch dictate terms to you," Norman said, becoming animated. "This is your daughter's life we're dealing with."

"I'm fully aware of that." Michael picked up the handset again. "I know who I can call," and he began punching in the number from memory. "I should've done it right at the very start. He'll know what to do."

Michael hoped Jude wouldn't mind too much at being disturbed at five past midnight, but these were exceptional circumstances and he was sure he'd understand. The phone rang several times, and for a disheartening moment Michael was worried that it wasn't going to be answered. Then the ringing stopped and he heard the familiar voice speak into the other end.

Such was his relief, Michael almost yelled at him as loudly as he had to Maria earlier. "Jude! It's me, Mikey."

"Hello cuz," Jude said. Michael figured that he was probably at home in bed, as his voice sounded slightly muted and there was only silence in the background. "I heard you'd been discharged from hospital. What's the matter? You sound as if something's wrong."

Michael paused for a moment. He knew Jude didn't think an awful lot of him, their relationship was pretty tender at the best of times, and he wondered, now that he really needed his assistance, whether he would take this moment to exact revenge for that incident all those years ago and refuse to help. "I, uh, I'm sorry to ring you at this time of the night," he said. "I'm in a spot of bother."

"No problems, Mikey." He sounded more willing than Michael had anticipated. For some reason, he could imagine Jude grinning from ear to ear. Then he heard Jude cover the mouthpiece of his mobile phone with his hand, as if talking to someone else he didn't want him to know about, probably one of his many girlfriends. "Have you been a naughty boy?" he said, after a brief moment. "Been caught drunk driving and you need your cousin to bail you out, is that it?"

"No, nothing like that," Michael said, running a hand through his hair, still unable to fully believe what he was about to say. "Jude, my daughter's been kidnapped."

Jude expressed his shock and demanded to know more. Michael told him how he had been lured out of the house under false pretences and returned to discover that someone had abducted his baby. He also knew the kidnapper's identity. She was returning to pick him up; for some reason they had to leave Adelaide.

"Maria Sanchez is our number one suspect at the moment," Jude said, after Michael had finished. "She's a clever girl, but she's gone one step too far this time, like they all do in the end. Has she said what she wants, a ransom or anything like that?"

Norman had gone to the window and was peering outside through the curtains. He had heard something Michael hadn't, or was anticipating the early arrival of Maria. Michael watched him turn around after a few seconds and make his way back to the couch, parking his considerable rear end on an armrest.

"No, nothing, absolutely nothing," Michael said to Jude, now turning his attention to the wedding photo on top of the piano. He wondered just how he was going to break the news to Angie later tonight. He would have to be gentle; this news might really kill her. "I don't know what to do. That's why I rang. I saw you on the telly and knew you were in charge of the investigation. I'm sorry to bother you, I know it's late, but she said that if I called the cops… sorry, police, that Jessica was as good as dead. I thought I'd call you first, considering… well, technically you're family, not police."

"You've done the right thing," Jude said. "I *am* the best person you could have called."

Michael paused. Being part of the family had never been high on the list of Jude's priorities, and yet he now seemed positively eager to help in any way he could. Why the sudden change? Had he suddenly developed a sense of remorse?

Michael bit his bottom lip, stopping this line of thinking. He was being cynical and it wasn't important what Jude's motives were. The fact was, Jude was willing to help and he should be grateful for that. He was right. He *was* the best person to call. It was a good thing that they were family. Having Jude immediately on the case took a massive load off his mind, and now what Michael really wanted to know was what the next step should be.

"Is there anything you want me to do?" he asked, swapping hands that held the telephone. "Should I call the police department and have someone come over and take a statement?"

Michael heard the sound of a jingling dog collar beyond the closed curtain outside. He figured gramps and Jack were slowly returning from whence they came. "Don't worry about that," he heard Jude say, just as the voice of the old man calling out to Jack to hurry up floated through the window. "Let me liaise with the police department. You just stay put. When she arrives, try and stall her. I'll be around to your house shortly. Don't let her talk you into leaving, okay? Your baby's life depends on it. I'll be there in about forty to forty-five minutes, just after one, okay?"

"Okay, thanks cuz," Michael said, now thinking of Maria and trying to figure out just what the hell she was up to. "I owe you one."

The distinctive chug of a VW Beetle drove past the window, reminding him briefly of his burnt out car now lying somewhere in a wrecker's yard, then faded into the distance. He hung up and turned to his friend sitting on an armrest of the couch, thinking this night was never going to end.

# CHAPTER 15

A S SEEMED HIS habit tonight, Michael returned to pacing back and forth between the two walls of the lounge room, from the Elvis clock and luggage bags to the glass-fronted drinks cabinet, then back again, wearing a path on the already thinning blue carpet. Norman was now slumped on the couch, watching him with tired, droopy eyes.

"You're going to wear the carpet out," he said, slumping even further into the cushions. "Why don't you sit down and have a rest? You must be tired."

Back and forth Michael continued. "I'm not tired. I could run a marathon the way I feel at the moment." He glanced once again at the Elvis clock. "She said she'd be here already. Where the hell is she?"

"I'm here," Maria said.

Michael spun around and Norman bolted upright in his seat. Maria was standing in the doorway pointing a handgun from her waist with what Michael guessed was a silencer screwed to its barrel. She was wearing a black dress and her dark hair was falling straight to her shoulders. He looked at her, then at the gun, and then back at her again. Even though he had made her acquaintance on numerous occasions at the hospital, he was still struck by how petit she was, at least half his size. Michael figured all he and Norman would have to do was rush her when she wasn't looking, and this whole charade would be over.

She must have sensed his thoughts because she pointed the gun at him, and said, "Don't even think about it. I'll use this if I have to." To emphasise her point, she stepped into the room and quickly turned the gun toward the Elvis clock. There was something in the way she moved, smooth and effortlessly, like a glide, that was startlingly familiar. She pulled the trigger. The shot sounded no louder than a polite fart, and Michael flinched as chunks of plastic, springs and bits of metal spewed out of Elvis like robot intestines. The time of Elvis's death was 12:46 a.m. His hips swayed no more.

Maria turned the pistol back toward them as quickly as the bullet had smashed into the clock. Michael saw Norman gulp, and any thoughts of trying to force the gun out of her hands went to pieces like the unfortunate Elvis clock on the wall. Michael ran a hand through his hair.

"Why don't you take a seat Mr. Joseph?" she said. "Next to your friend here."

Michael didn't move. For a moment he was at a loss with what to do. Then he remembered what Jude had told him over the phone—stall her.

"Go on," she said, waving the gun menacingly in his direction. "Don't make me use this again."

Michael did as he was asked, slowly. After he was seated, Maria took position in front of the TV where he had just been standing, keeping her gun cautiously trained on both of them. "How did you..." Michael began.

"Be quiet!" she said, now edging her way to the window. Michael shut up and watched her quickly peeked outside between the curtains. Not once did the gun leave its mark... him. She seemed happy with what she saw at the front of the house and made her way back to the area in front of the television.

"I hope you don't mind," she said, "but I felt it best to let myself in, considering the circumstances, that is."

"How did you get in?" he asked.

"An acquaintance of yours had me make a set of your house keys when you were unconscious in the hospital," she said. "It wasn't difficult."

An acquaintance? Sure, Michael mused. He was probably going to hear a thousand more lies over the next few minutes. It was safer to believe nothing she said. That way he wouldn't be lured into whatever trap she was trying to set.

"I don't believe you," he said. "You did it all on your own as part of your sick little fantasy."

221

Her face suddenly hardened, and for a second Michael thought he was going to get a bullet between his eyes. "Why don't you shut up and let me tell you about fantasy?"

"I'm not going to listen to the ravings of a lunatic," Michael harrumphed. Norman shot him a glance, silently pleading with him not to patronise her. Michael ignored him. He had to stall her. He had to try to eek out as much time as he possibly could before Jude arrived with the cops.

"Where's my daughter?" he asked. "I want to see her."

Maria smirked, a cynical grimace as ever he'd seen. "She's safe, Mr. Joseph, thanks to me," she said. "Unfortunately, your wife's daughter was sacrificed so that your daughter could live."

"What? You bitch!" he shouted, standing. "What have you done with my baby?"

"Sit down, Mr. Joseph. Before I'm forced to use this thing." She spoke with an air of indifference, not caring too much for his antics. "Now!"

Although the gun was aimed straight at him, Michael was caught between two minds. He was caught between following his maddening urge to throttle her on the one hand, and the calm sense of reason to do as she said on the other. Reason finally took hold. Michael sat down, firing Maria a look that could kill as efficiently as the gun she was holding.

"I'm sorry to have to tell you this, but Jessica is dead," she said, and to Michael the news was like a shot to the head. "She didn't die in vain. She was a decoy for your child."

Michael caught his limp expression on the television screen behind Maria. His well-defined jaw had sagged, leaving his mouth gaping in a wide O, and his eyes had that rabbit blinded-by-the-headlights stare about them. It was a look of utter disbelief. He blinked, scrunching his eyes tightly, and wondered if he hadn't actually woken up from his accident at all, if this wasn't, in fact, part of a fantastical illusion created by his comatose mind. Was insanity contagious? He looked up at Maria and at first couldn't speak; his voice, like the clock on the wall to his right, was silent and inactive. He kept looking up at her, staring blankly.

"You, you murdered his baby?" he heard Norman ask.

"I never did such a thing." Maria flicked her eyes to Norman, then back to Michael. They were as steely hard as the gun in her hand. "Dr. Rouben killed Jessica."

She was insane, Michael thought. Not only had she abducted his child, she had built an elaborate web of lies to deny she had done any wrong. It was inconceivable what she was saying. "Dr. Rouben has done nothing but help me and Angie this past year, and now you accuse him of murdering the child he helped conceive?" he said, almost spitting. "It doesn't make any sense. Why would he do something like that?"

As hot as Michael was with anger, Maria seemed as cool with collected poise. "We don't have time to go into details here, Mr. Joseph. We have to go and collect your daughter. She's still in danger."

Michael sat forward in his seat and rested his elbows on his knees, looking directly down the barrel of the gun. The hole at the end of the silencer stared back, cold and black and silent. He scratched his temple, confused at to what she had just said. Had he heard her correctly? Maybe she was so caught up in her own web of deceit that she didn't know what was true or false anymore. "But, but you just told me she's dead," he said.

"I said Jessica is dead," Maria said, glancing at her watch, "but she isn't your child. Your baby is alive and well... for now."

Michael held back a disparaging sneer. It was risible, completely and utterly risible. He shook his head, discretely covering his mouth with his hand. Was this not proof of her insanity? Had she not lost all semblance of reality? Talking with her was like talking to someone on LSD; logic was no longer relevant, and trying to reason with her was pointless. The psychiatrists were going to have a field day when they got their hands on her after all this was over.

"If Jessica's not my child," he said, and threw his hands wide, "then whose is she?"

"You're incapable of siring children, Mr. Joseph," she said, without a trace of sympathy or condolence. "You're infertile, not your wife. Dr. Rouben falsified the investigations. He fertilised Angie's eggs with his own sperm in the laboratory. Jessica was his child."

Michael ran a hand through his hair, doubting whether she could make her lies any more elaborate. She was obviously unstable. He had no doubts she was capable of using the gun she was still pointing at him. But how far could he push without her cracking and pulling the trigger? She now had an expression on her face that suggested she had been here long enough talking, yet he had no idea how far Jude was from the house, nor how much longer could he stall her. He still had to take the chance, though. He still had to keep her occupied and stop her from hurrying him up.

"You're lying to me," he said, his voice emphatic and defiant. Out of the corner of his eyes, he saw Norman bring his fingers to his mouth. "I don't believe you."

"You mean you don't want to believe me. Why do you think he paid such a keen interest in you and Angie? Do you think he treats all his patients with the same level of care?"

To be honest, Michael thought, he hadn't paid it any real consideration. In the end, did it really matter? "If that's the case, why would he murder his own child?" he asked.

"Because he thought it was yours."

Unable to hide it this time, Michael laughed scornfully. She wasn't making any sense; she had just told him he was infertile and was now contradicting herself. He chuckled and shook his head disbelievingly. "You're not consistent," he said. "You've lost track of all your lies because everything you've told me is all in your head. It's all a deranged fantasy."

"I wish it was," she said, staring vacantly. For a moment Michael thought she was going to cry. She inhaled deeply, and when she spoke again her voice was strong and vibrant. "But Jessica didn't have her heart ripped from her chest because of a fantasy."

Norman's hand dropped from his mouth, slapping into his thigh. Maria immediately turned the pistol in his direction and Michael followed its direction. Norman's face had turned white and pasty, and his were eyes bulging from their sockets. "She... she had her heart ripped out?" he asked, spluttering, almost gagging on his own words. Michael could tell he was about to bring up tonight's pizza all over the carpet any second now. Sweat beaded on his brow and his Adam's apple bobbed forward as he swallowed what was probably a mouthful of saliva. "She... she had her heart," Norman began again, and then his eyes suddenly widened even further and he sprung out of his seat with his hand covering his mouth.

Michael was powerless to stop him running out of the room. He could only watch in surprise as he disappeared down the hallway. It didn't matter. He couldn't have thought of a better way to stall Maria if he'd tried. The bathroom door slammed shut moments later.

"Never mind," Maria said, having also watched him exit the room. She turned back to Michael and waved the gun in the direction in which Norman had just left. "We have to leave," she said. "There's no more time to waste. Your daughter's in grave danger."

As she finished, Michael heard footsteps approaching on the path outside. He looked up. Jude was here, he thought, finally. Maria edged her way back to the curtains, the gun continually pointed at his head. Once again her movements were reminiscent of something he'd seen before, something he was still having trouble recalling. She peeked between the crack in the curtain and after a second or two stood back to draw them closed, giving Michael the chance to glimpse through the gap and see who it was. To his deep disappointment, it was a woman scuffling past the front of the house in the direction of the city. She was clad in a short mini skirt, fishnet tights and precarious high-heeled boots. Reflecting the orange rays from the streetlight, her broth of hair took on the appearance of candyfloss. Maria continued to watch her go by, and Michael could hear the echo of the woman's high heels fading long after she herself had disappeared from his sight.

Maria relaxed, flicked the curtains closed and moved back in front of the television, still pointing the gun as she had. "Come on, we have to go," she said.

"Wait a minute," Michael said. He had to keep stalling. Jude couldn't be too far away now, surely. "Why do I have to leave?"

"Your daughter's in danger."

"You've completely lost me. I don't understand. What daughter?"

Maria sighed. "Do you believe in the Immaculate Conception?"

Michael frowned quizzically. What was she going on about? She sounded like a brainwashed zombie. Maybe that was it. Maybe she belonged to a religious cult, something like that crazy UFO-worshipping freak show half the actors in Hollywood seemed to belong to at the moment. She certainly had that serious, "I've seen the light and you haven't" look in her eyes, a look that was as deadly serious as the bullet that had shot Elvis on the wall.

"No, it's bullshit," he said, after a moment. "What has it got to do with all this anyway?"

"Everything," she muttered. "Absolutely everything."

"Really?" Michael smirked. Now that he had engaged her in conversation once more, it was just the opportunity he needed to put her off her guard. "Do you know what I think?" he said. "I think you're off your rocker."

His comment didn't seem to faze her, as if being crazy was the least of her problems at the moment. She just cocked an eyebrow, and said, "What would it take for you to believe?"

Michael scoffed. "A miracle, that's what."

"Miracles happen every day," she said with a tone as serious as before. "They just need to be seen in context. You choose not to see them. What would have to happen for you to acknowledge that they exist?"

Michael rested his elbows on his knees and sank his face into his hands. He was suddenly very tired. "I don't know," he said. "I haven't thought about it."

"Isn't it about time you did?" Her stare was as demanding as it was agitated, and Michael wasn't sure whether it was due to his amateurish efforts to stall her or his sacrilegious ignorance. "If you were Joseph two thousand years ago," she said, "would you believe it if your wife came to you and said that God had impregnated her?"

Again Michael scoffed, recalling similar conversations with Angie on the same topic. He wasn't perturbed; no matter what was said, the conclusions were always the same. "No, if I were Joseph, I wouldn't believe her," he said. "The Immaculate Conception is pure fiction. It was conceived by a woman desperate to hide her infidelity and save herself from getting stoned to death."

Maria brushed his comments aside with a contemptuous harrumph and an upward flick of her eyebrows. "And what if Joseph went to Mary and said that he had been impregnated by God and was going to have a baby?"

Michael glanced up. "Now you're being stupid. That's impossible."

Maria simpered, and Michael was suddenly struck with the idea that she was hiding something, something secretive and coy. "No, that would be a miracle," she said. "Would you believe the impregnation of a man constituted an Immaculate Conception?"

Michael had no idea where this was heading, but he was happy enough to continue with it as long as it prevented her from leaving before Jude arrived. "Well, yes, I would," he said, smiling as she had just done. It was his turn to be coy and secretive. "But it's never going to happen because God doesn't exist."

"What would you say if I told you it's already happened?"

"I wouldn't believe you."

"Why not?"

"Because I'd have to see it with my own eyes first."

Before Maria replied, someone spoke for her, and it wasn't the voice Michael had expected. "Well, Michael," said the stranger, "I saw it with my own eyes. Do you believe *me*?"

Michael spun around. The stranger was standing in the doorway, pointing a gun and silencer directly at Maria. He was clad in a long white robe, the hood pushed off his head and the right cuff stained with several splattered drops of red. Blinking with shock, Michael felt his jaw drop. It was his dream coming alive. It was all there; the gun; the white hooded robe, everything. He suddenly understood why, in her black dress, Maria had seemed so familiar—she was the black shadow that had been stalking him all along. In the dream, he had always been unable to see the faces of the men chasing him, but not any longer. The face beneath the neatly slicked hair was clearly visible.

"Dr. Rouben?" Michael said. "What are you doing here?"

Dr. Rouben continued to look directly past him, his dark eyes watching Maria fiercely. To Michael, they were the eyes of a leopard stalking its prey. "Put the gun on the floor... slowly," he said to her, ignoring Michael. His voice was calm and controlled. "Your double-cross didn't work. The game's over."

If she had moved quickly, Michael thought, Maria might have had an opportunity to take a shot at Dr. Rouben and get away, but she had been caught by surprise. She was trapped. She hesitated in putting the gun down, as if still contemplating a quick shoot out, but it was too late. If she made any sudden movement her intestines would be spewing out onto the carpet like the innards of the Elvis clock before she even heard the shot. After her guts, it would be her brains, Michael reckoned. The game, as Dr. Rouben so eloquently put it, was over.

Michael tried to stand. "What's going on?" he said, turning his head from Maria to Dr. Rouben.

Dr. Rouben continued to stare past him. "Stay seated, Michael," he said. "If you don't want a bullet in your own skull." Then to Maria, "Hurry up. Before I lose my temper."

Maria slowly bent down and put her handgun on the carpet in front of her. She edged near the drinks cabinet on the far wall, her hands in the air. Dr. Rouben instructed Michael to pick up the gun and hand it to him. Michael obeyed and was then ordered back to the couch. Dr. Rouben scrunched up his robe and tucked Maria's gun into his trouser belt, all the while his eyes and his pistol never leaving Maria. She stood motionless, her arms bent at the elbow and her hands pointing to the ceiling, reminding Michael of a human pitchfork. Her lips were pinched tight and the colour had drained from her face. The corners of her mouth, like her fingers, were trembling slightly.

Michael found his voice and turned back to Dr. Rouben. "What the hell is going on?"

"Something beyond your control," he said, dismissively. "It's beyond all our control, isn't it Maria?"

Maria said naught, just stared, unmoving, her hands in the air.

"Will somebody at least tell me something, *please*?" Michael looked at Maria; there was nothing doing. He faced Dr. Rouben, who remained impassive.

"You're the father of a baby born of Immaculate Conception," he said.

Like Maria earlier, the doctor's lips twitched into a simpering smile. Michael didn't like the look of it. "I know," Michael said, "you helped Angie and me to conceive her…"

Dr. Rouben's smile faded as quickly as it had arisen. "Not Jessica, she was my baby." For the first time since he had arrived, he unclamped his stare off Maria and glanced at Michael. "I'm talking about the baby that came from you," he said, and then to Maria, "And you're going to tell me where she is."

"What baby?" Michael felt like screaming and pulling his hair out.

"You're a modern day Mary, Michael. You've given birth to the Second Child of Jehovah."

At first Michael thought he was joking, but the obstetrician standing in the frame of the doorway wasn't laughing. "What are you talking about?" he asked, recovering himself. "Has everybody gone stark raving mad? When was this supposed to have taken place… and where?"

"The night you were brought into the hospital after the accident. You've got the scar to prove it." Dr. Rouben glanced again at Michael. It was only fleeting, but it was enough for Michael to realise he wasn't making any of this up. His frankness was chilling. "You're the final link in a two-thousand year cycle."

Michael turned to Maria, absently rubbing the scar on his belly through his jumper. She was still standing mutedly, hands raised. She nodded to him, confirming what Dr. Rouben had just said. He still couldn't believe it, though; it was just too far-fetched. What he also didn't want to believe, but what was becoming increasingly obvious with every second that passed, was that Dr. Rouben was part of some diabolical plot to kidnap and sacrifice his child. It was undeniable. The stains on his cuff were more damning than a self-confession; the man he had begun to trust like a father had murdered Jessica. Michael knew that now. He also knew that Dr. Rouben would stop at nothing to find out where Maria had hidden the baby he really wanted, the baby that they were unbelievably implying had been gestating inside his own abdomen.

Michael ran a hand through his hair. Maria had been on his side all along, so it seemed. She had obviously been part of Dr. Rouben's original plans, but something had happened between them, some kind of falling out. Maria must have taken the other baby for herself, using Jessica as a decoy. She must have double-crossed him, as he said she did, and swapped the babies right under his nose, but why? What could she want with the other baby?

The more Michael thought about it, the more he confused himself. He turned to Dr. Rouben and stared into those coal-like eyes again, still absently rubbing his scar. Michael felt mentally numbed, like his brain was momentarily paralysed. In fact, he probably wouldn't even react if Dr. Rouben shot him. Could he truly believe what Dr. Rouben and Maria were saying, that a child had been wrenched from his own belly?

"The Second Coming has occurred. I admit I was fooled when you told me Gabriel had visited you in a dream. I thought he meant Angie's baby, *my* baby," Dr. Rouben said. "But he was really talking about the baby that came from you." Dr. Rouben then focused on Maria. "And now I want her. The prophecy must be fulfilled tonight."

Suddenly, Michael heard the creak of a floorboard in the hallway. Before he registered what was happening, there was a flurry of movement followed by a sickening crunch of bone being struck with wood. Dr. Rouben's dark eyes rolled to the back of his skull and the gun fell from his grip. He sank to his knees and collapsed head first onto the floor.

# CHAPTER 16

THE SOUND DR. ROUBEN made when he hit the floor reminded Michael of a boxer receiving an uppercut to the solar plexus: a meaty thud followed by a winded groan, and Michael briefly wondered if he had sounded like that when he fainted in OR3 the day this man impregnated Angie with ovum fertilised with his own sperm. From the couch, he stared in shock at the slumped, prostrate body. Dr. Rouben's neatly slicked hair was matted with blood at the back of his head, and a thick rivulet had begun to congeal as it dripped onto the nape of his neck, as if a crimson tapeworm had tried to crawl out of his brain. Michael tore his eyes away from the grisly sight and glanced up at the murderer. Like a knight brandishing a sword, Norman was still wielding what appeared to be a rolling pin, as if about to strike out at anyone who dared to come close.

"Bloody hell! I think you've killed him," Michael said. "How hard did you hit him?"

Tittering nervously, Norman lowered the rolling pin. "I knew you shouldn't trust a doctor who calls himself Billy."

Maria, who had initially seemed surprised by the sudden attack, dropped her surrendering hands and rushed over to feel Dr. Rouben's neck for a pulse. "He's still alive," she said, looking up at Norman. "You didn't hit him hard enough." She half-rolled the unconscious body over, lifted up his robe, removed the handgun holstered between his belt and Armani shirt, then pointed it at his head and said, "I'll finish him off."

Michael was horrified. He jumped up from the couch and grabbed the hand with which Maria was holding the weapon, pulling it up and to the right just as the bullet left the silencer with a soft puff. It entered the Steinway with a spray of fine splinters and a jingle of one or two jolting cords, leaving a small hole in the piano's flat wooded face, as if a carpenter had bored a half-inch drill neatly above the keys.

"What the hell do you think you're doing?" he said, almost shouting. "It's murder."

"It's all the bastard deserves." Maria tried to aim the gun back at the unconscious head at her feet, but Michael's grip was too strong. "Let me go. It's for your own good."

Michael held firm. "Maybe, but that just makes you the same as him," he said. "I'll let you go if you promise to put your gun away." Maria made a half attempted tug with her hand, then relented. "Put it away," he said.

Maria glared at him. "Okay, but you're making a big mistake."

Michael relaxed his grip, warily at first, thinking she was going to pull the trigger again despite her words to the contrary. When she lifted her black dress and slotted the gun into a leather holster strapped to her upper thigh, Michael felt better.

"Okay, good," he said. "Let's get out of here before he wakes up. Let's get my baby."

"Wait a minute." Maria bent down and picked up the handgun Dr. Rouben had dropped when he collapsed. It had fallen beneath the small foot table adjacent to the piano. "Here," she said, handing it to Michael, "you might need it."

"What do you want me to do with this?" he asked, grimacing. "I've never fired a gun in my life."

She took it out of his hand. "This is not just any handgun," she said, and began quickly displaying its parts. "It's a Colt Mk IV Series 80. Single action. Seven rounds of 45's; clip's in the grip. Here's the safety." She caressed the grip safety with the tip of her thumb. "It's off, see. The bastard would have shot you without a second thought." She cocked the locking mechanism and handed him the gun.

"Why don't you just keep it?" he asked.

"Because I have my Colt Defender," she said.

Michael eyed the gun with disapproval and took it with only marginally more confidence than before. He flicked his eyes towards Norman. He still looked in shock at what he had done to Dr. Rouben.

"Thanks for saving our lives," Michael said, then looked back at the white robed figure lying on the ground, absently pointing the gun at him. "But, how did you know he was, you know, responsible for Jessica?"

"Watch where you point that thing, Mikey," Norman said, warily. "I know he's not your favourite person at the moment, but I don't think you want to spill more blood on the carpet, do you?"

Michael glanced from side to side, searching for a place to put it down, then decided to holster it in his belt like he had seen Dr. Rouben do with Maria's.

Norman visibly relaxed. "When I came out of the bathroom I heard his voice on the baby monitor in the kitchen," he said, nodding his head toward the grey transmitter sitting on top of the piano. A small red light on its side flashed on and off when he spoke. "I heard everything."

Michael ran his hand through his hair. "And what do you think?" he asked, after a moment. Part of him wanted Norman to tell him that it was all a load of rubbish, that there was another, more believable explanation. Yet, there was another part of him that wanted Norman to agree. There was some kind of perverse comfort in knowing that someone else was having just as much difficulty grasping to reality as he was. If Norman thought it believable, then he reckoned he might not feel so crazy.

"What do I think about you being a mother and a father at the same time?" Norman shook his head. "It's all above my head," he said. "In fact, I'd rather not think about it. All I know is that he was willing to kill you to get your baby. I had to stop him somehow." He turned the rolling pin over in his hand and examined it. Michael looked too. There was a small indentation surrounded by a splattering of blood where it had made contact with Dr. Rouben's skull. "I found this in one of your kitchen drawers."

Maria had moved to the window whilst they were talking and was now peeking outside through a slender crack between the drapes. She suddenly became agitated. "We've got company," she said, quickly closing the curtains, frowning. "It's your cousin, the Chief Inspector. We have to think of something."

"But that's great," Michael said, his face brightening. "He can arrest Dr. Rouben. I'll call him in."

"Don't be an idiot," she said, just as Michael was about to exit the room. He looked at her with mild surprise. "He's part of it all."

It was Michael's turn to frown. What she said was unthinkable. He was a cop. He was family. There was no way he would be an accomplice to Jessica's murder. "We're talking about my cousin, Jude, aren't we?"

Maria came away from the curtain and once again Michael was struck by her prettiness. "I'm afraid so," she said.

In spite of the recent admissions from Dr. Rouben, he still didn't trust her completely. He had to see for himself. He went to the window and peeked outside. Sure enough, on the pavement beneath the streetlight, he saw Jude's distinctive athletic figure dressed all in black. He was smoking a cigarette and acting much as Michael figured a lookout would. At first he didn't want to believe his own cousin was involved in all this, but his presence outside was proof enough. He closed the curtain.

"I shouldn't have called him," he said.

"You did what?" Maria stared at him with utter disbelief, as if he had destroyed every hope they had of getting out of this mess. "Is that how they knew I was here? I thought I told you not to call the cops," she said. "What did I say would happen if you did?"

Michael lowered his eyes. "He's not technically..."

"Not technically?" she said, interjecting. Then realising she was raising her voice a little too loudly, she lowered it to a hush. "What in God's name is a Chief Inspector if it's not *technically* an officer in the police force? What were you thinking?"

"I was thinking about getting my daughter back!" Michael said, his voice hushed like hers. He hoped Jude couldn't hear. If he suspected Dr. Rouben was in trouble and came inside, Michael knew there would be a shoot out and more than just a drop or two of blood on a rolling pin being spilled. "What was I supposed to do? I thought you were responsible for all the abductions and murders and kidnaps and whatever..."

She held up her hand for him to stop. "All right. What's done is done. There's no point in arguing," she said. "I think I know what we can do." She hurried around the couch and stepped over the collapsed figure in white to get to the phone. "Let's hope they haven't gone too far."

Norman looked over at Michael who looked back at him and shrugged. Maria dialled a number seemingly from memory. She spoke briefly. Michael could only hear part of the conversation, but not enough to know what it meant.

"Who was that?" Michael asked when she hung up.

"Friends," she said. "Your cousin may die tonight. Does that bother you?"

Michael stepped away from the window. "What? Of course that bothers me."

"Lower your voice, or it'll be you, not him."

Now whispering with restraint, he said, "What's going to happen to him? Who were you just speaking to, hit men?"

Maria managed a smile. "No," she said. "As I said, friends. Nothing will happen to him if he cooperates. We're not murderers." She looked disdainfully at the figure lying at her feet. "Not like this scum."

"What about all those babies you kidnapped?"

"I did what I had to." She went to the window once more. "I'm not proud of it, but it was necessary."

"Necessary for what?"

Her eyes were like brown ice when they looked at him and he felt their chill run up his spine. "For your daughter to survive," she said. She peeked outside between the curtains again to check on Jude's movements. Michael could see over the top of her head. Nothing had changed, thankfully, except that Jude had stopped smoking and was nervously eyeing the street with his hands on his hips.

Maria flicked the curtains closed. "Now, when my friends arrive, we have to move quickly, okay?"

Norman and Michael nodded in unison. She told them what needed to be done.

FIVE MINUTES LATER, Michael was watching Jude through the crack in the curtains. With his back to the house, Jude brought another cigarette to his mouth and exhaled a large, wispy O-ring, which floated above his head and lingered like a dirty halo. As he watched it disintegrate into the night air, Jude suddenly heard something and spun his head to see what had made the noise. Michael strained his ears, and a moment later heard the jingle of a dog collar and the unhurried footsteps of someone approaching from up the street.

"Good boy, Jack," gramps said from the dim gloom.

As the old man neared, Michael could make out the shadow of his hunched gait, closely followed by the dark shape of a dog wiggling its tail. He wondered whether Maria was in place. She had exited the rear kitchen doors a few minutes ago and should have sidled along the side of the house to the front by now. Unfortunately, the porch was blocking his view of the nearside driveway. He could only see Norman's white Ford Falcon. Angie's car was out of sight.

Jude stubbed out his cigarette on the pavement and immediately lit another one, watching the old guy and his waddling black Labrador with arthritic hips. Michael knew he hated dogs, and that if this one tried to hump his leg he would probably shoot it. The Labrador seemed to sense his antipathy towards it and stopped in his tracks. It looked up at him with the kind of sad eyes women went gushy over. Its tail, too, had stopped wagging.

"Got lost old man?" Jude asked the old guy, taking a drag.

"No, sonny, just going for a walk with Jack."

Jack was still looking at him with those sad eyes and sniffing him from afar. Jude exhaled a lungful of smoke. "Bit late to be going for a walk, isn't it?"

Suddenly, Michael saw a movement in the shadow of Norman's car. It was Maria, hunched down in front of the hood. With professional stealth, she crept up behind Jude and pushed the barrel of her gun into his back. Jude's shoulders sagged the instant he felt the hard metal shaft between them.

"Bit late to be visiting your cousin, isn't it?" Maria said. There was a tad of self-satisfaction in her voice, as with the smile that was on the old guy's face. Her voice then turned as hard as the gun imbedded between Jude's shoulder blades. "Drop the cigarette and put your hands in the air, nice and slow." The cigarette fell to the path and he raised his arms above his head.

This was Michael's cue. He faced the lounge room. The unconscious obstetrician was lying on his stomach between the piano and the couch, which was blocking Michael's view of the lower half of his torso. He was stripped to his underwear, his white robe and clothes tossed absently over the back of the couch, and Norman was now bent over him, tying his wrists behind his back with some rope. Michael quickly called his friend over. Norman grabbed the white robe and slipped it over his head, hurrying across the room to take position in front of the window. Standing behind him, Michael reached around and covered Norman's mouth with his hand, gagging him. Next, he removed the gun from his belt and held it to Norman's head. Then he said okay and Norman opened the curtains.

Outside, Maria glanced over her shoulder and nodded to them, almost imperceptibly. "Now, before you get any funny ideas in your stupid head about using that gun you're carrying," she said to Jude, "just remember your precious master has a gun trained to his head as we speak. One false move and it's… well, it's good night nurse. Now turn around, nice and slowly does it."

She took a step back and allowed him to do as she ordered. "Oh, don't look so disappointed Jude," she said when he eventually faced her. "Didn't the priest always tell you to expect the unexpected?"

He glared at her, then flicked his eyes towards the window. Michael knew that if Jude didn't take the bait, they wouldn't get further than two streets before the whole of the state's police force descended on them. Jude looked at Norman, then raised his eyes toward Michael. It was only a brief stare, but Michael could feel the hatred in those blue eyes. He struggled to fathom how anyone could be filled with so much loathing.

"Okay, Maria," Jude said to her, "what do you want? Whatever it is, you know you won't get away with it. We're too powerful."

"Shut it!" she said. "Or you'll get a chest full of holes. You'll be dead long before those disgusting cigarettes will do it for you. Got it?" Jude snorted scornfully, but said nothing. "Pat him down," Maria said to gramps.

The old man's bent back was suddenly erect and he began to move with the litheness of someone half his age. Jack began to wag his tail once again and, to Jude's obvious distaste, began sniffing around his ankles. Jude held his peace as the old man patted him down and removed the gun holstered inside his belt, along with the cell phone, cigarettes, lighter and wallet from his front pockets. The old man inspected the contents of the wallet, and, seemingly satisfied that there was nothing but cash and credit cards, threw it and the lighter and cigarettes onto the street. The cell phone, he handed to Maria.

"That's it. He's clean," gramps said, pressing the gun into Jude's spine.

Maria nodded. Stepping back, she dropped the cell phone onto the footpath and crunched it with the heel of her shoe. She kicked it into the gutter, and said to Jude, "Where's your car?"

Jude pointed down the street with a disdainful nod of his head. Maria looked over her shoulder and Michael followed her gaze. On the very edge of his vision, two houses in the distance, he saw the vague outline of Jude's Chrysler Valiant. It was parked in the dark shadow between two streetlights, directly opposite Maria's yellow Renault. Maria then stepped onto the road, the gun steadily maintaining its aim, and waved to someone at the other end of the street, the same direction from which the old man and Jack had emerged.

Almost immediately, Michael heard the distinctive chug of a VW Beetle come to life, breaking the quiet of the night. Within seconds, it pulled up beneath the streetlight in front of Michael's house. Maria went to the driver's window and spoke to the driver, a woman with a mess of hair that looked like candyfloss. He tried to listen as hard as he could but their voices were lost murmurs over the chugging of the engine. After less than a minute Maria was standing before Jude again, her gun pointing directly at his heart.

"You won't get away with this," Jude said.

"Didn't I tell you to shut it?" Then, over his shoulder to the old man, Maria said, "Take him to the driveway."

Gramps put a firm palm into the small of Jude's back and marched him to the white Ford Falcon. "Spread 'em!" he said, and Jude spread his legs wide. "Hands on the roof!"

Maria turned to the lounge room window. She gestured to Michael with a wave. Jude tried to look over his shoulder, but was clipped in the ear with the back of the old man's hand. "Bring that murdering bastard to the car," Maria said to Michael.

With Michael's left hand still gagging Norman, and his right hand holding the Colt to his head, they exited the house onto the porch and slowly crossed the front lawn toward the street.

"Don't do it Mikey," Jude said, speaking over his shoulder to him. "You don't know what you're doing."

Michael didn't answer. Maria had warned him earlier that Jude would target him. He could feel a surge of cold hatred rush from his chest toward his cousin like the day they witnessed the death of the Great Dane through the hole in his backyard fence. Like that day, he felt a compelling need to lash out and smash his cousin's jaw, this time with the butt of the gun instead of his fists, but he did no such thing, knowing that the slightest deviation from Maria's plan could mean the death of his daughter. He kept his anger in check and his voice mum, shuffling behind Norman onto the pavement. Half a minute later, he opened the rear door of Maria's car and bundled Norman in. Then he slammed it shut and waited for Maria to finish her business.

"Okay, it's all set," Maria said to the old man. Her voice was barely audible over the chug of the Beetle. "You can go now. She knows what to do. She'll fill you in."

Gramps stepped slowly back. His gun remained trained on Jude as he opened the passenger door and leaned the seat forward. Tail wagging, Jack jumped into the back seat, albeit with a little help from his master. Then the old man got in and Michael watched the Beetle engage into gear and accelerate past.

"Don't even think of making a move," Maria said to Jude, as the chug of the Beetle faded into the distance. She edged her way to the street, keeping her eyes and gun firmly fixed on him, and when she felt the distance between them was safe enough she turned and dashed toward Michael and her car. Michael jumped into the front passenger seat, Maria behind the steering wheel. They accelerated off, wheels spinning.

Maria spent the next minute zigzagging through the back streets of

Tusmore, randomly turning left or right at whatever intersection they came upon in case Jude had decided to give chase. After the seventh or eighth turn, she pulled the Renault into the shadowy pool beneath the overhanging branches of a large eucalypt, killed the engine, and flicked off the headlights.

"We did it!" Michael said, facing Norman first, then Maria. Her demeanour remained serious, but Michael saw a glimmer of a smile.

"We're still a long way from safety," she said.

Norman pulled the white hood off his head. "Christ, I thought he was going to figure us out," he said, smiling as broadly as Michael. With the unbloodied cuff of the robe, he armed away some sweat off his brow. "I don't mean to be rude to your family, Mikey, but how the hell did he make it to the ranks of Chief Inspector being so stupid?"

Michael shrugged, still smiling.

"Let's say he has very powerful friends in low places," Maria said.

"Who was the old man?" Michael asked. "And the lady in the Beetle?"

"Just friends," she said, their eyes meeting. "They belong to *The Fold*."

Michael recalled his initial thoughts of Maria when she had unexpectedly arrived at the house. He figured he probably hadn't been too far off the mark. "*The Fold?* Sounds like a cult."

Maria smiled a little. "It is, kind of, but not what you're thinking. They've been keeping an eye on your house for several months now. It's how we knew you and Angie were being watched." The smile lingered a little before fading away. "But we don't have time to discuss it now," she said, rather abruptly. She leaned over and reached beneath the front passenger seat, felt around the floor for several seconds, and then finally found what she was looking for. It was a switchblade knife. "You know what to do?" she said to Norman, handing it to him. "You still want to go ahead with it?"

"Yeah, yeah," he said, taking it from her. Once out of the car, he took off the white robe, flinging it on the back seat. Norman stuck his head in through the open door. "I'll slash the tyres of Jude's car to stall them and then see you at the arranged spot in an hour."

Michael looked at his friend with admiration, and said, "I don't know how to thank you, mate. You're risking your life for something we have no idea will work out."

Norman gave him a wink and a cheesy grin. "Mikey, this is the best thing I've ever done," he said. "So hurry up and find your daughter before those bastards do, okay?"

Before Norman closed the door, Michael smiled lopsidedly and nodded in appreciation. He watched Norman disappear over his shoulder as the Renault accelerated away and turned left into a side street.

MARIA STEERED THE car into a driveway several streets from the hospital and into an open garage, parking next to the VW Beetle Michael had seen gramps and his dog jump into ten minutes ago.

"Come on," she said, getting out. "There's someone I want you to meet."

Maria closed the garage and ushered him through a door that opened into the kitchen at the back of the house. It wasn't that dissimilar to his own house and kitchen, he noticed. Maria hurried him down the hallway to the lounge room, where gramps and the woman with candyfloss hair and mini were waiting, seated on the couch. The curtains were drawn and only a small lamp was on, the light so dim Michael could barely see Jack lying at his master's feet, his head between his front paws. Gramps was stroking Jack's head and the woman was cradling a baby. They greeted each other with a curt nod.

"Here she is, your little girl," the woman said, standing up and holding her out for Michael to take.

Eyes closed, dressed in a white cotton pyjama suit, the baby made not a sound. Michael hesitated in accepting her. She looked too delicate, too fragile, like a Botticelli angel, and touching her seemed defiling in some way.

"Go on, take her," Maria said. "Her name's Ananda."

Finally, he did. On the front of her pyjama suit was a large emblem drawn with a black felt marker, reminding him of a Celtic rune: a large circle in which an equilateral triangle was drawn, the three points of its apex and base neatly touching the inner edge of the circle, and another smaller circle drawn to fit precisely within the borders of the triangle itself; circle, triangle, circle.

"She seems very sleepy," he said, cradling her in his arms and staring at her with a mix of astonishment and bedazzlement.

"Don't worry about it. It's just the antihistamines I've given her," Maria said. "They'll wear off in two to three hours."

Caressing her cheek with the tip of his index finger, Michael looked up, alarmed. "You've drugged her?"

"I had to," Maria said. "If she cried while I was bringing her here…" and her voice trailed off before picking up again. "Let's just say all our efforts to save her would have been for nothing."

Michael's emotions were now getting to him. He cleared his throat, which seemed to have constricted tightly, as if someone had grabbed him from behind and was now in the process of slowly throttling him. "Don't I get a say in what she should be called?" he asked.

"Not with this baby," Maria said, rather matter-of-factly, and Michael heard gramps chuckle quietly. Maria caressed the baby's scalp. "She's the Second Child of Jehovah. Her name was chosen by God before time began." She halted and looked up at him, quizzically. "What's the matter?"

"I, I'm just a bit overwhelmed, I think." His throat still felt tight. "I mean, I'm not even sure I believe in God," he said. "I'm not sure I can believe He has a child."

"Do you always deny what's so obvious?" she said. "What will it take for you to believe I'm telling the truth, another miracle?"

Angie had that same demanding tone of voice, Michael mused, when she thought he was being stubborn and pigheaded. "I, I don't know," he said.

Maria went to the TV and switched it on. "I want you to see this, before it's destroyed." She pushed the PLAY button on the VCR atop the TV and turned up the volume. "It's the video of your operation. Dr. Rouben thinks I've already deleted it."

Michael watched the video flicker on. The camera had captured the scene from up high, somewhere near the ceiling. Peering closer, a little squeamish, he could see himself lying on the operating table, unconscious and ventilated. He counted four others (three men, one woman), dressed in surgical gowns and hair-caps, standing around the operating table. A doctor, presumably the anaesthetist, was barking orders at the head of the operating table. Behind him, atop the ventilator, an ECG monitor beeped loudly. The anaesthetist leaned over and silenced it whilst a nurse busily attached a bag of blood to the T-bar above his head, then turned and disappeared off the screen. While this was happening, another nurse stood at the foot of the operating table readying a set of surgical equipment. Next to her, a fat guy was holding a pair of retractors, waiting for the surgeon on the opposite side to begin. Michael watched the short surgeon slice through his bruised, distended abdomen. Just as the scalpel reached the groin, a gush of blood vomited out of the incision like a flooding river breaking its banks. Everyone jumped back with surprise. The ECG monitor alarmed hysterically.

"Flat line!" yelled the anaesthetist. "Start CPR, now!"

"We canna do it," the surgeon said with an almost incomprehensible Scottish accent. His surgical facemask only partially covered his red beard. "We 'af t' feend the bleed."

Michael kept staring at the screen, still cradling Ananda, his stomach turning somewhat. The images were as graphic and as disturbing as when he had seen Angie for the first time in the ICU, yet as surreal as a dream. It was more than a little weird watching your own operation, and he didn't need a medical degree to know that he had been in bad shape after the crash.

*Someth'ns wrong with Mikey*, he thought, giggling nervously. *I think he's dyin', Mikey.*

On the video, the nurse at the foot of the table immediately inserted a suction probe into the wound and began sucking the blood out of it, the sound of its slurping loud enough to drown out the mechanical breaths of the ventilator. Wasting no time, the anaesthetist rushed to operating table next to Scottish surgeon, almost elbowing him out of the way. Michael watched him reach into the incision, his hand disappearing from view as it groped toward the centre of his chest. Like a background narrator on some reality TV show, Michael now heard Maria explain that the anaesthetist had grabbed hold of his heart and was squeezing it in his palm like he would a tennis ball. At that moment, he was clinically dead.

The nurse continued to slurp up the blood with the suction probe. Michael could now see most of his intestines. "I think we're losing him," the anaesthetist said to the surgeon. "You have to find the bleed. He can't cope with the loss of volume."

"Just a wee minnit," the surgeon said, peering into the messy gash. "Okay, sister, stop f'r a wee moment."

The nurse removed the suction probe from the open stomach and the operating room fell suddenly quiet. The surgeon grabbed several loops of bowel and plonked them on the chest of his patient. He lifted several more loops out, then suddenly stopped. "Oh... my... God!" he said, staring unblinkingly.

From the angle of the camera, the fat guy was obstructing its view and Michael was unable to see the whole of his opened abdomen. He saw the nurse peer in. Like the surgeon's, her eyes immediately widened. She dropped the suction probe and it clattered onto her foot. The other nurse suddenly walked in from off the screen cradling several blood bags to her chest. She took one look at the patient on the operating table and emitted a scream that could have curdled the contents of those bags.

The fat guy suddenly fainted, flopping onto the floor like a shot pig. Michael could now see what everyone else saw.

Out of his open wound, its umbilical cord attached to the yellowish, curtain-like omentum of his stomach, the Scottish surgeon held aloft a healthy baby girl. She began screaming immediately, red in the face, her eyes scrunched tightly and her mouth opened as far as it could go. "Get me Dr. Rouben," the surgeon said. "Now!"

"He's in OR3 with an emergency C-section," the anaesthetist said to the nurse who had just entered. Seemingly grateful for the opportunity to leave, she darted off screen.

Maria went back to the VCR and fast-forwarded it, saying she only wanted Michael to see a little bit more. Gramps and the woman with the candyfloss hair remained silent. Jack had his eyes opened, his head still lying between his front paws, watching everything that was going on. Maria stopped fast-forwarding at the point she and Dr. Rouben rushed into the operating room. They had just finished operating on Angie, she said.

Michael watched Dr. Rouben step forward and take hold of the baby. He was calm, as if he had seen this sort of thing every day, or, as Michael was beginning to suspect, he'd been expecting it.

"I'd appreciate it if word of this didn't get out," Dr. Rouben said to the others, cutting the umbilical cord with a scalpel and then wrapping the baby in a green surgical towel the assisting nurse had handed to him. "We have to think of the best interests of the child, do you agree?" Everyone nodded, no one saying a word. Michael saw him glance up to the video camera as he handed Maria the baby. "Good. If anyone asks, what you saw here today was nothing but a tumour growth that had to be surgically removed, okay?"

Everyone nodded again and the anaesthetic monitor suddenly stopped beeping. All attention in the room was momentarily focused on the ECG trace, which seemed to have reverted back to normal. Then, all at once, they began to work feverishly where they had left off, as if Michael's reversion to a normal heartbeat had kick started their own hearts and minds back into action. It was as if nothing had ever happened.

"Why didn't they say anything?" Michael asked.

"It's too confusing for them." Maria switched off the VCR and ejected the cassette. She handed it to gramps, and said, "You know what to do with it." Gramps nodded.

She was absolutely right, Michael thought. They had seen a miracle and no one wanted to believe it. It was easier to believe in fairytales than the truth they had just seen. He couldn't really blame them though, could he? Until this moment, it was exactly as he would have behaved.

"Why don't we go to the newspapers?" he asked. "We have the video. Once her story is out, she'll be protected."

Maria shook her head. "The papers can't help," she said. "Anyway, who'd believe it? They'd say the video was a fake. That's why Dr. Ruben wasn't too worried if the news of her birth leaked out. It wouldn't get past the editor's desk."

Michael ran a hand through his hair, not altogether convinced.

There were several UK tabloids he could think of off the top of his head that would have a field day with this story. "So where do we go now?" he asked. The baby in his arms was still sleeping quietly.

Maria asked the other woman whether she had the briefcase. The woman shook her head and apologised, claiming she hadn't been able to get to Maria's room in the nurses' quarters because of the increased police presence. Maria seemed to take this information badly, but she kept her troubles to herself. She closed her eyes, silently collecting herself.

"Looks like we have to make a slight detour when we get your wife," she said to Michael, after a moment. "But we have to be quick. Your cousin and Dr. Rouben are probably on their way to the hospital as we speak. They would have assumed you'd want to get Angie." She paused briefly. "We just have to hope Norman was able to complete his task. Otherwise…"

She didn't need to finish her sentence.

# CHAPTER 17

MICHAEL CRADLED ANANDA to his chest in the passenger seat as Maria reversed out of the garage. Less than five minutes later they were on John Street, heading toward St. Mary's. Michael tried to push the memory of the last time he drove down this street out of his thoughts, its impact still too fresh and painful to allow it to linger for too long.

"Why is tonight so important?" he asked.

"Today is November the 28th," she said, concentrating on the road ahead. "As it happens, it coincides with this year's celebration of Thanksgiving Day in the New World."

Michael absently scratched his head. By the expression on her face, and the tone of her voice, it was obvious she thought he should recognise the importance of the date and its underlying implication. He didn't, and she seemed to sense the confusion in his eyes.

"It's exactly two thousand years to the day that the First Child was born," she said.

Michael kept scratching his head, then realised what he was doing. "But it's only 1996," he said, lowering his hand. They had just passed the spot where he had crashed into the eucalypt, he noticed. "There's still over four years to go until December 2000, and it's not even Christmas for another month. The dates are all wrong."

The car sped on. The twin buildings of St. Mary's Hospital now dominated the view through the windshield. "No, they're not. Jesus was born in the year 4BC," Maria said. "The monk who calculated the date of his birth made a mistake. His name was Dennis the Little, and I don't know how but it seems he lost four years in the calculation. He also rearranged the actual month and day of Jesus' birth to coincide with the Roman festive celebrations of the winter solstice. I guess he wanted to manipulate the pagans into believing Jesus was the true Messiah. He shouldn't have, but he did, and it means we've been celebrating the wrong date for nearly two millennia."

"And what does Dr. Rouben have to do with all this?" he asked. Maria slowed the car as they approached the main hospital gates. "Why does he want to get his hands on my baby?"

"Dr. Rouben is the head priest, the mastermind, of Satanism in the New World." Maria pulled past the sleeping security guard and into the parking lot, where there were no more than two-dozen cars. "He's in it for the power, and believe me he has an awful lot of it. He has an insatiable lust for it and if he drinks the sacred blood of the Second Child on this day he will gain power never before seen on this earth. If he does," and she paused, like someone not wishing to consider the consequences if he succeeded. "If he does, then Satan will rule for the next two thousand years, until, that is, the cycle is repeated and Jehovah's Third Child is born. They missed their chance last time because they were weak and badly disorganised, but not now. Now they're as powerful and as organised as a corporate business. We've been lucky so far. He made the classical blunder all megalomaniacs make at some point or another, totally underestimating the guile and will of his enemy, us, *The Fold.*"

Maria parked as close as she could to the main entrance, a beacon of whiteness in the dark night. Michael remembered seeing the light halo the journalist's hair on the television when she stood in front of the sliding glass doors reporting on the latest abduction from the hospital, an abduction perpetrated by the woman who was now acting to save his, and his daughter's, life. Maria got out, leaving the keys dangling in the ignition. They would be needed later for a quick getaway.

Michael followed her with the baby across the parking lot and into the hospital lobby. When his eyes finally adjusted to the brightness, he saw only one other person, a woman, sitting behind the reception counter with bored, tired eyes. Michael hurried after Maria, their footsteps echoing around the empty vestibule as she led him past the shuttered shops to the stairwell adjacent to the elevators, deliberately keeping her face turned away from the receptionist. On the door, and written in green, was: EMERGENCY EXIT ONLY. They quickly entered the stairwell, which was less well lit than the lobby but more than sufficient to see the steps in front of them. To his surprise, Maria began descending toward the basement.

"Where are you going? The ICU's on the eighth floor," he said, pointing upward.

"To my room in the nurses' quarters first," she said. "We have to get the briefcase before we get Angie."

"Then why didn't we go through the front entrance to that building?" he asked. "Why do we have to go this way?"

Maria stopped, already half a flight down. "There's a security guard on the door," she said, looking up. "The police might have tipped him off to be on the lookout for me. We can bypass him this way."

The basement was grim and grey and it immediately gave Michael the creeps. Once or twice as they weaved along the corridors toward the nurses' building, Michael felt the hairs on his neck raise, as if he could sense the presence of someone watching him. It wasn't the same feeling as being watched by security cameras, which Maria expertly pointed out and avoided as they went; it was a different feeling, atavistic, as if he just *knew* that he was being observed, like he sometimes knew who was calling him before he picked up the phone. The faint rush of air in the large air-conditioning pipe above his head didn't help matters; it sounded uncannily like voices whispering to one another, whispering about *him*. Irrational as it was, he felt an uneasy, child-like desire to get out of this place as quickly as possible.

They finally arrived at the elevator-well. He reached out to press the call button, but Maria grabbed his wrist and pointed to the closed elevator door with a quick nod of her head. "Cameras in the elevator," she whispered. "We'll take the stairwell."

They ascended another set of emergency stairs as quietly as they could, tiptoeing behind the security guard on the ground floor, and onto the sixth floor. Getting inside had been a lot easier than he imagined it would. At the door marked 6E, Maria began unlocking the first of its five locks, starting with the top. He remembered Jude saying on the telephone that Maria was the number one suspect and wondered why the police hadn't broken the door down yet to investigate her room.

Then again, he figured, Jude had probably instructed them not too. She was, after all, supposed to have been Dr. Rouben's accomplice.

"What's with all the locks, anyway?" he asked.

"Don't hurry me," she said, not looking up.

Michael stood behind her, checking the corridor to his left and right. He was feeling too vulnerable in the open, as vulnerable as he had been feeling in the basement. "Don't you trust the security in this place?" he whispered, his eyes darting from side to side.

The last lock clicked and Maria entered the room. Michael hurried in behind her. "Would you trust the security in this hospital?" she whispered back, gently closing the door. When she turned he saw the cheeky smile on her face. "Haven't you heard of all the babies going missing here?"

Michael wasn't sure if that was funny or not, but he matched her smile. She squeezed past him and he surveyed the room, wondering how anyone could live in such a cramped, tiny space with barely any creature comforts: an old wooden closet, a single mattress bed with grey blankets, a small bedside table and a telephone. With the old, dirty curtains draped across the window, the picture was complete—the place was a prison.

It was her idea of wallpaper, however, that made him gape with surprise. Plastered across every inch of space along the walls and ceiling were various, assorted pictures of Jesus—a Divine Montage. The room was a gallery to the Lord. Some depicted him on the cross, others as a baby held in his mother's arms. One, he saw, was a nativity scene, another, the Sermon on the Mount, and directly above, the Resurrection. There were hundreds of them, all different sizes and shapes. He had never seen anything quite like it. It was something, he imagined, like a miniature version of the Sistine Chapel.

"How long have you been living here?" he asked.

Maria was now on her knees and reaching below the mattress. She dragged out a black briefcase. With two hands she lifted it off the floor, plonking it on top of the blankets. It made the mattress spring up and down a couple of times when it landed. "Five, nearly six, years. Before that I lived in Melbourne," she said, spinning the digits of the combination lock with her thumb, first the three digits on the left, then the three on the right. "I used to be a cop in the Victorian Police Force, before *The Fold* reassigned me to study nursing in Adelaide."

"A jack of all trades," he said, smiling, and impressed. "What next?"

Still on bended knees, she turned to look up at him over her shoulder. Her expression was grave. "Nothing," she said, with a tone of voice that scared him; it was flat and lifeless, as if she was already resigned to the realisation that she had come to the end of her time on this world. "My job is complete." Her eyes glazed over for a brief moment, and then quickly sparked back into life. "Come here," she said. "Look at the code." Michael read the combination over her shoulder. It was Ananda's birthday—06-11-96.

Maria clicked the briefcase open and his jaw dropped further than he knew it could. "There's almost one million dollars in used one-hundred dollar bills here," she said, giving him several seconds to feast his eyes on the money. "All untraceable."

There was something else, too, he saw. Almost hidden, a white envelope poked out from the inner sleeve of the case's lid. It couldn't keep his attention for long, and he returned to gape at the money, almost dropping his sleeping baby. Doing so shook him out of his awe-drenched stupor. "How… how much?" he asked.

"One million Aussie dollars." She snapped the lid of the briefcase shut, clicked the locks into place, and then spun the combination so that the numbers were randomly arranged.

"Where the hell did you get that sort of money?" He was breathless. It was becoming increasingly difficult to distinguish reality from illusion the longer the night went on.

Maria got off her knees. "Don't you mean where in heaven? I have friends too, you know, but they're in high places." She picked up the briefcase and held it out to Michael. "Now, take it and leave," she said. "You have to go."

Michael cradled Ananda in the crook of his right elbow, knowing his right shoulder wouldn't be able to take the strain of the briefcase. As it was, it was already protesting with the weight of the baby. "But where do I go?" he asked, taking the case with some difficulty. Ten thousand bank notes were a lot heavier than they looked. "Aren't you coming with me?"

"No. There's something else I have to do here. Inside is an envelope with the address of a convent in Melbourne." She put an arm on his shoulder and led him to the door. "They're expecting you. They know all about Ananda," she said. "You can trust them; they belong to *The Fold* and they'll give you further directions from there."

Michael stopped. "You mentioned *The Fold* before," he said. "Those other two we saw tonight, the old man with the dog, and that lady with the hair, you said they belonged to it too."

Maria nodded and continued to the door. "Yes, there are many of us," she said, grabbing the knob, "and you will meet many more, if all goes according to plan."

"But I've never heard of it before."

"Good. We're a highly secret organisation, just as the priest's … Dr. Rouben's is. It's been around for thousands of years. You've heard of the Three Wise Men who visited Jesus in Bethlehem when he was born?" Michael nodded. "They were Mages, high priests from Babylon, members of *The Fold* sworn to protect the Child of God. But not even they were original members. *The Fold* existed for centuries before them. No one knows exactly how old it is or who began it, but there's a veiled mention of it in the Old Testament." She opened the door and peeked outside. "The coast is clear," she said, staring back into Michael's eyes. "Come, you must leave now. Time is not on our side."

She opened the door wider and Michael exited into the corridor with Ananda and the briefcase. He could tell she thought they had spent too much time talking. "Just one last thing," he said, speaking quickly. "I promise, no more questions."

"Okay, but make it quick," she said, checking the hallway left and right.

Michael saw the anxiety in her eyes and realised, perhaps for the first time, the urgency of the situation. "You said before that there will be a Third Child in the future."

"Yes, there will be seven in all," she said. "John, the disciple, was given a vision by God." She paused, as if pondering whether or not it was safe to wait another minute or two, and then seemingly decided it was worth the risk. She ran to her bedside table and picked up a thick, leather-bound book upon which the telephone was resting. "Here it is," she said, returning to him and spreading its pages. It was the Bible, Michael saw. She traced the sentences with the tip of her finger and spoke with reverence, "Revelations one verse twelve: 'When I turned to see who was speaking, there behind me were several candlesticks of gold. And standing among them was one who looked like Jesus who called him the Son of Man, wearing a long robe circled with a golden band across his chest.'" She paused briefly, though continued to run her finger along the sacred passages. "'He held seven stars in his right hand and a sharp, double bladed sword in his mouth... This is the meaning of the seven stars you saw... The seven stars are the leaders of the seven churches.'"

They met each other's gaze and the reverence he had heard in her voice sparkled in her eyes, like first love. "And Ananda is the second of those leaders?" he asked.

"Yes, and the last to be born on this earth," she said, gently shutting the bible. "A new threat to mankind is rising. The world is at crossroads, just as it was in Jesus' time. He came to teach us about God's Love, and indeed was the essence of that Love here on earth. Ananda has come to reinforce that lesson. She is a prophet and her life will be a reflection of that Love, of His life, and we shall call her Bliss. For that is what Her name means, *Bliss*." She reached forward and caressed the baby's hair as if she were her very own. "She will lead the Second Church, as Jesus lead the First, into the next age towards peace and the stars, towards the heavens. And in two thousand years time, the human race will once again be at a crossroads and the Third Child will be born, but not on earth, on a distant planet far from here."

She glanced up into his eyes and then down at the baby. "Do you see this sign?" With her index finger, she began tracing the symbol drawn on Ananda's pyjama suit.

Michael saw her finger follow the lines of the outer circle first, then the triangle, and finally the smaller inner circle. "Yes. I saw it before," he said. "What is it? It looks Celtic."

"No, it isn't," she said. "It's her symbol, and it's called a *ki*. The outer circle represents the infinite universe of God. The triangle represents humanity's place in that universe, and its three points symbolise the triune of mind, body and soul. The inner circle represents the Infinite

Spirit that resides within us. As you can see, the *ki* is a Holy Trinity." Maria stopped tracing the lines on Ananda's pyjama suit and drew her hand away, looking up and meeting Michael's gaze. "You must go now. Follow the instructions I have written down for you in the envelope inside the briefcase."

Michael nodded. "Thank you for everything. I'll take good care of her."

Maria put her hand on the door and took a step back. "I know you will, you're a good man, Michael," she said, then hesitated. "There's one more thing I should tell you before you go. Jessica, your wife's baby," and he felt his brow ripple at the sound of her name. It would be some time before he was able to accept Jessica's death, he supposed. "Do you believe in a soul?"

"I guess so."

"And do you accept that the soul exists on a different level of consciousness than what you and I are normally aware of?"

Michael shrugged. It was difficult holding the baby and the briefcase, and his shoulder complained once again. "I guess, yeah, but what does this have to do with my... with Jessica?"

"Jessica was never meant to live longer than she did," she said. "Angie probably has no idea, but her soul made a contract with God before Jessica was born. Jessica was a decoy so that Ananda could live."

Then suddenly, Maria's words resurrected the memory of a dream many months ago that had been the cause of numerous arguments with his wife, a dream of an Angel who had told him he was to be the father of a child born of Immaculate Conception. All the signs had been there, he mused. All he had to do was accept Ananda's birth for what it truly was—a miracle. He felt like Adam, the first man, when he stared at his reflection in a still pool of water and realised who he really was. Awakening, he now knew, was shocking.

Michael blinked several times and opened his eyes. It felt like he was emerging from a deep sleep or hypnotic trance, and when he spoke his voice had a dreamy, translucent resonance. "I, I finally understand what's been happening to me," he said. "What's happened has always meant to happen."

Maria stared at him with deep knowing. The corners of her lips twitched and spread into the most beautiful smile Michael had ever seen. Even more beautiful, and he felt a tad guilty about admitting this, than Angie's on her wedding photo.

"Now you understand. Jessica made the ultimate sacrifice; her place in heaven is assured," Maria said, and Michael could feel the solemnity on her face.

Suddenly, she was alerted to the squeal of tyres drifting through the window and her smile was erased, quickly replaced with a frown. Michael had no doubts as to who was in the vehicle outside. She ran to the window and peered out.

"They're here," she said, turning to him. "They've come in the van. You have to go, now. Quickly. You know what you have to do."

Michael nodded. He was now as alert as Maria, who hurried back to the door. The anxiety in her eyes was as sharp as he had seen that night. He could now hear voices drifting through the window. It sounded like Dr. Rouben shouting orders.

"Go through the basement. It's the quickest way," she said.

Michael turned and made his way down the corridor toward the fire exit, but before he did, he thanked Maria and told her he would never forget what she'd done. She smiled once more and closed the door.

Michael cradled Ananda with his right arm and carried the briefcase containing the money in his left. It dangled by his side and bounced awkwardly against his left knee. He didn't know how much it weighed, but it felt like a ton after three weeks lying in a hospital bed recovering from a major accident. He eyed the stairwell, then the elevator to his right, weighing up his options. He didn't fancy his ability to carry Ananda and the payload all the way to the basement without resting and, considering the urgency Maria had relayed, he reckoned the best course of action was to take the elevator and pray it didn't open its doors in front of the security guard on the ground floor.

He pressed the call button and the elevator wasn't long in coming. As he stepped inside he heard hurried footsteps echoing up the stairwell and wondered if it was Jude and Dr. Rouben. He was in no mind to hang around and find out. He put the briefcase on the floor and pressed the button marked B, praying Maria had the good sense to lock her door.

MICHAEL HASTENED THROUGH the winding corridors of the basement to the elevator-well directly beneath the hospital lobby. He pressed the call button and tapped his foot impatiently. He watched the indicator lights above the door move slowly from 2 to 1 to G, then stop for what seemed an eternity. He pressed the call button again, tapping his foot and glancing over his shoulder to make sure he wasn't being followed. Thankfully, there was nothing apart from the empty corridor, and he turned back to watch the indicator lights above the elevator door. The light flashed off the G and for a brief moment there was no light showing at all. There was no way of knowing whether the elevator was ascending or descending.

To his relief, the light flashed onto B. Seconds later, the silver doors parted. He got in, put the briefcase on the floor by his feet, and pressed the button for the top floor. The elevator rushed him straight there, but the moment he got out he almost tripped over the suitcase. As it transpired, it was a fortunate near-accident. He suddenly heard the doors to the ICU down the corridor burst open, then footsteps running in his direction. Thinking he had walked straight into a trap, he stopped in his tracks, suddenly lost for ideas. He felt his heart up its tempo, now drumming so hard against the baby cradled to his chest he was afraid it might wake her. Only now was he glad that Maria had sedated her; if she cried, it would be impossible to hide. As it was, no one, thankfully, had seen him come out of the elevator, including the cleaner who was polishing the corridor floor with his back to him, but the footsteps were now nearly upon him. He couldn't stand here looking like a stunned rabbit. He had to take cover.

He looked to his left. Angie's room was open, but there was no way he would be able to cross the corridor without being seen. To his right was the door to the emergency exit, adjacent to the furthest elevator. It was his only option. He hastened there, soft of foot, closing the door behind him but keeping it slightly ajar. Squatting on his haunches, he peered out through the crack between the door and the frame.

Two policemen stopped outside Angie's room, knocked, and then entered without waiting for her to invite them in. Michael cursed his luck. If he had arrived five minutes earlier, he would have had Angie out of bed and downstairs into the car before the cops arrived, but he had no one else to blame. It was his own stupid fault. Maria had warned him of the urgency of the situation and he hadn't listened. Now he was backed into a corner like a mouse trying to hide from several hungry cats. He hated it, but there was nothing he could do apart from wait.

He leant forward, anticipating the worst. From his position, he could see most of what was happening inside Angie's room. In the dim light, the policemen were vague shadows standing at the end of the bed. "Did I hear you correctly?" Angie asked, clearing her throat and rubbing her eyes with her knuckles. "You're placing me under arrest?"

Michael's ears pricked. In the corridor, the hum of the cleaner's floor polisher carried easily to him, and although it muffled Angie's and the cops' voices, he could still hear most of what was being said.

"Yes, Mrs. Joseph," said the taller of the two officers. "We've been ordered to keep you under guard pending further investigation."

Michael was stunned. He could only imagine what was going through Angie's mind. "Further investigation of what?" she asked.

"Of infanticide," the officer said, rather meekly.

Angie burst out laughing. It sounded, as Michael knew she intended, replete with derision. He had to smile. Her directness was starting to make the policemen feel awkward and he was glad he wasn't in their shoes at this point in time; he had been on the receiving end of too many lashes of that tongue.

"Are you both stupid?" she said, turning her head from one to the other.

The two policemen visibly squirmed, especially the taller one with the broad shoulders standing beneath the television set, and Michael could feel a degree of perverse delight.

"I haven't left this hospital for three weeks," she said. "I can barely walk or brush my teeth, and now you're saying I'm responsible for the murder of a child? Get real."

"We're sorry, Mrs. Joseph." The shorter of the two policemen had taken position near the open door, lest she decided to make a dash for it. "We're only following orders."

"Whose orders?"

The two cops shared awkward glances. It was the taller one who answered. "Chief Inspector Joseph."

Angie laughed again. "Bullshit!" she said. "Are you aware that I'm his cousin through marriage?" From the way that they shuffled on their feet, Michael figured they weren't. "There's no way he would order my arrest for something so outrageously inane as this," and then she paused, struck by a sudden thought. "This is a prank, isn't it? Jude put you up to this as some sort of joke, didn't he?"

"No, Mrs. Joseph." It was the tall one again. "This is not a joke. We haven't been put up to do anything. We're just following orders."

Angie paused like a barrister silenced with the unexpected appearance of a surprise witness. She crossed her arms and glared at them. Then, suddenly realising she had them on a point of technicality, she said, "Have you got an arrest warrant?" She held her hand out, palm up. "I'm a lawyer. I want to see the authority by which you're arresting me." Once again the two cops shared embarrassed glances with one another. "Uh ha," she said, "just as I thought. You boys are really pathetic, aren't you? If you persist in going ahead with this contemptible course of action, I hope you're backed up by a pretty decent legal team because I'm going to sue you and whoever is responsible for this sham for every cent I can."

As much as Michael enjoyed listening to his wife's humiliation of the two cops, he knew he couldn't stay here in the emergency exit all night. Someone was bound to find him sooner or later, probably a doctor or nurse on night shift, and demand to know why he was lurking in here like a thief. He needed to formulate a plan. If he had to, if there was no alternative, could he leave Angie here, guarded by the police and left to the mercy of Jude and Dr. Rouben? Could he escape with Ananda to Melbourne without his wife? He didn't think he could. Leaving without her was not a viable option. What then?

Not for the first time that night, the decision was made for him. As seemed a stroke of providence, the urgent voice of a radio operator squawked over the cops' walkie-talkie handsets hitched to their belts. There had been a homicide at the nurses' residence and they were needed urgently.

*My God*, Michael thought, *the bastards have killed Maria.*

It took him a moment to comprehend what had happened. As he listened to the operator give the police a physical description of the chief suspect in the homicide, he knew instantly he had been framed. Jude was going to stop at nothing to hunt him down.

The tall cop unhitched his walkie-talkie and brought it to his mouth. "Hear you loud and clear," he said, making his way towards his partner and the door. "Will immediately investigate. We're on our way now. Over." He hitched the walkie-talkie back onto his belt, and said to Angie, "I'm sorry, Mrs. Joseph, but we have to leave you for the time being."

"You're damn right you're sorry," she said, glaring at them as they exited the room, and then shouting at them, "If you come back, you had better bring your lawyers."

They were already out of the room, and Michael could tell that they couldn't leave quick enough. The taller officer pointed toward the fire escape, telling his partner they needed to hurry. Michael's eyes almost bulged out of their sockets and he momentarily stopped breathing. They were now heading straight for him.

"No," the shorter officer said, grabbing his partner by the arm. "Look, the elevator's here."

Michael held his breath until the elevator doors closed behind them, gasping for air like someone whose head had been held under water for too long. He wasn't cut out for this, he mused, nor had he asked for it. All he wanted was to get his wife, go home, and pretend this whole thing never happened.

The memory of the radio operator's voice on the walkie-talkie brought him back to his senses. Things were never going to be that way. His life had changed irrevocably. Maria was dead, he was the main suspect, and if he didn't hurry and get his wife out of this place his parents would be reading about his arrest on the front pages of the *Adelaide Sun* tomorrow morning over breakfast. He had to get moving, and he had to get moving with haste. It was now or never.

Without worrying whether or not the cleaner saw him, Michael exited the emergency exit and headed across the corridor, tiptoeing into Angie's room.

"What are you doing here?" she said, obviously surprised. "You wouldn't believe what's just happened."

No, he thought, neither would she. He gently closed the door, shutting out the hum of the polishing machine and most of the light from the corridor, then made his way to the side of the bed. "We haven't got much time," he hushed, putting the briefcase down on the floor next to him.

"What are you talking about?" Angie asked, turning her attention to the sleeping baby in his arms. "And who have we here? Is this my little girl coming to pay her mummy a visit?" She reached out to take her. "And what have you both been up to? Have you been a good little girl?" Then she frowned, querulously. "She looks different. What's happened to her birthmark?"

Michael gave the baby to her, glancing nervously over his shoulder at the door. "I'll tell you later. Where are your things?"

"What things?" she asked. "Why are you whispering?"

"Because we have to get out of here. We have to leave, now."

"Leave? Has everyone gone mad? I've just been arrested by the police and now you come to me in the middle of the night and want me to abscond like a…"

"Angel, shut up!" He looked over his shoulder again, hoping he hadn't spoken too loudly. When he turned back, Angie's mouth had dropped to the bed covers.

"Don't you…" she began.

He didn't give her time to finish. "I don't have time to explain," he said, and pulled back the bed sheets. She was wearing only a hospital gown. "Come on. Get up. We're leaving."

Angie complied, seemingly too stunned not to.

Michael's hand was on the door handle when, to his horror, he heard the elevator open with a *ding!* Michael ducked behind the cubicle door as two sets of feet rushed across the floor. At first he thought it was the policemen returning until he heard the familiar voice of Dr. Rouben. Michael figured it had to be Jude he was talking to and braced himself for the impact against the door.

But the expected arrival didn't occur. Miraculously, they jogged straight past toward the ICU. *They don't know Angie's been moved*, he thought, listening to their footsteps fade down the corridor. He turned to Angie who was struggling to put on her bathroom gown.

"Quickly, hurry," he whispered, "we have to go."

She glared at him. "I *am* hurrying," she whispered back. To Michael it was like the hiss of an angry possum.

Ignoring his wife, he hastened to the bed. He cradled Ananda and picked up the briefcase in one motion, and said, "Come on, follow me."

They crossed the corridor to the elevators as fast as they could. Out of the corner of his eye, Michael saw the cleaner look up, sweeping his floor polisher back and forth. Michael could only hope he wouldn't tell Jude and Dr. Rouben that he had seen them, but he pushed his concerns out of his mind; it was something he could do nothing about. The doors to the elevator Jude and Dr. Rouben had come up in, he saw, were still open. He stepped toward them, then stopped.

"Let's take the stairs," he said

Angie frowned at him. "Why? I can hardly walk…"

"Just trust me," he said, and dragged her by the elbow to the emergency stairwell, figuring it to be a much better option; they were far less likely to be trapped should the elevator open without warning in front of any policemen. Two flights down, however, as he feared might happen, Angie was forced to stop and rest, despite his supporting arm.

"My head's spinning," she said. "I can barely walk. I need to stop for a minute."

Michael glanced over his shoulder toward the top of the stairwell, then back at Angie. She was breathing heavily, almost too exhausted to stand. Michael could tell that her wobbly knees were going to give way at any second, and before he could do anything about it, she sat down heavily upon the step. She held her head in her hands, supporting it with her elbows resting on her knees, and for a worrisome moment he thought she was going to faint.

After a few seconds Angie looked up at him, taking several deep breaths, but Michael wasn't prepared to give her any more time to rest. He grabbed her other hand and tried to pull her back up. "Come on, you have to get up. We have to leave. Now!"

She snatched her hand back and stared defiantly at him. "No, stop it!" Her anger was comparable to when the two policemen had woken her up and placed her under arrest. "I've had enough of this nonsense," she said, brimming with tears. "I'm not going anywhere until you tell me what's going on."

Michael once again glanced up to the door on the eighth level. He was expecting Dr. Rouben and Jude to burst into the stairwell any second. "Angel, we don't have time to go into all the details right now. We're in a lot of danger, especially Ananda," he said, conveying his urgency with his eyes. "There are people who want to get their hands on her and…"

"Who's Ananda?" Angie asked.

"Who? What? Oh, her," he said, pointing to the baby with a nod of his chin.

"When did you change her name? We agreed on Jessica, didn't we?"

"Look, I'll explain later." Michael grabbed her arm again and lifted her on to her feet. "Come on, please, you're just going to have to trust me on this one, okay?"

Angie allowed herself to be pulled up, and by the expression in her eyes Michael knew he was going to have to do at least a week's worth of explaining before she understood anything of what was going on.

They harried down the remaining stairs and were just about to leave through the bottom door of the fire escape when they heard the slamming of the top door against the wall. It reverberated down the stairwell like a thunderclap, and Michael cursed beneath his breath. He looked up and saw Dr. Rouben's face peering down at him from over the railings on the top floor.

"Quickly!" Dr. Rouben said. "There they are!"

Jude and Dr. Rouben's feet thudded down the stairs. Michael elbowed Angie in the back with the arm he was carrying Ananda and pushed her through the outside door so hard she almost tripped over. She complained vociferously, but Michael ignored her in his quest to locate the car. In the dark, his eyes seemed to take an eternity to adjust from the brightness of the stairwell; everywhere he looked was like staring into the mouth of a deep cave, nothing but stark blackness and amorphous shapes. Footsteps thudded down the stairs behind him. He searched. He scanned, but there was nothing apart from blackness.

Then his eyes finally adjusted. The car was there, to his utter relief. They rushed across the asphalt, but when he jumped into the driver's seat his heart sank into its springs. The keys weren't in the ignition.

He searched the glove compartment. He searched on top of the dashboard. They were nowhere. He got out of the car again, thinking that he might have accidentally sat on them. They weren't on the driver's seat either. Then his eyes saw a glint of light reflecting off something near the brake pedal; the keys had fallen out of the ignition onto the floor. Michael grabbed them and jumped back in, starting the engine before he even settled properly behind the wheel. Barely a second after it roared into life, he stepped on the accelerator pedal and reversed the car, just missing the delivery van parked behind. Angie was in the passenger seat holding Ananda to her bosom, the briefcase by her feet.

"Slow down Mikey!" she said, jerking to the side with the change of movement of the car. "You're driving like a maniac. Do you want to get us all killed?"

Michael ignored her and sped out of the hospital grounds onto the main road, glancing over Angie's shoulder as they passed the front of the hospital. He saw Jude and Dr. Rouben pointing and gesticulating wildly to the two police officers he had seen Angie give the third degree to. They were standing around a squad car parked at the main entrance, behind which was a white van with a sign on its side: MAD HATTER'S LAWN MOWING SERVICE—MAD SERVICE AT A MAD PRICE! Jude held what looked like a CB radio to his mouth, and Michael realised, to his alarm, that he was calling for reinforcements.

He drove as fast as he could without breaking the speed limit, careful not to draw any unwanted attention to the vehicle, and moments later crossed the intersection with Greenhill Road at the edge of the parklands. The roads were empty, and thankfully there were no signs of any more police. At the next intersection, Michael steered diagonally left up Glen Osmond Road on a direct bearing toward the freeway. He saw the red taillights of a car a few hundred yards or so ahead and, even further in the distance on the opposite side of the road, two white pinpricks of light of an approaching car. Though he wanted nothing more to plant his foot to the metal, he kept his cool and maintained his speed at the legal limit. Half a minute later, at the base of the dark hills in the distance, he saw a flash of green from the traffic lights that led onto the freeway, less than a kilometre away. They were getting closer by the second. Less than a minute and they'd be there.

"We might have done it, Angel," he said, patting Angie on the thigh. "We just might have done it."

He kept staring through the windshield. The row of streetlights marked the dark empty road like a runway, and like a plane that had just touched down, the headlights of the other car approached with disquieting speed. To his alarm, it was a police car, and before he could think of what to do, it was already upon them. Michael ran a hand through his hair. If he turned off the main road, he'd still be seen; he couldn't do anything except grip the steering wheel and hope that they hadn't as yet been alerted to the vehicle.

Unblinking, Michael watched the cop car out of the corner of his eye. It flashed past in a blur of blue and white metal, and Michael breathed a sigh of relief, watching it get smaller in the rear-view mirror. Suddenly, its red and blue lights blazed on top of its roof. A second later, Michael heard its siren begin to wail and the screech of its brakes as it prepared to make a U-turn. Then, with frightening speed, it was heading toward him, accelerating fast, its bright headlights looming large in the mirror. His heart sank. He didn't know whether to laugh or cry. There was no way he could outrun the cops in this car. His only hope was to pull over and try to talk his way out of it, or otherwise… and he reached down and caressed the cold, hard metal of the Colt tucked into his belt.

The headlights of the police car flashed him with high beams. Michael steered to the side of the road and stopped, pulling the gun from his belt and sliding it beneath his thigh. He turned to Angie, who stared at the gun with wide, frightened eyes. "I'm sorry I've got you into this mess," he said. "I should have left you in the hospital."

The cop car was now upon them. He watched it in the driver's side mirror, readying his hand on the butt of the gun. He felt surprisingly calm, almost kind of righteous, like he thought Joan of Arc must have felt as she burned at the stake, or even Socrates as he willingly sipped from the poisoned chalice. He thumbed the safety lock off and waited for the inevitable.

To his bewilderment, the cop car roared past. Just several hundred yards ahead, it caught up with the other car and screeched diagonally in front, forcing it to the side of the road. The two font doors of the squad car flung open and two cops jumped out, pointing their handguns at the driver and passenger. As he watched through the windshield, Michael could just hear their faint shouts to the occupants of the car to keep their hands on the dashboard.

Michael took a moment to think what to do. Just past them was the turnoff to the South-Eastern Freeway. Should he reverse and try to find another route onto it? He didn't like that idea. There were probably more cop cars on the lookout for them, and when the cops up ahead realised that they had the wrong suspects, he might not be so lucky with the next one that passed. There was really only one option. Michael drew a deep breath, put the car back in gear, and accelerated slowly ahead.

As he approached the gun-wielding cops, he saw that the other car was in fact Maria's yellow Renault. He drove past, staring straight ahead and allowing plenty of room between him and the arresting policemen. Angie stared out of the passenger window, turning her head to watch what was happening.

"Wasn't that Norman and his wife?" she asked when they eventually overtook, facing Michael. "Now that I think about it, aren't we in his car? And why was it parked at the back of the hospital, and not at the main entrance?"

Michael smiled lopsidedly. They were now at the turnoff; freedom was barely several yards ahead across the intersection. The traffic lights turned green and he accelerated onto the freeway, passing a sign that read: MELBOURNE 780 KM.

"I'll tell you all about it as we go," he said, turning to his wife and baby.

Ananda, he saw, was peacefully asleep.

# Other Titles By
## Scott Zarcinas

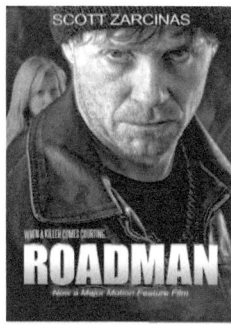

*Roadman*
by Scott Zarcinas

ISBN: 978-0-9943054-3-5
eISBN: 978-0-9943054-2-8
Publisher: DoctorZed Publishing

Available in print and ebook.

*Now a major motion feature film.*

Lorraine Jackson is a single white female looking for Mr. Right. But when the Roadman knocks on her door, she isn't prepared for the secrets he's been hiding... and would kill to keep them hidden.

*www.roadman.doctorzed.com*

*Samantha Honeycomb*
by Scott Zarcinas

ISBN Parent: 192120702-7
ISBN International: 0 9775969 3 1
eISBN: 097759630-3
Publisher: DoctorZed Publishing

Available in print and ebook.

*"Enchanting and full of joy."* ~ Inner Self magazine.

Wrongly punished for breaking the ancient laws, Samantha Honeycomb is expelled by the queen into the wild and untamed Crazy Lands. Her only hope of redemption is an impossible quest—to find the fabled hive of Beebylon and bring back its secret of Infinite Richness. But there are others who would see her fail.

Evoking the wisdom of the ancient sages, Scott Zarcinas reveals through the trials and tribulations of Samantha Honeycomb that the surface appearance of unpleasant and torturous experiences are, in fact, essential ingredients in the melting pot of our future joy, security and acceptance—our destiny.

*www.samanthahoneycomb.doctorzed.com*

*The Golden Chalice*
by Scott Zarcinas

ISBN: 978-0-9875975-9-5
eISBN: 978-0-9775969-2-8
Publisher: DoctorZed Publishing

Available in print and ebook.

Fleeing the dreaded plague that has struck his village, the orphaned Giacomo heads to the mountains and its mysterious Golden City in search of the Elixir of Life, the only thing that can save the village and the woman he loves.

His quest brings him face to face with the Six Thieves, cunning enemies who will stop at nothing to see him fail, and even with the Angel of Death herself.

In the tradition of The Pilgrim Chronicles set by *Samantha Honeycomb*, *The Golden Chalice* is a compelling adventure story of self-discovery.

*www.thegoldenchalice.doctorzed.com*

*DeVille's Contract*
by Scott Zarcinas

ISBN: 978-0-9924473-5-9
eISBN: 978-0-9-872495-4-8
Publisher: DoctorZed Publishing

Available in print and ebook.

Louis Hugo DeVille, CEO of the giant pharmaceutical company, Global Resolutions Network, suffers a heart attack in his office, only to wake up in the underground tunnels of LeMont International Enterprises.

Louis has been headhunted by The Boss of the mega-corporation to help restructure its flagging corporate image, with the promise of limitless power and money.

There's only one catch. He must sign an unbreakable contract, one that will bind his services to The Boss for an awfully long time. For eternity.

*www.devillescontract.doctorzed.com*